**Gua**

"A thrilling new ... se sexy warriors!"

—*New York* ... owalter

"Caris Roane powers into the paranormal romance genre with a sexy, cool, edgy, romantic fantasy that gleams like the dark wings and lethal allure of her Guardians of Ascension vampires. Prepare to be enthralled!"

—*New York Times* bestselling author Lara Adrian

"The latest Guardians of Ascension romantic urban fantasy is a great thriller . . . another fantastic entry in one of the strongest sagas on the market today."

—*Midwest Book Reviews*

"An amazing author with a unique twist on vampires."

—*Bitten by Paranormal Romance*

"Roane's world-building is complex and intriguing, and in addition to her compelling protagonists, she serves up a slew of secondary characters begging to be explored further. The Guardians of Ascension is a series with epic potential!"          —*Romantic Times* (4½ stars)

"A super urban romantic fantasy in which the audience will believe in the vampires and the Ascension . . . fast-paced . . . thrilling."          —*Alternative Worlds*

"A great story with a really different take on vampires. This is one book that is sure to be a hit with readers who love paranormals. Fans of J.R. Ward's Black Dagger Brotherhood series are sure to love this one too."

*—Red Roses for Authors Blog*

"*Ascension* is like wandering in a field of a creative and colorful dream. There are many interesting, formidable, terrifying, beautiful, and unique images. They surround and envelop you in a story as old as time."

—Barnes and Noble's *Heart to Heart Romance Blog*

"Incredibly creative, *Ascension* takes readers to another level as you learn about two earths, vampires, ancient warriors, and a new twist on love. I felt like I was on a roller-coaster ride, climbing until I hit the very top, only to come crashing down at lightning speed. Once you pick this book up, clear off your calendar because you won't be able to put it down. Best book I have read all year."

—SingleTitles.com

"Tightly plotted and smoking hot . . . a fantastic read."

*—Fresh Fiction*

"Nail-biting romance . . . hot sex . . . I can't wait to see what's going to happen next." *—Bitten by Romance*

Also by
Caris Roane

# SAVAGE
# CHAINS

CARIS ROANE

St. Martin's Paperbacks

This is a work of fiction. All of the characters, organizations, and events portrayed in this novel are either products of the author's imagination or are used fictitiously.

Previously published in eBook form as *Captured: Savage Chains: Part 1, Scarred: Savage Chains: Part 2,* and *Shattered: Savage Chains: Part 3.*

SAVAGE CHAINS

Copyright © 2015 by Caris Roane.

For information address St. Martin's Press, 175 Fifth Avenue, New York, NY 10010.

ISBN: 978-1-250-03799-2

Printed in the United States of America

St. Martin's Paperbacks edition / April 2015

St. Martin's Paperbacks are published by St. Martin's Press, 175 Fifth Avenue, New York, NY 10010.

10  9  8  7  6  5  4  3  2  1

# CHAPTER 1

Angelica stood in front of Briggs's Ocean Club in Newport Beach, staring up at two well-lit palm trees that
flanked the entrance. Her heart hammered out a few unsteady beats, since her reasons for being here involved a
certain walk of shame she hoped to make sometime the
next morning.

But now that she was here, her knees felt watery and
the butterflies in her stomach had staged a massive riot.
She hadn't been with a man for a good long stretch of
road. So why was she aiming for dark and dangerous
when any number of hardworking males around her office would scratch this itch just fine? She might even fall
in love, make some babies, have a life.

Except she didn't want that kind of life.

Putting a hand to her stomach, she drew a deep breath.

She'd finally admitted to herself that only one man would do: Brogan Reyes, a six-five god who looked like he ran black ops missions in his spare time. Piercing blue eyes, massive shoulders, and a scruff that made her tongue tingle just thinking about licking a line straight up his jaw.

Despite her self-confessed need, she remained outside the club, knowing he could be inside. For whatever reason, she couldn't make her feet move.

She didn't really have time for a man in her life anyway. She had a demanding job as an accountant in a big firm that kept her insanely busy. She should just show some sense, head back to her apartment, pay some bills, drink a tumbler of Patrón Silver, and get some rest. Besides, her stilettos pinched like hell. She wasn't used to dressing up like this, showing a ridiculous amount of come-and-get-me cleavage. And she was way out of flirting practice.

Yet her feet wouldn't move backward, either.

Her life had become a serious rut, and if she didn't do something to shake things up she thought she might go mad.

A sudden offshore breeze gave her a small push and she finally set her feet in motion, straight for the doors. She wanted this for herself, if only for one night.

And Reyes was the man she wanted.

Taking a deep breath, she lowered her chin and crossed the foyer threshold, her black sequin clutch held tight to her side.

The hostess smiled. "Welcome to Briggs's Ocean Club. Can I help you with your reservation this evening?"

The club had a variety of venues, including an upscale restaurant, a huge bar and lounge, and an outdoor patio, as well as live music and dancing.

Angelica waved a hand to the left, indicating the lounge, and the hostess smiled and nodded. She made her way to the short staircase that descended to the large, noisiest part of the club: the bar.

As she walked down the five steps, she quickly scanned the tables and long, polished oak bar, but Reyes wasn't there.

She picked a stool at the end nearest the stairs, and perched.

The bartender made his way over. "Angelica, great to see you again."

"Hey, Marcus."

"You haven't been here in a while." A concerned frown followed. "How's your mom?"

"She's doing much better, but thanks for asking. My aunt's in town to look after her, so I have a reprieve, at least for a couple of weeks."

"Well, that's great."

And it was. Angelica could breathe a little and tonight, she could indulge.

"You're one of my favorite people, you know. Lot of spoiled rich kids in this joint. So what can I get you?"

"Gin and tonic, please."

"You got it." He moved away to prepare her order, then returned swiftly, drink in hand, laying down a silver coaster first. But he was off almost as fast, greeting a new group and taking orders.

Marcus had worked at the Ocean Club for years and knew everyone who frequented the upscale, sexy nightspot that served the young and wealthy of Southern

California. A gem-like array of bottles ran floor-to-ceiling behind the bar in every color imaginable, a beautiful mosaic against a mirrored wall. Low lights and deep maroon glossy walls gave an intimate feel to what was a large space full of linen-covered tables, comfortable chairs, and chattering guests.

When several customers got called to their restaurant reservation, a lull allowed Marcus to come back to her. He had shoulder-length black hair, dark eyes, and a warm smile. "You look good in red." His gaze fell to the low cut of her neckline, and he waggled his brows. "Hot. Very hot."

She felt a blush climb her cheeks, but she smiled. "Thank you." She lifted her drink to him. "I needed that."

She'd dressed for the occasion in red silk, sleeveless and cut low. She wore more makeup than usual and had dressed her thick dark-brown hair to flow away from her face.

"So can I help you out tonight? Anyone you want to meet?"

Marcus had a sixth sense where people were concerned, and he had never steered her wrong. She trusted him.

Squaring her shoulders, she jumped in. "I'm wondering what you know about Brogan Reyes." Just mentioning his name caused the ever-present butterflies to make a few dive-bombing runs.

His brows rose. "One tough hombre, but I have to say I don't know much more than that. Not sure anyone does. He comes from European money or maybe South American—even that's unclear. But he must have been educated somewhere in the States because he has no accent to speak of. He's usually in the lounge on Fridays so

I would expect to see him and I have asked around, but he keeps his cards close. All I know is that he's wealthy, doesn't make a show of it, and meets business associates here. And no, I don't know what kind of business. My only concern, but it's a mild one, is that some of the people he meets give off the wrong vibe."

She knew what Marcus meant—more than one person he'd had drinks with, though well dressed, had a predatory look. "You know what it is? Some of the people I've seen him with do a kind of strip search with their eyes. The last time I was here, I felt like I was being visually weighed and measured, summed up. Make any sense?"

He nodded. "That's a good way of putting it, but I've never seen Reyes pull that kind of shit. I'll give him that."

"I agree. He's definitely a cut above the company he keeps."

He leaned his forearms on the bar. "So is he the one?"

Again her cheeks warmed up. "I'm not sure, but I'm determined to find out."

"Good for you and for what it's worth, despite his I-can-beat-the-shit-out-of-anyone look, I like him. He doesn't play games and he treats women decently, which says a lot."

Another throng of customers arrived, and Marcus moved away to take more orders.

Angelica swiveled in her seat. The dimly lit room was full of laughter and lots of flirting. Windows lined the lounge, with a pair of double doors that led to a crowded patio beyond. Outside, tables and chairs surrounded a massive tree covered in white mini lights.

Music filtered through from the dance club, sometimes with a strong rhythmic beat and other times a slow, sexy groove.

As the band moved into the latter, the erotic rhythm of the bass guitar and drums sent another shiver through her.

Marcus called her name, and when she turned toward him, he winked, then jerked his chin toward the stairs. "He's here."

For a second she couldn't breathe, as though all the air had been sucked from her lungs. She let her gaze move slowly toward the entrance. There he was, standing at the top of the short staircase, looking sexy as hell dressed in a black leather coat, blue silk shirt, and tailored slacks.

Awed as she was by his physical presence, she reminded herself that he was the reason she'd come here tonight. She sat up a little straighter, drink in hand.

He scanned the lounge, just as she had, his gaze moving slowly, then landing on her. She smiled and lifted her glass to him. She'd hoped for an answering curve of his lips, some indication he might be interested. Instead he frowned, though holding her gaze steadily.

Not the most encouraging note.

But the moment of truth had arrived. Was there a chance in hell she could persuade a frowning man to at least have a drink with her?

She felt in her gut that her life was poised right on the head of a pin, and what she did next would either catapult her forward or send her back to her apartment and a sad bottle of tequila for comfort.

Despite his frowns, she made a quick decision.

Grabbing her clutch, and setting her drink down, she slid off the bar stool and headed in his direction. She'd come here to talk to him and talk to him she would, even if all he did was tell her to get lost.

As she mounted the stairs, he turned back in the

direction of the foyer with a slight jerk of his head. With that small movement, hope soared.

She found him in the foyer, standing near the tall water feature. As she drew closer, his gaze fell to her cleavage. She watched desire spark in his eyes, and an answering response raced through her body.

Still very nervous, she pushed her hair away from her throat, and his gaze followed, his nostrils flaring. He blinked and his lips parted. She hadn't been wrong about him; he was interested in her. Yep, he was the one.

"I was hoping to talk to you tonight. I've seen you here before, of course."

He searched her eyes. "What do you want?"

Angelica's turn to frown. She'd hoped for a little ice-breaking chitchat, maybe the promise of a smile. Instead his jaw stiffened as once again he held her gaze, frowning.

But she wasn't about to give up, at least not yet. "Can I buy you a drink?"

He shook his head slowly. "Not interested."

Well, that was a lie, so she pressed on. "Let me buy you one anyway."

His eyes narrowed. "What's your game, Angelica?"

Her heart skipped a couple of beats. He knew her name. That meant something.

Swallowing hard, she drew in a deep breath. "I don't have a game. I just wanted to talk to you, maybe get to know you."

"I never took you for a fortune hunter. Guess I was wrong."

"What do you mean?"

"Why else would you be talking to me like this?"

She didn't understand why he suddenly sounded so hostile. It made no sense. "You think I'm after your money?"

"Sure. Why not?"

He was being incredibly rude. "How do I know you even have a nickel?"

He snorted. "Women like you always know."

"Women like me?" She shook her head. This was not how she'd imagined her first conversation with him going. "You know, I asked around and no one knows much about you except that you have ties to Europe and maybe South America. Your last name sounds Spanish enough. And you dress well, but even a monkey could put on a fine suit and Cartier watch, and look well shod."

Something passed through his eyes—amusement maybe, she couldn't tell. But for a second he seemed almost human.

His steely expression returned fast enough, however, and he squared his shoulders. "Let me speak plainly."

"Oh, you haven't been?"

"All right, let me speak more specifically. You don't belong here in this club and when I saw that you'd stopped coming, I thought, *Good, one less gold digger to worry about.*"

She compressed her lips but lowered her voice. "I'm not a gold digger. You've got me wrong."

"Then how about you just stick to your own kind?"

"My own kind? You mean people who work hard, take care of their families, that kind?"

He snorted. "Go home, Angelica, to your little apartment and to the numbers you crunch all day long." So he knew the details of her life. That meant something, too, but it also made her a little nervous. Had he been checking up on her?

He leaned close, though his voice sounded a little softer, not quite so mean. "Go home and live your life. Find some guy who can set you up in a suburb and make babies with you. Isn't that what you really want?"

The question brought her up short, maybe even going to the heart of why she'd come to the club tonight. She decided to be honest with him. "I could have had that, I suppose. Yet somehow, you were what I wanted. I came here for you."

He seemed taken aback, surprised even. He huffed an exasperated sigh and took her arm in his hand. "For fuck's sake, just go home."

But the sudden physical contact had a strange effect on her as she met his gaze once more. Desire for him flowed all over again, an unstoppable wave of need that brought tears to her eyes. She couldn't explain it as anything other than a bone-deep inner knowing. She knew the man's cruel words weren't truthful. He was merely trying to drive her away.

"Reyes," she whispered softly. "You're not indifferent. I can sense it. And I promise you, I'm not after anything, except this." She leaned up and kissed him.

His lips were moist and sensual and for just a moment, he leaned into her and returned the kiss.

When she finally drew back, his eyes flared once more and the grip on her arm increased. "Who are you?" His voice was now hoarse and deep.

She wanted to ask him to take her somewhere, anywhere, but he released her arm and once more adopted a hard expression.

"You're making a mistake, Angelica. And I'm begging you to leave this club and never come back. You belong tucked up in your safe, very normal life. This one, I promise you, this one will destroy you."

Before she could ask what the hell he meant, he moved past her back in the direction of the bar.

Angelica didn't know what to think. His words seemed to suggest she was in some kind of danger, or at least she would be if she stayed here.

For a long beat, she considered following after him, but the moment had passed. She'd given him plenty of opportunity to engage with her, but instead he wanted her to go away.

She moved forward toward the open front doors of the club. The cool ocean breeze cleared her senses as more customers flowed into the large foyer.

She couldn't believe she'd kissed him. She'd wanted to shake him up, and she was sure she'd succeeded, at least a little. But apparently not enough for him to ask her to stay.

Walking toward her car, almost in a daze, his words kept playing over in her mind: that this club or maybe this part of society would destroy her. But what bothered her the most was his reference to her safe life.

As she reached her modest Camry, a very *safe* car, she drew her keys from her clutch but got no further. She didn't want to go back to her usual routine, to her normal life. That's what went through her head, and it made it impossible to put the key in the lock.

She knew the kiss had touched him, opened him a little. She couldn't be wrong about that.

She also thought it possible that if she left now, she'd never see him again, and that was the last thing she wanted. She had to break through his icy barrier, get him to talk, and maybe at the very least to explain why he thought she was in danger.

She put her keys back in her purse and turned around. She had to make one last attempt to reach him.

The parking lot was well lit with lots of people coming and going. Though there were two rather large, imposing men at the end of her row of cars, she had no reason to feel at risk. There were just too many people around for anything to go wrong.

She moved quickly in the direction of the club, and at the same time the two men pivoted toward her. A jolt of fear went through her, an instinct that almost turned her feet around once more. But even if they meant her harm, what could they possibly do with so many witnesses nearby?

She therefore straightened her shoulders and kept on going. However, just as she drew near, she swore the air around them grew oddly distorted, the way heat would look on sun-blasted asphalt.

She blinked and the next moment one of the men grabbed her arm, hauled her against his chest, and held her tight. The other pressed a cloth over her nose and mouth. The smell nauseated her, and she struggled hard, kicking and screaming, certain that someone would come to help her or, if not, at least call the police.

But her mind started spinning, she couldn't feel her feet, then she was falling.

Three days later Brogan Reyes sat in a very different kind of club deep in the Como cavern system, his nerves on edge. Sex slaves of every human ethnicity worked the club table-to-table, while a live stage performance kept the customers on the verge of release.

From the earliest time he could remember he'd survived by playing a role, and tonight was no different. But if all went well, he'd get the one thing he wanted above everything else: an invitation to become a member of the Starlin Group.

Just a few nights from now Starlin would host another gala event, and if he played his cards right, he was in. He'd purchase his first sex slave and become part of the inner circle of one of the most heinous slavery rings in his world.

Once inside the organization, he intended to bring the whole damn thing down.

So he played his role, watching the live stage show and behaving as though he liked that the woman screamed in pain. The dom, covered in leather, used a variety of implements to draw blood. He knew the progression of torture well; given her pallor, she'd drop into unconsciousness soon, then another slave would be brought out and the process would begin again.

Part of him wanted to rush the stage, grab the woman, and get her permanently out of this hellhole. If he did, however, he'd destroy decades spent building a reputation as a man fully into the lifestyle. He had to perpetually think beyond the present moment, to the thousands of women and men who lived caged in this part of the world, serving the sadistic needs of a hungry, perverse, but well-paying vampire clientele.

The club appealed to high-end slavers, with black marble on the walls layered with swaths of emerald crystals. Soft lighting hung suspended over numerous linen-covered tables, creating an oddly intimate atmosphere for the horror taking place not just on stage but all around him.

Many of the clientele brought their own slaves with

them to perform fellatio while they enjoyed the evening's entertainment. Ecstatic moans occasionally rolled through the club as waitstaff kept the drinks coming.

This club was at the dark end of the lifestyle, where the slaves lived constantly with the threat of torture. But other clubs were worse, involving a snuff element. Those, he avoided. He'd sacrificed a lot to create his cover, but he drew the line at watching slaves murdered for the purpose of sexual gratification.

He lifted his now-empty glass to a passing female slave, toggling it slightly. She came toward him on a quick step, eyes flaring. With that one brief signal, he knew her type: She might have entered the world as a slave, but she'd fully embraced the lifestyle and learned the fine art of turning pain into pleasure.

On his periphery he saw that two Starlin men sat at a nearby table, no doubt assigned to observe him. He therefore had his own little performance to give, and this slave would be perfect for what he needed to do.

She was Asian, with straight black hair to her shoulders, and wore a costume made up entirely of chains crisscrossed over most of her body. The chains left nothing to the imagination, revealing bare breasts, buttocks, and a narrow black landing strip.

"What's your pleasure, Master Reyes?" She held her small round service tray toward him.

With one hand he placed the tumbler in the center, but with the other he grabbed the chain that ran from the middle of her chest, downward between her legs, then rose to connect high on her back. He pulled, one hard tug.

She gasped, her chin quivering.

He watched her face as the pain transformed into something sweeter, and in a slow rhythm he worked the chain up and down. "What I want right now is your mouth on my dick."

With her dark eyes glittering, she set her tray on his table, then dropped to her knees.

She did all the work, unbuckling his pants, licking him, teasing his balls. With his eyes on the stage, she took him deep, her head doing a slow bob as he leaned back in his chair.

He wasn't happy about the situation, which meant he struggled to physically enjoy the process, but he kept his eye on the prize: proving to the Starlin spies that he'd adopted the slaver way of life.

She paused for a moment, looking up at him, and whispered. "You're legendary, master." She rubbed her thumb slowly over his crown. "Take me home, later? My owner won't even charge, not if he knows it's you."

Her words pleased the hell out of him, not because she applauded his sexual prowess, but because she'd inadvertently told him that her owner would treat him just like he did all the big boys at Starlin. He'd worked a helluva long time to achieve this position, spending a large portion of his fortune securing the goodwill of the various club owners.

He smiled and leaned close to bite her ear, sinking his teeth hard until he tasted blood on his tongue. He repressed the part of him that wanted more of the sweet-tasting elixir, that wanted a deep draw at her throat, then sat back once more.

She looked up at him again, her lips swollen as she breathed hard, clearly enjoying his attentions. "Please, master."

"We'll see. Take care of me now and we'll discuss terms."

She smiled and went back to work, head bobbing once more.

His hatred of the sex-slave world went deep, so to sustain his arousal, he let his mind drift into dangerous waters: into the recent past when he'd seen Angelica at the Ocean Club.

The mere thought of her brought pleasure flowing and his hips flexing slightly.

Angelica.

She'd be his salvation in this heinous situation; images of her would see him through.

He recalled her red dress and the most beautiful display of cleavage he'd seen in a long time. She had looked so damn sexy, so beautiful when he'd first seen her sitting at the bar, her long legs crossed at the knee, her gaze fixed on him. He'd recognized the invitation and wished like hell he could have taken her up on it, taken her home, made love to her. God knew, he'd wanted to.

The more he focused on those memories, the more his body responded, so he stayed with them. She'd looked even prettier up close, with large brown eyes, made up just right, her lips shiny with gloss. Then she'd kissed him, one of the biggest surprises of his life. He'd wanted to keep on kissing her, to lay a line of kisses across the mounds of her breasts, to run his hands up her dress, to sink his fingers deep inside her wetness.

He moaned and the mouth that worked him sucked just a little harder, a little faster, a perfect response.

He saw Angelica naked, her layered hair shoved behind her creamy shoulders, her throat exposed, pulse beating in her neck.

Desire flowed as he saw nothing but her, imagining the feel of her breasts beneath his fingers and his mouth sucking each nipple repeatedly until her body responded with heavy undulations.

With these thoughts, pleasure soared. He cupped the back of the slave's head. She knew the signal and sucked faster. But his mind was full of Angelica now, her long legs, his knees spreading them wide. He was over her now, pushing his cock inside, pumping into her, faster and faster.

His lower back tightened and the release came, streaking like lightning through his cock.

*Angelica.*

She was the one. The one he'd wanted, desired, needed.

As his pleasure peaked he groaned, not caring if he was heard above all the other sounds in the club.

Angelica.

His breathing slowed and he leaned back in the chair, his mind still spinning with the images he'd created.

He frowned as he thought of Angelica, of how much he wanted her, how much he wished she were here right now, with him. That would never happen, of course, not in a million years.

After a moment the slave leaned back on her heels. She gently tucked him inside his briefs, zipped him up, fumbled with the button, then buckled his belt. All neat and tidy.

Though she smiled, he saw her drawn cheeks, the pinch at the corner of each eye as she worked to hold back her emotions. He knew what it was to be in her position, to have to engage sexually on demand, often several times a night.

Fuck this horrible situation and the way this slave had been brutalized. He took her chin in hand and, leaning down, he whispered in her ear, "You brought me beautifully. Thank you."

When he leaned back again in his seat, her dark eyes grew haunted and she spoke quickly. "Master, please buy me. I would give anything to serve in your house. I know my owner would allow it. Like I said, he'd do anything for you. He says you're to be the next Starlin member. Please. I need to get out of here."

He felt her desperation, but with the Starlin boys watching him, he still had his role to play.

He steeled himself and took on a bored expression. "All I want from you right now is another Maker's Mark, neat."

The light of hope died swiftly in the woman's eyes. She nodded, rising to her feet and moving away as fast as her shackled ankles would allow.

He made himself a promise that as soon as he brought Starlin down, he'd start destroying clubs like this one until they were all gone and slavery was a thing of the past in his world.

Thank God he'd been able to warn Angelica away from the Ocean Club. What she didn't know, what he hadn't been able to tell her, was that she perfectly fit the bill for Starlin acquisition. Not just because of her beauty, but more important because she had no money to speak of and her closest relative was infirm.

Earlier in the year he'd seen the Starlin team scoping her, so he'd done his own surface investigation and learned the basic details of her life. He understood her vulnerability. Fortunately, at least until a few days ago, she'd stopped coming to the club and he'd been relieved.

But the moment he'd seen her, he knew she was in

danger. She'd never looked more beautiful or sexier and the Starlin team had already arrived, hunting for the right women to snatch.

He'd watched her leave the club, then he'd taken off in the opposite direction, heading back to his home in Italy. He just hoped to hell that in the future she'd stay away. The one thing he'd learned was that the acquisition teams worked clubs almost exclusively, all over the world, grabbing women and sometimes men to sell at auction. Witnesses at clubs were notoriously unreliable—another perfect aspect of the whole setup.

His server returned with his drink, but her eyes were now passive, no longer pleading. She moved away slower this time. He felt her despair like a palpable weight in the air, but he kept his gaze fixed on the stage.

He drank his whiskey in slow sips and after a few more minutes, from his peripheral vision, he watched the Starlin spies leave their table. They would make a full report. If the gods smiled, he'd get that fucking invitation.

He needed to get the hell out of the club, take a hot shower using plenty of soap, but he remained where he was just in case there were others tracking his movements and reporting, spies he didn't know about.

After another hour, and another whiskey, he was about to leave when a slave brought him an embossed envelope. He recognized the Starlin insignia, an *S* with a chain in a circle around it.

He strove to calm the surge of adrenaline that rocketed through him. This was it, what he'd been working toward all these years.

Breaking the gold seal, he pulled out the card and read. *The Starlin Group extends the warm hand of fellowship and requests your presence at all future events. Congrat-*

*ulations and warmest wishes to our newest member.
Your fellow slaver, Master Engles.*

He glanced up at the male slave, whom he knew to be one of Engles's many assistants. Engles was the man to impress and Reyes had apparently gotten the job done, but it had taken years. "You may tell your master I am most grateful."

The slave, his face also a familiar mask of impassivity, nodded once, then left.

Reyes remained another half an hour, a powerful euphoria flowing through his veins. His forearm rested over the invitation, the physical reminder of what he'd accomplished.

His gaze sought out the slave he'd used earlier. As she dropped to her knees in front of yet another slaver, a woman this time, he promised himself he'd get her out along with all the others who had served him while he built his heinous reputation.

His plans were finally falling into place. The next auction would take place on Friday, followed by several gala parties. On the block would be beauties gathered from every corner of the world, and to cement his reputation he'd buy his first slave, or even a group of slaves.

When the woman on stage finally passed out, the dom tossed her over his shoulder and hauled her away. A round of applause rippled through the audience, along with calls for more drinks. Another group of slaves entered the stage to clean up.

Reyes finally rose to leave.

Pulling a well-packed money clip from the pocket of his pants, he dropped several thousand on the white linen, then headed home.

* * *

Angelica lay on a hard mattress that smelled of blood and urine, her hands bound behind her. She couldn't keep her eyes open and her head felt as if spikes had been jammed through the top of her skull. Mostly her arms were killing her in this position.

She sensed that considerable time had passed since she'd last seen Reyes at Briggs's Ocean Club, but she had no idea how much. Days, at least.

She also had vague recollections of being awakened, forced to drink things she didn't want to, then shoved back down on the same mattress to sleep for long periods of time.

Her arms hadn't always been bound like this—only after she'd tried to claw one of her captors' eyes out.

She still didn't understand where she was, what was happening to her, or how long she'd been in what she could only describe as some kind of jail cell set in a cave, a very large cave.

"How's Sleeping Beauty?" A woman's voice reached her, sweet and melodious. A spurt of hope swept through her.

"Coming 'round, mistress."

"Well, get in there, strip her down, and let me have a look. The Starlin acquisition team said she's worth at least two million."

"Yes, mistress."

Hope crashed.

Angelica tried to sit up. She wanted to fight whoever it was that intended to follow the woman's orders, but she'd only made it to her elbow when a hand grabbed her arm and hauled her to her feet.

"Hey." Her protest came out slurred.

For this one word, she received a hard slap across her mouth.

"How many times have I told you not to hit the face? Humans don't heal fast."

Angelica processed this statement, but couldn't make sense of it. What did the woman mean by *humans* not healing fast?

"Sorry, mistress."

"Bring her closer."

Angelica's face throbbed as her captor dragged her to the front of the cell, then pulled her upright for inspection. Between the pain in her head from whatever drugs she'd been given and the new blow to her face, she could barely open her eyes.

"Closer."

Blinking, she had a blurred view of the bars of her cell and a figure beyond.

"Aw, why are you crying, sweetheart?" The woman clucked her tongue. "He didn't hit you that hard."

"Not crying," Angelica managed through thickened lips. She might have been, she wasn't sure, but like hell she'd give this she-devil a reason to think small of her.

"Well, at least you've got some spirit." The woman tilted her head—that much Angelica could determine, but her vision still wasn't working right.

"Get her clothes off. I need to see the goods."

At that Angelica's instincts took over. She thrashed in the man's hold, kicking at him and screaming. Of course she couldn't do much with her arms bound. Still, she fought him hard.

Something struck the back of her head and all went black.

She woke up with a pungent smell wafting beneath her nose. Again she came up fighting, but she didn't get far since restraints held her down, flat on her back.

And she was naked.

She breathed hard, trying to twist, but her ankles were pinned as well.

"You need to relax, princess."

The woman of the melodious voice had returned, only now she was inside the cell.

She drew close to the bed and sat down on a stool beside the putrid mattress. She put a hand on Angelica's throat, stroking down the side of her neck. "Your blood has a wonderful smell, very rich. I'm tempted to sample you myself. Unfortunately, we always promise pristine, never-before-bitten goods to our clientele."

Angelica rocked her head back and forth. "Get the hell away from me."

She could finally see, despite how badly her head ached.

The woman smiled at her, but her dark-blue eyes held a cruel glint, truly malevolent, despite her otherwise angel-like appearance. She looked like something out of an old painting, with light-red hair in a mass of curls, pale skin, small pink lips, and large cornflower-blue eyes.

Angelica couldn't battle the woman, but maybe she could reason with her. "Listen, I don't belong here. There's been some kind of mistake."

The woman's small lips curved into a bow. "Of course you belong here. You're built exactly right for our needs."

A chill ran through her. "What do you mean *needs*?"

"You're a woman. Figure it out."

The statement confirmed her worst fears. "Sex."

"Of course, and all sorts of variations so you'll never be bored."

Angelica shuddered. "Can't you let me out of these restraints?"

"No, I can't. You almost blinded one of my workers. You must be obedient while you're in our care, do you understand?"

The woman slid her hand down Angelica's chest and began caressing her bare breasts, moving in slow circles. "You have very full, exquisite breasts, by the way. Does that feel good?"

Angelica squirmed, trying to get away from the unwelcome touch. "I'm not into women."

"They all say that at first, but pretty soon you'll be doing a lot of things you never thought you'd do. And given your spirit, I feel compelled to offer a taste of the kind of pain you'll experience if you don't do as you're told."

The woman took hold of Angelica's left nipple between her thumb and forefinger and pinched harder and harder. Angelica twisted, trying to get relief, but the pressure increased.

She looked at the woman's face and saw a kind of euphoria in her features. She was enjoying hurting her.

"Sorry, precious, but this is gonna get worse before it gets better. Try to relax."

"It's bad enough already." She spoke the words between gasps.

Something that felt like fire began to burn through Angelica's nipple, a burn that kept coming, kept increasing. She heard screams, then realized they belonged to her.

"Beautiful," the woman said softly. "I really am tempted

to keep you for myself. Let's see how much you can take. I hadn't meant to go this far, but you've got some chops, my dear."

The fiery pain broadened, expanding through her breast. She shook, cried out, and wept. The pain was beyond bearing. She was sure it couldn't get worse, then it did.

"What stamina. I swear I haven't seen someone of your potential in more than a century. You'll do extremely well on the block, just wait and see. But you'll need to rein in your spirit if you want to survive, and don't ever say I didn't warn you."

Her vision began to blacken. As Angelica slipped into unconsciousness once more, she saw the woman smile, a final image she'd never forget.

# CHAPTER 2

On Friday night Reyes straightened immaculate cuffs, held together by black onyx links. His Brioni tux, ordered months ago, fit like a glove and looked like the fortune it had cost. Shoes, Italian leather. Watch, limited-edition Cartier.

He'd left nothing to chance. What he accomplished at the auction tonight would be the final door he'd use to enter the Starlin world for good. He'd worked toward this moment for a long time, building his bad-boy, player reputation and finally gaining membership.

But having access to all the Starlin events was only the beginning and he knew that. There could be no easing off. If anything, he needed to work just a little harder to make sure that the front man for the operation, Damien Engles, totally bought his cover, the reason he intended to purchase a slave tonight.

Once he had Engles's support, he could begin pushing the boundaries of the corporation to find out once and for all exactly who was behind the Starlin Group. Only then would he know what steps he'd need to take to destroy an organization that had enslaved, tortured, and murdered hundreds of thousands of innocent people, human and vampire.

His heart thrummed with excitement and with a familiar deep need to pay-it-back-in-fucking-full. The slavery he'd endured himself for a full century had created his profound wish to change the status quo. Slavery had gone on for millennia and maybe that was part of the problem: Time had given it a certain acceptability and tolerance.

Not that he cared. He had one purpose in his life, and he meant to see it through even if he died in the attempt.

His reasons were personal since he'd never found his captor. She'd eluded him all this time, staying one step ahead of him, living her life in secrecy, perhaps knowing that once he found her, he'd kill her. However, she had a lot of powers in her arsenal, and one of them was the ability to create intricate disguises.

She'd bought him at auction, or so he'd been told. He hadn't been conscious by the time he'd been taken to the actual bidding block. He'd fought his captors hard, something that had appealed to her sadistic nature. The only way they'd been able to manage him was by binding him with a dozen chains, all enhanced with preternatural power.

Sweet Dove, the only name he'd ever known her by, had offered the highest bid in sex-slave history. Then she'd torn him down, one drop of blood at a time, one inflicted wound after another, depriving him of sleep and of sustenance, until he'd become a mass of incoherent thoughts.

She'd rebuilt him with sex, chaining him up and making him come repeatedly with every part of her body, until his soul shut off and he became the animal she'd craved.

He'd engaged with her then, fully and completely, holding nothing back.

Yet some part of him had remained intact, and began a painfully slow resurgence, a process that took over a century. By the time he escaped Sweet Dove's cavern lair, he'd had only one thought: to get rid of her kind forever, the sex slavers who used humans and fellow vampires like animals.

Maybe he hadn't found her yet, but in the meantime he'd undermine the world she'd helped create and no doubt continued to sustain with her wealth and patronage. As far as he knew she had no association with Starlin, but this arm of the sex-slave trade functioned in a way that felt very familiar to him, with layers of secrecy he hadn't seen since his time with her. Though he believed that a man headed up this organization, somehow he wouldn't have been surprised to find she was a major contributor, at least on some level.

Half an hour later he arrived at the auction site, deep inside the underground cavern system. The large ballroom-sized space was beautifully decorated with carved slabs of polished black granite embedded in the rock walls and surrounded by intricate carvings. The floor was made of the same granite. The house displayed large photos of each of the slaves on easels spread around the room, so that buyers could look over the twenty women who would be auctioned that night.

Servers came up to him, offering drinks and anything else he wanted, bare-breasted beautiful women and men who always revealed what they had to offer. Some even looked him over and made overtures.

He refused them all, politely, but carried a whiskey as he moved around the large cavern.

Given that he'd been gradually making himself known in the darker sex-slave clubs, the presence of so many owners at the auction with their slaves in tow seemed par for the course. Most of the captives wore painful collars with leashes attached and very little or no clothing; they bore plenty of bruises, cuts, and bite marks. Public sexual exchange was a given, part of the allure of the lifestyle, so that couches in different configurations were scattered around the room, as well as wingback chairs.

Like the club he'd been at earlier in the week, moans sounded through the room.

The truth was, when he'd first witnessed the overt nature of the lifestyle, he'd questioned his ability to go through with his plans. As sadistic as Sweet Dove had been, she hadn't taken him to public events like these and put him on display. Of course, she'd held brutal private parties and he'd endured much worse than anything he was witnessing tonight. But what he'd learned later was that because Sweet Dove had feared losing him to an aggressive competitor, who might have done anything to get his hands on Reyes, she'd kept him hidden.

Now, after decades of being in the clubs while he built his reputation, he was fairly immune to the suffering around him, but only because he made nightly promises to himself that he would get rid of this scourge no matter the price.

Most of the female slaves paraded by proud owners were vampires, prized because they could outlast their human counterparts by decades. But for those men and a few women who wanted the excitement of the more fragile human slaves, who bruised and screamed more easily, the auctions featuring the best human wares brought almost everyone to the monthly events, if only to watch the bidding wars.

Some of the slaves sold tonight would die quickly at the two-week mark, a weakness of the human race that couldn't be predicted or helped.

Others would perish at a six-month transition, another human phenomenon and one that many who enjoyed the slave lifestyle paid to watch, a sort of snuff version of the vampire world. Fortunes changed hands over the betting that went on during transition weeks.

When Reyes had escaped, he'd changed his identity, and because Sweet Dove had kept him locked away, and also because he'd shaved off his long hair, no one recognized him now. The facial scruff he wore also enhanced his altered appearance.

He worked out as well, so that his presence tended to dominate most rooms, so different from what he'd known as a slave. Sweet Dove had kept him in a weakened state. About a decade ago, he'd added a series of tattoos to further establish his new identity. He now sported a hawk with wings that stretched across the top of his back, and a collage covered his upper right arm and shoulder, of foliage and symbols that had great meaning to him.

Now he was here, playing his role as a slaver and a Starlin member. Many came up to congratulate him and even to offer the use of their slaves. He thanked everyone, his face almost as impassive as the slaves on their leashes.

He ignored the sex going on all around him and took his time viewing the pictures of the slaves who would soon be auctioned. He paused before each nude image, feigning deep interest, but he barely looked at the women. They were heavily made up, another sign of their enslavement, but even looking felt like a violation.

The auction had two parts. The first involved the individual slaves; in the second, several groups of five women sold for one price.

He'd already made up his mind to focus his efforts on purchasing a group of slaves since he'd save five women instead of just one.

He continued to move slowly, sipping his whiskey. The auction had become a time to preen, something popular among this wealthy set. Most would go to Engles's after-auction party to celebrate the purchases that would take place tonight. Those who successfully bought a slave, or even a group of slaves, would be expected to show off the prize, and especially to demonstrate dominance.

He'd made a complete circuit by the time he reached the last photograph, a woman with dark-brown hair and, as he'd come to expect, heavily made-up eyes. For a moment, however, as he stared at the portrait, his mind filled with flashes of Angelica at the Ocean Club, of her red dress and soft lips as she kissed him.

He stepped closer to the photo, frowning now. He wasn't focusing very well, and a strange red haze had started to flow over his eyes. His arms tensed up, then his thighs, his body reacting to what he was looking at before his mind could catch up to what he was actually seeing.

The woman in this photo looked like Angelica.

A terrible sinking sensation grabbed his heart and pulled hard. He shook his head once. He couldn't believe it was true, this couldn't be true, couldn't be her.

Angelica.

He'd told her to leave the place and never come back. Then she'd kissed him. He could still feel her lips on his, a soft humming against his mouth.

Afterward, he'd watched her leave the club.

Angelica.

He wanted to be mistaken, but he would know those eyes, that nose, the shape of her lips as well as his own. She'd been captured by the Starlin Group despite his efforts. How the hell had this happened? How had he not known?

"She's the one."

He turned, his mind still free-falling, to stare into Engles's face. "Pardon?"

The man narrowed his gaze, then took a sip from his tumbler. "Just thought I'd let you know that she's mine. The Starlin acquisition team who found her somewhere in the States said they had a live one, a real fighter."

Angelica would have fought her captors. He knew that about her, knew her spirit would be part of her appeal. She might seem innocent and have a kind, even vulnerable appearance, but she also had strength of will and courage. Hell, she'd kissed him despite his abrasive attempts to get rid of her.

He needed to adjust quickly to this reality, to pull himself together, because the man claiming Angelica for tonight's auction was Damien Engles. He was the one man whose good side Reyes needed to cultivate above everyone else in this soul-sucking room.

Taking a deep breath, he reordered his senses.

He shoved his hand out and Engles took it. "Brogan Reyes and you're Master Engles. Very nice to meet you and I want to thank you for my membership. I look forward to many years of, shall we say, pleasurable association." He even smiled.

His mind might be in turmoil, but yes, he could smile. Decades of service to Sweet Dove had built up a fine skill set.

Engles held his gaze. The man met him eye-to-eye, straight on, putting him at a similar six-five. His grip was solid. He then added a bit more pressure before he released Reyes's hand, a familiar signal that he considered himself top dog and wanted Reyes to know it.

Starlin's front man wore a tailored tux, finely cut but of a shimmering dark-blue silk that made him stand out, no doubt by design. He had dark-brown wavy hair that he combed away from his face, thick arched brows, and round, almost innocent brown eyes. His nose was large and aquiline, giving him the look of a predatory bird. He had a deep cleft in his chin. Oddly, he looked like the man he was, as though even his features had conspired to reveal a man of violent intention with just enough innocence to lure his victims into a false sense of safety.

Reyes turned back to Angelica's photo and he sipped his drink. "She's very beautiful."

"Yes, but it's the expression in her eyes, don't you think? I know what they put these women through to get them ready for auction, yet in this photo just look at the glint of rage in her eyes. Yes, she's the one."

Reyes took deep breaths. He knew Engles's preference for fighters, just like Sweet Dove. He wanted someone he could break to his will.

The thought of Angelica falling into Engles's hands nearly undid his resolution. He didn't want her hurt like that, her mind and soul destroyed, her body tortured. In addition, Engles's human slaves never lived very long.

But he had a job to do, a big one, that went way beyond what would happen here tonight—and that included Angelica's fate.

He had to stick to his plan, he had to remember that he was working to save thousands of women from the fate she would soon endure. Whatever happened tonight would be a tragedy for her, but he couldn't jeopardize his mission for a lone human female.

And if she survived her captivity, he'd make it his mission to find her and take her out of her hell, but right now, he needed to stay tough. More than just Angelica's life was at stake.

He lifted his drink to Engles. "I'm sure this woman will be all that you're hoping for."

He'd intended to walk away, but Engles held him back. "Are you bidding tonight?"

Reyes smiled, a broad comprehensive smile he'd learned to offer all those years ago. "I came for no other purpose, but I'm looking for more of, shall we say, a group experience."

Engles clapped him on the shoulder. "Good man."

He took one last look at Angelica's photo and saw what Engles had meant and what would make her tonight's star. She had a defiant expression in her eye. A slave with spirit always tempted the most sadistic owners. Angelica would have done better to have appeared broken and submissive because she would have gained one of the more humane owners. Her chances at survival would have increased tremendously.

He felt sick in his gut suddenly, that the woman who had kissed him, who had for a brief moment filled him with something like hope, would be sold to Engles tonight.

He cursed mentally as he signaled to one of the servers.

"What can I get for you, master?"

"Maker's Mark, neat. Make it a double."


Angelica feigned a drugged-out state in the hope of finding her way out of captivity. For the first time in a week, she was outside her prison cell, all her attention focused on her surroundings, on trying to figure out where she was. She searched every wall, looking for a doorway or some kind of access to the outside world. The trouble was, she seemed to be in some kind of cavern system, which severely limited the number of ways out.

She stood in a long line of women, each dressed differently in strange costumes that left very little to the imagination.

She now understood that she'd fallen into some kind of sex-slavery ring, operated within a very strange secret society, that kept its women inside a kind of prison. She didn't know where she was or even what part of the world. She'd been one of dozens of women in the same situation, all held in separate cells in the same prison-like facility.

Her captors had put her through hell over the past several days. She'd been stripped of her clothes and tied down, then beaten for screaming that she wanted out. To her surprise, none of the other women had put up such a racket, but then maybe her screams when tortured had taught the rest to keep quiet.

In the end they'd drugged her. At least then, she'd slept.

But a few hours ago the male servant assigned to her had prodded her awake and forced coffee down her throat. The final prepping had begun, as she was bathed, manicured, coiffed, made up, and finally adorned with her costume, such as it was. She wore only a headdress, draped with a long gauzy floor-length scarf in a leopard print. She could appreciate the artistry, except that she was otherwise completely naked.

All the other women had adopted submissive attitudes, which pissed her off. If they all fought their captors together, maybe they'd have a chance of escape.

The line moved intermittently, and the several male servants in charge spoke quietly into headphones, prodding the women as needed. No one talked. No one dared. The men carried Tasers with them.

At the same time a number of shirtless men, real bodybuilder types, who wore black leather pants and carried whips, lined the walls. She didn't need to be a genius to understand the threat. Even so, she kept looking for a means of escape.

If only she could find a doorway, anything she could slip through, no matter where it led; she'd take the chance. Every instinct screamed that this would be her only opportunity to escape.

Hope dimmed, however, when the line reached what looked like the backstage area of some kind of theater. She hadn't seen a single door or hallway—nothing that could have taken her away from this.

But what were they doing in a theater? Would each of them be required to perform in some kind of strip show?

She glanced down at her breasts, beaded in the cold

cave air, and she would have laughed if her situation hadn't been so horrific. If she was supposed to strip, what would that involve? Taking off the scarf?

As she moved by the wings of the stage, past several rows of curtains and backdrops, she saw the first of the women walking down a runway of some kind followed by applause.

Definitely a show of some kind.

But the next words froze her heart. "We'll begin the bidding on this fine Chinese ware at ten thousand dollars. Do I hear ten thousand? Yes, the gentleman on my left. Do I hear eleven? To the gentlemen in the green blazer. Very nice. Twelve?"

When she'd first realized that she was being held a prisoner, she'd had many thoughts about what was happening to her. But not one of them had involved being called "ware" by an auctioneer, or hearing an audience applauding each bid.

Reyes sat at a small glass table, one knee crossed over the other. A server hovered nearby just for him. On the other side of the stage, Engles sat directly opposite and had already raised his glass, making it clear to Reyes yet again that he expected no competition for his bid.

But Engles was safe from him. He'd long since made his decision and would stick with his plan, despite the fact that his nerves had grown ragged with waiting. He dreaded seeing Angelica walk down the runway.

The bids had already started and he feigned his interest in each woman, knowing that as the newest Starlin member he would be watched for a long time. Even sex slavery had a probationary period.

Many would be curious about him. Others, like Engles, would want to know how his loyalties fell. He had an organization to protect so no doubt everyone, including Reyes, would require continual surveillance and monitoring.

How did Reyes know? Because he would have done the same thing, left nothing to chance. Engles struck him as the same type of man, in complete control.

Reyes finished his whiskey, then ordered another, just to keep the edge off. The parade of captive women disgusted him. They were frightened by what was happening to them, and more than one had stumbled in her stilettos on the way down the polished wood runway.

He just had to get through the night, win his bid for one of the groups of five, then get the hell home.

But when the gavel came down to indicate that number nineteen had just been sold for one-million-five, his stomach twisted into a knot. The new owner lifted her off the stage and carried her to a dark corner. A muffled scream followed.

Reyes struggled to suppress his rage, reminding himself for the hundredth time to take the long view, that one day this organization would be toast.

Then Angelica appeared at the top of the runway and he fell to a place of intense stillness. Time flowed to a stop as he stared at her. He forgot for a moment where he was. He saw only her, the shape of her brown eyes, her straight nose, her full lips. She was an incredibly beautiful woman and carried herself like none of the others. He'd been right about her: even now her spirit showed.

Suddenly he wanted to be back at the Ocean Club, but instead of warning her away, he wanted her in his arms, wanted to take her home, to make her his. He could have protected her then, if only he'd known what was in store for her.

His gaze drifted down her body, to full breasts peaked in the cold room, her narrow waist, and the elegant line of her hips and legs. She had a narrow landing patch.

Unlike all the others, she at first refused to move, which caused the tension and interest in the audience to rise. But two doms with whips nudged her, and she finally moved forward.

Time resumed when the auctioneer started running through a list of assets, including her womanly dimensions and how many sex partners she'd had.

She moved slowly, glancing around the tables. No other slave had done that. Her expression slowly filled with disdain, her upper lip curled, her cheeks drawn back.

He wanted to warn her that these outward displays would only enflame the audience, but there was nothing he could do. He could only stare, like everyone else.

Her hair had been piled high on her head, revealing her long tapering neck, while a very long, leopard-patterned scarf, just a few inches wide, trailed from a feathered headdress over her right shoulder, partially covering one breast. She held the scarf in place by wrapping it around her arm as though she kept this one part of her body sacred.

She had no idea that an attempt at modesty and the look of defiant disgust in her eyes would have the opposite effect, making her more and not less desirable.

He felt the interest of the vampires around him like a wave through the room as the tension level ratcheted up.

She paused halfway down the runway and threw her arms wide. "You're all a bunch of fucking perverts.

What's wrong with you people? Can't you see that what you're doing is vile? That it goes against every honorable code of humanity?"

The crowd erupted, not in disapproval, but rather in a sudden flood of bids. She looked confused now, not understanding what was happening.

But Reyes did. She'd just set herself up as a sadist's dream, an innocent, worthy woman ready to fight.

The auctioneer shouted above the din, "I have two hundred thousand, do I have three? Three, do I have four?" The number kept escalating, and quickly.

He saw her mouth move and extended his hearing. Her voice had dropped to a confused whisper. "What's happening? I don't understand."

He glanced at Engles, who was now on his feet, his face red as he called out a bid that launched the number to two million.

Two million. So fast.

Slowly, Angelica lowered her arms. She searched the crowd, trying to make sense of her surroundings. She pivoted, looking perhaps for one person who would stand with her against this terrible crime.

Reyes rose to his feet and moved next to the runway as so many others had, needing to see her defiance close up. He now stood no more than three yards away from her.

When she met his gaze, her lips parted. She shook her head several times. "No," she murmured. She looked at him with a question in her eyes; then the answer seemed to dawn on her and her gaze grew cold. "So you're one of them."

He nodded slowly, still staring at her as the bids kept climbing toward four million, Engles leading the way. She searched his eyes and he saw profound disappointment, but she couldn't possibly know what it would cost him to support her right now.

He had a role to play and lives to save. He had his cover to protect.

But even as he made up his mind, a different kind of drive rose up in him, one that involved getting her off the stage so that all these other men would stop looking at her.

In a strong voice, and against every ounce of reason, he shouted, "Five million."

"I have five million from one of our newer bidders, Reyes of the Venezuelan system."

The crowd fell silent.

"Do I hear five-million-one-hundred-thousand?"

Engles suddenly called out. "Reyes, what the fuck do you think you're doing?"

Reyes glanced at Engles. "I want the woman." He even offered a show of fangs, just to let Engles know he meant what he said.

Engles met his gaze, staring at him hard, but Reyes kept glaring back. "My bid stands. You offering more?"

Engles slowly shook his head. "You'll regret this one day."

Reyes turned in the direction of the auctioneer. "Five million," he reiterated in a loud voice.

That old saying, *a pin drop,* fit the moment. No one contradicted Engles who didn't have a death wish.

The gavel came down in a hard crack. "Sold, the human Angelica, to the bidder Brogan Reyes."

He moved swiftly toward the stage and held out his hand to Angelica.

"Fuck that." She turned away, moving toward the stage

proper. The two doms now stood at the top of the runway, whips in hand, ready to take charge of her if needed.

She topped in her tracks. "Shit."

His decision to buy her might have been impulsive and incredibly stupid, but if he didn't want to lose the entire game, he knew exactly what he had to do. He had to make her submit to him right now, in front of his peers.

Rising into the air, he levitated in her direction. Her eyes opened wide as she stared at him. "You're flying. Are you on wires or something?"

She didn't even know the truth about the world she'd entered. As he landed, he caught her around the waist in a grip so tight that she cried out in pain. "You're hurting me."

A slight roll of laughter moved through the audience. "Just the beginning, sweetheart," a voice called out.

"Fuck you," she shouted at the crowd.

But he gripped her harder until she turned to stare at him and felt silent. "Let's get something clear right now. You belong to me from this night forward. You're my slave, Angelica. Got it?"

He hated that this worthy woman would also have to learn the art of adopting a hated role, but it couldn't be helped. He'd just saved her life, although that was something she probably wouldn't understand for some time yet. But more than anything, he needed her to submit to him in front of his fellow Starlin members.

She turned to stare at him, her eyes wide with horror. "Why are you doing this?"

"Because I just bought you at auction, you're my slave, and you need to learn your place. I want you to show these fine people that you understand your new role."

Using a pressure point between her shoulder and neck, he pinched hard.

She cried out in pain. Inwardly, he recoiled, disgusted at himself for hurting her, but it couldn't be helped. He pushed down on her at the same time so that she began to lower to her knees.

A spattering of applause rolled through the club.

He kept up the pressure until she'd landed on the wood runway, her hand gripping the back of his leg for support.

"Stop, please stop."

"What do you call me, Angelica? Use the correct address, and the pain will go away."

She looked up at him, tears rolling down her cheeks. "I can't believe this is who you are."

The look in her eyes of pain and disappointment tore at him, but he couldn't stop now. He'd already made an enemy of the one man he'd needed to keep on his good side; if he didn't uphold his cover now, he'd never get inside the Starlin inner circle, find the name of the man who ruled this group.

"Then I guess you never really knew me." He smiled, still pinching her hard. "Now what's my name? What do you call me from this moment forward?"

He increased the pressure so that she cried out again.

"I don't know. I don't know what to call you."

"It's simple: master. You call me master. Say it, loud enough for everyone to hear."

"Master."

"Louder, slave."

"Master. Master."

"One more time. What do you call me?"

"I call you master."

"We finally understand each other. Good."

He released his hand from the slope of her neck and she fell forward, facedown on the runway.

Applause resounded from the ballroom, letting him know he was on the right track.

Turning to the doms, he called out, "I want shackles brought to me right now, for both wrists and ankles, preternaturally charged." When they stared at him slack-jawed, he shouted in a resonant voice, "Do it now."

The men leaped like he'd struck them, though they were thirty feet away. Angelica remained prone, only partially conscious. Half a minute later the doms returned, levitating in swift flight down the runway. A few seconds more and the job was done, the shackles sealed and cutting into her skin.

A third burst of applause sounded and he knew he'd finally done his job well enough. Though he would be wise to stay and parade her around, Angelica was in serious pain now and he'd had enough.

Leaning down, he gathered her up in his arms.

She moaned softly, regaining consciousness. "My arms and legs hurt and I think my wrists are bleeding." Her speech was slurred.

He hated that he'd hurt her so much. Unfortunately for her, things were about to get even more complicated. For one thing, he intended to shift into altered flight, a form of teleportation that would allow him to pass through solid matter. He'd be moving fast to get her out of the building, but that level of speed always hurt the average human.

"Sorry," he whispered. "But this next bit is really going to cause some pain."

Without trying to explain further, he flew her straight through the cavern wall. Her screams echoed in his ears, but she might as well get adjusted to her new reality as soon as possible.

Within his mind, he formed a picture of the two-story mansion he'd had built not far from the Starlin headquarters and like a homing beacon, the location drew him in. Within seconds he landed in his foyer.

He was about to explain that they'd be heading to Engles's after-auction gala, but Angelica pulled from his arms, whirled, and threw up all over his entry rug. She shook head-to-foot, the long scarf trailing in the vomit.

Holding her arm in a strong grip, he held her upright.

His housekeeper appeared. "Master Reyes? What's going on?"

"Mathilde, we have an addition to the household, a human. I just flew her in and she's airsick."

Mathilde frowned as her gaze took in the shackles. "Master, what have you done?"

"Just fix her some tea and get her a robe. Do it now."

"Yes, master." She left the room, heading back to the kitchen.

Angelica groaned and tried to lift a hand to her head, but the shackles prevented her. She stared at them. "You've bound me with chains? Oh, God, my head hurts almost more than I can bear. And my arms feel like they're on fire."

"You'll be fine in a few minutes."

He reached up and unpinned the headdress, letting it fall to the carpet away from her feet.

A moment later Mathilde and several of her housekeeping staff returned to help with Angelica. The women bundled her up in a robe and led her away. Even one of the maids turned and scowled at him. They'd all been slaves at one time or another and each knew exactly what preternaturally charged shackles felt like.

Of course, they couldn't know he'd just saved Angelica's life by buying her at auction.

For five million.

His turn to groan. What had he done? What impulse had led him to throw so many careful plans to the wind?

He could have saved five women tonight and cemented his position in the slavery community at the same time. Instead he'd used up a helluva lot of goodwill to rescue just one. And he'd made an enemy of Engles, the one man he'd needed to placate.

A string of obscenities flew through his head.

Mathilde returned. "We can't get the shackles off. Master, where did you get this woman?"

Two of the servants returned with buckets of water and sponges to work on the rug.

He moved past his housekeeper, a woman who had been with him for two decades now, and gestured with a wave of his hand for her to follow him. Part of him felt a compulsion to tell her the truth or at least some part of what had happened, but more than anything he needed to salvage his efforts to get into the belly of the Starlin Group.

Which meant he needed to figure out what to do with Angelica.

He moved into his library and waved her in, shutting the door behind her. "This woman is my slave and will be until I tell you otherwise."

Mathilde glared at him. "Your slave? I can't believe it. You, of all men, when you've been so tolerant."

"The past doesn't matter. She's my slave now, this is

my domain and you're my servant. And you are not to question my decision or to speak of this to anyone outside my employ. Do you understand?"

"Yes, master."

"You'll be receiving a large parcel from Starlin in the next few minutes. I want everything unpacked as soon as possible."

"Yes, master." She pinched her lips together. "I just don't understand how you could do this. I lost a most beloved sister to slavers."

He kept his face impassive, but her horror and disgust mirrored his own. "I will treat her kindly, Mathilde. She will come to no harm on my watch, you for one should know that. I will only tell you that had I not bought her, Engles would have had her."

She gave a small cry, a hand pressed to her chest. Engles had bought Mathilde's sister at auction, and by all accounts she'd died in the middle of one of his sessions with her. Afterward he'd dumped her in the nearest ocean graveyard.

Tears touched her eyes. "These are terrible times in our world."

"Yes, they are, but she's to be my slave now."

Mathilde nodded, but her shoulders sagged. "Very well, but the shackles have hurt her. Can you at least have them removed?"

"Of course. I'll do it now."

# CHAPTER 3

Angelica lay on a bed in what the housekeeper had told her was Reyes's guest suite. The kind woman had taken the pins from her hair, removed her ridiculously thick false eyelashes, and wiped her face. For all of that, she found herself grateful. Despite the amount of pain she was in, she wanted out of this horrible costume, every bit of evidence removed and destroyed that she'd ever been on that disgusting runway.

"The master will be here soon to remove the shackles. I'm sure of it."

Tears streamed from her eyes. She hadn't wanted to cry, but she was in physical agony from the steady pulse in her head as well as the horrible sensations flowing up both her arms and legs. A painful sensation, like an electrical charge, emanated from the point that the shackles pressed against her skin.

And Reyes had done this to her, the man who just a week ago she'd wanted to take home with her, the man she'd kissed, the man she'd thought was *the one*.

Now she had an entirely different view of him. It seemed he wasn't a man at all, but a beast, an animal, just like her jailers and all those people who'd participated in the auction.

She squeezed her eyes shut, forcing the tears to stop.

She realized that she had truly known nothing about the man she'd craved for months. The darkness she'd seen in him, which she'd understood as some kind of black ops background, had been far worse than anything she could have imagined.

Brogan Reyes was a slaver.

A slaver in some kind of alternate world that she found herself trapped in. The way they'd flown here and all the oddities she'd witnessed during her captivity confirmed it. When the housekeeper and the other servants left the room, she would have started looking for an escape route if she hadn't been in so much pain. As it was, she could only lie still and endure.

The door opened and her captor entered the room.

"Angelica, turn toward me and I'll get the shackles off."

Cringing at the sound of his voice, she rolled on the bed, unable to pull the robe around her; once more she lay exposed. The shackles were heavy, and a short chain between each set prevented much movement.

He looked damn serious as he knelt beside the bed with a tool in his hand that sort of looked like a screwdriver.

"Is this going to hurt more than it already does?"

But he didn't say anything. He just scowled as he placed the tool against the bolt holding together the manacle on her left hand. He tapped and at the same time, some kind of energy flowed.

And so did the pain. She screamed.

"Mathilde," Reyes shouted. "Get me a goddamn healer here. Now."

"I already called. She's on her way." The housekeeper moved back into the room to stand beside Reyes. She was very short and wore thick blond braids wrapped around the crown of her head. She sported an equally serious expression.

He pulled apart the first shackle. Though the weight was no longer there, the pain pulsing up Angelica's arm remained, and the skin at her wrist bled even more than before.

She wanted to tell him how much it hurt, but she didn't see the point. He was no longer someone she could ever think of as a friend. He'd bought her at auction and now no doubt thought of her exclusively as his property.

He glanced at her. "Preternaturally charged shackles cause a lot of pain, even when they're gone. That's why I called for the healer."

She didn't want a healer, which sounded very new age and probably wouldn't be of much use. She wanted a medical doctor, an emergency room, painkillers. And what did he mean, *preternaturally charged*?

She nodded, but she didn't know what else to say. She'd entered an extremely sadistic world, an experience that had begun with her abduction, moved on to a strange woman with curly red hair sending shards of pain through her breasts, and ended at an auction with Reyes controlling her through the shackles he was now removing.

He repeated the process with the other manacle, and she screamed again. And just as Reyes had said, the removal of the shackles still left her arms feeling as though fire burned up to her shoulders.

He turned and went to work on her ankles. When she heard the punch of the tool against the shackle, the same electrical charge ripped through her leg so that she screamed all over again, then started sobbing.

The last tap of the tool sent pain flowing through the rest of her body. She writhed and screamed. "I hurt. Oh, God, I hurt."

"Master?" Another woman's voice this time.

"About time you got here. Dammit, help her."

"Yes, master."

Reyes drew back to allow the new arrival to take his place. She had light-brown hair and pinched gray eyes. She knelt beside the bed the way Reyes had done. The moment she put her hand on Angelica's head, however, sudden warm waves started passing through her; like magic, the fire in her arms and legs drifted away as though it had never existed.

The relief was so great that Angelica sobbed all over again.

But the woman continued to work on her, releasing some kind of healing touch with her hand so that in slow stages, even the terrible pain in her head eased up.

Angelica finally started to breathe again, deep draws into her aching lungs. She lay on her back so relieved that for a long time she couldn't even speak. Finally, she managed a weak "Thank you."

The woman nodded. "How do you feel?"

"I'm very tired, but my arms and legs no longer hurt and my headache is completely gone."

"Good. I'm happy to have been of service."

She rose to leave, but Angelica grabbed her arm and pleaded with her. "You have to help me. I'm a prisoner here."

The woman met her gaze, removing Angelica's hand gently at the same time. "I'm sorry, mistress, but I treat a lot of slaves. I can't do anything for you other than to tend your wounds. Have the master call me again if you have any other difficulties."

"Please, I can't stay here. I'll die if I have to live under this roof."

At that, the woman bowed to her, a strange, formal movement, but averted her gaze. "I have to go now. I wish you well." She then turned and hurried out.

"Please don't go."

Reyes appeared in the doorway, thunder on his brow as he slammed the door shut. "Don't ever do that again. Don't ever try to enlist either my servants or anyone else who comes into this house to help you to escape."

"I won't stay here. I promise you I'll never stop trying to get away from you." Her whole body shook as she spoke, but he ought to know the truth: that she wouldn't remain a victim, that she'd never give up trying to leave.

"You intend to just walk out the door?"

"That would make the most sense." She'd walk out, then she'd make her way to the nearest police station.

"And where exactly do you think you are that you can just open a door and leave?"

She looked around, then up at the ceiling. She blinked several times at an intricately carved flow of rock, beautiful in its way, but like nothing she'd ever seen before.

She kept having her thinking knocked sideways at unexpected moments, and this was one of them. Other parts of the room looked quite normal: flat walls made of drywall, painted up, trimmed with baseboards and molding around the doorways.

Though the door was closed, she remembered seeing the hallway when Reyes had brought her into this room—she'd had a glimpse of another intricately carved rock wall. She'd seen similar walls while moving from her prison cell to the backstage of the theater.

She knew then she wouldn't find a door to the outside anywhere in this house. Reyes had built a very large mansion in the middle of a cave.

Finally, her gaze returned to him. "Where am I? What is this place? And how did we get here?"

He only shook his head, still very grim as he stared down at her.

A terrible sensation descended on her that she was in a place even worse than the prison cell she'd inhabited for the past week and the large room where she'd been auctioned.

She met and held his gaze as she leaned up on her elbows. "Tell me . . . *please*."

"The Como cavern system, in Italy, deep underground. Miles underground."

For the first time since she'd awakened in her cell, she felt truly and completely trapped. She stared for a long moment at her captor, a man she'd thought she'd known well enough to want to take him home with her, yet he lived underground. She'd never heard of such a thing. Other things that didn't make sense returned to her. "You said the chains had a preternatural charge."

He nodded slowly, holding her gaze, his expression solemn.

"One of my jailers spoke of wanting to take a draw from my throat. What did she mean?" The word hovered just at the edge of her consciousness, but she couldn't bring herself to think it.

He seemed almost angry as his jaw worked. But a moment later he parted his lips. She didn't at first recognize what she was looking at until his nostrils flared and his upper lip curled back.

Fangs. Like the ones he'd shown while making his bid and yelling at the other man. Fangs. They were real.

"Vampires," she said barely above a whisper. "Oh, God, this is a vampire world."

"A very secret one."

The room seemed to grow warm and even spin a little. She leaned her head back against the pillows once more and closed her eyes. This couldn't be true, couldn't be happening.

For the past week she'd tried to assimilate the horror she'd landed in, but her mind had refused to catch up. Instead she'd operated on some kind of raw instinct that had kept her from knowing the truth, from understanding where she was and what exactly had happened to her.

"Angelica."

When she opened her eyes, Reyes stood right next to the bed, his blue eyes dark in the dimly lit room. At least his fangs had disappeared.

She held a hand up as though to ward him off, but as she thought back on everything that had happened, one thing really didn't make sense to her. "I need to know something. Will you at least answer a question?"

He nodded.

"At the auction, when I said what I said, calling all those people perverts, why did that jump-start the bidding? Why did that make me such a hot commodity? I thought it would have the opposite effect, make me less attractive."

"You really must be naive—or were you just not paying attention? Think for a moment. What do you remember about the audience, those who had come to bid and to observe the bidding. What was going on?"

"I saw a lot of naked flesh. Women, and even a few men, walking around with barely anything on, like those of us on the stage." Her stomach roiled. "And there was sex as well, in at least three different places. So that was some kind of sick sex club."

"Keep thinking back. Did you hear screaming as well?"

She nodded, turning everything over in her mind. "So we're talking sadism."

"Exactly."

"And you belong to this club?"

He lifted his chin. "Just joined, and you were my first buy."

She stared at him, once more feeling like she'd been body-slammed. A week ago, she'd wanted to sleep with Reyes, and now he owned her. He'd hurt her as well, pinching her shoulder to force her to the runway floor, then putting on the painful shackles. She just couldn't believe this was who he really was.

He scowled heavily now, his nostrils flaring.

She realized suddenly that Reyes was angry, but she didn't know why. In fact, he seemed downright hostile toward her, which made no sense at all. He was the one with all the power in this situation. He could hurt her, use her, even torture her if he wanted to. She should be the only angry person here.

"Why are you so pissed off?" She sat up and swung her knees over the side of the bed. "I'm the victim in this situation, the slave."

"You want to know why?" He took a menacing step toward her, bumping against her knees, a hard light in his eye.

She nodded, but he scared her like this. She pulled her robe tight across her chest.

"Because you've just fucked up my plans."

"What are you talking about? What plans?"

Reyes stared at her for a long moment, wishing Angelica had a little less spirit. He had no intention of sharing his mission with her, but she presented a serious dilemma for him. He needed to take a very submissive slave to Engle's after-auction party, not a willful human female full of questions and outrage.

In order to sustain his cover, she'd have to be obedient to him, even frightened of him, throughout the entire event. He'd all but made an enemy of the one man who could lead him to the power behind the Starlin Group. But if he took Angelica to the party in her present condition, Engles would know the truth, that all this time Reyes had been fronting, and his cover would be blown.

Right now he had to get away from her, to think, to figure out just how to get her to submit to him. "You're to stay in this room until I summon you."

He turned on his heel and walked swiftly out of the guest suite, heading in the direction of the foyer and the broad, curved staircase. More than anything, he loathed that she thought him a slaver, but he saw no other way around the issue. He needed her to play a role, and the only way that made sense was if he brought her into submission so that no matter what, she'd do as she was told.

When he reached the foyer, he pulled his phone from the pocket of his tux and called his head of security, ordering guards to be placed at each door of his mansion. To keep Angelica safe, he had to make certain she didn't try to leave his house. This exclusive section of the Como system housed a lot of Starlin members, and if she was caught on the run, Angelica could disappear into another slaver's house and never be seen again.

Runaways were fair game.

He wished to hell he could tell her the truth, but he'd be risking too much, which meant he had to make her believe that she truly was his slave and her survival depended on doing his bidding.

Which meant he had to break her will and do it fast. Most of the time, it took very little to make a human submit—a threat of pain coupled with the taste of great pleasure beneath his fangs if she obeyed. Angelica wasn't the typical human female, however, and he worried that if he started down this road he'd be forced to do things to her that would make him as bad as Engles.

A cold shudder went through him, but he really didn't have a choice.

As he started up the stairs, he heard her bare feet slapping against the slate floor. She called out, "This isn't right and you need to let me go. I don't care that you bought me at some kind of freak-ass auction. I'm not a slave and you can't make me one."

Pausing on the third step and gripping the handrail, he turned to stare down at her as he considered his next move. He'd intended only to retrieve the outfit she'd need for the party and bring it to her, and afterward make her a couple of serious threats that he hoped might bring her in line. But she'd just proved yet again that breaking her will would be no simple thing.

Two of his guards arrived and took up positions on either side of the massive wood front door.

She watched them, her brows raised. He thought their arrival could work in his favor because the men were one more signal her brain clearly needed to help clarify her present reality.

He held a hand out to her. "Come with me. I think it's time we had a heart-to-heart."

She looked wary and didn't move for a long moment. But after glancing once more at the guards, she finally put her feet in motion.

He led her up the stairs, then to the east wing that housed his private quarters, recently renovated to enhance his slaver identity.

He threw the doors wide, then passed by his bedroom, taking his time so she could see the level of his wealth. Money was power, another piece of information she clearly needed to figure out.

He had a sitting room on the right, then his exercise and massage rooms, and finally an expansive bathroom with a deep soaking tub in addition to a walk-in shower.

She didn't say anything, but she'd slowed her movements to look around, which he took as a good sign.

The last room had cost him over a million, having required the dredging out of tons of rock. But the investment had speeded up his Starlin membership since the room had met the approval of several Starlin men who'd come to make an inspection.

As he grasped the door handle, he looked back at her. Most of her makeup was long gone, and her hair had come down to hang about her shoulders. She was in a state of disarray and looked ridiculously vulnerable as she held her head high. Even like this, with reddened eyes, she was damn beautiful. How he hated that fate had somehow put her in this heinous position.

She met his gaze. "So what's beyond the door? What is it you need to show me? I'm guessing it's some kind of oversized closet for your billionaire wardrobe."

"See for yourself."

He pushed the door wide, flipped on the lights that dotted the wood ceiling, then stepped aside to make way for her. "This is the game room, a place you and I will be spending a lot of time, starting now, actually."

She moved in slowly, then gasped. "Oh, God. What is this?"

He'd designed the space based on one of the rooms Sweet Dove had kept in her sprawling home. She'd taken him there on an almost nightly basis. The result was essentially a padded torture chamber full of masks, whips, a variety of implements for cutting, two different kinds of tables with straps and stirrups, and a wall of chains and manacles.

Taking hold of Angelica's arm, he pulled her into the room, then turned to lock the door. He'd positioned the dead bolt high so that no slave could reach it.

She turned to him, wide-eyed, a frown between her brows. "You can't be serious."

He could explain everything to her, or he could show her. He knew she'd been through a lot, but she needed to get with the program now. If he wanted to sustain his reputation in this lifestyle, he needed Angelica on a leash and her demeanor properly subdued by the time he took her to Engles's home.

"You're going to learn to obey me, Angelica. I won't have you fighting me, not here in my home or in public. I own you now, you're my slave, get used to it and do it fast. I've been working for years to gain admittance into the Starlin Group and I'm not about to let you fuck it up.

"Now, we'll be going to a party in a couple of hours, and while we're there I need you on your knees the moment I tell you to get on your knees."

A look of horror passed over her features. "To do what?"

"I think you know exactly what that means."

She shook her head. "This can't be happening and like hell I'm going down on you in public. I'd rather die."

He'd hoped the mere sight of the room would start softening her belligerence. Instead she was more obstinate than ever.

Time for phase two.

He shifted to altered flight, scooped her up, and slapped her against the wall that dangled with chains. He bound her up vampire-fast so that she was once more shackled, and spread-eagled within seconds, her robe gaping wide, her body on display, her feet on the floor. The only difference was that these shackles weren't preternaturally charged and except for their weight wouldn't hurt her.

"What are you doing?"

He got up close. "I've already told you. I'm helping you get a good picture of your new life so that you can adjust your attitude accordingly. I want you submissive and meek, and it looks like you need a lesson or two to get you started.

"But feel free to shout. Scream your head off. This room is soundproof and if one of the servants happens by, well, let's just say that everyone in this house is loyal to me and serves only me. You can't turn a single person in the immediate twenty square miles against me. You can't escape, you can't run, you can't hide. I'm here. I'm your master. And you'll do as I say. Do we have an understanding yet?"

"I understand that you can go straight to hell."

He let out a roar of frustration, but her gaze never wavered from his. Shit, this was going to get ugly if he had the smallest hope of breaking her will.

"Let me go home."

"Not gonna happen."


Angelica stared at Reyes, her captor, a self-proclaimed slaver.

Her mind was still working to make sense of all that had happened to her. She knew she was still in shock, yet she had to pull herself together enough to withstand his attempts to break her.

She got that the man she'd kissed not long ago, the man she'd wanted so badly, was a monster, the worst kind, sadistic and brutal. The room spoke of the kinds of things he intended to do to her. In addition, the nature of the auction, as well as the horrible acts going on in that room, made her future clear.

Yet she rejected all of it, with every ounce of her being.

Her heart pounded in her chest. "I'll never stop trying to escape this captivity. You have to know that. No matter what you do to me right now."

He moved in closer and pressed a hand to her throat.

"Do you know how easily I could kill you, snap your neck, or just choke you to death?"

He squeezed her windpipe, making it hard to breathe. She felt his latent strength and trembled.

"All I want you to do is submit to me. That's all."

Though tears bit her eyes, she refused to bend. If she had to die, then so be it.

She closed her eyes and waited, but after another few seconds the pressure eased up.

She blinked and stared into cold blue eyes.

"How did you enjoy that, Angelica? I can choke you repeatedly without taking your life. How about I do that to you for months or years, only each time I'll take you just a little closer to death. How does that sound?"

"Go to hell." Her voice was hoarse as she spoke. "I despise you."

"What you're not getting is that I don't care what you think of me. All I need is for you to say 'Yes, master,' and mean it." His hand slid down her throat to her breasts. He caressed her, in much the same way that horrible woman had done earlier in the week.

"Does that feel good?" He was even using the same line the woman had used.

"I hate that you're touching me."

"You can learn to love my touch, or fear it, the choice is yours." He pinched her nipple and the same kind of fire that had penetrated her breast at that woman's hand touched her again, a threat that could get much worse. But now she understood that this was some kind of vampire ability.

"All I have to do is let my energy flow and you'll be screaming. Is that what you want? Pain so bad that you'll pass out?" He leaned close. "I don't want to do this to you and you can make it stop. Just submit to me, because, trust me, I can keep this up for hours."

"She did the same thing to me, only much worse, and I didn't relent then," Angelica said. "Why would I give in to you now?"

He released her breast, frowning. "What do you mean, *she*?"

Angelica's knees had started feeling rubbery, and she was grateful he'd backed off. He hadn't hurt her the way the woman had, but he could have and might yet. "The woman at the prison, with this cloud of red curly hair. She came to see me, said she was tempted to buy me herself. I didn't get it, then, but I do now. She's a sadistic slaver, just like you."

He didn't say anything for a long moment. Finally, he said, "Describe the woman. What did she look like, besides her red hair?"

"Why should I tell you?"

But the moment the words left her mouth, his hand was around her throat again, squeezing. "What did she look like?" His eyes were wild. "Goddammit, Angelica, what the fuck did she look like? You've got to tell me. This is important."

She blinked several times, stunned by the sudden intense look in his eye. The woman meant something to him, something really bad. "Her eyes were a dark blue. She had a small mouth, pale skin. She was beautiful and ugly at the same time. She hurt me."

"And she was at the prison, where you were held?"

She nodded.

She didn't know why, but Reyes released her throat, then stepped away from her, sweeping a hand down his face. He bent over as if in sudden pain. After a moment, however, he rose up and straightened his shoulders, coming back to himself. Whatever memories this woman had evoked, he appeared to have shunted aside.

He met her gaze again, his eyes narrowed as though contemplating his next move. "If pain doesn't affect you, maybe the opposite will."

When he moved toward her this time, she trembled all over again but for a different reason as his gaze roved her body. He drew close, pushing her robe aside. "You have beautiful breasts. That dress you wore at the Ocean Club still gets me going when I think about it. But what would please you, I wonder?" He leaned down and suckled her breast.

"Don't do this," she whispered. She'd had fantasies about Reyes before her abduction, all of which she'd enjoyed.

But right now she was horrified that he would do this to her while she was chained to a wall. For some reason it seemed worse to her than the feel of his hand at her throat, or the fire at her breast, that while holding her captive, he would pleasure her.

In a louder voice, she said, "You sick bastard, stop it. I hate what you're doing."

He slowly dropped to his knees, looking up at her at the same time. "You don't get a say in this, slave. You've felt the stick, now let me show you the real advantage of surrendering your will to mine."

His tongue swirled over her sensitive navel, then began a low, purposeful glide toward the flesh between her legs.

"No, please don't."

The shackles held her prisoner and there was nothing she could do to stop him as his hands glided up and down her legs. But before his tongue found her most tender flesh, he rose up in front of her.

As much as she hated him, there was no denying how handsome the man was, his eyes like the clearest water as he held her gaze.

Then his nostrils flared as his gaze roved her throat. He slid a hand around the back of her neck, and to her horror she watched as his fangs emerged.

"Don't bite me. Don't you dare fucking bite me."

"You think you've felt pleasure before? You have no idea what's about to happen, and once I've given you this ride you'll be begging for more."

She had little strength left to fight him when he tilted her head to the side, then struck with his fangs.

She winced at the sudden sting, but a moment later, as he began to draw from her neck, a new layer of desire rushed through her, a kind of euphoria she'd never known before.

She wanted to scream her frustration at feeling so many unwelcome sensations, but he was right: the pleasure she felt grew more intense with each draw from her neck. It hit her like the strongest drug, and while part of her raged against it, she was powerless to stop the waves of bliss that overtook her.

He suckled greedily, groaning as he took her blood down his throat. She felt each draw in a heavy pulse deep between her legs. He slid an arm around her now, caressing her bottom once more, then anchored his hips against hers.

Through his pants, she felt the thick rope of his erection and groaned once more. He arched his hips, pressing into her flesh in just the right way so that she cried out.

Maybe it was the complete despair of the moment, or

the fact that she was fully aroused, but her body took over and she writhed against him, an orgasm building. Her whole body felt sensitized so that as his hips pressed into her repeatedly, pleasure ran up and down her arms and legs, her back, and over her breasts.

His hips moved faster, pummeling her now with swift strikes that brought her closer and closer to the edge. Even his suckling increased in speed.

The sound of the moans he made added another layer—so that suddenly she flew straight over the cliff, crying out once more as a lightning flow of ecstasy rushed through her, taking her high into the stratosphere.

Pleasure peaked, fell back, then peaked again. He kept working her body, kept drinking from her throat, and she cried out repeatedly, pleasure, just as he'd promised, rolling through her again and again.

She finally came back to earth, her body growing quiet as he released her throat.

He planted his hands on the wall on either side of her head, staring into her eyes, his expression as serious as ever. He was breathing hard, his brow pinched. She knew without having to be told that though he'd been aroused, he hadn't come and the experience had no doubt left him in pain.

For that, she couldn't feel bad. He ought to suffer.

Her legs didn't want to support her and her arms had started to hurt. Not that her captor cared.

Her mind spun in circles. She'd gone from Reyes frightening her to giving her the most incredible release she'd ever known.

But her stomach boiled with anger and disgust. Just because he'd brought her didn't mean she'd thank him for it, or even value what had just happened.

On the contrary, something about having been worked up sexually against her will served to strengthen her determination.

"You'll never break me. You can tear my flesh apart with one of those whips, you can give me a thousand orgasms, but I promise you, I will never submit to you willingly."

# CHAPTER 4

Reyes stared into Angelica's hard brown eyes. He'd just introduced her to a new world of sensation that would have taken any other human female to her knees. Instead she glared at him.

He knew from his own experience that every man or woman could be broken, given enough time, and he knew that eventually he could make her submit. However, given her spirit, the process would require days, maybe even weeks to accomplish, and he didn't have that kind of time.

He knew something else as well. He couldn't do it. What he'd done tonight had been something he'd promised himself he'd never do: force either a human or a vampire to do anything against his or her will.

Yet that's exactly what he'd done.

Worse still, when he'd sent a light preternatural charge through her breast, giving a hint of the kind of pain he was capable of inflicting, she'd told him something that had sent him reeling.

If he was right, the woman who had hurt her might very well have been Sweet Dove herself. The physical description matched and the terrible truth was that he'd learned from her how to focus his power into a debilitating stream in order to cause pain. How many times had she hurt him in just that way, sometimes to create sexual pleasure, other times to torture him just for her gratification?

Guilt and shame washed through him, and slowly he set about unlocking Angelica's shackles. When she was free, she rubbed her wrists, then tied up her robe. She moved slowly to sit on the nearby padded table.

Her shoulders were slumped with fatigue, but her eyes still sparked defiantly.

Despite his guilt over trying to break her, he knew by the look in her eye that he'd done the right thing in buying her. If Engles had won the bid, he would have battered her senseless by now, savoring how hard she fought him. But she would have died within a few days because he would have beaten her, broken her bones, cut her to ribbons.

One of only two things was going to happen from this point forward. He would tell her about his mission and either she would agree to help him or the game was over. There was simply no way he could take Angelica in her present state to Engles's mansion and have anyone believe that he'd brought her under his command, that she was truly his slave.

But would she ever agree to help him after what he'd just put her through?

He removed a soft linen handkerchief from the pocket of his pants and wiped any remaining blood from his lips. He'd almost come at least three times while taking down her life force. She'd tasted as sweet as her blood had smelled and he was satisfied—another reality that filled him with guilt.

He paced slowly, trying to find the right way to tell her the truth and to ask for her help. At this point, however, he'd be stunned if she ever believed another word that came out of his mouth.

Finally, he moved to stand in front of her, then swept an arm to encompass the room. "So none of this really frightens you?"

She glanced around. "Actually, I'm frightened out of my mind, I'm just too worn out to show it. Any chance you can leave me in peace for a while? Let me get some sleep?"

"I wish I could, but there's something I need to explain to you. I'm not a slaver and you're not really my slave."

She held up both hands. "You're driving me crazy. What does that mean, I'm not your slave? From the time you brought me here, you've messed with my mind. You hurt me badly, then did all that shit to me while I was chained against the wall, and now you're telling me you're not a slaver?"

"I need you to listen to me. For a long time now, I've been working to infiltrate the Starlin Group, the same outfit that abducted you and forced you to walk down that runway. This organization is one of the most powerful sex-slavery rings in our world.

"When I told you to leave the Ocean Club that night,

I was trying to warn you that you were being scoped by a Starlin acquisition team, a group trained to hunt all over the world for beautiful but vulnerable women who could be removed from their lives without significant repercussions."

She blinked. She looked exhausted, which of course she would be. She'd already been through hell before he'd brought her into his home, then he'd added to her misery.

Her shoulders fell a little more. "But you told me you joined this group, that I was your first buy."

"Both of those things are true, but I didn't buy you to keep you as a slave."

"Then what did you buy me for?"

"For one essential reason, to uphold my reputation as a slaver."

"But you just said you're not a slaver."

"No, I'm not."

She glanced at the chains on the wall, the whips, the knives. "So what is all this? Are you saying you don't use this room?"

"Never, not until tonight."

She shook her head in disbelief. "You're lying. You're a fucking, lying bastard and you're messing with me again. How can I believe you? You hurt me just now, or at least you showed me how much you could hurt me if I didn't do as you said. Then you used your fangs on me. I'm just surprised you didn't shove your cock between my legs and take the whole thing the rest of the way."

"I wanted to. Believe me, I wanted nothing more."

She released a heavy sigh. "So you drew the line at raping me."

"Yes. I did."

"You're disgusting."

He saw the level of her revulsion and knew he wasn't explaining things well enough yet. "I bought you to support the role I'm playing as a slaver."

"What role?"

"I have only one goal here, Angelica, to bring Starlin down. And I still want to. When I succeed in destroying this slavery ring, I'll be saving tens of thousands of lives, maybe more. These auctions will end forever. That's how I've justified, until this moment, doing to you what I just did. I don't know how else to say this to you, except that I'm deep undercover and I have a plan. A damn good one."

"And that's what you meant when you said I fucked up your plans?"

He nodded. "That's what I meant. What I did in buying you has put me an inch away from blowing my cover."

"And I'm supposed to believe you?"

"Yes, because it's the truth, the only one that matters right now."

"And it's Starlin who abducted me and all those other women there tonight, parading our bodies and selling us at auction."

He nodded again. He could see that she was turning all this new information over in her mind, so he waited.

Finally, she met his gaze straight-on. "Let's say I choose to believe you for now. So tell me about this Starlin Group. I take it they're a significant player."

"One of the biggest."

He gave her numbers, something an accountant would appreciate: The Starlin Group moved twenty thousand human women through its organization every year. Between the prostitution houses they owned in a number of countries worldwide, as well as the auctions they sustained in the vampire world, they generated eighteen billion dollars a year.

Then he added the worst stat of all: without exception the human slaves died, so the inventory had to be replaced at a quick, steady pace.

She stared at him, a deep frown drawing her brows together. "All of them?"

He nodded once, slowly.

"How? Why?"

"In a slave situation, a certain percentage of humans, about fifteen percent, will not live beyond the two-week mark even if they're treated well. Ultimately, it's a matter of the will."

She pressed a fist into her cheek, her eyes pinched. "And after the two-week period?"

"A second transition occurs at six months, but the survival rate drops to fifty percent. Beyond that, only a handful live past two years."

"Oh, dear God. So my life expectancy, in the best of circumstances, would have only been two years."

He nodded. "But I also want to stress that in the Starlin Group, the percentages are much worse."

"Because of the sadistic element."

"Yes. The torture. Humans just don't hold up well."

"Are there other auction houses in your world?"

"A few, but not at this level."

"And you intend to take this beast down."

Again, he nodded.

"Are you working alone?"

"Pretty much."

"But how can one man really bring down an entire organization?"

"It will still take time, but the most critical element is

that I need to find out who runs this show. The head guy, the brains behind the operation, must be eliminated first. After that, I'll use my resources to take every single member of this club down, one by one, until nothing is left.

"Despite my efforts to find him, the man who's behind Starlin remains one of the biggest secrets in our world. He goes by the code name Scorpion, and to my knowledge only one man has access to him, a man called Engles."

She frowned slightly, tilting her head. "Do you know, I used to think you had to be involved in black ops missions of some kind. You had that look. I'm beginning to think my first assessment of your character was right. So are you some kind of military man in your world?"

He shook his head. "No, not at all."

She looked him up and down. "You're big enough. You look like you could take anyone down, which means the real question on my mind right now is why you're so intent on breaking up the sex-slavery operations in your world? Why are you so determined to destroy Starlin? Why do you even care?"

She got right to the heart of the matter, he'd give her that, but just how much he should tell her, he wasn't sure.

On the other hand, he suspected that to hold back now, to not tell her the truth, would be the last straw for her. And because he was so close to really getting inside Starlin, he decided to risk it all. He'd tell her what he'd never told another living soul, vampire or otherwise.

He drew a deep breath and held her gaze steadily. "I was a sex slave once, held by my captor for over a century. I know what it is to endure abduction and sale on the block. Everything you would have suffered as a slave, had another man won the bid and brought you to a room like this, I experienced at the hands of my captor. But worse." She opened her mouth to speak, but he held up a hand. "I'm not willing to talk about what happened to me, except that it was bad, as bad as it gets. That I survived is nothing short of miraculous, but every day I promised myself that if I ever escaped, I'd tear this depraved part of our world down, if I had to do it with my own bare hands."

Angelica wondered if she'd ever be able to blink again. She still sat on the table, her hands clasped tightly together, staring at Reyes, and trying with all her might to process so many revelations: his mission, his reason for buying her, and the fact that he'd suffered as a sex slave himself.

She looked away from him, letting this new tsunami of information sweep over her. That feeling of having been tackled hard and slammed to earth struck her again.

She met his gaze once more. "So if I've truly understood you and if I can believe you, then you saved my life by buying me at auction."

"More than you know. Damien Engles, the man I referred to earlier, had made it clear to me before the auction began that he intended to purchase you and that I was not to interfere. But I already knew his reputation. Human slaves don't live longer than a week in his house. He savors the killing element as part of sexual gratification. The worst kind of monster."

"And he was intent on having me."

"Absolutely. He liked your fighting spirit, your defiance."

Reyes turned suddenly, crossing to a nearby shelf and picking up what looked like a small leather bag. When he returned to her, he pulled out a weird-looking glove, then slipped it on. "I want you to take a good look at this."

Her gaze moved slowly down to his hand—and what she saw forced all the air from her lungs. Each fingertip held a sharp steel claw. She tried to breathe, but couldn't. Every part of her body felt frozen, immobile. Nothing she'd been exposed to in this world had truly sunk in, not even his comments about sadism and torture, until she stared down at the leather device. The middle finger had two claws, about a quarter inch apart. "And this group uses this thing?"

"Some do. Engles, most certainly."

She shook her head, staring at him. He tucked the glove back into the bag and in a quick flick of his wrist tossed it back on the shelf.

She pulled the lapels of her robe tight together once more. Her voice came out on a whisper. "You didn't just save my life, you saved me from a kind of torture I can't even begin to imagine. My God."

For a long moment, she covered her face with both hands. She didn't think she'd ever be able to get the image of that glove out of her mind. But maybe that was a good thing, given her present circumstances.

She'd thought Reyes an absolute monster when he'd put a hand to her throat, giving her a warning about what he could do to her if he wanted to. But he hadn't actually hurt her. Of course, he'd definitely caused her pain on the runway, but now she understood why he'd felt compelled to do so: to show he could command his newly bought slave. He was playing his role, supporting his cover.

"Angelica, I need to be honest with you. I hadn't intended to buy you like I did, especially since my plans depended on Engles having his way. I acted on impulse when I started bidding for you, because I knew that not only would you be tortured, but you'd be dead within a few days and I couldn't have lived with myself. But dammit, Engles is the key to my mission." He shook his head several times in a row. "Now, however . . ."

"This could already be a shitfest for you."

"To put it succinctly. I bid against the most powerful man in the organization, short of Scorpion himself."

She frowned as she met his gaze again. "You're asking for my help, aren't you? That's why you've told me all this."

"Yes, but there's something else you should know before you make a decision. These people, Angelica, they're evil personified. If they question who I am and what I'm doing, I'll be dead and you'll be auctioned again. So you'll need to think about that."

He ran a hand through his hair and glanced at the place he'd chained her up, shaking his head. "Shit, I should have been up front with you from the beginning. I should have asked you straight out for your help, the moment I brought you back to my home. I should have laid it all out as soon as I removed the shackles in the guest room."

At that, she slid from the table and punched him in the shoulder, a thump that caused his brows to lift as he stared down at her. "Yes, you should have, and why didn't you? Did you think I would refuse, especially knowing that you saved me from a true sadist like Engles? I would have forgiven what you did. Now I don't know what to do."

"I thought I had a better shot at pulling the whole thing off if I forced your submission. If you're not willing to cooperate, or you can't pull it off, though, all the work I've done is for nothing."

"Can't you just go to the party without me?"

He snorted. "There'd be no point. I'm on thin ice as it is. If I didn't show up with you, the whole thing would be over."

"So it's all on me."

"I don't want you to think of it that way. That's unfair to you—you never asked for any of this. If you can't continue, I'll walk away. I'll figure out a new strategy and rebuild. It'll mean a shift in direction, no question. But this current plan will be dead, that much is true, and right now I'm okay with that. No one deserves to be ripped from their lives and I promise you that if you decide to return immediately to your old life, I'll see to it that you're safe from Starlin."

She nodded several times, processing, running the numbers, thinking through everything he'd told her. Reyes needed her to play the role of a woman bought at auction to sustain his mission. And if everything he'd said was true, on some level she owed him. But she'd have to be subservient to him, willing to do anything in public to prove her submission.

"How long have you been building this cover?"

"Decades."

"Seriously? It took you decades to be able to join this freak show?"

He nodded. "They're extremely protective of their organization. I've done things I'm not proud of to prove that I've embraced the lifestyle."

"Jesus." She rubbed her forehead with her fist. "And you'd give this all up if I said the word, if I said I wanted nothing to do with it, if I couldn't play this role, if I just wanted to go home and be done with it all?"

He nodded solemnly, and she believed him.

Angelica searched his eyes, seeing once again the man

she'd been so attracted to back at the Ocean Club, for all those months. She hadn't been wrong about him after all, even if he was a different species and his cover meant that he did things she knew she wouldn't approve of.

But could she really do this? Could she step into the role of sex slave and perform well enough to secure his reputation? Could she keep her opinions to herself, her eyes lowered, her voice submissive as she spoke? Or worse, if the situation called for it, could she engage in certain activities publicly in order to sustain his cover? Or would she end up jeopardizing his mission by saying or doing the wrong thing at the wrong time?

Beyond what her role would entail, however, was the prospect of returning home. He'd just told her that she could go back to her life if that was what she wanted.

She was an accountant who worked long hours in her firm, but wasn't that crazy about her occupation. Mostly she worked the kind of overtime she did to help support her mother, who'd been ill for years. Her aunt was with her now, so Angelica wouldn't truly be missed for another week or more, but all of those essentials reminded her why she'd gone to the Ocean Club in the first place.

Her life had become a rut.

If she went back now, nothing would be materially different. Of course, she had no idea if her job would be waiting for her when she returned, but she could always look for another accounting job. It was more than that, though.

As she stared into Reyes's eyes, she understood his purpose, why he felt called to stop others from being abused as they had been. "How long do you think you'd need me in this role?"

His eyes lit up. "Just for tonight. After that I could fake

your death, which would go a long way with Starlin. I just need to parade you at the party for a few hours. It won't be pleasant, however. That much you really do need to understand."

"But it would only be for tonight."

"Exactly."

She thought about the other women who'd been auctioned off tonight, and somehow she came to her decision. The least she could do was give Reyes's plan a chance.

"Okay, then. I could do this for one night. I know I could, and I think I owe you that. It's clear to me that you saved my life and that if you hadn't bid against Engles, well, I don't want to think about what I'd be going through right now." She glanced briefly at the leather pouch on the shelf and repressed a shudder.

"Angelica, I don't know what to say, except that I'm grateful and I'm equally sorry that I put you through all that earlier."

"You were doing what you felt needed to be done." She clapped her hands together. "Okay, so, what happens next? Although to be honest I wouldn't turn down a meal. I'm starved." This was the first time in the past week she'd actually had an appetite.

"I'll have my housekeeper send up some homemade soup. How does that sound?"

"Perfect."

He moved past her, heading in the direction of the door. "Your measurements were taken while you were imprisoned. Starlin always provides an initial wardrobe for the auctioned women, including makeup and all kinds of lotions and hair care products. By now my servants will have unpacked everything for you."

He led her to his bathroom, which proved large enough

to roller-skate in. White marble covered the floors, walls, ceiling, and a long vanity area. Two sinks had gold fixtures. Given all that she saw, she had no reason to doubt the gold was real.

She followed him as he moved into what proved to be a large closet with a dressing area and a full-length mirror. Most of the space was empty except for a row of barely-there garments that made use of leather and sequins, feathers and chains, and a variety of sheer fabrics.

Reyes went through them, sliding the hangers along the rod in quick swipes, his expression as grim as ever.

He chose the red costume that seemed to have the most fabric, and that wasn't saying much. From a row of shoes, he picked up a pair of matching red sequined pumps with five-inch stilettos. "These will have to do. I'll apologize now, but the truth is I'm going to hate everyone staring at you."

She glanced at him and realized there was a hint of jealousy in his tone, but she didn't say anything. As at the auction, once again, most of her body would be on display no matter which outfit he chose.

He took the costume and hung it back up, putting the shoes back on the rack. "While Mathilde prepares a tray for you, why don't you have a bath?"

She glanced at the soaking tub and nodded. "I'd really like that."

"I'll leave you alone, then."

He left the room and she immediately turned on the waterfall-filling feature and poured in some bubble bath. As the tub filled she hunted through the drawers and found that he'd described things exactly right: she had more cosmetics, lotions, powders, oils, and hairstyling implements than she could use in a decade. After finding a brush she took her time getting rid of the tangles, then pinned her hair up off her neck.

The bubbles were a beautiful mound when she returned to the tub. She let her robe fall to the floor and climbed in.

For the first time in a week, her body relaxed. She sank to her neck, closed her eyes, and let out a deep, shuddering breath. For the moment, she was safe, and if all went well she'd be home by morning.

After she'd soaked for a few minutes, Reyes knocked and asked if he could come in: her meal was ready.

Relief once more rolled through her. She was no longer a slave, but had the simple right of granting or refusing permission for anyone to enter a bathroom. With bubbles covering her head-to-foot, she thought it could do no harm. "Come in."

His brows rose as he saw her. "Better?"

"A little. Yes. Thank you." She felt nervous suddenly. He'd already seen her completely naked, yet somehow this felt more intimate.

He held the tray cradled in one arm, and opened the door the rest of the way with his free hand. She watched him set the tray on a chair, then adjust a nearby rolling table to bathtub height. When he had the height to his satisfaction, and poised over her chest, he placed the tray on top.

The soup smelled heavenly, and her stomach growled. He'd provided a small glass of red wine as well. He said nothing as he left the room.

She scooted up to a better sitting position and pulled the table closer.

The soup proved to be a flavorful lentil, and each spoonful tasted like heaven. For the first time in a week, she ate without the fear of having one of her captors show up and start demanding things.

And by all appearances, Reyes intended to honor her basic boundaries.

Without warning, her mind slipped back to the moment when Reyes was drinking from her throat, the absolute bliss of it and the attending sexual need. Now that she understood him and his purpose, a powerful wave of desire swept through her once more, despite all that she'd been through.

After months of fantasizing about the man, how strange to think that he wasn't a man at all—or at least not a human male. He was a vampire, from a secret world that most of the human population knew nothing about.

With her meal consumed, and her skin starting to wrinkle, she finally left the tub and started getting ready for the after-auction party. She went into the closet and found a clean robe to replace the one she'd worn earlier, this one a beautiful jade silk. She returned to the vanity area and the overstocked makeup drawer.

She sat on the cushy stool and debated how to do her makeup. In the end, for her own sanity, she chose to keep it simple. Despite the revealing nature of the costume, being able to select it herself gave her a sense of control.

Maybe she would have to parade around in a sequined outfit that barely covered her nipples and didn't cover her ass at all, but she wouldn't do up her eyes like they had for the auction, with false eyelashes that looked like a pair of small black fans.

Having wept off most of her makeup earlier, she added back a little gray eye shadow, a thin line of eyeliner, some mascara, and just a hint of blush.

As for her hair, she took some time with a curling iron,

then arranged it all in soft layers the way she usually wore it. She finally worked herself into the minuscule, snug red costume, then stepped into the sequined stilettos and headed to the sitting room.

Time to start playing her new role.

Reyes sat in a brown leather chair, opposite the bedroom. He sipped a different scotch this time, a Bowmore '64. He'd acquired the taste for fine whiskey during his captivity, Sweet Dove having been as generous as she was sadistic, a real fucking paradox.

He swirled the amber liquid, sipped, savored.

He still felt guilty that he hadn't done a better job at warning Angelica away from the Ocean Club sooner, but he couldn't change the past. He also knew he'd made the right decision by telling her about his mission.

He'd get her home as soon as he could, but she'd only truly be safe if he took the Starlin Group down. He heard the door to the bathroom open and the sound of her heels on the hardwood floors.

He leaned back in his chair. He really didn't want to see Angelica in a fantasy outfit. He already lusted after her, so having her soft curves on display without much covering her up was going to make the situation something of a trial for him.

She appeared and time slowed to standstill as his gaze drifted over her body. The barely there costume made use of a handkerchief's worth of sheer red fabric, along with a few sequin-embellished triangles that covered her nipples, her peach, and little else. A few narrow straps held everything together.

She put her hands at the hem of the material that dipped just below her navel. She flipped it up and down a couple of times. "Feels a little breezy, otherwise it fits quite well."

At that he smiled. This was the woman he knew, the one who had kissed him at the Ocean Club, who'd made him think that maybe his life could be more than he imagined.

Her legs went on about a mile, slender and shapely. Red-painted toenails peeked through the cutouts in the front of her sequined shoes.

He set his tumbler on the table at his elbow and stood up.

He wasn't going to even bother concealing his arousal, though the coat helped.

Even so her gaze took him in, and her brows rose. "So does this mean you don't find anything wrong with this getup at all?"

He shrugged. "Only that we have to leave this room. As I said before, I really hate the idea of other men seeing you like this."

"Vampires, you mean."

"We're all males. Human or vampire, we think with our dicks."

She chuckled but after a moment, she frowned slightly. "Will everything else do? I saw about ten sets of false eyelashes but I couldn't bring myself to use them."

He loved her appearance right now with just a little makeup, the same way she'd looked at the club, fresh, earthy, very feminine. "You look fine. In fact, I think you look wonderful."

A short leash, also covered in red sequins, dangled from her hand. She held it up. "I suppose I have to wear this."

He crossed to her and took the leash. "It's probably the

most important thing you will wear tonight. In its way, it'll protect you, because it will keep us connected."

He unbuckled the collar, from which several thin loops of silver chains hung. Pushing her hair over her shoulder, he reached up behind her neck and secured it without making it too tight.

When he was done, she planted her hands on his arms, which surprised him.

"Reyes, I'd like to thank you."

"What for?"

She took a deep breath. "I've had time to think, to process, and I realize now what you've done, that you really did risk so much to save my life. I also think it's incredibly selfless of you to be working on behalf of all these enslaved men and women."

He cleared his throat and pulled away. "I think it's generous of you to say that, but you may be cursing me by the end of this evening. You're going to see some shit tonight, and it can't be helped. You might even be required to perform, if you get my drift. Are you sure you're up for that?"

"I've already told you I am. I'll do whatever's needed."

"Okay, then."

She surprised him all over again. His threats and sexual violation had accomplished nothing, but asking for her help had brought him more success than he would have believed possible.

He clamped the other end of the leash around his right wrist. "Before we go, is there anything you'd like to know?"

"Actually, there is, and I think it has something to do with your world. While I was at the parking lot of the Ocean Club, I got the feeling that no one actually saw my abduction even though there were plenty of people coming and going. How was that possible?"

"Many of us have an ability to create what we call a disguise. I'm sure the men who abducted you did exactly that. Nothing that happened to you would have been visible to anyone but them. And if they had sufficient power, which they probably did, it would've been invisible even to other vampires."

She nodded slowly. "Well, that would explain it. I had a bad feeling about those men, but I was sure I was safe. The next minute they grabbed me, put a cloth over my mouth that smelled medicinal, and now I'm here."

"Angelica, there was nothing you could have done. My only regret is that if I'd understood you were marked to be taken that night, I would have walked you to your car myself. As it was, I took off shortly after I thought you'd left, after I believed you were safe. And frankly, I blame myself or maybe that red dress you were wearing. You looked amazing."

Her lips parted as she met his gaze. For a moment he felt the way he had back in the foyer of the club: He wished he could take her home. And now, ironically, she was in his home.

He looked away because as always, he was drawn to her, but not a damn thing could come of getting close to the woman right now. She was human, not fit for his world, and in the morning he'd take her home.

"One last thing. There's something I want to try with you before we go. It could make it easier on both of us during the party. You're a strong woman, which tells me there's a chance we could do this."

"Do what?"

"Telepathy."

Her eyes went wide. "Seriously?"

With a smile, he sent the words straight into her mind. *Why not?*

She blinked, gasping slightly. "Did you just say, 'Why not?'" She put a hand to her forehead. "Oh, my God, I heard you."

He nodded and his lips curved. Damn, the woman had chops, more than she knew. *Now you give it a try.*

*How?*

He chuckled. *Just like that. You're a natural.*

*Then, right now, I'm speaking to you, inside your head?*

*Yes, you are. Now tell me something about yourself, something I may not know.*

*I like to drink tequila when I'm alone in my apartment.*

Aloud, he asked, "Why the hell do you like drinking tequila alone?"

"Because I do." She glanced past him. *And I'll bet you drink whiskey while you're alone.*

*Yeah, I do.*

She shook her head. "Wow. This really is a different world."

"But this is good news. We'll be able to communicate with each other throughout the evening. I can warn you when I have to put on a show and command you to do something. And you can let me know if any of the other guests try to manhandle you while I'm not looking."

"Well, that does sound like an advantage." Then suddenly she was in his head. *So I'll be able to communicate with you at any time.*

*That's exactly right.*

*This is amazing. Will anyone else be able to listen in?*

*Not even a little, so don't worry.*

He drew close and held out his arm. "As for how we're getting there, I'll be using altered flight. Now put your arm around my neck and step onto my foot."

"Oh, Reyes, no, I'll puke all over everything."

He chuckled and for just a moment he almost felt like a regular guy taking a woman on a date . . . except of course that she was dressed like a stripper. "I promise that it'll be very different this time. I'll go really slow, unlike when I took you out of the auction house. You might feel a little dizzy when we arrive, but that should be all."

She drew in a deep breath and settled herself on his shoe with great care, apparently making sure she didn't puncture his expensive leather footwear with her stilettos.

Holding her tight against his side, he told her to close her eyes. "Let me know when you're ready. Again, I'll take it slow."

He felt her take a deep breath "I'm ready."

From his peripheral vision he could see that her eyes were closed. He opened his power and entered altered flight, heading straight through both the bedroom and the cave walls. Just as he'd promised, he flew at a crawl, the picture of Engles's mansion burned in his mind, a true homing beacon, typical of his world.

He slowed on approach, and felt the resonance of others arriving at the same time. He gauged where he needed to be without colliding with anyone or anything else and landed near a large fountain that rose thirty feet in the air. Engles liked to display his wealth.

Angelica blinked and released him. "You're right, just a little dizzy."

She glanced up at the well-lit structure that had water cascading from a central bowl. "Wow," she murmured. Her gaze skated around the massive, vaulted cavern and her eyes widened further. "I hate to admit it, but this is beautiful. The sculpted rock walls are exquisite. I take it that stonework is a highly prized art form in your culture."

"It is."

"And I didn't expect to see so many women in gowns, though I can see that there are an equal number of slaves present." He felt her shudder. "So many of them are bruised."

"That's usually how you can tell if the slave is human. Vampires self-heal."

She turned to look at him, but surprised him by shifting to telepathy. *Reyes, should I have a few bruises? Would that have made you look better—you know, to keep up appearances?*

He was incredulous as he stared at her. *Sorry, but I draw the line at beating the shit out of you.*

She smiled faintly. *Just as well. I probably wouldn't have gone for it anyway.*

His lips curved. *No, I don't think you would have. But there's something else you should know.* He glanced around. *You're the star of this party.*

*Great. Every girl's dream, to be the main attraction at a sex-slave blowout. No pun intended.*

# CHAPTER 5

Angelica took a moment to calm down. She was nervous as hell and trying hard not to show it.

Sticking with telepathy, she asked, *So how do we do this? Do you want me next to you? Although I'm not seeing any of the other slaves doing that.*

*Walk just a little behind me and keep your head slightly lowered.* He took a couple of steps forward and glanced back at her. *Good. You look submissive. Just remember that I won't be able to see what's going on behind me, so if anyone touches you, tell me telepathically. And for God's sake, don't address anyone directly. Let me do that. I'll protect you tonight.*

*Got it.*

"Oh, shit."

"What?" She looked around.

"Engles is at the head of the stairs, waiting for us. It's time."

*So that's the monster? I remember him from the auction. His face had a ruddy color at the time. I guess he was pretty worked up.*

*And furious.*

She let him get half a foot ahead before she fell into step at an angle behind him. He tugged on the leash and she tugged back.

With her head down, she continued to glance at what had to be a huge mansion tucked into some corner of the cavern system.

The area where they'd landed sported a waterfall, a small lake lit by torchlight, and dozens of potted trees and shrubs, creating a sort of outdoor garden. The trees twinkled with small blue and white lights.

All this led up, through a series of wide stone steps, to the house itself. The front facade appeared to be fifty yards across and at least four stories high. Mansion, indeed.

She was struck again by how beautifully gowned the women were. Most of them wore not just necklaces, but intricate chains.

*A lot of chains around here.*

*Yes, some of them are blood-chains.*

*Okay, that's new. What's a blood-chain?*

*The single blood-chain creates a tight bond—the couple can't be more than a few yards away at any given time. I've never done it myself, but if I was a controlling sadist as some of these men are, I'd chain you.*

*If we were chained, I wouldn't be able to run away, would I?*

*Not even a little.*

She noticed one woman who wore a gold double-chain, linked together with loops. A large diamond pendant pulled the chain toward her cleavage. *You said single-chain. Are there double-chains as well?*

*Yes. These are deep bonding chains, usually indicating a married status.*

*Ah, married slavers. How charming.*

*There are a lot of women equally into the lifestyle. You'd be surprised.*

*After that redheaded she-devil who hurt me, I guess I'm not.*

He didn't respond, but at the mention of the woman, she felt he'd tensed up again. Reyes's owner had been a woman. The subject no doubt hit some buttons.

As she drew closer to the entrance, she saw that massive white marble pillars supported the front structure, leaving it completely open to the air. She began to understand something important: she hadn't fallen just into a world of vampires and sex slavery, but into an entire civilization as well. A profoundly skilled architect, accompanied by master builders, had created this extraordinary house.

*And this is Engles's home?*

*Yes, it is.*

*I'm guessing Starlin earnings built this house.*

*You guessed right.*

*And he's really not the one running things?*

*He's a front man. Don't ask me how I know, but I know. Call it an instinct. He's smart enough and manages things quite well, but he's not an empire builder. He's too much of showman. Building and sustaining an empire requires finesse and, to a degree, secrecy.*

Angelica thought it a great irony that so much beauty had been built on the deaths of tens of thousands of slaves. *He has excellent taste, I'll give him that. But I wouldn't mind seeing him tortured for a decade, then his head chopped off, for all that he's done.*

*Have you been reading my mind?*

She heard a faint whimpering sound and glanced to her right. She recognized one of the women from the auction, a tall blond Russian. She had bruises on her arms and legs. She'd been worked over but good, and her new owner had his fangs buried deep in her throat sucking hard—too hard by the looks of it. The slave stared up at the cavern ceiling, tears streaming down her cheeks.

As Angelica walked up the steps, however, she noticed that when some of the guests, especially the men, looked at her, they frowned, then glanced at Reyes.

*I think we should have figured out a way to give me those bruises. You're losing your street cred because I'm still intact.*

He glanced at a group of men and nodded to them. *I don't give a fuck what any of them think. I only have to impress Engles—and mend fences with him, if I can. The rest can go to hell.*

His words reminded her again just how different Reyes was from the rest of these cretins. She had to work at holding her head down and sustaining her long-suffering expression, because right now she felt nothing but admiration for him.

*Do I look submissive enough?*

He glanced back at her once more. *You're doing great.*

*And so are you, master.*

\* \* \*

Reyes liked Angelica in his head and he was proud of her for bearing up well, but he'd expected nothing less. He knew her history, because he'd had her investigated, that she was the sole support of her infirm mother and had sacrificed a lot to take care of her. She hadn't had an easy life.

She was a woman of great strength, another reason why he hated that she'd gotten caught in the Starlin trap. And one more reason why he needed to bring this organization down.

As he led her up the broad stone steps to the entrance, Engles stepped out onto the expansive porch. He had his usual Dubonnet in hand, a leer in his eye, and a smile Reyes wanted to wipe from the bastard's mouth.

"You haven't chained her yet?" Engles narrowed his eyes as he took another sip. His gaze drifted the full length of Angelica. "She's not even bruised."

Reyes took a step closer to her. "Unlike you, I intend to take my time."

Engles shifted his gaze to stare hard at Reyes. "I've always had my doubts about you, pretty boy. And I think you may have just proved my opinion again tonight. And by the way, anyone's membership can be revoked at my sole discretion."

Reyes had known men like Engles his entire life. They taunted and bullied at every opportunity, no matter the situation or the person. But he knew something else as well: if he showed the smallest sign of fear, Engles would go after him. Nor could he appease him. Engles would see that as a sign of weakness.

A real rock and a hard place, so he opted for a different tack.

He held Engles's gaze for a long moment, then wheeled

on Angelica, hoping like hell she would follow his lead without flinching. He caught the back of her neck with his hand and telepathed, *Drop like I'm hurting you. Whimper, groan, cry, anything you can do.*

Aloud, he said, "On your knees, slave."

She immediately obeyed and gave a decent performance, crying out as she crumpled at his feet.

While keeping one hand on Angelica's head, he met Engles's surprised stare. "The thing is, I've already laid out a plan for this slave. And if I don't hold back, she'll be dead before I've even started. I may not have the same punching style as the rest of your bidders, but I like my meat seasoned over a period of time, then chewed slowly in my mouth for about as long. I take no pleasure from a quick slice-and-drain. I want the woman's pain to serve me for months." He lowered his voice. "More important, I want to get her to a second auction at the six-month mark. I intend to set a new record and recoup my investment."

Engles's eyes widened as his gaze fell to Angelica. He actually seemed impressed as he licked his lips. If Reyes had been at all serious, Engles would no doubt have been the first in line to bid for Angelica at her six-month transition.

Engles tugged at his chin. "All right, then. I look forward to what the future holds."

"As do I." He pulled on the leash and Angelica slowly rose to her feet, wiping away tears. He gave her a shove, setting her in motion as together they moved into the foyer.

*You okay?* Oh, God, had he hurt her?

*How'd I do?*

*So you are okay.*

He swore he heard her snort inside his head. *Did the bastard buy it?*

*Yeah, he bought it.*

He glanced at her, meeting her gaze for a fleeting moment. *You're doing great.*

An odd blush covered her cheeks. He wished like hell circumstances had been different, because he really liked this woman.

But this thought stopped him up short. What circumstances? Angelica was human, and—except for the extremely rare mating between the species, involving love, marriage, and offspring—vampires didn't date humans.

Beyond that, his background made him about the worst sort of man she should ever get tangled up with.

Moving Angelica into the house proper, he heard her swift intake of breath and watched her eyes skate to the tall ceiling. Massive crystal chandeliers illuminated the space, more for effect than necessity. Vampires could easily see in the dark.

*Too bad this was all built on slave blood because it's a beautiful home.*

*Yes it is and you're right, Angelica. This dwelling is a travesty.*

As he led her to the top of a large descending staircase, applause began to build through the gathered partygoers below.

*Is this because of the auction?*

*Of course. Again, you're the star.*

*I think I'm going to be sick.*

*Just keep your eyes lowered and stay one step behind me.*

*No problem.*

Reyes knew how to square his shoulders and give a

show. His captor, Sweet Dove, had trained him well in a number of different ways, and one of them was the importance of holding an attitude. Most of the women watched him, lusting, as did some of the men.

All around the audience, the slaves were apparent in their usual revealing garb, like Angelica's, sporting sheer fabrics, chains, and leather. Lots of sequins. A few feathers.

The female slaves, most with naked breasts, often had rows of dots tattooed around their nipples that in turn were stained varying shades of burgundy. Many of the male slaves were also naked and kept in a state of arousal, usually through a variety of drugs.

The room was jammed, some attendees standing around and drinking, others seated in several love seats. Many of the new slaves sat beside their owners, cut up and beaten, eyes glazed.

Reyes repressed the deep disgust that threatened to rise like bile up his throat. There would be time later to punish each and every slaver. For now, he needed to stay focused on doing all that he could to discover the man in charge and take him down.

Scorpion had kept his identity secret from the time Starlin came into existence. Once Reyes found out who the man was, he could begin the process of working his way into his inner circle. Beyond Scorpion's identity, he needed the documents that detailed every aspect of how the organization worked. After that, he'd know exactly how to destroy Starlin from within, step by step.

As he moved through the room, attention became increasingly focused on Angelica.

When he'd told her earlier that he hated the idea of other men looking at her, he meant it. Some caveman part of him had already laid claim to her, so to have other men openly lusting after her scraped at his nerves.

Angelica's voice pierced his thoughts. *Calm down. I can feel your agitation like it's rubbing against my skin.*

*It shows?*

*Well, that fist you're making is at least one clue.*

He relaxed his hand and stretched out his fingers.

*That's better.*

For the next hour, he greeted most of the members by name, essentially working the room. What wasn't lost to him was the goodwill that flowed in his direction. He realized that a lot of slavers here liked what he'd done by winning the bid, beating out Engles.

By the time he'd made a circuit of the large, ballroom-like space, Engles waited once more back at the top of the stairs. He gestured for Reyes to join him.

*Engles wants us.*

*Got it.*

Once Reyes was standing beside Engles—with Angelica on his other side, though as always slightly behind him—Engles caught Reyes's hand.

Lifting it high, Engles called out, "Our winning bidder for our most sought-after slave."

Heavy applause and a few whistles and shouts sounded through the room.

When the audience settled down, Engles turned to him. "And now, my friends, I have a surprise for my guest of honor." He pivoted toward Reyes. "A theatrical performance from the owner of The Ruby Cave. The famous Eve said she knows you well and agreed to bring one of her troupes here, to perform for you tonight. Now follow me."

Turning to his right, Engles led the way down the sloping path of the theater, settling them in a front-row love seat. The stage was situated just a few yards away, raised up only a foot, so that all the action would be at eye level.

More than one of the couples in the audience had already gotten busy, slaves on their knees. *You need to prepare yourself. This whole thing might erupt into an orgy.*

He heard her sigh. *Great. Will I be expected to join in?*

*It's standard courtesy that slaves be shared with other members of the club. But I won't let that happen tonight.*

*Won't they suspect you if you don't participate?*

*We'll cross that bridge when we come to it.*

He didn't glance around but he knew damn well everyone in the theater would be watching him, and his slave, throughout the performance.

The lights dimmed, and at the same time the stage spots lit up the area to the left. Eve appeared, wearing red leather from head to toe. She was a tall woman with long blond hair that ranged past her knees. Tonight she wore it pulled on top of her head to cascade behind in a ponytail. But even that rope of hair landed mid-buttocks.

Eve owned The Ruby Cave and had been one of the leading performers of The Erotic Passage for a long time. She had a melodious, carrying voice. "Hello, my lovelies, and welcome to a performance by the Ruby Theater Players. Knowing that my good friend Reyes would be here, I designed a show just for him and for his lovely date."

Eve was a major star in The Erotic Passage, otherwise known as The Passage. She was heavily into BDSM, but played the game by her own rules. He knew her well: she didn't approve of slavery, but she had a no-judgment rule about everyone. Of course, it hadn't failed to reach his notice that she often bought slaves, putting them to work in her club for a period of time, then eventually setting them free. By his count, she'd saved thousands.

He trusted her—so much so that she was one of only two people who knew of his mission. The other was the owner of The Passage, a short Italian vampire named Rumy. Both could keep a secret, and each had promised to help if he ever found a way to bring Starlin down.

On a more personal level, Eve had been trying to get him on her table, chained down, for a long time. She'd told him repeatedly that after everything he'd been through, a good dominance session would work wonders for him, give him the kind of release he'd been needing for a few decades now.

He'd never do it, of course. He'd made himself a promise that never again would a woman chain him down.

Angelica crossed her legs, grateful that at least for now, her body for the most part wasn't on display. She relaxed against the soft cushion of what looked and felt like a regular old love seat. To her right another slave from the auction house was already bending her head down into the lap of her lord-and-master, and the show hadn't even gotten started.

She drew her hair close to her face to block as much of that image as she could.

She was also grateful that Reyes had pulled her close so that she was pressed up against him. The cave wasn't freezing, but without even a decent shirt or pants on, she was cold.

The woman, Eve, had an exotic appearance. She wore stiletto boots that rose past her knees, snug red leather pants, and a tight red leather bustier that supported large breasts.

She carried a long black whip. Swinging it once over her head, she cracked it at the end of the stage.

Angelica jumped.

At the same time, a sound track started up that had a deep thumping rhythmic bass, a strong guitar, and a beat that spoke of sex and not much else.

Angelica put a hand to her stomach. She didn't want to be affected by what she was about to see, but Reyes's warm body, her never-ending desire for him, and the sexual nature of the music rippled through her. She felt things she didn't want to feel, more so because she knew Reyes had tensed up the moment Eve had said this performance was meant for him.

Even his thighs flexed and released.

At first, she thought it was a sexual reaction; then she realized it had to be something else because sex was not the sensation she got from him right now. If she had to define it, she'd call it fear. But what did Reyes have to be afraid of in a theater like this?

From the back of the stage, two men in loincloths rolled a massive wall to angle toward the audience, locking it in place on the floor. Chains with manacles, meant for wrists and ankles, hung from the wall, similar to the ones Reyes had put her in earlier.

Another woman, also carrying a whip, entered the stage completely nude.

The two loincloth men returned, dragging a third man in a black tux. The spotlight focused on him as the first two chained him up.

The completely nude woman, a very athletic vampire,

used her whip. The first crack caught the man's coat in a deep tear.

He winced, and the audience knew the whip had stung.

Soft groans moved around the theater, but Reyes's tension level ramped up. The female repeated the process in quick succession, her arm and eye trained to strip the man of his clothes while leaving very few significant cuts behind.

The male servants tore the strips between strikes so that more and more of his well-muscled body appeared.

The music continued to beat the erotic rhythm and the whip kept time so that even Angelica could see the exquisitely orchestrated artistry of the performance.

But what surprised her the most was that once the servants pulled the torn pants away, the man was fully erect behind a pair of snug briefs. He clearly enjoyed the experience, the fear, the pain.

She was pretty sure the entire audience held its breath as the female, on the beat, and in two quick successions, cut to either side of the man's groin and sent his briefs falling to the floor. The two men gathered up his torn-up clothes and left the stage.

Angelica covered her mouth with her hand. Despite the fact that the man was clearly enjoying the performance, she couldn't get past the public nature of the spectacle.

The woman moved forward and, no surprise, began fondling his arousal.

The whip, the chains, the seductive female, drew Reyes into the past, his years as a slave. He'd belonged exclusively to Sweet Dove to use as she saw fit, to share him when it pleased her.

She had places of punishment and of pleasure, so that over time his body became confused. What hurt him often dealt out reams of exquisite sensation, and what should have been pleasurable caused him a terrible agony of his mind and his vampire soul.

Sitting in front of a show, beside a woman he'd desired intensely for months now, had his body in an uproar. The whole time, guilt and shame tightened his chest.

The sight of the woman now caressing the slave's thighs and groin, her lips surrounding his erection, sent shock waves through his body. He wanted to look away but couldn't.

Eve walked around the performers, cracking her whip to the beat of the music. The tempo increased, and the woman rose from her knees.

On cue the two servants returned and lifted her, poising her split legs over his cock. The man struggled in the chains, thrashing his head back and forth, feigning his unwillingness.

She mounted him and the man grew still, his eyes rolling in his head.

How many times had Reyes known this moment with Sweet Dove, trying to restrain his desire only to have all the physical sensations, both brutal and sensual, coalesce in an erotic wave of pleasure.

She wrapped her legs around his waist. Once she was secured with her hands on his shoulders, the servants drifted back into the shadows.

She rode the slave hard, using her vampire strength to work his body. She shoved his head to the side and he in turn shouted his pleasure as the woman bit into his vein and started to drink. No playacting, either. This was the real deal.

But at the moment that the play should have climaxed, the wall began to tremble and the slave's arms flexed. The woman cried out, a long lingering groan that turned to a scream as the slave broke free of his chains.

The audience gasped, crying out in shared ecstasy as well.

The slave, now free of his manacles, whirled the woman in his arms and with his hips pistoning hard drove relentlessly into his owner.

This time, he bit into her neck, returning the favor, grunting as he pushed inside her in heavy, powerful thrusts.

The woman's face looked pained at first; then her arms wrapped around him and she began to moan, then utter cries of ecstasy.

Finally, the man lifted off her neck and pounded into her so that her whimpers turned to screams as she came and as he shouted his release.

Reyes watched unblinking as both pairs of hips settled down, the music subsided, and the lights grew dim. The couple on stage breathed hard.

Reyes gripped his thighs, his fingers digging in deep.

A single spotlight followed Eve to the front of the stage. She met and held Reyes's gaze. "May you know the pleasure one day of release through domination. And may you break free of your bonds."

The lights went out and the audience applauded wildly.

Reyes could have adjusted his vampire vision, but he didn't want to; in fact, he couldn't. He sat, unable to calm his erection, his body trembling.

Angelica's voice once more slid through his mind. *You're shaking.*

He couldn't speak, not even telepathically, as though the nature of the show had scrambled his neurons.

The crowd had already started moving around. Someone stood in front of him speaking his name, but he couldn't make it out, couldn't focus, couldn't think.

He lifted his gaze slowly and in the recess of his mind recognized that Engles now stared at him.

"Reyes?" His name sounded as if spoken underwater, only with long echoes.

The performance had taken him back at least a century in time, to the middle part of his captivity when despair had made him contemplate chewing off his own hands, halting the healing process, and welcoming death.

He felt a hand slip around his elbow and squeeze, a tender touch that startled him blinking.

*Reyes, come back. You've got to come back. Engles looks suspicious. I don't know what you've got planned, but you're about to blow this whole thing.*

He turned slowly to stare at her, horror-stricken. *Why are you touching me?*

He couldn't believe anyone would want to touch him. He was a filthy slave, used so many times by Sweet Dove and her friends that he was unworthy of ever being touched again. But then Angelica didn't know the complete truth of who he was, how many times he'd orgasmed on command for Sweet Dove, or how many men he'd fucked during his captivity in hell.

And with that his mind shut down completely.

# CHAPTER 6

Angelica watched Reyes turn away from her to stare blankly at the now empty stage. Something had happened to force his mind inward. Maybe the performance had been too much.

She glanced around and saw that all eyes had turned to them, waiting expectantly.

She used telepathy again. *Reyes, come back to me. You have to do something.*

When he didn't respond, panic set in—not just that his plans might be disrupted but for her own safety as well. If Engles attacked right now, Reyes wouldn't be able to defend himself, and she knew enough about the bastard to know that Engles would take command of her if he could.

She made a quick decision and aloud, said, "Yes, master, I've heard your command within my mind and I'll do as you say. I'll obey you in everything."

With all eyes in the theater now on her, she felt nauseated as she rose up slightly, trembling, and moved in front of him. She lowered herself to her knees as so many other slaves had already done that evening.

She spread his legs, moving between to undo his pants. Not surprising, he was firm and ready for her. Without allowing herself to think about the horror of the moment, she focused on Reyes, knowing that if he didn't get with it, he'd lose his standing with Engles and the rest of the Starlin members and she'd be caught in a madman's power.

She slid her mouth over his cock, shutting out the movement and increased groans all around her, even the nearby approving comments.

*Reyes, you feel so good in my mouth. You're a big man and hard as a rock.* She reached between his legs and fondled his balls as she sucked, then stroked the length of his stalk.

*I've wanted you from the first moment I set eyes on you. I've hungered for you, craved your cock.* She tongued his crown, sliding over the ridge, teasing the most sensitive parts.

She kept her ministrations tender, hoping that the feel of her tongue would bring him out of his mentally locked-up state. Maybe then they'd both survive.

She also blocked everything else out of her mind. She recalled her fantasies of having his body beneath her hands and let herself go there again, pretending she was alone with him.

*You have a beautiful cock, thick and long.* She took as much of him in her mouth as she could, working him with her hand at the same time, slow upward pulls.

*Reyes, I've wanted to do this for months now. How many times I've longed for your body moving over mine, your cock buried deep, your hips thrusting harder and harder. I could come like this. I'd only need the pressure of your hand pressed between my legs and I'd be screaming with pleasure.*

She moved faster, her head bobbing up and down.

He started to respond, his hips rocking slowly.

*Yes, that's it. You like what I'm doing. Come back to me, Reyes. Let me know I'm pleasing you.*

Reyes began the long journey back because pleasure rode his thighs, his abdomen, and his cock. A warm, wet mouth worked him.

With his eyes closed, he heard a voice in his head, a woman's voice. With a start he recognized Angelica, but what was she saying? His mind felt muddy and strange. She talked about loving his cock, wanting to come like this.

Like what?

He strove to make sense of what was happening. Mostly, he felt like he was waking up very slowly from a sex dream.

*Angelica?*

*I'm here. Just enjoy what I'm doing. That's it. You're so hard. I can feel you're close to release.*

Her mouth sucked a little harder, but her hand worked him faster at just the right pressure. He slid his palm to the back of her head and flexed his hips, pushing as she sucked.

He loved that she was sucking him.

Other images intruded, of Eve and her red leather, of the dominance show, of the theater in Engles's home.

Tension flowed through him, not in a good way, as reality returned. *Angelica, what the hell is happening?*

But she didn't pause in her movements. *Just go with it, Reyes. I've got this. Engles is watching and you need to come for me.*

*This isn't right.*

With her free hand, she dug her nails into his abdomen, drawing his attention low.

He opened his eyes as her voice once more penetrated his mind. She met his gaze, staring up at him. *I've wanted you like this. Did you know that? I've wanted all of you in my mouth from the time I first saw you. I've pleasured myself repeatedly with thoughts of having your cock right here, my tongue swirling over you.*

Reyes finally returned to reality and in a brief flash realized all that Angelica was doing for him in this moment, the sacrifice she was making. As a slave, he'd been in this position, having to perform against his will, against his morality. But she'd chosen to do this for him.

He stroked her head and set his mind on nothing but the woman on her knees in front of him. He recalled the kiss she'd given him in the foyer of the Ocean Club, the way she'd looked in her red silk dress, the hopeful expression in her eyes.

She was so damn beautiful and he wanted her. He let his desire for her take over. Aloud, he said, "Suck me harder now, slave."

She responded, moving faster as well.

"You've obeyed me, slave. That's all that matters."

*Angelica, your mouth is like fire.* He thrust his hips now and she moved even faster. His balls tightened. *I'm coming.*

*I can feel it.*

She stayed with him, with his movements, holding her head and the suction of her mouth just right as he pumped all that he had straight into her mouth. The orgasm had him shouting at the cavern ceiling, eyes closed, refusing to acknowledge anyone else around him.

As he settled in his seat, Angelica drew back, swallowing and wiping her lips. But she wisely kept her eyes downcast. He saw tears on her cheeks as she tucked him back inside and carefully zipped up his pants.

He'd had enough, and he was sure she'd just reached her breaking point.

Ignoring the sudden burst of applause all around him, and not caring what repercussions might follow, he caught her up in his arms.

In a loud voice, he said, "I need you in my game room. Now."

More applause.

Shifting to altered flight, he flew through the cavern walls, taking it slow for her sake as he sped in the direction of his home. He dropped down into his master suite once more.

He laid her on the bed, but she turned to her side, swiping at her face, to look up at him.

The crowd's approval still worked like a sickness in his gut, twisting him up. His guilt rose, heavy guilt over his past, over all the things he'd done through the decades.

And now an innocent like Angelica had performed in public, sucking him off.

The erotic show had messed with his mind, making him long for things that couldn't exist, like breaking free and having power over what had controlled him for so long.

After the first months of his freedom, he'd thought that if he could track down Sweet Dove and kill her, then he'd be free.

But Sweet Dove wasn't to be found. He quickly learned that very few people even knew of her. Even the men who'd visited her, who had also used his body, had disappeared from the vampire world.

He now believed that Sweet Dove had killed them, or ordered the killings, though doing the job by her own hand would have suited her equally as well. Since then, nothing he'd done to try to locate her had worked. She'd slipped into some well-disguised cavern system and disappeared.

Maybe she was dead. Or maybe finding Scorpion would help lead Reyes to her. After all, Sweet Dove had been with Angelica. She'd known all about her. It was highly possible that Sweet Dove knew Scorpion.

Angelica shivered.

"Are you cold?"

She nodded.

He moved to the fireplace and lit a well-constructed stack of newspaper, kindling, and logs. When the fire burned hot, Angelica shifted to sit on the side of the tall bed. She stared up at him, the comforter loose about her waist as firelight played over her perfect cleavage and the red sequins covering her nipples.

"Angelica, I'm so sorry for what happened just now, but I'm beyond grateful, too, because you saved the situation. I got lost for a few minutes, and you brought me back. Is there anything I can do for you?"

She released a weary sigh. "I know this is going to sound odd, but I'd really like a shower."

He nodded. "Actually, that makes perfect sense." He'd been there a thousand times.

She pushed the comforter back and headed to the bathroom.

Angelica let the water flow over her head for a long time. She soaped up repeatedly, trying to scrub some of the experience off her skin and out of her pores.

Her job was over, the part she'd agreed to, and sometime the next morning Reyes would take her home. He'd even said he'd do all that he could to keep her safe from Starlin in the future.

She should have felt relieved, and maybe she was. But a large part of her was still stuck at that horrible party where at least a hundred slaves had milled around dull-eyed and on leashes like hers. Except their obedience and submission were real, unlike hers. She only had to feign her captivity. She shuddered, trying hard not to think about what the rest of the night would be like for the other women.

Despite this brutal reality, she was proud of what she'd achieved tonight. She'd saved Reyes's reputation and protected his cover. He could go forward with his plans and fulfill his mission, and in the process save tens of thousands of future slaves.

Then why didn't she feel more satisfied?

\* \* \*

Reyes leaned his forearm over the tall mantel, drawing deep breaths. He could recall everything now, how he'd watched the show and fallen into a strange trance as images of Sweet Dove's torture had overtaken his mind.

Engles had stood nearby watching him like a hawk, waiting for a sign of weakness, hoping to tear him apart.

Dream-like, he could even see the moment Angelica had made the decision to go down on him, pretending that she obeyed his orders.

Horror rolled through him in waves at what might have happened had she not jumped in and played her slave role as brilliantly as she had. But it wasn't the possibility of failing at his mission that distressed him; it was the simple fact that Engles happily would have appropriated Angelica as his slave once he was assured that Reyes wasn't up to the task.

He couldn't be certain exactly what had happened to him, why he'd checked out for those few minutes. He supposed Eve's show had been too real for him. Or maybe the overall stress of the evening had finally gotten to him.

He squeezed his eyes shut and for the present worked at letting it all go. Angelica had saved the situation and now he had her home, safe and sound.

In the morning he'd take her back to Newport Beach, to her apartment, back to helping her mother and working all the long hours at her accounting job. Maybe it wasn't a great life, but it sure as hell wasn't the dangerous and potentially fatal one he'd brought her into.

He ignored certain other thoughts that had stolen into his mind as well, ones that involved keeping her with him for the next few weeks.

He had no right to ask anything more of her.

Even so, he moved to the wall unit to the left of the

fireplace, laden with a host of books on shelves. A set of drawers made up the lower portion of the unit.

Opening the top drawer, he pulled out a red leather case and popped the lid. On a bed of scarlet velvet lay a pair of identical dark-metal chains. He touched each in succession and felt the powerful vibrations they carried. When created, the chains had been infused with his blood and carried his DNA, which meant that he could bind Angelica to him if he wanted to. He could keep her close to him with a range that rarely extended beyond ten feet.

The chains would prove he'd brought her under his complete control. But they would do more than that. He'd have a sense of her at all times, and she'd know exactly what he was feeling moment to moment.

Everything about their current relationship would be heightened, including his desire for her, his longing for her blood, his need to bury himself inside her.

He knew she desired him, so in turn, what she felt for him would be enhanced exponentially as well.

The thought of taking Angelica to bed as a willing partner while bound in blood-chains caused him to groan.

"You okay?"

He closed the lid, then the drawer.

Pivoting in her direction, he met her gaze. She wore a robe, tied up tight at her narrow waist. Her hair was slicked back, wet from the shower, which made her eyes look huge, enhancing her vulnerable humanness.

He really couldn't ask this of her.

He couldn't.

Instead he answered her question. "I'm fine. Tired, maybe."

"Will I be sleeping here tonight?" She dipped her chin

toward the bed. With a towel she rubbed the ends of her hair.

He nodded. "I can sleep in the guest room."

Her gaze roved over the bed. "I think that would be best." But she frowned.

"What is it?"

"Nothing." At that, she smiled as she met his gaze once more. "I could use some sleep. Maybe a decade's worth."

He realized then that whatever she could do in terms of helping him reach his Starlin destruction goal, there was another reason he didn't want her to go. She eased something inside him he couldn't define.

And he wanted her to stay with him, at least for a little while longer. "I need you."

"What?" She tilted her head.

"I need you." There, he said it again, flat out. "I want you with me for the next few weeks. The Starlin Group is hosting a festival, like your New Orleans Mardi Gras, with parades and parties in many of the local sex clubs. It culminates in a masked ball."

"I don't understand. What are you saying?"

He dove in. "I want you to stick this out with me, to share a blood-chain bond—which will help keep you safe. I think with you by my side, I'll be able to finish my mission. In fact I'm sure of it. Angelica, I want you to stay, to continue to pose as my slave, to be with me."

Angelica drew close to Reyes, trying to understand his meaning. She frowned so hard that the muscles of her face hurt as she stared once more into clear blue eyes. He was pleading with her, something she hadn't expected from him.

And he wanted her to stay.

But how could she remain in this world? She'd already been through so much. That last episode, when he'd mentally checked out, had almost put her square into the hands of a madman.

"I can't. You know I can't. I have to go home. I have my mother to think of, and my future. If I stay, there's a good chance I won't make it out alive."

He drew her into his arms and kissed her, then nuzzled her neck. "Angelica," he murmured against her throat. "You made everything possible and I want you with me. I need you with me. Please stay." He kissed her again.

She sensed how desperately he wanted her with him.

She pulled away from him, rubbing her forehead with the palm of her hand. "I'm sorry, I can't do this."

He turned back to the drawer he'd closed and pulled out a red case. Opening it, he let her look at a pair of chains.

"These are blood-chains, aren't they?"

"Yes, they are. We would each wear a chain and once bound, you'd be able to siphon my power, sense where I am at all times, and to some degree what I'm feeling and thinking. And I would experience the same with you. It would make working together much easier on every level. And if I bound you, I'd gain credibility with Engles."

Even without touching them, she sensed their power.

"I want you with me more than anything in the world, more than I've wanted anything in my life. And I know you've felt it, too—it's what brought you back to the Ocean Club and why you didn't leave my world when you had the chance. We belong together, Angelica. Please stay by my side. Help me bring Starlin down."

Her heart lurched as she met his gaze once more. She

was so drawn to him. She hated that he'd once been a slave himself, that throughout the first part of his life, he'd endured decades of torture. And now all he wanted was to make a difference, to end the horrors of sex slavery.

She thought back to the Russian slave, whimpering in pain as her new owner sank his fangs into her neck and drank from her with the intention of hurting her. Reyes had taken her blood, but it hadn't hurt at all. Instead she'd never known such exquisite pleasure.

And there was the other, sensual side of the equation: She wouldn't just be partners with him, she knew he'd become her lover, the thing she'd wanted more than anything else over the past several months.

But he'd spoken of her staying with him for weeks? She couldn't be away from her mother for that long. And despite Reyes's assurances, what if she died? Who would care for her parent then?

Did she really want to enter such a completely intimate relationship with a vampire? Even if she survived, would she like the person she'd become by the time it was all over?

She couldn't do this. She felt in her bones that to choose a blood-chain bond with Reyes would alter her life forever, that she'd never be able to go back to her human world.

"I can't, Reyes. I wish I could, but I can't. I'm not strong enough for this. Trust me."

"You have more strength than you know."

She shook her head. She'd made up her mind.

Then as if from a great distance, she heard his spirit calling to her.

*Stay.*

She didn't know how she knew, but this wasn't telepathy, not like before. It was a plaintive cry straight from his heart. And for that reason alone, she wanted to say yes, but how could she?

*Stay, Angelica. Please stay . . .*

# CHAPTER 7

The expression in Reyes's clear blue eyes pierced Angelica's heart. He was pleading for her to remain with him, to help him bring down the Starlin Group, the organization that abducted tens of thousands of humans every year and sold them into slavery.

She'd been with him long enough to understand that he walked this path alone and that he never asked anyone for help.

But he was asking her now.

He still wore his expensive Brioni tux from the after-auction party, and it didn't help that his broad shoulders tapered to a narrow waist or that he was so easy on the eyes. He had a striking appearance with thick black brows, straight nose, and soft, sensual lips. He had a sexy scruff, and his cheekbones angled sharply, adding to his don't-mess-with-me look.

She tried to be sensible. She had an obligation to her infirm mother that couldn't be ignored, a life to return to, a very human life. Even though Angelica knew she needed to make changes, to get out of the rut of her accounting job, of too much overtime and not enough social life. But she was still young and she could fix whatever needed to be fixed.

But if she stayed with Reyes she could die.

The truly sensible thing would be to run. Yet she hesitated.

He'd asked her to stay with him during the upcoming Starlin Festival, to continue playing her role as his slave for a few more days or possibly a few more weeks. If she left now he would have a hard time sustaining his cover, but if she stayed she'd have to form a blood-chain bond with him. The bond would help keep her safe from other slavers intent on manhandling her, would increase her ability to siphon his power, and would help her to know what he was feeling from one moment to the next. In the same way, he'd have a clearer view of everything she experienced.

Her own reasons for wanting to stay were far more complex. She had little to gain personally, except the knowledge that in playing her role and supporting Reyes she could possibly save thousands of lives.

The ominous risk to her life, however, kept her locked in a terrible place of indecision.

He stood close to her, the red leather box in his hand, the one that displayed the bonding chains. He wanted her with him badly.

But how could she possibly stay?

She glanced at the blood-chains one more time. Once bonded, the chains would create a proximity issue. From what he'd said, she'd have to remain at all times not more than ten feet away from him. Something about the bond didn't permit either person straying beyond that distance.

So close.

Something she had to admit: she wanted to be that close to Reyes. And there would be no reason for not engaging sexually with him anymore, no holding back. Sudden desire, always a breath away, sent a shiver through her. She'd wanted him badly from the first, and she had no doubt that the blood-chain bond would take them the distance.

Extending her hand, she touched the chain on the left and immediately felt a strong drift of power, a vibration against the tip of her finger, like electricity. Everything about Reyes's world was so strange, the hidden caverns in which an entire vampire civilization lived, the way they could travel with altered flight and pass easily through stone as though it were air and not solid matter, and now the chains infused with his blood.

But could she do this?

Still touching the chain, she lifted her gaze to Reyes. His lips were parted and she could sense what he was feeling, that he desired her and something more, that he called to her from so deep in his soul that her heart seized.

His voice moved softly through her mind: *stay.*

*I want to, Reyes, but I'm scared.*

*I know.*

Then suddenly, as she continued to touch the chain, as the bonding sensation flowed through her finger, she felt drawn into the past. His past. She couldn't explain exactly what happened, but she saw Reyes as he'd been well over a century ago, when he was a teenager, as the young man abducted by slavers and sold at auction to the sadistic woman known as Sweet Dove.

The image sharpened in Angelica's mind, and she knew it had to be some kind of vision.

Her breathing grew short as she stayed in the past, seeing him as an innocent youth, full of fire and drive, stacks of books all around his cavern bedroom, as well as a bench, a rack, and barbells for working out. He looked so serious, even back then, so driven.

She didn't know how she was able to see into his past, but she kept looking and watching. He was lean and looked to be about fifteen. He barely had a beard, compared to his current scruff, but he was clearly proud of what was there, a typical boy in his teens.

She scanned the space and saw that many of the titles dealt with justice and the law. Even then, his purpose had been fixed.

She released the chain, and the image disappeared. She wasn't sure what had just happened, but she needed to know if what she'd seen was real. "When you were young, before you were abducted, did you live in a cave with rough, jagged walls, an arched doorway, and books stacked high, all scattered around the space?"

His eyes widened. "Are you telling me when you touched the chain that's what you saw?"

She nodded slowly. "You had workout equipment in there as well, a bench, barbells. Many of the books had to do with government and the law."

He stared at her. "You saw all these details?"

She nodded.

"You've just described my bedroom, the one I had

growing up. And you say this happened when you touched the chain?"

"Yes. I felt a sort of electrical charge; then the image just came to me, of you when you were young."

He seemed more distressed than ever as he clamped the lid shut on the chains, then shifted to sit on the end of the bed. He scrubbed a hand through his short hair.

She pivoted to look at him. "So, I didn't imagine what I just saw?"

He lifted his gaze to her. "I was fourteen when I started collecting books from the European and American libraries. I wanted to know about government and about how various societies dealt with criminals, with the rights of the individual. All we have is a corrupt court system in our world."

"Then you'd already made the seeking of justice your mission even before you were abducted?"

He leaned forward, planting his elbows on his thighs. He clasped his hands tightly together, flexing his jaw several times. "A year prior, my father, a very powerful Ancestral, tried to take a stand against the injustices in our world, in particular the increasing sex-slave traffic. Shortly after he'd made his tenth speech to what had become larger and larger audiences, he disappeared. My mother and I never knew what happened to him, but we suspected he'd been assassinated, then dropped into the middle of the ocean somewhere to remove all traces of his existence. But we had no recourse, no one to turn to for help in finding out what had been done to him, never mind holding anyone liable for the crime."

Angelica hardly knew what to do with this new piece of information. Just before Reyes had been abducted he'd already had to endure his father's apparent murder.

"And you'd planned that one day, you would take his place?"

He looked up at her, his blue eyes glittering. "I had. I was planning on studying in the human world, at one of the major European universities, when I was drugged and abducted."

She thought about this for a moment, about mother and son surviving the disappearance and probable death of a worthy husband and father. "Your mother must have been devastated when you disappeared."

"If you're asking what happened to her, she didn't survive. I think you might even say she died of a broken heart. Sweet Dove kept me informed, though, the gentle soul that my captor was, telling me how she'd stopped meeting her blood-needs, fell into madness, then perished."

Angelica, standing close to him, shaded her face with her hand. She saw all that he was in this moment, from the orphaned youth to the tortured slave under Sweet Dove's cruelty and to the current warrior on the brink of rectifying a terrible injustice in his world.

And all he had asked was that Angelica stay with him for the duration of Starlin's festival, attend a few functions, share a chain-bond and quite possibly his bed. Her life suddenly seemed so small because here was a man standing alone against an organization that earned billions each year from its crimes.

"Why was I able to see into your past like that? What was it I saw? I don't understand."

"It's called a revisiting vision. Some humans have markers in common with basic vampire DNA."

"And these humans can see into the past?"

"It's very rare, but apparently you have exactly that kind of capacity, which could be useful."

"And that's why this whole thing bothers you even more."

"Yes, because you're who you are. You're an amazing woman, and to top it off apparently you have this unique ability in my world."

She glanced at the leather box next to him. "So just by touching the chains, I could see the past. Would I see even more if I wore the chains? If I was bound to you?"

"I don't really know. This is new territory even for me."

"So you've never bound anyone before."

He shook his head. "Never wanted to. Never thought I would just on principle." He rose up and faced her once more. "All these questions, Angelica. Does this mean you're considering saying yes to my proposition?"

She nodded, but her throat grew tight. "There's just one thing. If anything happened to me, I would need to know that my mother was cared for."

"Of course," he stated, taking Angelica's arms gently in his hands.

"Not to put a damper on things, but what if you died as well? I really don't want to leave anything to chance here."

"I'll have papers drawn up immediately, so that she'll never lack for anything as long as she lives."

Angelica was so stunned that her mouth fell agape. "You would do that, without question?"

"It's the least I could do given the situation, given what I'm asking of you."

"At the Ocean Club, you accused me of being a gold digger."

He shook his head, a sad smile on his lips. "I knew you were no such thing. I was just trying to warn you away."

"And if only I'd gotten in my car and left." But she felt her lips curve; then tears started suddenly to her eyes and she began to weep, though she didn't really know why. The whole situation overwhelmed her, including Reyes and all that he'd been through. That alone, what he'd suffered even before his abduction, made her want to help him.

Reyes surprised her yet again as he rose up, drew her gently into his arms, and just held her. He rubbed her back, letting her feel whatever it was she needed to feel.

"You're exhausted," he said against her cheek. "Why don't you get some sleep and we'll talk about this again when you wake up? If you still think you want to stay with me through the Starlin events we can work out all the details, including an arrangement that will protect your mother's future. You can ask anything you want about the blood-chains and, perhaps more importantly, what will be expected of you in the coming days and nights. For now, bedtime."

At the mere mention of sleep fatigue settled into her bones as much from the mental stress as anything else. "You're right."

After getting ready for bed Angelica crawled beneath the comforter. Reyes gave her some much-needed space, leaving the room to take care of other business.

As she fell asleep what slipped through her mind didn't have anything to do with concerns for her mother or even what she might have to do if she stayed in Reyes's world but, rather, her own heart. She already felt a connection to the man, so what would happen if she joined him in a blood-chain bond? Most certainly he would become her lover, but what if she grew even more attached to him than she already was? What if she fell in love with him? How would she ever be able to leave this world after that?

Later, long after Angelica had fallen asleep, Reyes lay on top of the comforter next to her. For her sake, though he usually went commando, he now wore pajamas and a robe. He didn't want her to assume for a moment that he had any expectations, and he was pretty sure the last thing she needed to confront right now was his naked male body.

With one arm slung over the top of his head, he thought back to the cave she'd described, to the bedroom from his youth that reflected his plans to take up his father's cause.

Despite the fact that his father had been killed by his enemies, Reyes had embraced his calling to bring down the vile elements in his world. How ironic that Reyes had then been enslaved by a sadistic female owner for over a century.

Now Angelica was here and she was considering remaining with him.

With his mind reeling at this unexpected turn of events, that Angelica would have an added power if they forged the chain-bond, he finally left the bed and paced quietly in the opposite sitting room.

He poured himself another Bowmore and drank deeply, his gaze shifting to the bed. Angelica had thrown the comforter back and lay on her stomach. She wore a short dark-blue silk nightgown that rode up, exposing much of her white creamy skin and the curve of her buttocks.

His constant need for her flooded him in a sudden wash of desire. For just a moment he imagined kissing that curve and running his tongue in the erotic crease where her buttocks met the backs of her thighs.

He shifted away from her and sipped his scotch again. He needed to get hold of himself, to stop lusting after the woman. If she chose to remain, more than anything he would want her to feel respected.

When Angelica woke up she lay on her back staring up at a carved ceiling. Reyes's world made use of stone in ways she'd never seen before, sometimes a reflection of the actual makeup of the cavern, sometimes added. In this case, she wasn't sure. An angled flow of black granite, speckled with silver, stretched across the entire cavern space. Parts of the room appeared to be squared up with drywall, but other parts had been carved out of rock.

Reyes was nowhere to be seen, but his bedroom suite was larger than her entire apartment, so he could be anywhere right now. She listened hard, wondering if perhaps he was in the workout room or the bathroom, but nothing returned to her.

She drew up her knees and crossed her ankles, resting her hands in her lap. The comforter was a beautiful burgundy silk and felt expensive. But then Reyes had money. He'd paid $5 million for her.

She pressed her hands to her cheeks as she once more processed all that had happened to her over the space of a week. She'd had her life turned upside down and was even now considering donning a blood-chain and binding herself to a vampire.

Her brain still had trouble making sense of the word *vampire*, despite the fact that Reyes had already sunk his fangs and taken his fill. If she bound herself to him he'd be doing more of that, which of course sent a shiver down her neck, and desire bloomed yet again.

What would it be like to really be with Reyes? To share his bed, his body, all that he was?

She slipped from bed and moved to the bookshelf opposite. Reyes had left the box in plain view, and she wanted to look at the chains once more.

As she flipped the lid there they were, two simple dark metal chains, each with loops about a half inch long. She recalled the revisiting vision and wondered if she would experience something similar again.

She touched the links, but nothing happened, perhaps because Reyes wasn't nearby; she didn't know.

She closed the lid, returning to the bed this time to sit down on the edge, her gaze fixed to the box, to the chains, to the tough decision she had to make. She'd hoped that when she awakened she'd know which way to fall, whether backward to her life as a human with a job that bored her and to the care of her mother or forward into the dark unknown, into what looked like a world that had enough evil to fill up a universe.

Instead, Angelica was as much on the fence as she had been the night before.

Her instincts told her that if she bound herself to Reyes what happened between them afterward wouldn't be simple. Her attraction to him hadn't dimmed in the least, despite the horrible nature of the events that had occurred after the Ruby Theater Players had put on their little production.

Her cheeks grew hot all over again as she recalled going down on Reyes in front of a bunch of strangers. She would be foolish, however, to fail to consider that something similar or perhaps even worse might happen if she agreed to stay.

As thoughts of Reyes came to mind, even going back as far as kissing him at the Ocean Club, she realized that what bothered her the most was her vulnerability to him. Her heart already leaned in his direction and had tilted even further when she'd learned that instead of being a slaver, he was intent on bringing down this part of his world.

For that reason, she couldn't have admired him more.

But she also knew that she and Reyes lived on opposite sides of a deep gorge, with a very flimsy rope bridge between. The human and vampire worlds didn't mix.

She simply didn't know how to make this decision.

Reyes sat in his office, at his large burl-wood desk, going through page after page on the Starlin Group private Web site. Now that he was officially a member, he'd been given access.

So far his cruise through the site had essentially confirmed what he'd learned about Starlin over the decades, that Engles was Scorpion's link to the rest of the group and that Scorpion remained the most powerful force behind the organization. But the Web site had at least given Reyes the names of all the Starlin board members.

His next step had to be getting on the Board of Governors, a process that would no doubt take a long time to achieve. And as much as he'd like to get this whole thing settled as fast as possible, he'd already accepted that his mission might require years, if not decades, of patient effort. But being on the board would give him access to the information he needed to bring the entire organization down.

When he'd opened up the Web site the first thing he'd checked was a slave mortality counter from the recent auction. The counter was still set to "zero," which meant that none of the slaves had died yet. That number would change, but the fact that it sat on the Web site, with a flashing graphic around it, was one more indicator of the perverse nature of this group.

A link next to the mortality counter led to a secondary site for placing bets on which slaves were likely to die next and when, down to the minute. He'd clicked on it to familiarize himself with every aspect of Starlin's operation, but what he found there only deepened his disgust, something he hadn't thought possible. The site had pictures posted of every slave and her stats as well as information on the slave owners, including their known levels of abuse toward the humans they'd owned previously. Both he and Angelica were listed there, which meant that his cover held. He'd fabricated a reputation of having kept and killed over thirty-eight slaves over the past two decades, preferring slow-kills to short, brutal ones. Odds changed constantly, an indication that serious betting was going on even now.

As he scrolled back to the home page his thoughts turned toward Angelica and his senses told him she was awake. He almost shifted to altered flight and hurried to his bedroom in order to find out what decision she'd made about staying in his world. But he decided against it. He'd know soon enough, and the woman might want to have a shower first before confronting her vampire host.

He turned his attention, therefore, to the Starlin Festival and to the string of social events that would give each winning bidder more chances to display their newly acquired slaves.

He clicked on the Festival tab at the top of the Starlin Web site and found a rather lengthy list of parties that he could attend with Angelica, that is, if just this once the wind decided to blow in his direction.

Angelica still didn't know what to do. She'd never been so torn about a decision in her entire life.

She wanted to stay as passionately as she wanted to get the hell out of this insane world.

Once more, she rose up from the bed and crossed to the leather box.

This time, she took it back with her, sat down again, and balanced the box on her lap. Opening the lid, she decided to hold one of the chains this time. Maybe the blood-infused links would speak to her in a way that would help her make up her mind.

Several very small metal latches kept the chain in place, and once she removed them she drew the chain from the box. She set the red leather container aside.

She slid the blood-chain over her wrist and found that it had a nice weight. Only this time, perhaps because it rested against her skin, she experienced a faint vibration that *felt* like Reyes. She couldn't express it any other way. The chains reflected the way she thought of him, very powerful, intense, with a layering of determination that expressed his current goals.

She closed her eyes and forced her mind to relax. She posed the question silently: *Why should I stay here with Reyes? Why should I choose such an impossible path? Why?*

A single image rose swiftly within the center of her brain, of the Russian female slave from last night, the one who bore bruises all over her naked body. Angelica saw her clearly outside Engles's mansion, when her slave owner had attacked her throat and drunk from her neck.

Angelica opened her eyes. She could still hear the woman's whimpers.

From that memory Angelica's decision roared toward her with hurricane-force winds. Though she'd wanted to escape back to her ordinary life, she was needed here, maybe even for as long as it took to make sure that Starlin didn't abduct even one more vulnerable human.

She slid the chain off her wrist, holding it in both hands.

With her decision made, she simply slid the blood-chain over her head and let it fall around her neck. She pulled her hair from beneath until each link connected with her skin.

She drew in a deep breath as the chain began to vibrate softly and a sense of Reyes came into focus. She could even tell where he was in relation to the upstairs bedroom, as though some kind of vampire locator process had just clicked into place. Right now he sat in his office on the bottom floor.

She took another breath, and through the chain she began to siphon his power, letting it flow into her. She felt strengthened and renewed, something she hadn't expected.

Reyes had been so intent on reviewing all the parties to which he'd been invited that at first he didn't notice that his power was leaving him in a steady stream.

When he realized what it had to be he stood up abruptly and struggled to take a couple of breaths.

Angelica had put on one of the blood-chains.

Though he'd never been chained before, he knew

instinctively that this was exactly what had happened. He could sense it in the same way he felt the level of Angelica's determination.

She'd made her decision.

She was staying.

A wave of relief poured through him, as well as a thrill that he'd have the woman with him for at least the next few days.

But he had to calm down. His adrenals had released a huge amount of hormones, which had in turn ramped up his ever-present desire for the human. Glancing down at his jeans, he saw he had an uncomfortable bulge and adjusted himself because what shouldn't have been the least bit swollen was now rock solid.

He hadn't expected such a sudden, profound reaction. Maybe he'd wanted the bond and wanted her with him, but he'd set aside just how deeply attracted to her he was. Now, however, all that longing came into sharp focus.

But the last thing she needed was him coming at her in an aroused state.

Closing his eyes, he focused not on Angelica, but on his mission. That, at least, would help calm things down. He could finalize his itinerary now and choose which of the Festival parties to attend. There'd be a boat parade first in an extensive underground cavern that had over fifty mansions built on either side of a wide and very deep underground river. Engles had a place there, so his party would definitely be one of the stops.

Reyes was still the acknowledged guest of honor, and a variety of invitations had lit his in-box within the first hour following his winning bid at the auction.

Now Angelica would be with him. But how was he supposed to control his drive toward her?

At last calm, he shifted to altered flight and made his way slowly toward his bedroom, though he thought it only fair to give her a warning. *I'm coming to you.*

*I'm here.* Angelica still sat on the bed, the red leather box beside her.

She was suddenly very nervous. The chains would change everything. She'd known it instinctively, which was why the decision had been so damn hard.

But even as these thoughts rippled through her mind she could also sense Reyes's feelings and reactions. She smiled. His initial response had been full of sex, so much like a man.

She'd gotten that.

His desire for her had been like a warm wave easing down her body and making her feel things she shouldn't be feeling. But she'd known this would be a problem for her and for him as well. The chains merely accentuated what was already there, what had been simmering between them from that first kiss in the foyer of the Ocean Club.

When he arrived she watched him move through the solid wall and cabinet in the sitting room, appearing almost opaque at first, then solid, as he shifted from altered flight to mere levitation. He touched down near one of the brown leather club chairs but stayed put.

She rose to her feet to face him, suddenly aware that she should have at least gotten dressed. She'd been so caught up with her need to make a decision that she'd forgotten, until his gaze drifted up and down her body, that she wore only a short blue silk negligee.

"I'm sorry," she said.

"For what?" But his voice sounded hoarse.

"I should have put something on."

He nodded. "It's okay. I'm just so . . . grateful." His gaze fell to the chain around her neck. "Angelica, what you've done is enormous."

He moved toward her slowly, which affected her senses all over again. He walked like the powerful athlete he was, the outlines of his muscular shoulders and chest visible beneath a thin dark-blue V-neck sweater. He wore snug jeans and she couldn't decide whether she preferred this look, or the leather jacket he'd worn at the Ocean Club, or his tux. The man looked great in anything.

She touched the blood-chain, which vibrated more and more heavily the closer he got.

When he stood in front of her she caught a whiff of the ocean, like he'd been running along a seashore. The scent was very male and weakened her knees. His eyes were so blue, and once more the scruff over his jaw and chin made her tongue tingle.

"Angelica, I don't know what to say."

"You've already said it." She reached down and picked up the leather box, opening it once more so that it faced him.

He released the small clasps that held the second chain in place, then lifted it carefully with both hands. "The vibration is already so strong."

"And you've never done this before?"

He shook his head.

"Having reservations?"

He met her gaze. "I promised myself that I'd never be bound in chains again, of any kind, yet here I am."

She felt his distress, which caused her to reach out and settle her hand on his shoulder. "It'll be all right. It's just me."

At that he smiled ruefully. "You're right, but now I feel bad."

"Why?"

"Because I should be the one comforting you."

Her turn to smile. "As to that, I have a feeling you'll be doing a lot of that before we're through."

He held her gaze. "And it will be the least I can do."

She glanced at the chain he held in his hands. "So, what do you say? Now that I've made the decision, I'm dying to find out what it's really like."

He nodded and, using both hands, slid the chain over his head. It looked good on him, especially the dark metal against his blue sweater. She realized then that her vision had sharpened.

"I can see better."

"That would follow, but I can also sense your fear. I can almost feel your heart racing."

She nodded. "All that's true. I'm frightened half out of my mind right now."

"By me?"

"Oh, God, no, Reyes, not even a little. I trust you implicitly; otherwise I could never have done this. I fear what's likely to happen as we move forward with your mission. If the Festival events are anything like the after-auction party . . ." She let the rest of the thought hang.

At that he drew her into his arms, holding her tight, exactly what she needed. She slid her arms around his back, the sweater soft beneath her fingers. "See, you're comforting me already."

He held her like that for a few minutes, maybe waiting for her heart to settle down. He couldn't have known how much his big body and the latent strength of his arms eased her.

Finally, he drew back. "I want to test the proximity limitation. I think it'll be a bit of a challenge to get used to."

"Good idea."

He started backing away from her, one step at a time, and when he'd reached the ten-foot mark she felt the pull on her chain, a very strong warning tug.

"Do you feel that?"

He nodded but continued to inch backward. With each movement the tension increased. It was the strangest sensation, as though it would pull her forward soon and she'd fall flat on her face.

Instead of letting that happen, he took a couple of steps in her direction. "What did that feel like for you?"

"As though we had a taut rope between us and you were tugging. Hard."

"Same here."

What she didn't say was just how much of him she could feel, as though whatever thoughts he had or reactions he experienced automatically communicated themselves through the chains. It was both unsettling yet in a way thrilling. She felt strangely close to him right now. "So, what's on the agenda?"

At that he smiled as he returned to stand close to her once more. "The first part shouldn't be too bad. It's a boat parade."

She laughed. "A what?"

He explained about the underground river community where many of the wealthier members had homes and which was hidden behind a heavy, layered disguise.

"So these creeps can keep doing their thing without threat of jail time."

"Exactly. Although in our courts there isn't much risk of meaningful prosecution. Most of the judges are corrupt. Of course, if the entire vampire population knew what was going on there would be an uprising."

She considered all that he'd said. "No wonder you had to develop a cover over a period of years. With so much security in place, you couldn't have gotten this far otherwise. So tell me more about the festival."

"The parade lasts for several hours, with the boats coming and going and parties held at riverside. Most of these homes have landscaped front yards, patios, barbecues, and viewing decks."

"If I wasn't so horrified by what these people did, I'd be excited about seeing this place." She shook off the uneasy feeling about what would be ahead of her. "So you'll show me off, like you did at the after-auction party, which doesn't sound too bad." She felt the chain at her neck vibrate. "But you're worried."

"The situation won't be much different; that's true. The new slaves will be on display, forced to perform certain acts."

"And you're worried that we'll end up in a similar situation to the theater."

"I'll do my absolute best to avoid it; just be prepared."

"I understand."

He took her arm in his hand and squeezed gently. "I'll try to get us through without incident. The main thing is to make a show of being there. All we'll really need to do is appear at a number of the parties, talk to a few of the Starlin board members, then we can leave."

"I don't suppose we could avoid Engles." Angelica could only hope.

"He'll have to see you at least once, but we'll make it quick; then I'll bring you back here."

"So, how much time do I have?"

"We can go whenever you want. The parade has already started but lasts for hours, as do all the parties. Later is always better; that way we can make an entrance."

"I'm thrilled. Okay, I'll shower now." When she turned to go he moved with her, which brought her up short. "I think I can do this alone."

At that he smiled, but she didn't understand why. "Of course." He stayed put.

She moved on a quick tread, and the next moment the blood-chain bond not only gave a strong tug on her neck but also jerked her backward so that she fell on her tush.

Still sitting on the floor, she looked back at him and scowled. "You did that on purpose."

He chuckled. "I'm sorry. If I thought it would have done that to you, I would have said something. But I also thought that it wouldn't be a bad thing for either of us to experience the proximity problem of the bond." He slid a hand beneath her arm, lifting her to her feet.

She waved him forward. "Fine. Looks like you'll have to be in the bathroom with me."

"Hold on. Let me grab my laptop."

Without thinking he moved swiftly in the direction of the sitting room, and the next thing Angelica knew this time he was flying backward. She laughed as he rose to his feet, but she hurried past him, picked up his laptop, and handed to him. "It's really not that funny, is it?"

He narrowed his gaze at her, but his lips curved. "Let's go. I have what I need."

# CHAPTER 8

Once inside the bathroom Reyes had to keep moving himself and his laptop, tracking with Angelica, in order to sustain their distance restriction and avoid another tug at his neck. At least the toilet had its own small room for privacy, so that wouldn't be an issue.

He decided, however, that there were too many mirrors in the room. Though he could avoid watching her actually strip out of her short nightgown or hop in the shower, a couple of stray glances had allowed him too many glimpses of her naked body.

Fortunately, the shower was a walk-in separated by block glass tiles and he really couldn't see anything. He could imagine it, though.

He took a deep breath and opened his laptop, letting it sit on the side of the long marble counter. He returned to the Starlin Web site and once more perused the various parties he could attend.

Now that he knew who the board members were, he set up a separate document and listed the ten most influential. He then removed five whose human slaves rarely made it past the first week. He wasn't about to expose Angelica to the worst of the slavers if he could help it. That left him with five less-criminal party hosts, including Engles.

He found their homes and plotted a course along the river walk.

When Angelica finished her shower and donned a robe the real difficulty arose when she had to choose from the fantasy wear that the Starlin Group had provided for her. She sighed heavily over each of them as she pushed one hanger aside after another.

She glanced at him, wrinkling her nose. "Do I have to?"

It was such a normal response that he chuckled. "They're all horrible. Why not close your eyes and pick one? Either that or I will."

"I'll do it." But she actually did as he suggested. He watched her gather all the hangers and costumes into one tight group, then close her eyes. Waving her hand back and forth a few times, she reached out and grabbed one.

She groaned at the sight of the costume, but she didn't put it back. She'd randomly selected a very small outfit made up of a thong and a bustier of leopard print in black and turquoise. A pair of black thigh-high stockings, trimmed in matching leopard-print fabric, completed the barely there outfit.

Glancing down at the row of shoes below, she picked out a turquoise pair of what appeared to be a rather pain-inducing platform set with six-inch stilettos.

She scowled as she showed them to him. "You may have to carry me half the time."

"With pleasure."

Her gaze caught and held. "You know, you're exactly how I thought you would be. You're very kind, Reyes."

"You thought I was kind?" He was stunned.

"Maybe *respectful* is the better word. Even Marcus said that about you."

"Marcus?"

She nodded. "At Briggs's. He's one of the bartenders."

"Marcus, of course. And he thought I was respectful."

"Toward women."

Reyes nodded slowly. "That's an interesting view, though I'm not certain where he got that idea."

"Wait, what are you thinking about right now? Because I swear you feel really badly about something, but I can't imagine what that might be."

He held her gaze. He needed to remind himself that whatever he experienced, the chains would communicate his reactions. "I've used the slaves badly in this part of the world to build my cover, demanding sex from them, treating them no better than most of the other Starlin men who attend the sex clubs. I've watched women being hurt in sex shows and haven't lifted a finger to help. So somehow the compliment falls short of reality."

She grew very solemn, holding the faux-leopard costume against her stomach. "Did you ever hurt any of these women yourself?"

"Do you think it's necessary to cause pain in order to violate a slave? Every command is a violation."

She drew close, caressing his shoulder. "I understand."

"How can you? You've never been a slave."

She glanced at the costume in her hand, then let it drop to the floor. Meeting his gaze once more, she said, "You seem to forget that I was a captive for a week, even through the time that you seduced me while I hung in chains. Maybe it wasn't the level of torture you've gone through, but I experienced the same kind of overwhelming impotence and fear. I think it's one of the reasons I chose to stay here, to help you with your mission. It was such a terrible feeling . . ." She got no further, as tears filled her eyes. "I want to help. I really do."

He drew her into his arms once more. He remained silent for a long moment, then said quietly, "I was thinking about this Asian woman I used recently. She begged me to buy her, to take her out of that club, and I couldn't."

Angelica drew out of his arms and swiped her cheeks. "Why not?"

"At the time, I was still performing for a couple of Starlin spies. I hadn't been granted my membership yet. I couldn't take the chance."

"But you've been accepted since then. Is anything preventing you from buying her now? I mean, would that go against the rules?"

He felt light-headed suddenly. He hadn't quite adjusted to his new reality, that he was a Starlin member, a participant. He'd been vetted and approved. "You're right. I have a new set of options I didn't have before." When she reached down to pick up the costume and started to take it off the hanger he said, "Leave that. I want to do this now. I want to buy her before something terrible happens to her, if it hasn't already."

After Angelica put the leopard outfit back on the rod

he took her by the arm and guided her back out to the sitting area. He found his phone and called the club, asking for the owner.

The man gushed at Reyes's call. Of course he did, especially when Reyes offered a hundred thousand for the Asian slave. "She's still available, but working, Master Reyes."

But Reyes grew very quiet and with his silence let the club owner feel his displeasure.

"Of course, I can have her sent over immediately."

"That would be wise."

"Yes, master. Of course, master."

"I'll have the money wired within the next few minutes."

When he hung up he alerted his security staff of the woman's impending arrival. Closing his laptop, he made a second phone call to his bank, talked with the manager to exchange codes, and got the sum transferred.

A few minutes later, with Angelica by his side, he descended the stairs and opened the door to the woman who had serviced him so recently. Her eyes were wide with fear until she saw him; then she fell at his feet, sobbing. A stream of gratitude poured from her mouth.

Mathilde, his housekeeper, arrived with a robe in her hand and draped it over the woman. She had several bruises on her back. Some of the customers liked to get rough with the women.

A profound euphoria curled through Reyes that he'd finally been free enough to do what he'd felt an impulse to do a thousand times during the past several decades. From the moment he'd entered the sex-slave clubs he'd wanted to liberate every slave he'd encountered.

In some ways it felt insignificant, this sole woman

when hundreds of thousands had died. Yet at the same time nothing was more important than the individual.

"What's your name? Your real name?"

She lifted her face, wiping it on the robe. "Fei Yen."

"Welcome, Fei Yen, to my home. This is my housekeeper, Mathilde, and she will take care of you. For the present, you will serve here."

She glanced at Angelica, saw the chain around her neck, then lowered her eyes. "I understand."

Reyes figured out her mistake immediately, that she believed she would be expected to service them both from now on. He remembered feeling that way for a long time after he'd escaped from Sweet Dove, that every look, request, gesture by a normal person he interpreted through his sex-slave experience.

He understood, so he took Fei Yen's chin in his hand and lifted her gaze to meet his. "The only obligation you will have in my household from this time forth is to recover from your wounds and to do any small chores that my housekeeper will ask of you. And the only reason I have to insist on the latter is to make sure that I sustain my appearance in this world. Do you understand?"

"Yes." But tears once more filled her eyes. "No."

He could see she was in a state of shock and probably wouldn't believe the reality of her situation for a long time. He nodded for Mathilde to lead her away.

He led Angelica slowly back up the stairs, knowing that he had just changed the woman's life forever. Angelica took his arm and squeezed hard. *Thank you for this.*

He glanced at her and saw that her dark-brown eyes glistened with unshed tears. The chain at his neck vibrated softly, a pure reflection of her appreciation.

But he felt the same way, almost overcome. "I don't

think it would have occurred to me, so thank you. I know the sensation won't last, but I swear my heart feels as though a terrible weight has been lifted."

"You did good."

"You don't know how many times I've wanted to do exactly that."

"What will happen to her?"

"I have a connection who helps rehabilitate sex slaves and return them to their former lives. When the time is right, I'll send her to him."

Once back in his sitting room, he scrubbed a hand through his hair. "I guess we'd better get going."

Angelica settled a hand on his shoulder. "Not yet. Take a moment."

He held her gaze, that same shining light still in her eyes. "What are you thinking?"

"That you're an amazing man." Then, just as she had done at the Ocean Club, she leaned up and kissed him.

He closed his eyes, savoring the sensation, aware that what translated through the chains had to do with her admiration for him, the respect she'd talked about earlier. He hadn't bought the slave to gain Angelica's approval, nothing like that. Yet he drank in her approbation like a cool drink on a hot summer day.

His desire for her rose, a tremendous wave of need that threatened to swamp him. But for just a moment he let it flow, letting her feel just how much he wanted her.

He surrounded her with his arms and drew her tight against his chest. She moaned softly, so that he deepened the kiss, sliding his tongue into her mouth.

She responded, moving her tongue against his, stroking in a sensual way that made him think so many things at once that he had to draw back.

All he'd done was kiss her and he was hard as a rock yet again.

He leaned his forehead against hers.

"Reyes," she murmured.

He loved the sound of her voice. He couldn't recall the last time he'd ever allowed himself to stop long enough to have that thought, that a woman's voice could please him.

He'd been a lone wolf for a very long time, loping through the forest on a solitary track, hunting his prey.

Yet somewhere along the way Angelica had come into his life, an unexpected miracle who eased him.

But it was time to get to the boat parade. "I think I should warn you about something."

He felt a quick spurt of her anxiety through the chains. "What's that?"

"About the parade. There will probably be couples on the boats performing all sorts of sex acts. Just want you to be warned."

She shook her head and turned in the direction of the hall. "Well, come on then. Let's get me strapped into this heinous costume, then go celebrate with a bunch of pervs."

Angelica could never have imagined an immense two-mile-long cavern, or a river sixty feet across flowing down the center, or a soft wind that blew constantly so that the air smelled fresh and clean.

She siphoned Reyes's power in a steady stream now so that her vision kept improving. She stood beside him on a long wood deck at the river's edge, and though the cavern was dark, she saw everything as though it were lit by a soft glow of light. Given the height of her stilettos, she nearly stood shoulder-to-shoulder with him.

Wait staff brought drinks around, and she was careful not to ask for anything or to look anyone in the eye. Reyes held a whiskey in his right hand but held her tethered to him with a leash that ran from his right wrist to the front of her choke collar.

For the occasion he wore a short black leather jacket, though this one had silver boa skin across the top of the shoulders and down the arms. It wouldn't have been a first choice, but he looked amazing anyway. Besides, he fit in. This crowd didn't hold back when it came to clothes, and some of the men wore strange snakeskin shoes that showed the heads of the snakes on the pointed tips.

Her fantasy costume didn't cover much, and every breeze caused another round of goose bumps to rise on her bare ass. Oddly, the thigh-high stockings helped her to feel more covered up than she really was.

The turquoise stilettos had really bothered her until Reyes suggested she send some of the power she siphoned to her strained arches and bent toes.

She thought the idea brilliant, and after a couple of tries she finally succeeded in sending relief to her aching feet. Though not all the pain had disappeared, enough did so that she could walk without nearly as much agony.

She didn't understand how his power worked or how she was able to siphon it. Vampires possessed extraordinary advantages over their human counterparts, which made her wonder why, with so much power, his civilization hadn't conquered hers.

When she asked Reyes quietly he explained that while his kind lived very long lives, sometimes even millennia, they had poor reproduction rates. Their numbers ran in the low millions, compared to the billions of humans who populated the planet.

"Beyond that, we're not a highly centralized society. We still haven't figured out how to manage our psychopaths."

She glanced at the villas up and down the opposite bank. Each was very different yet had an ancient Italian feel. Knowing she and Reyes would raise questions if they continued in conversation, she maintained her submissive, head-lowered posture and switched to telepathy. *I can't believe all this is hidden from our world.*

Reyes kept his posture rigid, his feet apart, a very dominant position. He wrapped the leash once around his wrist but didn't make eye contact with her. *We have many Ancestral vampires who can create intricate disguises.*

*Ancestrals?* Here was something new. She found it difficult to converse without wanting to look at him.

*The most powerful in our world rise to Ancestral status, which is essentially the name given to that power.*

*Are you an Ancestral?*

*I have the genetic markers, but I haven't embraced that level of power. Not sure I'm going to, but I have the rest of my life to make that choice.*

She turned and held his gaze. *Why are you holding back?*

He scowled, though at first she didn't know why. *Angelica, remember your posture. Now.*

She lowered her eyes quickly to support his cover. *Sorry. Forgot for a moment.*

He gripped the back of her neck. *We're being watched. Pretend that I'm hurting you.*

She bent her knees and groaned.

When he released her neck she slumped her shoulders. *How's this?*

*Better. One of the men on the Board of Governors was watching us. He's smiling now and nodding his approval.*

*Bastard.*

*Yes, he is.*

Reyes turned toward the right and aloud said, "Another boat is coming. You may approach the rail to observe."

Angelica did as she was told but kept her head slightly bowed. "Thank you, master."

The fifteen-foot boat moved slowly and had an amazing array of purple lights that rose to a pinnacle, which in turn lit up like a fireworks rocket exploding. There was even an accompanying sound effect. But built up over the pilot's station was a platform on which a slave couple, both manacled, maneuvered through several sexual positions, as though performing an orchestrated dance. Maybe they were.

Once more Angelica averted her gaze. She hated seeing them like this, but at least it reminded her why she and Reyes were here.

*I can feel your distress. Why don't we to move to the next party?*

*Yes, please.*

He gathered up the slack in the leash and tugged as he drew her across the deck, heading toward the public walkway. The riverside path had been smoothed out of the natural surrounding rock, twelve feet in width.

Many offered their congratulations once more at both his acceptance into the organization as well as his winning bid.

A large portion of the slaves were completely naked, not even accorded the fantasy costume like the one she had on. At least the faux-leopard bustier and thong covered her up a little.

A female slaver walked by with a well-endowed male slave who had his hand on his upright cock, supporting himself as he moved. His eyes had a low-lidded, glazed appearance. Angelica looked away, trying to figure this one out. Was he enjoying himself or doing something else entirely?

*I can feel the question vibrating through my chain, Angelica. And the answer is yes, he must remain in an aroused state or he'll be punished.*

*Oh, God.* She understood a little about the male anatomy. *How is he able to do that?*

*There are a lot of tricks.*

Of course Reyes would know: he'd been a male enslaved to a sadistic female. But this slave was from her world.

Reyes continued, *Given that he's human, he's probably pumped full of a drug meant to treat erectile dysfunction.*

She didn't repress the heavy sigh that followed.

Reyes despised that Angelica had to walk slightly behind him. Her position also stressed him out, since he couldn't control what happened in his wake. If one of these partygoers, many of whom were drunk, decided to cop a feel Reyes was pretty sure he'd come unglued.

*Let me know if anyone touches you. I won't stand for it.* He moved his gaze from side to side, watching everyone who passed.

*Is that why my chain is vibrating like a Harley right now?*

*If any of these cretins put his hands on you . . .*

*Okay, ease down. I can see your neck muscles flex. That's not good for any man, and probably not a vampire, either.*

He cleared his throat. *You're going to make me laugh. You need to laugh more.*

*Maybe so, but right now I'm seeing another of the Board of Governors, a man by the name of Fitch, and I'll want to meet him. He's a few yards away, very tall. Wears his hair flowing around his shoulders. He has one of his slaves with him.* The blond woman was naked and stared dull-eyed toward the ground in front of her.

*Oh, my God, Reyes, she has cuts in perfect thin lines down her abdomen. He must have used the cat's claw.*

*Looks like it, but there's nothing we can do.*

*She'll die.*

*Not right away. He's known to take his time.*

Fitch approached. "Reyes. It is *Reyes,* right?"

Reyes once more picked up the slack on Angelica's leash and drew her close to his side. He extended his hand, and Fitch shook it. "How do you do, Master Fitch? I understand you're on the Starlin board."

"I am and your name keeps coming up at the meetings, has for some time. Keep up the good work and you might be asked to join us."

Reyes strove to check his emotions, but excitement coursed through him. He had one goal here, to get on the board, but he was prepared for his efforts to take years. Would it be possible to speed up his plans? "I'd like that. Starlin has set the bar in every sense."

"One day, we'll exceed even Briggs in volume."

Daniel Briggs was the largest slaver in the entire vampire world and his Dark Cavern system, which he owned and operated, moved more slaves than any other outfit. He was also untouchable as the most powerful vampire on the planet and currently now headed up the Council of Ancestors.

Once Reyes brought Starlin down, he fully intended to turn his sights on Briggs. The vampire owned hundreds of clubs from which he drew *new talent,* the current euphemism for fresh slaves. Briggs even owned the Ocean Club, which Starlin also used to gather its slaves, including Angelica.

Wishing Fitch enjoyment of the festivities, Reyes tugged on Angelica's leash.

As he moved past Fitch, however, Angelica's voice shot through his head. *Reyes, he just grabbed my ass.*

*Fitch?*

*Yes.*

Reyes didn't stop to think; he whirled, leaped toward Fitch, and had him in a choke hold on the ground, one knee hard into the vampire's sternum. "You don't touch my slave. Sharing is a courtesy but not a right. You ask first. Have you got that?" Board or no board, Reyes was setting some boundaries.

A crowd gathered quickly, but Reyes didn't care. He had to live this life for now and Angelica had already sacrificed so much to play her role, but like hell would he let any man touch her and not feel the consequences.

"Understood." Fitch's voice now sounded hoarse, like he had laryngitis. "Apologies."

Reyes released him slowly, then rose to his feet. He didn't wait to say anything more to the man, but Reyes did notice the startled look in the blond slave's eye and that tears welled quickly after.

Reyes understood. He cursed several times as he moved away. He'd just made it worse for the woman. Fitch was a bully, like most of these slavers, and he'd take his humiliation out on her.

*Reyes? Are you okay? What's going on?*

*I want you to move forward and walk in front of me; just keep your head down. I can't have that happen again.*

Angelica moved past him, unsteady in her stilettos. *I'm getting a feeling you're upset about Fitch's slave.*

*I am. He'll punish her because I humiliated him just now. I wasn't thinking, but I felt your horror rise up like a wave because he'd fondled you and your reaction jump-started my own.*

*Did you just ruin your chances with the board?*

*Don't give a fuck if I did. I thought I would be more tolerant, but not chain-bound.*

Angelica sighed. *Nothing about this is simple, is it?*

*No, it's not.*

At the next party a live band had just set up. Over two hundred guests danced on the largest outdoor patio Reyes had ever seen. Drinks abounded and by now several slavers were stumbling around. Others made a show of dominating their slaves, everything on display. More than one woman was being hurt.

Wanting to get Angelica away from as much of the cruelty as possible, he guided her toward the front entrance of the house. *Another board member owns this place. Master Kell.*

But the chains had grown very quiet on Reyes's neck. When he didn't get a response he drew close and stroked the back of her arm in such a way that no one could see what he was doing. *Hey, are you okay?*

She turned back to glance at him, then lowered her gaze. *I don't suppose there's someplace we can hide out for a while. I'm a little overwhelmed.* Her telepathic voice grew faint, *That man was raping his slave anally right on the lawn.*

*I know. Let's get you inside.*

The mansion, made of cream-colored stone and decked out with handsome pillars for support, went on for at least fifty feet in either direction and had two stories and a grand curved staircase.

A woman stood in the center of the foyer, wearing a sophisticated tight black dress. He understood her role as the housekeeper.

"How do you do, Master Reyes, and welcome to Master Kell's home."

"My slave needs the facilities."

The housekeeper nodded, her expression unchanging, then gestured toward the stairs. "You'll find several to choose from on the third floor."

He leaned close. "Which one would be most private?"

"Ah, yes, of course. You'll want to go left, then right. Master Kell has made this suite available to certain associates. Very private."

"Thank you."

Wishing this nightmare would be over, once more he gestured for Angelica to precede him. As she started up the stairs he was grateful to be following her because he could block at least some of the attention her nakedness drew. He hated that she was on display and the entire trip up the stairs brought dozens of pairs of eyes turning in her direction.

*Thank you, Reyes, for sticking close. I don't feel quite so exposed.*

*You're more than welcome.*

*This has to be hard on you and probably way too familiar.*

*You're exactly right. More than at any other point, I'm reminded of what it was to be a sex slave.*

When he arrived at the designated room he turned and locked the door. He wanted to apologize again to Angelica, but she flung her arms around him and thanked him. "I'm sorry, but I so needed to be away from all that, at least for a little while."

He wrapped his arms around her but slipped back into telepathy. *This place is probably videoed, so we'll need to keep up appearances.*

Her arms fell away, and the relief she'd felt was clearly short-lived. She dipped her chin. *Well, at least we're away from all the visuals. Just tell me what to do.*

*I should warn you, I'll have to really play up my role.*

*It's okay.*

Aloud, he spoke in a commanding voice. "Facedown on the bed. Now."

The décor was sparse, a round bed covered in a violet throw. Angelica stretched out.

*Just try to relax.*

She released a deep sigh, then put a hand over her face, shading her eyes. *I'll try. And despite that we might be filmed, this is still easier than having to watch what was going on outside.*

He sat down next to her and caressed her bottom. *Is this okay?*

*You mean besides the fact that it feels really good?*

*Yes, besides that.*

*It's fine. Whatever you need to do is fine. I trust you.*

Reyes couldn't really imagine what this was like for

Angelica, the horror of it, seeing all this perversion all at once. For the sake of those who were most likely watching he dropped to his knees on the floor behind her, spread her legs, and leaned over her.

"You're to stay in this position, slave, and do as you're told."

"Yes, master."

As he held her waist and kissed her bottom the chains at his neck vibrated, telling him that she liked what he was doing. His ever-present desire for her began to flow, hardening him, making him want to bury himself deep between her beautiful thighs.

*Reyes,* she whispered through his mind.

*I can make you come like this, if you want me to.*

*It would be wrong on so many levels.* Her hips flexed. *But I'd love it.*

*You're beautiful, Angelica. And these black stockings topped with faux leopard are turning me on.*

*Your lips are like heaven.*

Despite the horror of the festival, he wanted this for Angelica; he wanted her to know pleasure. This much he could do for her.

He slid one hand beneath her to cover her mound and began kneading her, pushing against her, teasing her clitoris. She moaned.

Wanting better access, he drew back and pulled her to the edge of the bed. He took his time taking her thong off, stroking her legs, then kissing her bottom in turns.

*Reyes, my God, Reyes.*

When her thong sat on the floor beside him he spread her legs wide and moved between. He ignored his own desire and made this all about her.

Using his tongue, he went to work while at the same time returning his hand to her mound and to the top of her clitoris.

But having his tongue deep inside her well and feeling her tight pulses brought his own need to a sharp, painful pinnacle.

He continued to drive his tongue into her and to massage her clitoris at the same time. She was gasping now, her face pressed into the comforter.

Aloud, he spoke in a harsh voice. "You'll come for me, slave; come now."

*Spank me, if you want.*

*I'm so tempted.*

*Do it, Reyes. It will help with the cover and, truthfully, I'd like it.*

He lifted his hand and gave her a sharp crack on her bottom.

She cried out as if in pain. *Reyes, oh, my God. Do it again.*

*Only if you protest.*

"That hurts, master."

"It's meant to, slave." He slapped her again, then went back to work using his tongue.

*I'm so close.*

*Whenever you're ready, Angelica.*

She panted, and because of the chains he could feel that she was on the brink. Using his vampire abilities, he flicked in and out of her faster than a human could go. She moaned heavily; then suddenly she was screaming her orgasm. He kept working her until she settled back against the bed.

*Reyes, that was wonderful. Thank you.*

Even within his mind she sounded loose and well-used.

*I'm going to issue some commands to help support what I'm doing, okay? Forgive me for the way this will sound.*

*No worries.*

"All right, slave, you're to stay in that position, your legs spread wide. Do you understand?"

"Yes, master."

He rose from his knees painfully aroused.

He drew a chair from beside the wall and moved to position it so that he appeared to be looking at her.

When he sat down he placed his feet on the insides of hers. *I'm going to force you wider, but let me know if it hurts.*

*I'm good.*

Slowly, he pushed her legs farther and farther apart. For a slave this would be a point of humiliation, but for him keeping Angelica in this position showed dominance.

*How's that?*

*Fine. Really, I'm fine.*

*We're just going to stay like this for a while. I may touch you now and then, just for show. All I want you to do is to take a breath, to relax, before we continue on. With this much drinking going on, I think things will get worse before we'll be able to leave.*

*You mean more like one orgy after another.*

*I'm afraid so.* Again he repressed the need to apologize. If he didn't hold back he'd be apologizing every other minute for what she'd have to endure.

Every once in a while he'd lean forward and caress her bottom or stroke her inner thighs, just for show. But he could tell by the chains that Angelica was finally relaxed.

*Doing better?*

*Much. That was lovely, Reyes. Unexpected. I think I needed that.*

*I know what you mean.* Of course the view of her, of where he wanted to be, wasn't helping his own situation, but he'd been well-trained and toughed it out.

*Do I have permission to turn over now?*

*Sure, but it will mean that in a few minutes we're going to leave this room.*

He released her legs, and drawing them together, she rolled onto her side and met his gaze. *Can I do something for you?* she sent.

He squeezed his eyes shut. When he opened them he shook his head. *Not right now. I won't lie and say I don't want you, because I've been in pain since we put these chains on. And I really appreciate the offer. But I have too much rage right now. Can't explain it.*

*And you don't have to. I get it.* Her eyes welled with tears. *Fitch is going to hurt that woman, isn't he?*

*Yes. Badly. He's an abuser, as most of these assholes are. They've given it a polite "Starlin" gloss, and built a lifestyle around it, pretending it's something that it's not. Some of them even believe that when slaves scream in pain it's merely because they're so emotionally connected to the ones who torture them, that everything is an act of love.*

She rolled slightly to lean her head against the comforter. *There ought to be a stronger word than* perversion *to describe these people.* After releasing a deep sigh she added, *I think I'm ready to leave now.*

*Good, and the sooner we get through this the sooner I can take you home.* He rose up. "On your feet, slave."

She put her thong back on, then her shoes. *Where are we headed to next?*

*Engles's place.*

She sighed. *Oh, goodie.*

Once more Reyes had to repress his amusement, but he loved that she'd lightened the mood yet again.

# CHAPTER 9

Angelica made the trek to what would be Engles's mansion in the platform stilettos and continued to focus Reyes's healing energy onto her achy toes and now tight arches. At least the stone path was smooth.

Because drunkenness was becoming an increasing problem, Reyes finally gave up trying to sustain a submissive distance and held her close to his side and well away from the foot traffic.

She still couldn't believe that just a little while ago Reyes had worked her body and brought her to such a perfect, thrilling orgasm. She didn't even know why she'd allowed it, except that his touch felt so good and maybe in large part because the whole time his own sexual need and desire had vibrated the chain around her neck in strong pulses. She'd been able to sense how aroused he was, and that's what had taken her the distance and made what should have been an impossible thing very possible.

And his tongue. She'd never experienced anything like that before. Wicked.

*Where have your thoughts gone?*

*Nowhere.*

*That's not what I'm getting.*

She didn't know why she tried to pretend. The chains wouldn't allow her to conceal that merely thinking about what he'd done had worked her up all over again. She'd desired him from the beginning and she'd known that the blood-chains would enhance what was there, but she hadn't expected to be catapulted into an almost chronic state of arousal.

*Angelica?*

*I don't know what to say. But I can't stop thinking about what you just did to me. It was amazing.*

*I pleased you.*

*Oh, my God, to say the least.*

*I want to do it again.*

She held the words back, the ones she really wanted to speak, what she'd always wanted from him, as in *I want all of you right now, your weight on me, your cock inside me.*

Instead, she overlaid his right arm, the one that held her tight to his side as they walked, and squeezed.

He guided her past three mansions, and after a turn in the path as the river shifted to a southeasterly direction Engles's home came into view.

She stared up at an incredible mansion built several stories high of white stone, reaching almost to the top of the cavern. The pyramid effect had vines trailing off several balconies and trees growing everywhere.

*Reyes, how does anything grow in these underground caverns without sunlight?*

*It's simple, really. We make use of modern technology and massive grow lights that run on timers. A community like this would have specified daily periods in which the entire cavern is ablaze with manufactured light. We have a lot of engineers in our culture.*

*It's truly amazing.*

She began to believe that from what she'd seen this civilization could do just about anything.

Another boat moved by, but Angelica didn't bother looking. She knew what to expect, and no matter how beautiful the lights or the artistic design of the set, the exhibition of flesh and sex would once again disgust her.

She walked beside Reyes in silence, working to sustain her submissive appearance. At the same time, a strange emotion vibrated through the blood-chain.

Something was bothering Reyes.

A chill chased down Reyes's spine as he stared up at Engles's massive riverside home. Though Reyes had never been to this part of the world before, he couldn't shake a bizarre feeling of familiarity, though he had no basis for it.

He thought the mansion a monstrosity, though he admired how the building actually molded itself to the shape of the cavern wall. The dwelling was the size of a small hotel, and he knew from gossip over the years that it boasted fifteen bedrooms, some of them equipped with smaller versions of his game room.

Engles stood alone on a secondary platform, away

from the river's edge by thirty feet and guarded by a security detail. He held a tumbler in his hand, probably his favorite, Dubonnet. A pair of female slaves, wearing nothing but chain chokers, stood nearby, heads bowed, bodies bruised. Engles represented the worst of his kind, depraved and self-involved, as though nothing else in the world should ever happen except what pleased him.

Engles had an odd, owl-like look with large dark eyes and a hawkish nose. He combed his thick mass of wavy dark-brown hair away from his face, had a deep indentation in his chin, and possessed a level of charisma that made him appear better-looking than he really was. His head swiveled in Reyes's direction, Engles smiled and waved his hand in acknowledgment but swiftly reverted his attention to the party below.

His gaze scanned the crowd on the deck that ran at least forty yards along the riverfront. Engles seemed methodical in his search, as though cataloging who had attended his event and maybe deciding to award favors based on that attendance. He wore a sharkskin coat and black slacks, an open-collared black shirt.

Reyes tightened his grip on Angelica. *Do you see Engles?*

*Yes. He's like a hawk, isn't he, looking for prey?*

Reyes nodded. *And we just need to avoid his talons.*

Repressing a sigh, Reyes held the leash at shoulder level, another dominant position, as he guided Angelica toward the steps that led to the curved stone platform. He moved in Engles's direction, intending to fulfill his obligation, when from the opposite side Engles's security detail called to Engles, handing him a phone.

Engles's face turned scarlet with rage as he shouted into the cell.

Reyes shifted direction, guiding Angelica toward the mansion. *I think we'll leave him alone for now.*

*Good idea. Besides, I was not looking forward to being anywhere near that man. There's something not right about him. Personification of evil, maybe.*

*I think that's exactly right.*

But as Reyes led her up the walk to the house another chill traveled down his back.

*What is it?* Angelica asked. *Because I'm getting this strange vibe from you.*

Reyes felt confused. *I honestly don't know, but I keep getting this feeling that I've been here before. Yet, I know I haven't.*

*Do you think someone has messed with your memories? I mean, is that even possible in your world?*

*Possible, yes.* His thoughts went immediately to Sweet Dove. The woman was an Ancestral, part of the reason she'd been able to gain such complete control over him, to hold him all those years. Some of his chains had been preternaturally enhanced with her power, a kind of binding that took decades to sever despite how physically strong he'd grown over the years.

But the question was, would Sweet Dove have taken his memories of being in this house before? If so, why?

*I find it awkward speaking to you but not looking at you,* Angelica sent.

*I know what you mean.*

*And I feel dizzy suddenly.*

He glanced at her. Though there were hardly any people near the house, he still held her tight, but he could feel her trembling. *What's wrong?*

*I don't know. I don't like this, Reyes. Something isn't right.*

*I'm getting that feeling as well.*

*What do we do?* She looked worried, a tight frown between her brows.

*We go forward. I want to know what's happening here as well, but I'll have to release you. It won't look right to be supporting you this way.*

*I know.* She removed her hand and he slid his arm from around her waist. Holding the leash, he gathered up the slack a little more.

When he crossed the threshold Angelica gasped, as she should have. Even he was stunned by the sight of split curved staircases that met at an upper landing. A massive crystal chandelier hung from a forty-foot-high ceiling.

Dozens of guests milled throughout the foyer and off to both sides. Elegant food stations ranged throughout, but he didn't see an open bar. Reyes thought he understood, that Engles might enjoy a good party, but the drunken revels could take place dockside rather than in his dwelling.

Engles liked control on every level.

Reyes accepted more congratulations on his winning bid, just as Angelica received the once-over again and again. He didn't like it and bristled more than once at a suggestive comment.

*Ignore them*, she sent.

Reyes shook his head. *Is it that obvious?*

*The chains speak your irritation every single time.*

He glanced around. *Are you hungry?*

*A little.*

*I'll have you pile up a plate and hopefully find some-place private. Unfortunately, for show I'll have to control what and how much you eat.*

*Don't worry about that. Let's do whatever we need to do.*

He passed by a seafood buffet and wended his way to a less populated room that opened on to a side garden. Another buffet sat in the middle with a spicy aroma.

*Italian. How does that sound?*

*Perfect.*

He ordered her to load a plate, then directed her into the garden. He wanted to have her stretch out on the chaise longue and kick off her shoes, but there were security cameras everywhere. He chose instead a chair and ottoman, so that she could take the subservient position in front of him.

*I'm pretty sure we'll be on video again, so follow my lead.*

She lowered her head, nodding, holding the plate with both hands.

*You're doing great. Just try to keep the fire from your eyes.*

Her lips threatened to curve. *The fire?*

*Yes, you have fire in your eyes, one of the things I value about you.*

*So, you value me.*

*You know I do.* He wanted to tell her more, but several people had entered the garden and he risked his cover by appearing to hesitate. *We should get this show started.*

*Ready when you are.*

He gestured to the ottoman. "Sit down, slave."

When she'd taken her seat he continued, "You're to feed me." *Can you make your hands tremble?*

*Sure.*

She did an excellent job, preparing bites of food for him, her fingers shaking, her head down. He ate two fork-fuls before he said, "You may have a bite, a small one."

She obeyed him.

By now they had an audience, one that continued to grow. In Starlin terms, they were both famous. He sat back watching her, forcing a hard expression to his features, just short of a glare. To her mind he sent, *You're doing great.*

*This whole thing is freaking me out, Reyes. Why have at least twenty people come to watch this?*

*They're hoping it will devolve into either violence or sex.*

*Is that what we need to do?* He could feel her mounting tension through the vibration of the chains.

*Doesn't matter. Not gonna happen.*

"You may prepare another small bite for yourself."

Using the side of her fork, she sliced a piece of corkscrew pasta in half, speared a pea-sized worth of prosciutto, and slipped it between her teeth.

*You're beautiful. Have I told you that, Angelica? And now you're blushing.* Aloud, he said, "I'll have a bite of the bread."

"Yes, master." She lifted the toasted sourdough.

*Look at me, Angelica.* She lifted her gaze to his, and the moment she did he opened his mouth and she slid the piece inside.

*Reyes.* She whispered his name through his mind and suddenly all he could think about was having her under him. He'd wanted her from the beginning, but in this situation, with her feeding him bits of pasta and bread and looking voluptuous in her black-and-turquoise leopard bustier, he was aroused all over again. In an effort to calm down he shifted his gaze to the row of nearby large planters that held thirty-foot cypresses.

*You okay?* Her voice and her concern did little to help his problem.

*Not exactly, but I think it's time you stopped feeding me.*

She settled the plate on her lap and folded her hands. *I don't suppose you could find us a dark corner somewhere?*

*What are you proposing?*

Her gaze flicked suddenly to his, then fell obsequiously to her lap. *You know what I'd like? I mean, really like?*

He could hardly breathe and he didn't dare try to stand up. *What's that?*

*Reyes, I know this is going to sound strange, but I'd love a first kiss. We haven't had that, you know. We've had other things, but I'd like a real first kiss.*

*Are you forgetting that you kissed me at the Ocean Club?*

Her chest rose and fell in a deep breath. *That's not the kind of kiss I'm talking about. That was just me showing you how much I wanted you.*

Reyes loved the idea of giving Angelica a first kiss. *I can find us someplace private.* He rose to his feet, took the plate, and set it on a nearby table. Gathering up her leash once more and without saying either a word to her or to the now-disappointed crowd, he led her back into the house.

Angelica felt Reyes's determination vibrate through her chain. He didn't dawdle, either, but moved as swiftly as her stupid shoes would let them. He even levitated her up to the second, then the third floor of the sprawling mansion.

A lot of the bedrooms were in use, but he didn't bother finding an empty one. They would all have cameras; that much Angelica understood extremely well about this perverse culture.

At last, he drew her out onto one of the balconies that proved empty of guests but had a lush garden. Guiding her away from the French doors, he pulled her off to the side so they couldn't be seen.

"Get rid of your shoes." He kept his voice low.

"Oh, can I really?"

"Hell, even I'm in pain watching you walk in them."

"I've been siphoning your power," she said, also whispering, "but it still isn't enough."

He supported her while she stepped out of the monstrosities. She flexed her feet and moaned. "Thank you for that. Although I'd be hurting worse if I hadn't been using your power to heal my feet along the way."

"I don't know how you women bear them."

"Not easily, but they're pretty."

"And these are unusually absurd."

He drew her into the shadows off to the side. "So you wanted a first kiss."

"Does that seem silly to you?"

"No, actually, it doesn't. This has all been assbackwards and I'd apologize again, but it doesn't change what's happened."

He slid his arm around her waist and pulled her against him, which sent a spattering of goose bumps traveling down her back. She settled her hands on his arms, aware yet again that he was heavily muscled and more man than she'd ever kissed before.

The lighting in the patio was very soft, but she siphoned a little more of his power and warmed up her vision so that she saw him perfectly. "Reyes," she murmured.

He tilted his head slightly and moved in. He met her

parted lips with a soft pressure of his own that went straight to her knees.

She slid her arm around his neck, and when he deepened the kiss she moaned all over again. His tongue dove within, causing her body to strain against him, needing more.

*Angelica.* His voice in her head felt like the softest vibration.

He gripped her waist tighter, then slowly ground his hips into her. She could feel the hard length of him and gasped as his tongue began to plunge in and out.

For a first kiss this one rocked. She couldn't get enough of the warm feel of his lips, his tongue searching the recesses of her mouth, then driving once more, of his arms flexing and releasing.

She let her thoughts flow. *I wanted to take you home that night at the Ocean Club.*

When he drew back he leaned his forehead against hers. "If things had been different, I would have gone with you, maybe even stayed all night." He caressed her arms. "I've wanted you badly, but this situation . . ."

"I know. So, how about we pay our respects to our elegant host, then get the hell out of here, if it's okay to skip those other parties."

He smiled. "We've made our appearance, so we'll be fine. You can leave the shoes, though. I'll carry you if have to."

"Can't you just fly me out of here?"

He shook his head. "There's a basic rule when there's this much drinking. Everyone walks."

"You mean you broke the rules flying me up the stairs?"

"I took a chance."

Angelica glanced behind her and saw that the room

beyond was empty; "Let's go then, because if I see one more naked woman on her knees in front of another self-satisfied slaver I may go ballistic."

He smiled. "Then we'd better get you home."

He led her on her leash into the hall, then down the stairs. More than one partygoer glanced at Angelica's bare feet and seemed to approve. She hadn't realized that her barefootedness might be received as a way to control her. How ironic that instead Reyes had saved her some pain. His fellow Starlin members would be extremely disappointed if they knew the truth, bastards that they were.

He'd just reached the open front doors when Engles's voice reached across at least forty feet of foyer. "Reyes, where have you been keeping your prize? Ah, you've stripped her of her shoes. I approve. Now if only she lost the costume."

She felt Reyes bristle as he turned in Engles's direction.

Engles, with a drink in one hand, caught Reyes's arm with the other, lifting it high. "Our highest bidder for one of our finest trophies in a long time." A burst of applause followed.

Angelica felt sick.

"I believe I now regret not exceeding your bid."

"You'll have a chance at her six-month mark."

"Ah, yes." He smiled, then glanced around at his guests. "You'll notice how well-preserved our beauty is despite that she was in the hands of a man like Reyes all last night. But he's assured me that he has plans to recoup his investment at her six-month transition. I suggest you all start saving your money for the chance to bid on her once she completes the process." He then turned to Angelica and took her chin in his hand, forcing her to meet his gaze. "For I have no doubt that you'll survive and when you do you'll become the perfect slave-companion. Again, I envy Reyes."

Angelica knew that those slaves who survived the six-month mark underwent a terrible sexual transition that caused them to fully embrace the slaver lifestyle.

As she stared into Engles's evil dark eyes her spirit rose up within her, demanding that she speak. Though he still had hold of her chin, she squared her shoulders. "But if all the rumors about you are true, I wouldn't have lived to see my six-month transition had I been in your hands."

Reyes's voice was suddenly in her mind. *Angelica, back down, now.*

Engles's nostrils flared and his dark eyes flashed. "You dare to speak to me in that manner, slave?" He released her chin but lifted his hand high, his lips pulled back, fangs showing.

She cringed, turning away from him, knowing she'd get hit.

When nothing happened she righted herself, appalled to find that Reyes held Engles's arm trapped in his powerful grip.

The two men glared at each other.

*Angelica,* Reyes called to her sharply, mind-to-mind. *Drop to the ground and prostrate yourself at my feet. Hold on to my ankles and put on the best begging-for-mercy show you can think of.*

She fell down instantly and began sobbing. "I'm so sorry, master. I forgot myself. Please forgive me. Forgive me."

"Silence, slave," Reyes bit out.

Angelica didn't dare look.

"You must discipline her!" Engles shouted. "Here and now."

"She will be disciplined. Beyond that, you have no rights other than my apology for my slave's thoughtless behavior."

"She shows no respect. You have not brought her into proper submission, which means that your current method doesn't seem to be working. All slaves are worthless and need to be taught well from the second you take possession. It's clear to me, you still have a lot to learn."

Reyes stared into Engles's hard, dark eyes. He held the man's arm high overhead, his fingers gripping Engles's wrist. But Reyes felt no give whatsoever.

"Relent," Reyes said quietly. "I will discipline my slave, and she clearly realizes now that she erred. Remember how much fight this one has. And again, I'm taking my time to season the meat. That is my way. And so far, she's proved savory. I'll have her in my game room next, for a few hours, teaching the lesson, as you suggest, that she so badly needs."

Finally, Engles started to relax, pulling his arm away. "And we do have our rules." He tugged on the cuffs of his silk shirt. "And I have no rights over your slave. But I would like to own her one day. I'd like her to learn a new set of lessons at my hands. In fact, I look forward to it."

Reyes dropped his arm to his sides and felt a little flattery might help. "I looked at several organizations before setting my sights on Starlin. What I always valued, that isn't true across the board, is that the owner has all the rights and members of the organization are not allowed to infringe on an owner's property, not where his slave is concerned, at least not without permission."

"You know our laws well."

"I do."

Engles once more glanced down at Angelica. His tongue made an appearance between newly emerged fangs. The bastard lusted after her, which sent off a warning bell in Reyes's head. Engles would do what he could to gain control of Angelica. More than at any other moment, Reyes understood Engles's mind and his purpose. The man was biding his time.

Engles gestured with an elegantly swept arm, encompassing the audience of at least a hundred of his guests. "We have resolved our differences. Please, enjoy the party."

Like magic, the crowd turned back to its various conversations.

Reyes glanced down and spoke to Angelica in a forced voice of command. "You may stand now, slave, well behind me."

She rose to her feet, her head bowed heavily. Her arms crossed over her stomach. He felt her remorse. More than anything, he needed to get her out of Engles's home.

He was about to thank Engles for his party when he said, "A word, Reyes, if you will, for I want you to know that despite your slave's unfortunate conduct, I have some good news for you. If you'll come with me."

Reyes wanted to protest, but Engles had already turned and now headed down the central hall that took him beneath the split staircase.

Angelica's voice broke into Reyes's thoughts. *Do we have to go with him? I despise the man.*

*We don't have a choice. He's the gateway to what I need for Starlin's destruction.*

Angelica sighed. *I know. My question was more rhetorical.*

*Believe me, if there was any other way . . .*

Engles led them deep into what appeared to be the private part of his home, unavailable to his guests except by invitation. The hallway was part of a much older section bored out of solid rock. Again that odd shiver chased down Reyes's back. Why did Engles's home seem so damn familiar?

*Reyes, you're feeling it again, aren't you? That you've been here before?*

The chains didn't lie. *Yes.*

*Are you sure you haven't?* She sounded worried.

*I don't think so.*

Engles led them to an alcove and through a doorway into a smaller room full of books and two maroon leather chairs. "Please sit down."

With leash in hand Reyes took a seat, gesturing for Angelica to stand behind his chair.

Engles poured out a drink. "I hear you like a good Bowmore."

Apparently, Engles had done his homework as well.

"I do."

Engles poured from a crystal carafe, then handed Reyes a heavy cut-glass tumbler. He held the scotch beneath his nose but never took his eyes off Engles as he sipped. "Excellent, but I must say I'm honored that you actually have the brand I prefer."

Engles planted his hand on his chest. "You do not have me to thank but rather Scorpion. He had you vetted and learned your proclivities and your background. I understand that you were a slave yourself once, but that you managed to elude your captor. I was stunned but, more than that, could not imagine how you escaped. So how did you?"

Reyes fell to a place of vampire stillness so that his mind could work on these swiftly rendered bits of his life. No one knew of his slavery, so how did Engles?

"I see I've stunned you." Engles smiled and poured his own drink. He sat down slowly in the chair opposite. Behind Engles's chair a slow trickle of water ran down the natural cave wall. Reyes watched the water, his mind turning in deep circles.

*Reyes, what's going on? It's as though you've disappeared.*

*I need a moment.* He needed several. What was Engles's game?

*But how did he know about your past?*

*I don't know.* He glanced around the room and felt uneasy once more.

*And this place seems familiar to you, doesn't it? I can feel it through the chains.*

*Yes. Like a dream I can't quite remember.*

Angelica touched the chain at her neck, focusing on Reyes and Engles at the same time, as well as this small, strange room. Suddenly it was as though the edges of the space began to spin and she felt herself drifting backward in time.

Another revisiting vision, a trip into the past.

After a few seconds the full vision arrived and she saw Reyes in this exact same space, because she recognized the narrow waterfall along the natural flow of rock.

There were no chairs, however. Instead, a hard wood

platform took up the same space as Engles's current chair. Reyes lay on the table, on his back. His face was bruised, his arms bound overhead. A familiar woman with a mass of curly red hair straddled him, riding him hard.

He cried out as if in pain.

Sweet Dove.

She lifted her hand, cloaked with the cat's claw, and dragged it down his chest, cutting deep. Blood flowed from Reyes's wounds. He screamed in agony.

Angelica felt faint. She wanted the vision to end, but she couldn't turn away. This was Reyes, and she needed to know something about this moment in time. She needed to understand.

She worked hard within the vision to take herself backward, to see more of the room. Someone else was present, but who?

Then she heard him: "Yes, Sweet Dove, make him come like that. It will be better for you both. He's taken enough for now. Focus on his cock. Slow down just a little. Let him feel himself low. The pain from the cuts will dim just enough and he'll start connecting pain with pleasure."

Angelica knew that voice. It belonged to the man opposite Reyes in the present.

Sweet Dove cried out. "He's hard, Master Engles. So hard. I want to come."

"Not yet. Lean down and take the blood from his chest. This is part of the process, the reward."

Still straddling him, she leaned forward and lapped Reyes's blood. Tears streamed from Reyes's eyes, which were now closed. He moaned as her hips kept working him low.

"You'll see. He'll grow to enjoy all of it, including the pain."

"And you'll slice his memories after?"

"Yes, as we agreed, so that he'll never think of me as his master. You were always a favorite of mine, Sweet Dove. And now you're becoming the master. How does it feel?"

Sweet Dove turned to him and smiled. "A bit like heaven."

Engles laughed.

Angelica had seen and heard enough. She released the chain at her neck and the vision faded.

Reyes, however, stood next to her now, his hand gripping her arm. "What's going on?"

She met his gaze, blinking hard, as though trying to remove from her eyes the sights she'd just seen. Aloud she said, "I think I blacked out. I don't know." But to his mind she added, *Reyes, I had a vision, but I can't talk about it right now. It involves Engles.*

"On your knees, and no more of this crying out."

*Did I cry out?*

*Yes. Just drop to your knees before Engles becomes suspicious.*

She fell quickly, bending over to plant her hands beside her knees. She felt so dizzy and sick at heart that tears once more welled, then plopped on the faux-leopard trim of her black stockings. She'd seen the beginning of Reyes's torture, and her heart hurt because of it.

Engles had trained Sweet Dove how to become a sadist.

Reyes's voice filled the room. "And be silent, slave."

"Yes, master," she whispered.

"Very good, Reyes." Engles's approving voice made Angelica cringe. "She's probably just in shock. Now, on to more important things."

His dismissive tone gave Angelica some relief. As long as Engles thought her worthless, he wouldn't assign too much weight to anything she did.

He cleared his throat. "Now that you've brought your slave under control, I wanted to let you know that Scorpion asked me to speak with you tonight. I see that you're surprised, but I'm happy to tell you that he has singled you out, hopefully for a quick promotion to the Board of Governors."

"I beg your pardon?" Reyes was clearly stunned.

"I think you heard me."

The leather chair creaked as Reyes shifted his weight. "I don't understand, Engles. I've been a member for two days now. What have I done to deserve that kind of elevation? I wouldn't say I've proved myself yet."

"I understand why you're skeptical, and in my view you should be. I don't agree with the concept generally. You're relatively new to the lifestyle and you have some growing to do. Our leader, however, believes differently and thinks you possess tremendous potential. And perhaps this will be an excellent means of proving yourself, since Scorpion has a requirement, something very simple and basic that I'm sure you won't have the smallest problem fulfilling."

Angelica's chain vibrated against her neck. Clearly, Reyes didn't like where this was headed.

"And that would be?"

"A bit of fun, actually. Scorpion commands a private show, just you and your slave, engaged in bondage play. The choice of dominance would be yours, chains, ropes, silk scarves, whatever you prefer. I will be there, of course, with my own slaves. Scorpion usually doesn't allow me to attend, but he's made an exception in this case. He knows how much I value your slave's attributes, and if you haven't figured it out by now, Scorpion and I are close business associates."

Angelica's mind blitzed out once more.

What had she been thinking when she'd agreed to stay? She had thought maybe she'd have to perform fellatio again. But something like this, having others view a full-on sex act while she was tied up, had been beyond the scope of her imagination.

*Angelica?*

For a moment she didn't realize Reyes had just contacted her telepathically. Coming out of shock, she responded, *I don't know what to say.*

*A simple* no *will end this now.*

*But you think you should accept?*

*I want access to Scorpion, to meet him, to understand my enemy. This is so much more than I'd hoped to achieve. If I could get on the board, I'd be able to gather the information I need to destroy this organization.*

Angelica didn't know what to say. She understood how much this could mean to Reyes, but she was having a hard time getting beyond the idea of performing in what would essentially be a sex show.

His voice was once more in her mind, but softer this time. *Never mind. I'm asking the impossible of you.*

She heard him draw a deep breath, preparing to refuse, but she was suddenly moving toward him on her knees. She bent over his lap, her hands on his arms. "Please, master, you must allow me to do this for Master Engles. I was rude before. I want to make it up to him and to you."

She knew that right now Engles had a clear view of her ass, with only a narrow thong covering her.

*Angelica, I can't do this. I wasn't thinking of you.*

With her head buried against his slacks she said, *But I agreed to be with you and we both know that if you refuse you won't get close to the leadership for months, maybe years, maybe never. Engles is not a man to be refused. Even I know that. Please say yes. We can argue later if you want.*

"Engles, I owe my membership to you, something I've sought for decades. The least I could do is oblige you and Scorpion in this."

Angelica leaned back on her heels. She watched Reyes lift his glass to Engles.

"Good man," Engles said. "I'll e-mail you the details. And now, I must get back to my party. Do you have other events to attend?"

"A few."

"Enjoy." He rose from his chair and held his hand toward the doorway.

Angelica trembled as Reyes tugged on her leash, and she gained her feet as well.

*A sex show. Oh, God.*

Reyes led Angelica out, but because Engles followed he kept her in front of him. He really didn't need to be battling Engles right now, but Reyes still wouldn't let the bastard touch her.

Reyes moved in a state of shock. So much had been said in that room that he didn't know which disaster to examine first, or the truly startling reality that a command performance could lead him to a seat on the board.

Once in the foyer, Engles parted from them with an easy wave of his hand. Reyes guided Angelica outside and commanded her to move down the slope of Engles's property to the riverside walk below.

Reyes realized she was distressed. *Are you absolutely sure you want to go through with this?* He could always cancel. *I can feel that you're trembling.*

She kept her head lowered. *I'm just overwhelmed, but I'll do better soon. As for the sex show, we have to do it because from everything you've told me, getting on the board is critical.*

*Good. Then we'll consider it settled. But what happened in there? Did you have another vision?*

*Yes, but I don't want to talk about it right now. How about when we return home?*

*Of course.*

By now they'd reached the stone path by Engles's dock. Reyes was about to tell her they could leave anytime she wanted, but she suddenly murmured, "No, oh no." Then covered her mouth with her hand.

At first he didn't understand what had happened. He looked at the raucous party and watched slavers and their captives moving back and forth. He glanced at Angelica and saw that her eyes had filled with tears. He tracked her gaze to the deck on the left.

The young Russian human stood beside her captor, very pale, too pale. Bruises covered most of her body, as well as partially healed cuts. Her eyes were dull as she stared at nothing in particular. The circles around her eyes were deep.

And just like that, Reyes had had enough.

He didn't care who saw him. He swept Angelica up in

his arms and shifted abruptly to altered flight. He took his time, not wanting her to be sick again, but he flew her the hell out of the cavern, rules or no rules.

Angelica's voice filled his mind as she clung to him. *She's going to die soon.*

*Yes.*

*And there's nothing we can do.*

*Not a damn thing.*

When he arrived back in his sitting room he sat down in his chair, pulling Angelica into his arms. She'd started to weep, and he didn't try to stop her. His own eyes filled with tears as well.

Suddenly he was overcome. Tears tracked his cheeks for the young Russian woman, for all the slaves, for his father, who'd given his life trying to protest the growing industry, for himself and the century he'd spent locked up, used, and tortured, and finally for Angelica, that her innocence continued to take such a horrendous battering.

After a time, she grew quiet and the tears on his cheeks dried. He ordered a meal, and though she'd lost her appetite, he made her eat what she could. He encouraged her to drink some water, then forced a few bites down his own throat.

Sharing the blood-chains with Angelica had forced him to look at the horror of the situation with fresh eyes.

After the meal he took her into the bathroom and ran her a bath, adding the bubbles she'd enjoyed once before. Maybe she could take some comfort in it now.

He had his housekeeper bring Angelica a glass of red wine. Once she was settled in the bath she took the wine and began to sip. He could feel her starting to let go.

With his laptop close at hand, he checked his e-mails. He wasn't surprised to find that Scorpion wanted the private performance the next night, at midnight, at Engles's home, the same place the after-auction party had been held.

Reyes had intended to respond right away. Instead, his mind got caught in the earlier loop of remembering the destruction of his family and the terror of living with a sadist like Sweet Dove and of the impending death of the Russian slave.

He needed to let all this go, but the muscles of his arms and back kept seizing. Maybe firing up his five shower-heads would help. Because the tub was close enough to allow for their constant proximity issue, he headed into the walk-in enclosure.

The chain at his neck had grown very quiet, another indication that Angelica was doing better.

As he let the hot water beat down on his neck what ended up bothering him the most was that he'd been aching to make love to Angelica for months now, but it looked like the first time would have to be in front of an audience.

# CHAPTER 10

Angelica was grateful for the wine, the food, the warm bath, and even the separation as Reyes took his shower. All of it had soothed and eased her.

But she was pretty sure that seeing the Russian in a completely emaciated, battered state would live with her the rest of her life.

Now that Angelica had some distance from the entire earlier experience, her resolve returned more firmly than ever.

The revisiting vision had explained why Reyes had a sense he'd been to Engles's home before and had also drawn a tighter line between Sweet Dove and Engles. The two had been connected for a long time, and as Engles's protégé Sweet Dove had learned her craft by enslaving and torturing Reyes.

Hatred lived in Angelica's heart now, aimed at both Engles and Sweet Dove for what they'd done to the man who had saved her from Engles's brutality by buying her at auction.

She needed to tell Reyes what she'd seen in this latest vision, but she wasn't certain how. For the past several minutes the chain at her neck had been vibrating heavily and she could feel that Reyes was locked in a level of rage and despair that he couldn't release. The last thing she wanted to do was tell him that Engles had been present at Reyes's initiation into the world of sex slavery.

Having finished her glass of wine, she rose from the tub, crossed to the shower, and moved inside.

Reyes faced away from her, his hands planted on the far carved-stone wall, the water steaming hot and pummeling his shoulders across the tattoo of the hawk. The chain at her neck still spoke of Reyes's anguish.

She went to him, grateful all over again for the worthy man he'd become despite the horror of his captivity. He was attempting the impossible and had been doing it alone for decades, to destroy something that had brought him a century of pain and that murdered humans every day. Her people.

Tears burned her eyes as she moved in behind him and slid her arms around his chest. He tensed up, because she'd startled him, but then he relaxed and she felt his chest rise and fall in what felt like a terrible tremor.

She hugged him hard. She felt his body shake as he let loose. He shouted, then pounded the stone wall with his fist. He wept like one whose heart had been torn from his chest.

Angelica never let go of him; she just held him, stroked his arms, his back. She said nothing. What good were words at a time like this?

But her presence might help, a physical representation that she stood with him in this moment and that he wasn't alone anymore.

At last, he stopped shouting and when the water grew cold he shut it off.

Slowly, he turned to face her, his cheeks drawn, his eyes haunted. "Are you ready to go back to Newport Beach, because I can't take you one more step down this road. I'm done. It was one thing when it was just me, but I can't do what's being asked."

"What's changed?"

He thumbed her cheek. "What Scorpion requires of us tomorrow night Sweet Dove used to demand on a regular basis. She loved to watch me tie down one of her female slaves and work her over, bring her to orgasm, repeatedly, the more times the better. She often instructed me how to get the job done, or how she wanted it done."

"Did you hurt them, the women I mean?"

He didn't say anything; he just held her gaze. "There, you see what I am? I've bruised women just to stay alive. Still want to be with me, Angelica? Still think I'm worth anything?"

He moved past her, grabbed a towel, and started drying off. She followed him as much by the necessity of being chain-bound to him as by the need to resolve their current situation.

"Will you be expected to hurt me during the show?"

"No. Engles would have been more explicit. Besides, I'm pretty sure by now he knows I would have refused."

"But I'll be tied down."

He shook his head. "Doesn't matter. We're not doing this."

As he wiped down his legs, taking the towel slowly to his feet, she felt his refusal like a brick wall between them. But she wondered if he understood her own current resolve.

He stood up, wrapping the towel around his waist.

She had things she needed to say. "I didn't know a woman could look like that, her eyes so dead."

"That's the way I feel right now. Dead."

"Anyone would in your situation."

He glanced at her, then turned toward her. She stood completely naked. He reached for a second towel and brought it to her. "What are you saying, Angelica? Because what I'm getting from the chain makes no sense to me."

"We have to do this, Reyes."

He shook his head. "No. We don't. I've changed my mind completely."

She moved closer to him. "I had some time to think while I soaked in the tub, about you and what you've been trying to achieve. And earlier, I felt the level of your relief, when the slave from that club went through the door and crossed your threshold, moving from slavery to freedom, because you know what that feels like." She held his gaze. "I don't, not really, except for what I can experience through you. I don't want to diminish how hard this would be for me, but I do want to move it out of the 'unacceptable' category and into 'shit that must be done in order to achieve the impossible.'"

He shook his head, a frown forming on his brow.

Putting her hands on his shoulders, she said, "What you're doing here, Reyes, no one else would dream of doing, of infiltrating the Starlin Group in order to destroy it. That doesn't even make sense by any kind of logic, except that sometime in the next twenty-four hours a young Russian woman, torn from her life, will be dead, just like hundreds of thousands of others who have perished, maybe even millions. And all I have to do to help you try to stop it is let you tie me down and make love to me in front of the head of Starlin, the man you've been trying to get to for decades. From that perspective, Reyes, it seems like a small sacrifice."

He grimaced. "You don't really know what this would be like."

"Actually, I take issue with that." She drew in a deep breath, wanting her next words to carry weight, a sense of her resolve. "If we did this right, it would be just you and me. I think we could block out our audience and engage in what I've been wanting to do with you from the beginning."

His eyes widened. "You're actually serious."

"On every count."

He turned away from her, forcing her hands to fall away. "Shit. You almost tempt me, but you still don't understand."

"Then make me understand." Again she moved close to him.

He whirled on her. "I don't want Engles to see you like that."

She shrugged. "He's already seen most of me. I did bend over your lap earlier in order to distract him with an eyeful of my ass."

At that Reyes's lips curved, but he quickly closed his eyes and suppressed his sudden amusement. "You're missing the point. I don't want him to see you aroused, to watch you experiencing pleasure. That's for me."

Her heart missed a beat or two. She loved this unexpected admission that he saw her as belonging to him, that he cared about her.

"There's just one thing I want first," she said.

"And what's that?" She felt his sadness like a stone he carried around in his heart. She wanted to smash that stone.

She slid her arms around his waist and held him but kept her gaze pinned to his. "I want you to make love to me first, before we do anything else or make any more decisions about how to move forward. No matter what happens, I want our first time together to be just you and me."

He stared at her as though stunned. "You want to make love with me?"

"More than anything."

He frowned as he slid a hand through her damp hair, easing his fingers through. "You amaze me. I hardly know what to say. I suppose more than anything I'd expected you to be freaking out; instead it was me."

She felt nervous suddenly. She had to tell him about the vision. "There's something else, Reyes."

"What is it? Because my blood-chain is telling me you're really upset when you weren't before, not even about performing a sex show in front of Engles. What the hell is it? What are you holding back?"

She felt Reyes's answering panic as though on some level he must have known. "I want a drink first."

She released him and moved past him to the closet. He followed the moment the chains tugged on her neck.

She grabbed a dark-green silk robe and wrapped herself up, then led him to the sitting room.

Grabbing two tumblers from the silver tray, she poured out his Bowmore, two fingers for each of them.

Turning back to him, she handed him a glass, then sipped her own. The whiskey burned and might not have been the best thing to put on top of the wine, but this seemed necessary.

She met and held his gaze but didn't know how to tell him what she knew.

His nostrils flared. "It's the vision, isn't it? The one you had back in Engles's library. You said it involved him."

"It did. Oh, God."

Reyes had a premonition that what he was about to hear would change things for him forever. Quietly he asked, "So, what did you see?"

She closed her eyes and drank deeply from her tumbler but came up sputtering. She dabbed at her lips with her fingers, then set the glass on the nearby end table.

Taking a deep breath, she began, "Do you remember how you told me you felt odd about Engles's home, that you knew you'd never been there, but felt like you had, sort of a powerful déjà vu?"

He nodded slowly. He didn't like where this was headed.

"Well, if what I saw was real, and I have no reason to doubt it, then I think Engles had taken us both into the older part of that cavern because you'd been in that space before and, by my estimation, many times."

His gaze moved slowly around different objects in his sitting room, the sofa and matching brown leather club chairs, the painting of his Venezuelan home, the carafe that held his Bowmore, a stack of books on the table between the chairs. He never stopped studying, reading, learning. When Sweet Dove hadn't been chaining him up he'd kept filling his mind.

Sweet Dove, always Sweet Dove.

"She was there, wasn't she? My captor."

"Yes."

He held Angelica's gaze. "Tell me everything. Tell me exactly what you saw."

Angelica straightened her shoulders, then recounted the vision, dwelling especially on the unusual waterfall as the definitive marker.

Sweet Dove and Engles. They'd known each other all those years ago. Engles had apparently owned Sweet Dove at one time or had found a woman with his proclivities and had trained her.

Reyes sank down in the closest chair. He felt ill all over again. He still couldn't pull the memory forward, but he believed that what Angelica had seen was real. It explained so much, and it also confirmed that somehow Sweet Dove was involved with Starlin. She'd been there early in the process, having checked Angelica out when she'd first been captured. So there was definitely a connection.

And Engles had taught Sweet Dove her trade on Reyes's body.

There would be a reckoning one day.

Reyes could see that his membership in Starlin and now an offer to meet Scorpion weren't an accident and maybe had even been planned for a long time, but to what end? Was it possible that Engles, as perverted as he was, had a sexual interest in Reyes, in bringing him into his own perverted circle of followers? Engles wouldn't be the first man to proposition Reyes.

What Reyes didn't know was Sweet Dove's role. Was she also a Starlin member? He thought it unlikely, since he'd never heard even a whisper about her in all these decades.

In the end, Reyes thought it likely that Engles and Sweet Dove were playing some game. He just didn't know what it was.

Angelica drew close, then sank to her knees beside him. "I'm so sorry, Reyes. I know this has to be yet another blow. But what I don't understand is why you don't have a memory of what I saw in the vision."

His chest felt tight as he met her gaze. "Sweet Dove is an Ancestral with great power. She could have erased any memory she wanted. Engles could have as well."

Angelica appeared to turn all this over in her mind. Finally, she asked, "Do you think it's possible you might actually know who Scorpion is? That you might have met him before?"

Reyes grimaced. "You mean that I might have fucked him at one of Sweet Dove's parties?" He needed Angelica to keep focused on the truth of who he was and the sick nature of his past.

She shrugged but didn't seem either surprised or particularly disgusted by the question. "At this point, given the level of cruelty and debauchery of this group of people, I think it's more than likely you did."

He shook his head, narrowing his gaze. "And this doesn't bother you?"

"In what way?"

She was actually serious, and the chain at his neck confirmed it. But he needed to know more. "You're not disgusted by the fact that you essentially saw me being tortured by my captor and that Engles probably got off on watching my pain and my orgasm?"

"I'm not disgusted by you," she stated flatly. "They committed crimes against you, whether you felt pleasure or not. They had power over you, something Sweet Dove had gained because she's an Ancestral who enslaved you when you were young. You were at their mercy and they were merciless, yet you survived.

"What's more, I'm beginning to think that you might have an unsuspected advantage over both of them. I'm now convinced each is so lost in their enjoyment of their lifestyle that neither can imagine for even a second that you haven't truly become a sadistic, self-absorbed slaver. Engles might taunt you by saying he has his doubts, but he's manipulating you, trying to get you to become as vile as he is. Reyes, he doesn't suspect you, not really. And in that way, we can continue to deceive him and therefore Scorpion."

Reyes stared at her hard, searching her eyes for the truth as well as the chains. He concluded that she truly believed what she said. But what astonished him the most was that she saw no real connection between the young man who had been chained in Engles's library and who Reyes was today.

He almost believed in himself because of it.

"Then you want to move forward? You're actually willing to have sex in front of Engles and Scorpion, despite the fact they'll both probably abuse their slaves while we're engaged."

He felt Angelica's resolve as she responded, "What I'm saying is that I believe it doesn't matter. If you're the only one touching me and making love to me I'm not going to give these bastards the satisfaction of thinking I'm distressed because they're watching me. These men are nothing. They're dirt beneath my shoes and will never be anything more. The only thing I care about at this point is crushing this organization once and for all."

The zealous light in her eye, her willingness to continue, as well as her belief in him, moved him.

He set his glass down, drew her to her feet, then took her in his arms. "You're actually willing to go through with this."

"Yes, I am. I want to see Engles punished for these terrible crimes, and if we can find Sweet Dove and destroy her as well, then all the better. Although I would like to see her in particular burned at the stake with a really slow fire. But there's one thing I need from you."

"What's that?"

"Like I said earlier, I want you to make love to me. I want you to pretend that we shared a few drinks at the Ocean Club and that we're on a date and that you've brought me here, back to your place."

His eyes fluttered and his groin heated up.

For a moment he was back in the foyer of the club and he felt as he had then, that she was giving him something that couldn't last, a hope, a desire for his life to be more than it was.

He had made the best of a truly horrible beginning. But he'd been a sex slave, and for the rest of his life his mind would be twisted and his heart scarred in just that way. He couldn't change his past.

But as he stared into her eyes and felt her desire for him, the scent of her sex perfuming the air, he shunted aside what would always be a deep blight on his soul. Instead, he kissed her, slanting his lips over hers.

Her hand traveled up and over his neck, caressing him. She ran her finger along his jaw, through his scruff. She moaned against his lips. *I've wanted this for so long,* she sent.

*I've craved you.*

She drew back. "You have?"

He groaned and dragged her against him, kissing her once more. *You have no idea.*

He slid his tongue between her parted lips, moving in and out as his hands pulled apart her robe. She lowered her arms and the robe slipped from her shoulders.

She tugged on his towel and the next moment nothing stood between them. Her hand found his cock. She drifted her fingers slowly up and down, letting him feel her nails as well.

He whispered, "You wanted me in your apartment."

She smiled. "In my bed. I used to have this fantasy that you'd break down my door."

"I like your fantasy a lot."

"What was yours, Reyes?"

He nuzzled her neck, kissing the lobe of her ear. Her hair was damp as he spoke softly against her cheek. "When I'd be in the shower, all soaped up and stroking what was very hard, I'd imagine my tongue deep inside you." He flicked in and out of her ear several times until she moaned and shivered. "I want to do that to you now, down low, taste you again, savor what's been tempting me for months. You don't know how much I enjoyed making you come while in that riverside mansion. So how does that sound? How about I feast on you?"

Angelica drew back and stared into clear blue eyes now dark with passion. She took his hand, turned, then led him toward the bed. Once there, she pulled the comforter back and stretched out, throwing her arms above her head. Slowly, she parted her legs.

Her gaze fell to his cock, now upright. He was big, which caused her hips to curl, especially since he thumbed the ridge at the tip. His gaze was fixed between her thighs, so she spread her knees even wider. She wanted him to see all of her, nothing hidden, everything exposed, just as it had been at the underground river.

He drew close, then knelt beside the bed. Sliding his hands beneath her thighs, he pulled her toward him, then kissed just above her landing strip. She glanced down at his thick, short hair and slid her fingers through. She couldn't believe she was here, with Reyes kissing her over and over. She could just make out the tattoo of the hawk on his back. She arched as his tongue made an appearance and dipped between, sliding along her folds, flicking at times, teasing her.

She moaned. "So, this was your fantasy?"

"Yes, only I'd do this for hours, bringing you to orgasm repeatedly until you were worn down to nothing but soft bones."

She moaned.

She'd wanted him for so long, and now he was here. She strained toward him as he kissed and licked her low. He'd done this earlier while she'd been on her stomach, giving her beautiful relief. But this felt like so much more, especially since this time she could watch.

He looked up at her as his tongue moved over her flesh.

She met his gaze, stroking his hair, then dragging a finger down his cheek to feel his tongue. He licked her finger, then her flesh, moving between the two, then drew her finger into his mouth and suckled.

Her hips rocked in a steady rhythm, longing for more of him. *Reyes, come here.*

He looked up at her, relinquishing her finger. She motioned for him with both hands to climb up her body. "Let me feel the weight of you."

At that he smiled. But he didn't exactly crawl. Instead, he surprised her by doing his vampire thing and levitating in a prone position. She didn't know what he meant to do until he floated above her. Using his hands, he slid them beneath her waist. In a single motion, he moved her up the bed so that her legs no longer dangled over the edge.

"Very clever."

He then lowered himself slowly. She spread her legs wide so that his knees landed between them as he stretched out on top of her. "How's that?"

"Like heaven. This was another fantasy, feeling you like this, seeing you above me." She smiled. "I was so into you."

"You're blushing."

She nodded, her head sliding against the sheet. "I suppose I am. It's just so strange to be admitting these things to you. And now here you are."

He nodded. "You're beautiful. Have I told you that?"

She looked into his eyes, savoring the moment, everything about him, the gorgeous color of his eyes, his sexy scruff, the varied tattoos on his left shoulder. She ran her finger over them. "Do these have meaning?"

"They're all elements from my Venezuelan home, the foliage, flowers, vines."

"Is that where you were born?"

He nodded. "Where we had our home before my father disappeared. Because of financial hardship my mother lost the dwelling, but I bought it back once I started making my fortune."

She caressed his face, his massive shoulders, then drifted her hand low to feel the solid curves of his chest. He closed his eyes and groaned softly as she teased his nipples. "Do that levitating thing again. I want my tongue right here." She rubbed a hand over his chest.

He obliged her and floated, lowering himself just enough so that her tongue could swirl over his pecs. She took turns with both, working the thick pads with her hands and sucking on his nipples. He moaned. "That feels amazing."

He started to float back down, but she stopped him with her hands. He looked at her, questioning.

"How difficult is this for you to sustain," she asked, "this kind of levitation?"

"Fairly easy, why?" He looked the nicest bit confused.

"Because if you move back, then go just a little bit farther, I could put my mouth on something else. Just take it slow so I can enjoy your body the entire distance."

He groaned, then glided slowly. She kissed him all down his rib cage. Guiding him with her hands on his waist, she let him know when and how to move so that she could kiss and lick different parts of his body. She mapped his abs, which he kept tense for her, another neat trick with gravity pulling the opposite direction. But the man was strong.

Lower she went, licking his navel until his hips flexed. Because his cock was fully erect, she didn't have far to go. She took the tip of him in her mouth and moaned at the velvety feel. She used her hands at the same time and explored all that he was, the entire length of his stalk, ending in his balls.

She suckled gently.

His entire body shuddered and suddenly he caught her hands with his, pushing them away, then drew his cock out of her mouth. "Too much," he whispered hoarsely.

She understood, smiling as he returned to land once more between her thighs. What surprised her the most was how much affection she felt for him, though she'd only been with him such a short time. But maybe sharing a disastrous situation could do that for any two people.

He held her gaze, his expression somber. He touched her damp hair, her cheek, then thumbed her lips. "I want to enter you."

She rolled her hips in response and cooed, "Yes."

Using his hand, he guided himself to her opening, then began to push.

She planted her hands on his shoulders, gazing into his eyes. She wanted to remember this moment forever, the first time he penetrated her.

Her lips parted as she drew in a deep breath.

"You're very wet." He thrust gently, each time going deeper.

"I've wanted this, Reyes, more than anything." Her breathing grew rough.

With each thrust of his hips Reyes felt more and more connected to Angelica. There was no question that he'd imagined doing this to her repeatedly. He was a man.

But he'd never been in this place before, desiring a woman not just with his cock but with his entire being. Planting his forearms and curling his hips with each thrust, he watched her move beneath him, her dark eyes glittering.

Her lips parted and a series of small gasps came out.

He watched pleasure stream over her face. He was doing this to her, giving her what she'd wanted for a long time.

Nothing seemed more important than that he please her. Her head rolled from side to side and she now had a hard time focusing. "That's it, Angelica; you're feeling me now, aren't you?"

"I am." Her words were hushed and hoarse. Her breathing uneven in the best way. "And I can feel how much pleasure you're experiencing at the same time. This is amazing."

He thrust faster and her back arched. She moaned, gripping his shoulders, her body tensing and releasing, getting ready.

She gripped him low. "Reyes," she whispered.

"I'm here. I'm with you."

"Do you want to come?"

"I want to see you come first. Can you do that, Angelica? Can you let go?" He leaned down and placed a kiss on her cheek, then her other cheek, then her lips. He played his tongue over her mouth, dipping in.

She moaned and he kissed her hard, driving his tongue deep. She cried out against his mouth and her whole body spasmed. *I'm coming. Oh, God, Reyes!*

He held back. Though he wanted to release, he'd been well-trained and kept himself hard for her. As he felt her orgasm reach a pinnacle, then finally ease down, he slowed his rhythm, yet still keeping the push-pull steady.

She kneaded the muscles of his shoulders, her fingers falling to his biceps. He flexed for her.

"My head is spinning," she whispered.

"Want more?"

"Do you know what I want?"

"What's that?" He kissed her again, a soft pressure against her lips.

"I want to watch you come, Reyes. That's what I want. That's the only thing I care about right now, seeing you have pleasure because you're inside me, because we're connected."

Reyes had never heard such words before, and for a long moment they didn't connect inside his brain. He'd never had a woman put his pleasure above hers or engage with him as though he had importance of any kind.

Yet he saw in Angelica's eyes and felt in the way she caressed his arms that she was truly thinking of him right now and not what she could wring from his body.

He moved faster. "You give me pleasure, Angelica, in everything that you say and do."

Small gasps once more broke past her lips. "I feel the same way about you."

His body heated up, a fire that raged through him, that made him want more than anything to release while ecstasy held her in its grip. He drove stronger now and deeper so that she cried out. "Reyes, will you come with me?"

"Yes."

He'd never been so hard as he drove faster and faster, slamming into her. She cried out in long, almost anguished sounds, pleasure building.

*I'm close,* she sent.

*And I'm ready. Look at me, Angelica. Look at me.*

He could tell she struggled to stay focused on him because her body raged with passion.

*Reyes.* Her gaze locked with his. *I'm coming.*

As he watched her tip over the edge his release rocketed. He shouted as his cock pulsed with heat and as pleasure streaked through him.

Angelica screamed, which in turn intensified the ecstasy that rushed through him in heavy pulses. And still he held her gaze. Emotion swelled within him as the moment rolled out and his hips flexed in rapid jerks.

*Reyes.* She spoke his name one last time within his mind, then finally relaxed beneath him.

He slowed his rhythm, then finally stopped, his body satiated.

Still connected deep, he kissed her, a long, lingering kiss, then looked at her some more.

He felt mystified, unable to comprehend what he was feeling. He'd never experienced anything like this in his long-lived life. He'd never been around someone like Angelica before, who actually saw him as a person and not as a tool to be used.

He frowned slightly as she caressed his face. "How was that for you? Were you satisfied?"

Her eyes popped wide. "Didn't I scream loud enough to make myself clear?" She laughed.

He chuckled. "Yes, I guess you did."

"Why the question?" She thumbed his scruff and sighed.

"Hard to explain, I guess I just wanted to be sure that I did well by you."

At that she leaned up, surrounded his neck with her arms, and pulled him down to her. "You were magnificent and that was beyond anything I've ever known before. But Reyes, I'm not talking about your technique. I'm talking about you." She fondled his arms, his shoulders, his neck.

He simply couldn't fathom what it was he felt, except suddenly he was taken back to a time in his youth when he'd been with his mom and dad. They'd taken him night-fishing on the Amazon. They'd all laughed so much.

And that's what it was about Angelica. She reminded him that before he'd been taken into slavery he'd known what normal felt like, when he'd been a typical kid and known how to laugh, what being loved had felt like.

"Where did you go?" she asked softly, still touching him, this time rubbing his back.

But it was all too much suddenly, too good, too normal. And it couldn't last.

He shook his head and lifted off her. "I don't know. I'm uneasy about what we have to face."

"Do we have to think about that now?"

"I do." It was only a partial lie. He just didn't want to be feeling so much for Angelica. He didn't want to live with the hope that his life could actually be different. He couldn't risk believing in the impossible.

But he wasn't about to hurt her in the process. He leaned down and kissed her. "I loved every minute of this. Thank you. You've been wonderful."

Slowly, he pulled out of her and rolled onto his back.

Time to fix his thoughts on the performance for Scorpion.

# CHAPTER 11

Angelica knew something had happened to end the moment; she just didn't know what. Although she was pretty sure she could guess. The vampire had a lot on his mind. For herself, she tried not to think about what would happen on the following night or how ill she felt with thoughts about what they'd be required to do.

But she also believed in present-moment living. Sitting up, she turned toward Reyes. He had his arm thrown over his face, his eyes closed. "Reyes, I'm starved. How about you?"

At that he shifted and opened one eye, his lips curving. "You need some food?"

"I do. And maybe another quick shower would not be unwelcome, either."

"Very pragmatic."

"It's either that or I'm going to start screaming at the top of my lungs out of fear about what we'll have to do tomorrow night."

He winced, sitting up as well, his gaze falling to her bare breasts. They were puckered in the cool air of the room. She didn't bother covering up. She wanted him looking. She wanted him to miss her when she was gone. She also knew her breasts were one of her finest assets.

She put her hands behind her back and arched just a little.

He met her gaze, his brows raised. "What are you doing?"

But she just laughed. "You were staring, so I thought I'd help you look at me better."

He reached for her, covering her breast with his hand and fondling her.

One thing led to another until he asked, "Think you can wait for your meal a little longer?"

"I think I can do that."

He made love to her again and again.

Later he called his housekeeper to have a tray sent up.

After a quick shower Angelica dipped into yet another fragrant soup and savored a glass of white wine. Reyes seemed preoccupied.

"Anything on your mind?"

He glanced up from a full spoon that had been sitting midair for about minute. Lowering it to the bowl, then leaning back, he drank from a bottle of beer. "Just the usual. I'm feeling the need to check the Starlin Web site, to see what's going on, if anything's developed that would require our attention."

"Good idea."

He rose, crossing to his desk, and brought his laptop back with him. He sat down in a different chair adjacent to his meal and watched the screen as he began tapping keys.

She watched his expression shift as some kind of video began running and the changing light played over his face. She heard laughter and shouts, lots of voices.

Suddenly he slammed the lid shut, shading his face with his hand.

Angelica had the worst feeling, and the chain at her neck vibrated with an emotion that ranged somewhere between full-out rage and a pit of despair.

She left her seat, rounding the table. She tried to lift the laptop lid, but he wouldn't let her. "Don't."

"Starlin, right?"

"Yes. On the fucking home page."

If this had been any other situation, if she hadn't already been abducted by the vilest people she'd ever known, she would have let it go.

Instead, she knew she had to see what had so swiftly taken him down. He rubbed three fingers across his forehead, digging in as though trying to force the images away.

"You have to let me see." How calm her voice sounded.

He stared up at her, that familiar haunted look in his blue eyes, the one that seemed to be the sheerest gateway to his soul and to what gave him the greatest pain. "I don't want you to see this. I don't want this for you. Dammit, it isn't right. You shouldn't have to know this kind of thing exists."

Angelica was torn. She valued that he was trying to protect her from what he knew to be the worst of his kind, and part of her wanted to stay in that safe garden. But another part, the part of her that had chosen to stay with Reyes through the duration of the Starlin Festival, had already gotten her hands dirty and didn't intend to stop now.

She drew close to him, then slid onto his lap and put her arms around his neck. She held him, not saying anything.

For a long moment, he did nothing as well but remained immobile, unyielding. But in the end, he wrapped her up in his arms and held her tight, even rubbing his hands every now and then up and down her back. She remained silent but let him feel her determination, knowing that their blood-chain bond would communicate what he needed to know.

Finally, she drew back and met his gaze straight on. "Show me, Reyes. I can take it."

"Just prepare yourself."

He shifted her on his lap, turning her toward the table, then lifted the lid, and the video began to play.

The young Russian woman's body, eyes wide and empty now, lay on a bloody sheet. She was naked and had cuts and bruises everywhere. She wasn't alone, either, which might have been the worst part, because there seemed to be a party going on in the background. Several pairs of naked muscular male legs surrounded her. Laughter ensued. Some cheering as well.

Her skin was pure white, with smears of blood on various parts, and fang-puncture marks that hadn't closed up. There couldn't have been a drop of blood left inside her. She'd not only been brutalized, but she'd also been drained.

"They killed her."

"Yes. And they were betting on the moment of death."

Angelica felt dizzy and sick to her stomach. She kept thinking she'd never be shocked again; then a new horrible event would knock her off her feet once more.

Closing her eyes, she worked at adjusting to the reality of the murder, that the innocent woman had died by torture and that there'd been nothing Angelica could have done to have stopped it. In this moment she thought she knew better than ever what drove Reyes to keep going and her resolve deepened.

When she opened her eyes she forced herself to witness the gruesome spectacle all over again.

But this time, as she settled her eyes once more on the laptop screen and started replaying the video, familiar waves began to flow all around the edges of computer. The actual images of the video began to grow indistinct and a revisiting vision arrived.

Uncertain what to do, she told Reyes what was happening.

"Just go with it," he said. "There's something here you're meant to see."

"Okay."

She watched, panning backward, and found that the room was full of about thirty people, most of them drinking. One part of the crowd was clustered around a series of flat screens that each held stats of one kind or another, typical betting windows.

Now that she'd moved into the past, Angelica could hear the young woman moaning and words spoken in what sounded like Russian. She told Reyes.

He held her tight. "You can stop anytime."

But she couldn't. She felt it now, what she was meant to see.

Hearing a voice that sounded familiar, she panned to her left within the vision and kept turning until she reached the arched doorway to the large room. "Your former captor is there, Sweet Dove, the one with the red hair. She's definitely a Starlin member. She's standing in a doorway and a man is with her. He has his arm around her, but I can't quite see him. I'll have to pan just a little bit more." She could almost see him. She shifted the vision slightly so that he came into view.

Engles.

She gasped, surprised all over again but not certain why she should be. If two people had ever been made for each other, it was Sweet Dove and her mentor.

"It's Engles, isn't it?"

"Yes. They're enjoying the moment, each holding a drink and looking nonchalant, as though nothing especially significant is going on."

"Typical slavers. Are they talking to each other?"

She nodded.

"See if you can hear what they're saying."

"Okay."

Even though what she saw had already happened, she trembled as she drew close within the revisiting vision. Evil lived in these two people.

Sweet Dove tweaked Engles's ear. "So you think Reyes will do it? Will he perform for Scorpion and for you? Because from everything you've told me, I don't think he likes you very much."

"I think he hates me, but that doesn't matter. He's been clamoring to get into Starlin for decades, and I saw how his eyes lit up when I mentioned the Board of Governors. You were right about him, my darling, and I confess you trained him well. He has more ambition than I've seen in a long time.

"But it was fun watching him jump through so many hoops, making him wait for over two decades, and it was absolute genius that you had me let him win the bid. He's very possessive of Angelica, which means that taking her away from him is going to be a lot of fun. But are you sure you still want him back?"

"I owned him once, remember? I will always think of him as my property, to do with as I please. So, yes, I want him back. Only now that he's embraced the lifestyle, and he's become a slaver, we'll have new territory to cover and it will be extraordinary."

"He's not the same man, not a youth to be seduced and trained."

"But he's not an Ancestral as I am, which means that I can handle him." Sweet Dove pulled at one of her long red curls.

"But he has Ancestral potential."

"And I'll make sure he never uses it."

"You are so beautifully corrupt, but when do I get my reward for doing your bidding?"

She held Engles's gaze. "Just be patient and you'll get your prize. I tested Angelica when she first arrived, so I happen to know just how much she can take, and yes, she'll break every endurance record. We'll both earn another small fortune through the gaming organization."

Engles smiled, his eyelids low. "I can hardly wait. She has so much fire." He then turned to Sweet Dove and nuzzled her neck, asking quietly, "But when do I get to meet Scorpion? Haven't I proved my loyalty yet?"

"Ah, yes, *your* ambitions." Sweet Dove turned and kissed him, then bit down hard so that he cried out.

Drawing away from her, Engles had blood pouring from a deep wound on his lower lip. He scowled at her. "What was that for?"

"For fun, of course, and to remind you that I won't be hounded or manipulated by you or anyone. When Scorpion is ready he'll bring you into our partnership, and not a moment sooner."

Engles drew a handkerchief from his pocket and dabbed at his lip. "And will you be present tomorrow night when Reyes performs for Scorpion and me?"

She shook her head. "Scorpion won't allow it."

"Yet you're partners."

"Scorpion always has his reasons."

But at that moment Sweet Dove got a funny look on her face and turned in Angelica's direction, almost as though she could see her. "Engles, my darling, I don't believe we're alone. Someone is here, watching us."

"What do you mean?"

"I don't know. It's just a strange kind of spidery crawl up my spine." She narrowed her gaze as though trying to see better.

Because Sweet Dove took a couple of steps in Angelica's direction, Angelica knew it was time to shut the vision down. She had no idea whether it was actually possible for an Ancestral of Sweet Dove's power to make contact over time and space, but she definitely didn't want to find out.

As Angelica disengaged the process, the vision faded slowly, then disappeared.

Reyes stroked her arm. "Are you all right? You're trembling."

Angelica closed the laptop. "I'm fine."

"You're frowning. What did you see?"

She met his gaze. "So much that I hardly know where to start." But she decided that the beginning was the best place and related the conversation point by point.

Reyes listened with hard blue eyes, then huffed a sigh. "My God. I had no idea. So, Sweet Dove is entrenched in Starlin and has some kind of partnership with Scorpion. But she also appears to rule Engles."

"Yes, it looks as though the student now schools the master. More importantly, everything they've done has been to bring you under Sweet Dove's control once more. Although it was clear to me that she fully believes you're a slaver now. At least that part of the equation is intact. Reyes, you've got to be careful."

He pulled Angelica tight against him and she leaned her head against his shoulder. "I never thought for a second that going after Starlin would lead me back to Sweet Dove."

"Maybe this is a good thing, because it seems likely to me that when you take Starlin down to rubble there's a strong chance you'll be able to bury her for good at the same time. And right now I want nothing more than to see that job done."

She felt absurdly safe held in his massive arms.

Reyes sighed heavily. "So Sweet Dove's plans are in play to bring me back under her control and she'll happily offer you up as Engles's reward. Sounds like the woman I knew."

Angelica frowned. "There's just one thing I don't understand. Engles said he still hadn't met Scorpion, so how will he be present at our performance without Engles ever meeting him?"

"He'll probably use a disguising shield. Some of the Ancestrals can create layered disguises that most vampires can't pierce. If after all this time Engles hasn't met him, that has probably been the process."

Angelica shook her head. Disguising shields, revisiting visions, and sadistic perverts. How had this become her life?

But she knew how and he had his arms wrapped around her.

With Angelica pressed against him, Reyes processed the revisiting vision. When she had first mentioned Sweet Dove torturing Angelica early in her captivity, he'd thought that his former owner might have had a distant relationship with the Starlin Group, like the rights to look over newly acquired slaves or something.

Yet at each turn, and especially thanks to the ability that Angelica possessed of experiencing revisiting visions, it was becoming clear that Sweet Dove was a significant player in Starlin.

His heart sank like a stone.

For a long time, he'd wanted to face his captor, to confront her head-on, even to choke the life out of her. But he wasn't alone anymore. He had Angelica to think of. He also had tens of thousands of slaves, present and future, whom he held as the beacon in his mind, the one idea that kept him on a steady course.

Now Sweet Dove appeared to be at Starlin's center.

His only consolation was that neither Engles nor Sweet Dove suspected his subversion. Engles had spoken only of Reyes as an ambitious man, as wanting a seat on the board, with a powerful desire to rise within the organization. He could breathe easy because it was clear his cover held.

As for Sweet Dove, he thought he understood her, that the last thing she'd ever believe was that he'd want her destruction. She truly believed he was a slaver and that she'd had a hand in helping him along that path because she'd been his torturer. How wrong she was.

His sole relief in the current situation was in knowing that Sweet Dove wouldn't be at the sex performance. He didn't think he could hold his rage back if he knew his former captor was watching and enjoying herself at his expense.

Her presence would have been a deal breaker.

Angelica grew very quiet and he remained holding her in his arms for a long time. No doubt she was processing all that she'd witnessed, both in the woman's death and in the subsequent vision.

Eventually, his thoughts turned to the difficult dilemma of managing the upcoming sex performance. He didn't lack for experience. But technique and even theatrical quality was one thing. Making love to someone he cared about for the perverse pleasure of others was an entirely different hole to dig.

He'd already been told that Angelica would have to be tied down. Though he refused to consider using chains or ropes, he thought he could handle silk scarves. The truth was, if Engles insisted on anything else Reyes would refuse. He wouldn't subject Angelica to the rigors of steel or iron bondage.

His phone dinged indicating a new text message, but his phone wasn't handy. As though reading his mind, Angelica slipped off his lap. He rose and headed into the bedroom, where he'd left his phone on his nightstand on the far side of the bed.

Because Angelica hadn't followed him, however, he

didn't get far when the blood-chain gave its tug. As he glanced back at her she seemed to awaken from her own lost-in-thought reverie, nodded, and moved with him. More and more they worked in tandem.

Once he retrieved his phone he read the text, then glanced at Angelica. "From Engles. I'm to wear dominance gear."

She touched the chain at her neck. "You're upset and you're scowling. Why? Isn't this what you expected?"

"It's all leather and shit, no shirt, usually a flogger. It's the idea of it I can't stand."

She shrugged. "It's fine with me, Reyes. Because it's you, I can handle it."

"I've already decided that there are lines here I won't cross with you. One of them is that though I'll be tying you down, I won't use chains or ropes, nothing like that."

"But you're okay with silk scarves, like we originally discussed?"

"Yes."

She drew close and slid her arms around his waist. "Scarves actually sound kind of nice."

His lips curved. "You're trying to put a positive spin on something hideous."

"Maybe. But I've been thinking. What if we practiced a little, set up some kind of overall rhythm to the event, something planned, more theater than actual lovemaking?"

He met and held her gaze; then he kissed her. "I think that's a brilliant idea."

The rest of the night was spent talking through what kind of order of sexual effort would most likely please a pair of sadists best. Which led, not surprisingly, to taking Angelica to bed for one last round, with gentle overtones and a series of climaxes that made him wonder how the hell he could ever let her go.

The next night Angelica flew with Reyes, her heart beating so hard she felt sure she couldn't take much more. She wore only a thin lavender negligee and Reyes's chest was completely bare, his tattoos on display. She thought maybe that during the upcoming ordeal she might be able to save her sanity by focusing on the collection of symbols and vines that curled around his shoulder and arm. Besides, she actually liked his snug black leather pants.

They'd talked for a long time about how to get through the experience, which moves he'd make and why, and especially what would be acceptable to each of them. Reyes, for one thing, would call a halt if Scorpion or Engles demanded anything extreme, like binding her with chains or inflicting any kind of torture.

The real problem was that neither she nor Reyes had any way of knowing how much Scorpion would be dictating what was about to happen. But Reyes assured her repeatedly that the moment any of their agreed-upon lines were crossed he'd shift to altered flight and get her the hell out of there.

When he touched down outside Engles's mansion, where the after-auction party had been held, Angelica once more looked around in awe. Engles might be a bastard, but he had an artistic eye. He'd created great beauty in the external landscape of his property with the lake and waterfall, the stonework and the palm trees all lit up, a terrible dichotomy.

*Ready for this?* Reyes's words ramped up her heart rate yet again.

She had only one response. *Hell, no.*

*You say the word, and we're outta here, no questions asked, no recriminations.*

*I know. I think it's the only reason I can put one foot in front of the other right now.* She wouldn't turn back, though, not with a seat on the Board of Governors at stake.

Engles met them in the foyer. He wore tailored slacks and a red silk shirt open at the collar. He held a familiar tumbler in his hand. His gaze skated over Angelica and the sheer negligee she wore. His eyes fell to half-mast and the bastard didn't try to hide his arousal.

She kept her eyes lowered.

"Looks like we're going to have some fun."

Reyes didn't say anything, but the chain at her neck vibrated heavily. He despised Engles anyway, but the man always seemed to be able to say the exact thing that would fill Reyes with rage.

Engles gestured for them to enter and Angelica almost took a step, but Reyes got in Engles's face so fast that she gasped. "You don't touch her. Have you got that, Engles? And I don't give a fuck who you are in this organization. She's mine to do with as I please. I'll only share my slave when I'm good and ready and not a second earlier. Understood?"

Engles smiled, sipping his drink as he returned Reyes's glare. "Of course. That's the Starlin way. But as you know, sharing is encouraged. You're an ambitious man, Reyes, so I hope you take the hint." Angelica heard the latent challenge in Engles's voice as their host pivoted, waving them forward. "And now, if you'll follow me."

Reyes addressed her mind-to-mind. *Stay behind me. I plan to keep a lot of space between the two of you.*

*Good idea. I might knee him in the balls, if he's not careful.*

Reyes laughed quietly and some of the tension left the moment.

As always, it wasn't a quick march to move in stilettos.

Engles guided them down the stairs where the main party had gathered last time, then through a bank of glass doors that led to a small garden and a shallow but very long rectangular pool that appeared to be about eight inches deep.

Some sort of table, draped with dark-green silk, rested on a platform in the middle of the pool. Four wood posts, intricately carved and dangling with strips of multicolored silk, rose from each corner of the table.

*We're going to do it there?* Angelica shuddered.

*Actually, this is more than I could have hoped for.*

*Why do you say that? It looks so exposed.*

Reyes glanced at her, holding her gaze briefly. *Because the pool surrounds the table. It's clear to me that this will just be a performance, that engagement won't be expected.*

Angelica wanted to take his hand. *Is that what you've been so worried about?*

*Of course.*

Engles stood on the pathway to the right of the pool and opposite the platform. He extended his hand in the direction of the table. "Scorpion has already arrived, but will remain hidden behind a layer of disguise. He may call out commands, in a voice that will be modified to sustain his hidden identity. You are expected to obey whatever he asks. I will be required to do the same, and Reyes, you would be wise to obey us both."

Without giving Reyes a chance to respond to this speech Engles turned and snapped his fingers. The lighting within the pool shifted from a soft white glow to a sensual red. At the same time, music floated through the air, a soft jazz with a blues undertone, very sexy.

Nervous, Angelica said, *I take it Engles is setting the mood for us.*

*Always a thoughtful host.* Reyes glanced around.

*At least there's no spotlight. Somehow I expected there to be lights blazing over us.*

Reyes turned toward her and made a pretense of gathering up the slack in the leash as he met her gaze. *You're doing fine. My problem is that if Engles doesn't stop smirking I'm going to break his face into about a thousand pieces.*

*I'd buy a ticket for that show.*

Reyes cleared his throat. *You're going to make me laugh again.*

*Sorry.*

*And keep your head down.*

Angelica obeyed. The part of her that was all nerves wanted to crack jokes, but Reyes was right. Laughter would not serve. *I'll be good now and I'll do my absolute best.*

*I know you will. Now step up on my foot. I'm going to fly us to the platform. Wouldn't want your shoes to get wet.*

Angelica bit her lip. *Hey, it's not fair if you try to make me laugh.* They were both nervous.

Reyes held out his arm to Angelica, and just for a moment, as she slid her arm around his neck and he drew her against him, he pretended he wasn't about to put her through hell again.

Slowly, he took her into the air, landing on the platform just to the side of the table.

Engles disappeared into the shadows, probably behind his own Ancestral layer of disguise.

Reyes could no longer see him at all.

He tried to warm up his vision, to see what was there beneath a tall shelf of rock, but more than one layer of disguise prevented him.

"Thank you for obliging me, Reyes." The voice that spoke sounded several pitches deeper than normal, with a metallic overlay.

Scorpion.

"As you are a new member, I'm sure my invitation for a private sex performance shocked you, but I confess I've been watching your career with interest, especially over the past year. You've provided me with ample entertainment as you used a variety of slaves in a number of our clubs."

So this was Starlin's founder and primary owner, the one who called the shots.

Reyes drew his shoulders back, refusing to be intimidated. "You've spied on me, then."

"Of course. Were you expecting anything less?"

"I suppose not. I knew you had your men watching me, but I didn't know you took such a personal interest in your members."

"Always, since I can't take the chance of letting anyone in who might not fully appreciate all that we do. And now, you may begin by telling your slave to undress."

He turned to Angelica. Removing the collar and leash, he tossed them on the wood floor that supported the platform.

"You've heard the command, slave."

Mind-to-mind, he gave her more specific instructions. *Strip slowly, moving the negligee up from the bottom, and just as you said, this is more theater than anything else. I'm going to touch you at the same time. Stay focused on me.*

*I understand. The music helps.*

She lifted from the hem.

Using the flogger, he tapped her hips. "Dance for me, slave. Make me want you."

She began to grind slowly to the music, and for a moment he stalled out. The sight of her landing strip coming into view as her pelvis rocked and her hips swayed did him in. She was a beautiful woman with soft, voluptuous curves.

She began to turn to the music, moving in a slow circle, so that after a few beats her hips and buttocks were on display and swaying.

He cupped her bottom and squeezed. *Just keep lifting the negligee.*

*Reyes, what you're doing feels so good.* She gyrated with her hips, swirling, then tilting her pelvis, rocking several times.

*Angelica, my God, you can move.*

*Thank you. I'm thinking about you, Reyes. About what you did to me last night.*

For a brief moment he forgot the performance. All he saw was Angelica's sensuality. Images of making love to her several times the night before rolled through his mind.

He stepped away from her and savored the way she finally lost the negligee, letting it drop near the leash and collar.

The metallic voice filled the air. "Bend over the table face-first, slave, and spread your legs."

Reyes froze. *You okay with this?*

Angelica didn't respond. Instead, she moved with a

sexy sway of her hips toward the table. She lowered herself slowly, stretching out until her hips connected with the side of the platform. In slow, measured sidesteps, again in time with the bluesy music, she parted as she'd been commanded. *Still thinking about you and what you did to me the last time I was in this position. Remember?*

*Hell, yeah.*

Reyes knew not to remain static but drew closer to her. He used the flogger to play over her butt cheeks and down the insides of her legs. He spanked her gently.

*Can Scorpion even see this?*

Reyes glanced around. *I'm sure he can, but you should also know that there are at least a dozen video cameras, all at a variety of levels, aimed at the table.*

*So, every expression of mine is being recorded.*

*Yes.* Reyes had to give her an out. *Want to stop?*

*No. I keep thinking about "her." I'm doing this for her.*

Reyes knew exactly what Angelica meant, that she referred to the Russian slave. *Me, too.*

Angelica ground her hips repeatedly against the side of the table, still keeping time with the music.

Though Reyes hated that other men were looking at what was very private, he stayed off to the side to allow the view he knew the men would want.

"Beautiful!" the metallic voice called out. "And your slave is performing well. She's pleasing me with her efforts. I congratulate you on your dominance of her. You may bind her now."

"You heard Scorpion, slave. Climb up on the table."

Angelica moved slowly, one knee at a time, stretching out a leg, arching her back, making it all work. Eventually she was spread-eagled on her back, and Reyes took his time lashing her wrists with the silk scarves loosely to the posts. He then bound her ankles.

"Take pleasure in her breasts," came the next command.

Still in his dominance leathers, he moved to the opposite side of the table, facing his well-disguised audience.

Glancing down at Angelica, he asked, *How are you doing?*

*Still focused on you, Reyes. Every move I make is for you and I can't wait for you to fondle and suckle my breasts.*

*You're making this easy for me.* He set his flogger aside.

*Not hard? Not even a little?*

*Don't make me laugh, but yes, I'm hard as a rock and I can't wait to be inside you.*

*This isn't so bad, you know.*

*No, it's not.* He drew close and caressed her breasts with both hands, then leaned in and slowly suckled the one closest. Her back arched and she moaned.

*Call me crazy, Reyes, but this is really turning me on. I love the music, and with my legs spread like this I'm feeling a lot of cool, moist air each time I grind my hips.*

He drifted his hand down her abdomen. *Let me make you feel even better.*

The moment his fingers touched her low, she cried out. He didn't hesitate but slipped one inside and begin to work her steadily while he sucked.

"Nice action!" the voice called out.

*Just ignore that.* He sucked a little harder and drove faster.

*This isn't quite what we had practiced, but you'll make me come like this.*

*That's the plan,* Reyes said. *I want to make it good for you.*

*You always do.*

He watched her arms tugging on the scarves now, her legs writhing. He moved his fingers faster, pistoning.

Moans now came from the metallic voice and a few quiet commands that Reyes knew meant that Scorpion was directing his own slave.

*Is that what I think it is?*

*Yep. Just be glad you don't have to see it.*

*I am.*

Reyes removed his finger in order to make use of two. When he slipped inside, Angelica said, *Oh, God, Reyes.*

*When you're ready, just let go.*

He moved faster until suddenly she cried out and he felt her tugging low on his fingers as her orgasm crested. A series of sharp gasps left her mouth. Then her eyes met his, her breasts rising and falling as she caught her breath. *That was so good. I didn't think I could do this.*

Other sounds, coming from behind the disguise, left no one in doubt of what was going on. A metallic shout brought the first round to a satisfied conclusion.

Engles, also hidden behind his own disguise, was heard grunting.

But Reyes knew how this would go. He'd participated in plenty of exhibitions like this one. No doubt Scorpion took opiates to sustain himself. Just like they did for humans, opiates did wonders for vampires.

*You did great.* Reyes released her nipple and kissed her breasts, then nuzzled her neck. He planned on drinking from her at the latter stage of the performance, also expected. *Your blood is calling to me.*

*Can't wait.* She was breathing hard. *Reyes, I'm loving this, loving that you have me trapped on this table. I didn't think I would, but it's sexy as hell.*

He rose up and waited for the next order.

The metallic voice called out, "Let's see what you've got, Reyes. I've enjoyed my share of men. And I've enjoyed seeing you in the clubs. I've looked forward to a private viewing for a long time!"

Of everything Reyes had done, this smacked so much of his captivity, of displaying his aroused girth for Sweet Dove's pleasure, that only in this moment did he hesitate.

Angelica must have known, because she quickly pierced his mind. *Do it for me, Reyes. Not for that bastard. Let me look at what you've got, what I had in my mouth last night, what I want between my legs desperately right now.*

Reyes turned slightly toward her, meeting her gaze. He knew the performance had to be geared toward Scorpion, but Angelica knew Reyes as well, and that he wavered.

*You can do this,* she added. *You're not a slave and right now you belong to me. Let me see you, Reyes. All of you.*

He met and held her gaze, then unbuckled the thick dominance belt. He unzipped and removed his pants. He was in a half-aroused state and his cock hung low.

*You're so beautiful. I could look at you for hours.*

The metallic voice intruded. "You're a big man, Reyes, a promise of good things to come. Now, release your slave to service you on her knees. You'll bind her again afterward, but a woman is at her best on her knees."

Reyes moved quickly, then climbed up on the platform. *Just let me know if you want to stop.*

*Hell, no. This is a trap we're setting for these bastards.
They're incredibly arrogant not to suspect what we're
up to. So, let's give them what they want, because at the
right time we'll make them pay. Besides, I already told
you that I wanted this, that I want to see you, and that I
want you in my mouth.*

He caught the back of her neck, and with his hips arching he fed her his cock.

She groaned.

"The slave knows a good thing when she sees it. I think
she's enjoying herself."

Reyes ignored Scorpion. He closed his eyes and focused on Angelica, savoring her mouth. He moaned as
she sucked, as her fingers moved over his thighs, his abdomen, his balls. She had a light, sensual touch.

*I love doing this to you, Reyes.*

He knew then that he could do this with her, even release into her as needed, and he began to relax. And all
because of her, because she kept bringing him back to
how this was an act between them, despite the circumstances.

Suddenly he felt movement and Engles was there,
naked and aroused, levitating to place himself behind
Angelica. "We're sharing, whether you like it or not." Engles's dark eyes were wild and glazed.

But something primal erupted within Reyes. A flush
of heat flowed through his body and he saw through a red
film that now covered his eyes. He levitated well above
Angelica, then launched at Engles, catching him hard in
the chest so that he flew backward between the two posts.

Reyes landed on top of Engles in the pool just a few
feet from the table. With his weight holding Engles down,
Reyes rained punches at his enemy. Fury raged through

him. He found Engles's throat and gripped him hard as he continued to pound his face, shoving most of his head below the waterline.

Reyes shouted, "Don't you ever touch what belongs to me!"

"Enough!" the metallic voice called out.

At the same time, two sets of powerful hands grabbed Reyes from behind, hauling him off Engles. Reyes tried to wrench free, but the men were part of Engles's security staff and built like tanks. Still Reyes fought, especially since Engles rose to his feet in the pool, as all the men were now, his eyes dark with rage.

*Reyes, stop! You've got to come back to me. I'm scared.*

Angelica. Shit, in his fury he'd left her alone and unprotected.

He stilled as he turned to stare at her.

She was still on her knees, though at the edge of the table, and very naked. But the security team now levitated in the air around her and he couldn't reach her.

She shifted her gaze to something beyond him. *Look out!* she shouted within his mind.

He didn't see the punch coming. Engles caught him on the jaw and he saw stars.

# CHAPTER 12

Angelica slid off the platform, jumped into the shallow water, then leaped toward Reyes. She'd half expected the security team to stop her, but they didn't.

When she reached Reyes, now held upright by Engles's men, his head lolled.

She reached for him, but Engles grabbed her arm and jerked her in his direction. His face was bloody and swollen, but he smiled. "I have you now. And there's nothing Reyes can do about it."

But there was something Angelica could do and right now she didn't give a damn for the consequences. She relaxed in Engles's grip and turned toward him. Adopting her most submissive pose and voice, she said, "What a powerful man you are."

He pivoted just enough. She leaned into him, and because he was so used to servility she was able to lift her knee in a hard jab. She caught him just right, because his eyes widened, then his mouth. He buckled and fell over on his side into the water once more but came up sputtering and holding his crotch.

The security team grabbed her as well.

Engles called out on a pained hiss, "Take them to the interrogation room. Now!"

But the metallic voice began to laugh, then called out, "You will do no such thing, Engles!"

Scorpion issued his own set of orders, sending Engles and his security team away. Angelica knelt in the cold water, supporting Reyes's head on her lap.

Scorpion's metallic voice once more called out. "Slave, try to bring your master around. I need a word with him!"

Angelica patted Reyes's cheek. She shivered as much from the icy water as from the knowledge that the head of Starlin, an extremely powerful Ancestral, was only a few yards away. She had no doubt that Scorpion could do anything he wanted to either Reyes or herself.

"Master, you must wake up. Please wake up."

She started rubbing his arms, chest, and shoulders vigorously. "Wake up, master."

After what seemed like ages, Reyes finally came around. And once awake he leaped to his feet. "Where the fuck is Engles?"

*Reyes, calm down right now. We're alone with Scorpion. Don't give us away.*

He pressed a hand to his face. "Scorpion, my apologies."

"The fault is Engles's. He did not have permission to disrupt the show and he's being punished as we speak. However, I was still extremely well-entertained. You stood up to Engles when no one else dared.

"I've had my eye on you for decades and have watched your excellent progress as a slaver. I believe you have tremendous potential in my organization and I'll be frank: I'm looking for a much more intimate association with you.

"I expect your attendance at the masked ball tomorrow night, and if all goes well I plan to reveal myself to you."

Angelica was stunned and the chains told her Reyes was as well.

Reyes frowned. "But even Engles doesn't know who you are."

"Engles will always have a specific role in my organization, but I'm looking for something very different with you. And there will be requirements which I expect to be obeyed."

Angelica wasn't surprised when Reyes bowed slightly and said, "Anything you wish, master."

"Excellent. And now you may go."

There was nothing elegant about the way Reyes simply picked her up, then shifted to altered flight, both naked. Unfortunately, as anxious as Reyes was to get her away, he moved too fast and pain pierced her skull.

She screamed. *Reyes, it hurts.*

He pulled back immediately, but the damage was done, so that by the time they arrived back at his bedroom she was dragging him toward the bathroom, where she promptly threw up. Naked, bent over a toilet, and vomiting. Exactly the way any woman wanted her man to see her.

Reyes was nothing but kind, however, as he stroked her back and apologized repeatedly for being so thoughtless.

This time, however, as she siphoned Reyes's power, she recovered much more quickly, so that within half an hour she sat next to him on the couch in his sitting room, both wearing robes.

He kept shaking his head. "I can't believe what Scorpion said to me, that he's been watching me and has plans for us."

"Sounds like he wants you for his boy toy."

Reyes grimaced. "I have no doubt that's his intention."

"I'd tease you if the whole thing wasn't so horrible. But it also seemed to me that Scorpion wants to bring you in as more of a partner than just a member of the board."

Reyes rubbed the back of his neck. "That's what it sounded like, but why?"

Angelica shrugged. "Like he said, he's been watching you."

"I've been careful," he stated, more to himself than her. "But this is an amazing turn of fortune."

"I assume we'll be going to the ball tomorrow night."

"Yes, of course. We have to go." He drew in a deep breath. "Do you know what this means?"

Angelica smiled and ran her hand lightly over the scruff along his jaw. "Actually, I do. You're close to your goal."

"All I need is to get at the documents detailing all the players, the clubs that Starlin owns, the bank accounts, the machinery for abduction, the holding-cell locations, and I can take them down."

"Reyes, this is amazing." That it all sounded too good

to be true wasn't something that she said out loud, but she felt uneasy.

His mood shifted suddenly, new, surprising emotions that had him grinding his jaw. She just couldn't imagine what it was he was thinking.

Finally, she said, "Say it out loud. Maybe that will help."

He groaned. "I'm still furious that I left you exposed on that platform. I keep thinking about how easily Engles or Scorpion could have hauled you away. I was unconscious, for God's sake."

"And therefore completely out of control, more than you'd ever been when I was with you."

Turning toward her slightly, he leaned his elbow on the back of the sofa and settled his head into his palm. His brow was lined with furrows, his body tense. She didn't know how to help him.

Finally, she decided on letting him know what happened after he got knocked out. "I kneed Engles in the jewels."

At that Reyes's brows rose. "You did what?"

She chuckled. "I kneed Engles hard. You were out cold and he so kindly told me that now I was his because you couldn't do a damn thing about it. So, I hit him where it hurt."

"I don't understand. If you did that, then either both of us should be dead or I should be dead and you should be bound to him right now."

"I think the whole thing amused Scorpion. He was laughing while you were unconscious. He was the one who broke it up. Believe me, we were both surrounded by Engles's security team, but Engles bowed to Scorpion's will."

Reyes stared at her for a long, hard moment; then his lips curved. "So, you nailed that bastard in the jewels."

"He crumpled like a little girl. I've never seen a face that red, and his cheeks were puffed out like a blowfish. He fell into the water and came up choking. It was a beautiful sight, despite the fact that I was scared out of my mind."

Reyes laughed, then slid his hand in her hair, cupping the back of her neck. "I hardly remember what happened except that the moment Engles landed behind you and touched you my brain funneled down to a narrow beam of pure rage."

"You knocked him so hard that both of you landed in the water. It was awesome. Of course I can say that now because we're both still alive. But it was one of the best moments of my life."

"You amaze me, Angelica. You're handling this whole thing with tremendous grace."

She stared into Reyes's clear blue eyes, once more caught by the man she knew him to be. Through this difficult experience she felt as though she was getting to know him and hoped that maybe she'd be able to help him see who he truly was. She knew he viewed himself in a bad light, as one who'd been enslaved and worthless.

For her, he would always be the man who, the moment Engles had touched her with the intention of rape, had defended her, putting both his life and all his plans at risk.

Her mind ran suddenly back to the platform, to making love with him, despite having an audience. She'd wanted him to complete the act then, and she wanted it now even more.

A delicious shiver raced through her. "You know, Reyes," she began as she pulled apart her robe and let him see her breasts, "we didn't exactly get to finish what we started and I have a feeling you need to feed."

"Angelica," he whispered.

He leaned toward, slanting his lips over hers. Passion erupted between them like a volcano.

He pushed her back on the couch and kissed her as though he were a starving man and she was his first meal in months.

She loved it. She flung her arms around his massive shoulders and shifted around so that her legs could accommodate his body.

She reached low, fondling what was already hard for her. She'd begun to feel that nothing was so beautiful as floating her fingers over the crown of his cock, then drifting the length of him. He would fit inside her and connect her to him, in the same way the chains had bound them together, the way his lips and his tongue formed a sacred seal.

When he entered her this time her body rolled in a languid arch, taking him in, feeling all that he was.

"I love doing this with you and I wouldn't have cared if we'd been on the platform. I swear it. All I wanted was to feel you inside, to be joined with you. I crave you, Reyes, every part of you."

He nuzzled her neck and she felt the sides of his fangs pushing against her throat in careful nudges. Knowing that he'd soon pierce her vein and take her lifeblood made her moan loudly. "Please, yes, please. Drink from me. I never dreamed it could be like this."

*Angelica, you feed me in so many ways and tonight you saved my life.*

He slowed his hips but kept up the seductive curl of his pelvis and thighs as he placed an arm over her chest to keep her still. He licked along her throat, encouraging the vein. She felt it rise as though reaching for him, as though needing this as much as he needed sustenance to survive.

*Yes,* she whispered through his mind.

His fangs struck and she cried out as her internal well tightened around his slowly gliding stalk. He felt so good and his scent, full of maleness and sex, rose to create euphoric streamers through her senses.

He removed his fangs and began to suck, pushing into her deeper now. The sounds of his mouth working her throat intensified her body's pull on him.

*See what you to do me?* She writhed beneath him. *I'm almost ready to come.*

He groaned; then with a movement that stunned her he drove his cock in quick thrusts, vampire fast, so that she was crying out, her body spasming before she realized what had happened. All the while he suckled her neck, somehow remaining pinned to her while her body arched and rocked.

The pleasure was so sharp, so intense, that she dug her nails into his back, which for some reason made him suck harder.

He slowed his hips but kept pushing into her. His control stunned and amazed her.

*This feels so good. You'll make me come again if you keep this up.*

Then, just like before, he thrust in quick sensual jabs and she rushed over the edge once more, crying out repeatedly. If he hadn't kept her upper body pinned, she would have thrashed just for the pleasure of it.

Reyes took fire down his throat, one of the most basic elements of life, of civilization, whether human or vampire. He took her essence, all that she was, and drank it in. He felt more vampire in this moment than ever before, as though something about the human, about Angelica, drove him back to his roots and helped him to know himself, all that he was.

He couldn't get enough. His hunger for her knew no bounds. Feeding for him had always been perfunctory, a necessary part of the process, but not something to be savored. He'd fed from Sweet Dove, but only when she allowed and only as part of her pleasuring process.

When she wasn't in the mood she'd throw him a half-dead slave from whom taking blood had been a difficult, soul-stripping process.

Now there was Angelica, her soft flesh, the sweetness of her blood, and the adoring way she caressed him. He'd never had an experience like this in his long-lived life. He hardly knew what to do or to think, except to continue enjoying her.

When he had his fill and released the serum into her blood that would replenish her supply swiftly he drew back and lifted up so that he could look at her.

He loved the euphoric expression on her face as he continued to push inside her, moving toward yet another orgasm. He had many techniques that could give her pleasure, and he rotated his hips so that his cock swirled within her, rubbing the sensitive areas just inside her well.

She panted lightly. "Reyes, my God!"

"I want you to come with me."

"Yes."

He held her gaze, watching pleasure float over her face, moving in a lift of the brows, a curve of the lips, then a faint almost painful grimace and back. Her breathing was beautifully erratic.

He started moving faster, thrusting into her in a long, steady drive.

"Yes," she whispered, still meeting his gaze.

Her lips were swollen with need and she looked ready to fly apart once more. He loved doing this to her.

"So close."

"Come with me. Now, Angelica. Come now." He leaned down and kissed her once, then drew back to watch the magic.

Her body arched. "Yes. Yes. I'm coming."

He sped up, a burst of speed that opened her mouth, and she screamed, a sound that caused him to erupt. Pleasure streaked and he roared as each pump of his seed left his body.

She held on to his shoulders, panting once more. Then suddenly she arched and screamed again. Her body held him tight down low, squeezing the last ounce of pleasure from him.

Rocking into her, he groaned heavily with the last few pulses of his cock.

Her abdomen fluttered. "Reyes. What you do to me."

He felt the same way as his hips settled down. He stared into her passion-drenched eyes, glinting in the dark, his vision warming her features. He smoothed her hair and kissed her again and again.

She kissed him back, her legs and body lax, her breathing slowly returning to normal. She slid her hands up and down his arms.

He remained connected to her for a long time, just looking at her, trying to understand how this miraculous thing had happened. For the first time in his life, he'd truly made love to a woman. He hadn't just sexed her up, using her for relief, but he'd made love to her.

He realized he cherished Angelica, that she'd become valuable in his eyes, a woman he could trust.

How different his previous experience with Sweet Dove had been. Nothing about her spoke of trust, of anything good. She was narcissistic and vain and was somehow connected to the most powerful man in the Starlin Group.

"Hey." Angelica's voice called him out of his reveries.

"What is it?" Reyes asked.

"You left me there. Your eyes glazed over and your lips turned down."

He huffed a sigh as once more he focused on her. "Sorry."

"No need to apologize. We experienced a wonderful distraction just now, but our situation will call on each of us quickly. Besides, I should apologize as well. I was looking at you; then suddenly all I could think about was what it would be like to finally meet Scorpion."

"And that's something we'll both do tomorrow night."

But Angelica frowned. "Reyes, don't you think it's odd that Scorpion intends to reveal himself to you when not even Engles knows who he is? And you were only recently made a member of his organization."

"I admit I'm uneasy, although he's already said he's been watching me for years. But worrying about any of it right now won't help. We'll know the truth soon enough."

The following evening Reyes dressed as a Roman gladiator and looked incredibly sexy. He frowned as he adjusted the metal brass armor over his chest.

Angelica knew that he'd had it made up weeks ago in anticipation of the Starlin event and that the brass works had taken a mold of his chest. She had a hard time keeping her hands off it, because even the nipples looked exactly like his.

"If you keep touching my chest armor with that kind of gleam in your eye, I'm not sure I'll be able to answer for what happens next."

She took a step back, lifting her hands playfully. "Don't you dare disturb either my costume or this hair." She patted the rolls at the back of her head carefully. "Your housekeeper spent hours getting me to look this way."

He wrinkled his nose. "And she probably used an entire bottle of hair spray."

Angelica laughed. "I believe she did."

His expression softened. "You look beautiful."

She wore a long white gown in the Roman style, though it was split in the front to the crotch and in the back all the way to the waist so that again, as usual, her bottom would be on display. Despite these flaws, it was far better than any of the other fantasy outfits she'd had to wear and no doubt a hundred times more modest than what most of the slaves would not-be-wearing at the masked ball.

She turned sideways to expose the full-length cutout of the soft white linen fabric. Only one strip of fabric three inches in width held the front of the gown to the back on each side. "At least I'm mostly covered."

His eyes fell to half-mast as he drew close and settled his hand on her waist. "Works for me."

She reached up and kissed him, intending it to be a quick touch of her lips to his. But he turned into her and surrounded her with his arms, his breastplate hard against her chest. When she parted her lips he deepened the kiss, which made her sigh and lean against him.

The more she was with Reyes, the more she wanted to do exactly this, to be close to him, to kiss him, to make love.

But it would hardly serve to extend the moment. Reluctantly, she drew back and addressed something very specific. "I know that the Starlin Festival lasts at least three weeks. But I thought it culminated in a masked ball. Is that still true? Will there be another one?"

"Yes. The final event is all in black and white and takes place at a location called the Crystal Cavern, another well-disguised Starlin location. But I'll tell you flat out we won't be going to that one. It's a full-on orgy, with lots of 'sharing.'"

She shuddered slightly. "Let's definitely find an excuse not to attend."

His gaze slid down the side of her gown from her waist to her hips and all the way to her ankles. "I like that you're covered as well, but all I want to do is to slide my hands beneath the fabric to feel what I can't see."

She stared up at him, enjoying this so much, that he was comfortable with her. "If we weren't leaving in a few minutes . . ."

"I know. I'd have you back in bed so fast."

"You know I'm a little sore, right, in a good way I mean?" She smiled.

He growled softly. "As you should be, since I spent so much time inside you before we fell asleep."

"I didn't know a man could do half the things you can do."

He leaned close and nuzzled her ear, whispering, "And there's more to come. I never told you this, but I can split into two beings."

She drew back and met his gaze. "What do you mean?"

"Some vampires, with sufficient power, especially those with Ancestral markers, have the ability to become two people at the same time."

"You mean . . . two of you?" Her chain vibrated at her neck so that she felt his growing desire.

He nodded. "Yes."

Angelica's cheeks grew warm, but not with embarrassment. The thought of having two of Reyes tending to her made her short of breath. "Sort of like a threesome."

He nodded slowly.

Her body stalled out, so that she wasn't even sure she could feel her feet. If she understood him, when they made love at any given time she would have two pairs of hands on her instead of just one. The thought was so intoxicating that she weaved on her feet.

He caught her arm, steadying her. "Hey, are you all right?"

"Oh, sure. Just had a couple of images of you that tripped my brain."

At that he took her in his arms again. "And what were you thinking? Tell me."

"All four hands on me, my breasts, my abdomen, my buttocks."

This time he listed and she had to keep him upright.

"Maybe we should go."

He drew back and forced himself to focus. "Yes, that's what we should do." After a couple of deep breaths, he added, "Time to put on your mask."

From the nearby table she picked up one of the smallest masks she'd ever seen, pure black and built more like a pair of glasses without the lenses. They slid into place and into her hair without disturbing the coiffure that Mathilde had so painstakingly created for her.

He donned his at the same, a similar small pair with a gold coloring that matched his chest armor.

After stepping onto his foot and with his arm holding her tight, he flew her slowly, protecting her vulnerable human physiology.

*You'll enjoy the resort where the ball is being held. It's on the Mediterranean in a massive hidden cavern open to the sea.*

*Sounds beautiful.*

*It is, especially at night.*

*Does that mean you've seen it during the day?*

*Of course. With altered flight I can go anywhere in the sunlight and not be affected. I'm only in danger when I touch down.*

They passed through more stone that felt like soft fingers grazing her skin. Once breaking through to the cavern, Reyes slowed down even more, which gave her a tremendous view of the scope of the resort. A cave shelf that stood at least a hundred feet high overhung the sea by at least fifty yards. A beach of light-colored sand met a bank of rocks, and several sets of stairs, carved into the seawall, led thirty feet to the main resort area. The coastline, beneath the shelf, curved, and all sorts of dwellings, including a massive hotel, held beachfront locations.

She glanced behind her and watched as more and more vampires flew in, many with their slaves in nothing but chains and feathered masks. Each couple landed in the same area or continued, as Reyes did, to levitate slowly through the air.

*Does this entire place belong to Starlin?*

*Yes. Impressive, isn't it?*

*I'm stunned.*

*My original plan was to purchase a home here as soon as I became a member. It would be another way to get close to the movers and shakers.*

*I keep forgetting that you're wealthy.* She glanced at him and saw that his lips curved. *And I like that about you very much. You've been chased,* she sent.

*Hunted.*

She chuckled. *But never brought down.*

He drew off to the side to make sure he didn't block incoming traffic. Holding her gaze while he hovered and kept her tight against him, he created a disguising shield. *Not until now.*

Her brows rose. *But I haven't been hunting you.*

At that he smiled fully, something rare for him. *I seem to recall a certain red dress . . .*

She planted a hand on his cool breastplate. *That was not hunting, Reyes. I only wanted a chance to be with you.*

*In your bed.*

*Yes, there's no sense pretending anymore. I wanted to jump you.*

His turn to laugh. He seemed so relaxed, something he hadn't been, even though they were going to meet Scorpion at some point during the party.

When Reyes removed the disguise he reminded her to adopt her servile attitude once more, then put them back in motion. She kept her head bowed but let her gaze drift over the sea on her right, then to the homes on her left, all staggered up the sloped incline toward the cave shelf and finally to the hotel with the entrance at the walkway level.

As at the underground cavern, what surprised her was all the plants, like this was any ordinary beach community with window boxes full of trailing vines, flowers, and even small shrubs. A few of the larger homes had small patches of lawns and large trees.

Another community that made use of grow lights.

*Your civilization never ceases to surprise me.*

*There's a lot to value in what we've achieved, but we've got a long way to go.*

He levitated to The Starlin Hotel, touched down outside, then took her leash in hand. *I really hate this.*

*Small price to pay, Reyes.*

*You're right, but you're the one who has to pay it.*

She stopped in her tracks and glanced at him. She didn't have her head down, which she could tell made him nervous. *You're wrong about that.*

He frowned. *What do you mean?*

*I know what this is costing you.*

He seemed so surprised. "Lower your gaze," he commanded sharply.

Angelica obeyed. She'd taken a risk confronting him like that, with so many people watching them. But she wanted him to know that she understood.

*Stop making me like you so damn much. You're driving me crazy.*

Angelica refrained from smiling, but her heart soared. She knew she was being ridiculous, that what she was experiencing with Reyes couldn't possibly lead to something permanent, but she never thought she'd hear him say she was driving him crazy. It pleased her feminine soul.

He led her straight through the lobby, past the check-in desks to either side of the foyer. Two costumed vampires, both extremely tall and wearing feather-trimmed dominance gear, made the ballroom easy to find.

Music poured from the space, enlivening the foyer.

As usual, Angelica had never seen so many naked

people before, and not just women but men with erect penises. She tried to look elsewhere, but because she had to keep her head lowered certain things were hard to miss.

Once she and Reyes were inside, the main ballroom area was in a sunken space surrounded by dozens of small tables and chairs, all at different elevations. A series of at least ten steps led to a dance floor alive with couples gyrating.

*So what do we do now?*

*We work the room and wait until Scorpion calls for us.*


Reyes made the rounds and let any number of prominent Starlin members stare at Angelica but postured to make sure no one else touched her.

He saw Engles once, but the bastard merely nodded, his eyes cold. Reyes knew he'd destroyed a lot of goodwill in that direction, but he wouldn't undo his actions even if he could. Engles had been determined to insinuate himself into the sex performance, and only a hard body slam like the one Reyes had delivered could have stopped Engles.

So Reyes ignored Scorpion's right hand, especially since the invitation still stood and he'd be meeting with Scorpion for the first time. More than once, however, Reyes wondered why Scorpion was taking such an interest in him when so many other vampires, having served on the board for decades, should have had priority.

He would soon find out.

He'd just finished his second tumbler of scotch when Engles finally approached him, looking none too happy. But Reyes met him stare for stare. Reyes supposed one day he'd have to battle the asshole for good, but not tonight.

"Scorpion is ready for you. Follow me."

He turned on his heel and moved quickly, but he looked mad as fire. Reyes caught Angelica against his side, then levitated swiftly after him.

Engles glanced at Reyes, then switched to altered flight as well.

Reyes tracked with him, passing through solid stone.

The trip didn't last long and Reyes's internal signal told him they were still within the beachside resort.

The suite was empty and nicely appointed with light-blue silk drapes and matching comforter, dark wood dresser and nightstands. Off to one side, an arched, darkened doorway led to a long corridor that sloped at a downward angle.

Engles gestured toward the bed. "Your instructions are there." With those words he shifted to altered flight and was gone.

On the bed was a box.

"What do you think this means?" Angelica asked.

"I don't know." Reyes drew close to the box and flipped the lid. Inside, a note rested on top of several folds of black leather as well as a flogger.

The flogger had a familiar style with a snake-head topper. Sweet Dove had owned an implement just like this one. His chest tightened. Was it a coincidence?

He unfolded the single sheet of paper and read: *"Your slave must wear the costume, though you may keep on whatever you wore to the ball. Through the arched hall, you'll find a lovely trip down memory lane waiting for you."*

A seal bearing a large *S* was stamped at the bottom.

Setting the paper aside, he lifted the leather costume,

then glanced at Angelica. The chains vibrated against his neck as she looked at it. Her heart rate had jumped.

"You're to wear this," he said.

She took the jumbled leather in her hands and lifted it up. "This reminds me a little of what your friend Eve wore during her theatrical performance, only she was dressed in red."

"You are being too familiar with me," he said curtly, then slipped into telepathy. *Remember that we might be watched.*

*Right.* She lowered her head. "I'm sorry, master."

*As for the outfit, that would follow. The costume is essentially a dominatrix outfit.*

Her brows rose. *Really? Scorpion wants me to be in the dominant position?*

*I don't know. I still have no idea what's going on here. Should I put it on?*

Reyes nodded. *If we're going to move forward with this you'll have to. Just remember, you can stop at any time.*

Angelica took the costume in hand. *I might need your help with this.*

In other circumstances, the process of helping Angelica get into any kind of fantasy wear would probably have landed him in bed with her. As it was, despite the fact that he pulled the bustier tight and zipped her up and that her firm breasts mounded so beautifully in the snug, too-small cups, his nerves kept him from enjoying the moment.

He had a bad feeling about this situation. Why was the flogger like the one that Sweet Dove had used on him and why was Angelica supposed to wear the dominant outfit?

The leather pants were an intricate combination of strips of leather, so that it took more than one try to get each leg through. Once the job was done and she wore the six-inch black stilettos he stood back. *I won't forget this image very soon.*

"She's like a wet dream, isn't she?"

Reyes turned, the sound of the woman's voice like broken glass slicing into his skin. She had frizzy red hair and deep cornflower-blue eyes, a small bow of a mouth, and cruelty emanating from every cell of her body.

Sweet Dove.

She turned in a slow circle. "How do I look, lover?"

She wore a cream silk skirt to midcalf, a sheer blouse with sleeves that ran to the wrists, ending in three-inch ruffles, and a gold metallic bra visible beneath.

Her hair was in a cloud around her head, gathered once behind with a gold clip, then flaring in more clouds and streamers down her back.

He hadn't seen her in decades, and now here she was somehow intimately connected to Starlin and even to Scorpion, the alliteration sinking deep suddenly, like a snake hissing. He wanted to say something to her, to rail at her for all the pain she'd caused him, but nothing would come.

He'd dreamed of this moment, of finally confronting his abuser, yet he stood immobile as though, even after all this time, she could still control him.

But it was Angelica who spoke first. "You're the bitch who hurt me."

She pivoted toward Angelica. Though Sweet Dove continued to stare at her, she addressed Reyes. "Your slave needs a lesson in manners. Would you like to teach her, or shall I?"

She extended her hand toward Angelica, but the threat against her moved Reyes out of his stupor. He caught his captor's wrist and turned her toward him. "What the fuck is this all about, Sweet Dove? I was told I'd be meeting Scorpion."

Sweet Dove smiled. "And you will. As for Scorpion, he and I are old friends, much older than even Engles and I, or did you not know that?"

Reyes made a decision not to tip his hand. There was no reason why Sweet Dove needed to know that Angelica had a revisiting vision capability. "I didn't know."

"I'm a little surprised. Somehow I thought you did. But before we get any further, I really must know how you got free of me all those years ago."

Reyes recalled the process and how it had taken two decades of slow, determined effort. He gave her the short version. "It was simple. Though it required time and patience, I seduced two of the men you brought in on a regular basis to join in our fun, that's how."

She held his gaze. "Actually, I'd already figured it out. But what distresses me to this day is that I never suspected. I thought you liked being with me. I made sure you had pleasure."

Reyes stared at her for a long, hard moment. Something that had never quite made sense to him now came into sharp focus. He'd always known Sweet Dove to be a pure narcissist, but until now he hadn't truly understood that she was actually surprised that he'd ever wanted to leave her. She believed what she said, that she'd thought he'd been fulfilled and content serving as her slave.

The woman bought her own propaganda.

But he refused to get distracted by her sense of ill-usage. "I looked for each of those men later, but they seemed to have disappeared."

She checked her manicure. She had long, sharp nails.

"I had to know the truth, so I tortured them. I was never so disappointed in all my life, because as much as they enjoyed inflicting pain on you in my presence, neither lasted very long when put under the cat's claw."

Reyes let these words slide off him. He didn't really care very much about the past, not anymore, especially with Angelica in the room and extremely vulnerable as a human. No matter what Sweet Dove's game was, he had to protect Angelica and because of Sweet Dove's Ancestral status she had complete power in the situation.

"And how are you connected to Scorpion and Starlin?"

She moved in his direction, reaching out with her right hand to touch his bare arm. But suddenly Angelica was right there, standing between them. In her stilettos she was taller than Sweet Dove. "Keep your hands off him. He's my master."

Sweet Dove's lips curled, her fangs showing. Then she laughed, a long trill of laughter. "What a stupid human you are, or do you not understand that I could rip you away from Reyes right now? I could have your blood-chains removed and throw you to the dogs or give you to Engles, though I suspect you would prefer the former."

Reyes felt Angelica ready to respond, but he took her quickly by the arm and pulled her behind him. Aloud he said, "Stand down, slave. You're out of line." Privately he added, *She can kill you with a single blow. Let me handle this.*

"How endearing that your slave has become protective of you, but we will get rid of her once you return to me."

He wanted Sweet Dove's focus off Angelica. "I belong to no one, Sweet Dove, or are you called something else now?"

"I am, as it happens. But I can see that you haven't

guessed, which surprises me. You never lacked for intelligence and you were always studying, which I thought endearing in its way."

He refused to get sidetracked. He had to get a clear picture of what he was dealing with. "What's your new name?"

She laughed once more. "I swear you've grown positively obtuse since you left me. How can you not know who I am?"

Reyes stared at her and then the pieces of the puzzle fell suddenly into place. It couldn't be, yet in his gut he knew it was true. He felt dizzy as he stated, "You're Scorpion."

She nodded. "I am. Do you like the empire I've built all around my favorite pastime? I think it sublime. I'm very proud of what I've created. The betting pools have been good fun and a real moneymaker, more than the auctions themselves. I won a small fortune on the little Russian. Of course, it helped to know the owner and to encourage him to increase or decrease his beatings. Power is a wonderful thing."

Reyes stared at his former captor, the woman who had beaten, raped, and tortured him for a century and whom he'd been unable to locate all this time. But there was one thing he had to know, whether or not she suspected his current ruse.

"After Starlin, you're my second most favorite achievement, you know." She drew close. "I've watched you especially over the past year, when Engles told me you'd applied for membership. I'm good at disguises, you see, and I watched that little Asian beauty suck you off. You bit her ear. Very nice. But what the hell happened at the theater performance?"

Again, Sweet Dove had taught him so much. Without missing a beat he responded, "I was thinking of you, of course, so I got lost in the memories." Would she buy it? Or would she suspect he'd almost lost his mind in that moment and blown his cover?

She smiled. "Of course you would have. I take it you telepathically commanded your slave to service you?"

He held Sweet Dove's gaze firmly. "Yes, that's exactly what I did. I had complete control of her and she performed for me just as I wanted her to."

Sweet Dove smoothed a hand over his breastplate. "So you were lost in thoughts of me."

"I was." How he hated her. He wanted nothing more than to snap her perverse neck. But she still had physical and preternatural power over him and she wouldn't hesitate to kill Angelica if it served her purpose.

"Oh, and I did so enjoy that even while in a fully aroused state you attacked Engles. I hadn't had that much fun in ages. You're both fit, beautiful men. It was like watching the Greeks of old wrestle."

He worked hard to process the truth that the woman who had enslaved him now led the organization he intended to bring down. It would never be enough to kill her outright. He had to get hold of the entire structure of her organization, all the players, everyone who got paid off, the names of the clubs, the betting organization, every damn thing.

Right now he felt stuck between a rock and a hard place. If he'd been alone, without Angelica, he could have maneuvered through easily, even setting out to seduce his former captor and gain the information he sought.

But Sweet Dove had been a fiercely jealous master and wouldn't tolerate Angelica's presence for longer than she had use for her. He needed to understand Sweet Dove's purpose right now and to somehow figure out a way to save Angelica.

"What do you want, Sweet Dove?"

"I want you back of course. I realize you'd never be my slave again, but we could become so much more as a couple. I've missed you. I've never had a man like you since you left.

"So for starters, I thought I would offer you what I know your ambitions crave: a seat on the Starlin board. That's what you want, isn't it?"

Her eyes glittered and in that moment he realized she didn't suspect him of any kind of treachery and a small part of him began to breathe, began to believe he and Angelica might just survive this night. "Yes, more than anything, I want on the board. I want what all of the governors have. I've made a small fortune on my own. But now I want what you and Engles possess."

She drew in a deep breath. "I knew it. You are my greatest accomplishment. I see it in your eyes. You match me in ambition now as well as in depravity." She smiled, a familiar penetrating smile that caused fear to run through Reyes. He knew that nothing good would follow.

"So, you may have a seat on the board of Starlin governors if you'll do one thing for me, one very simple thing."

His heart rate kicked up several notches.

Angelica's voice was suddenly in his head. *Reyes, I don't trust her. She smells evil.*

*I don't trust her, either, but we've got to play her game.*

Aloud he said, "What do you need me to do?"

"Actually, it's not what I need just you to do, but rather you and your slave. But you'll understand a lot better if I show you what I require." Her smile broadened. "I've prepared a surprise for you."

Angelica gripped Reyes's hand as she moved with him down the hall. The chains hummed low and hard, indicating a combination of sensations coming from him that she couldn't quite separate out. Beneath everything, however, rage boiled, the old kind that swam in deep currents of hatred and shame.

Sweet Dove led the way, walking with a confident stride in her cream skirt and gold bra, with her mounds of fiery hair.

The cavern hallway, sculpted with unique carvings in the stone walls and high curved ceiling, was at least thirty feet long. It sloped downward to a room that appeared to be lit with candlelight.

The closer Angelica drew to the light, however, the faster the chains vibrated at her neck, once more indicating Reyes's distress. He tightened his hold on her hand, and once they arrived on the threshold she was in pain. *Reyes, you're hurting me. You're crushing my fingers.*

She pulled, trying to disengage, but he stared at the room the way he had looked during Eve's theater performance, as if he wasn't all there. Something about this room had gotten to him.

Angelica turned toward him. His eyes looked glazed. "Reyes," she called sharply.

"I don't understand," Sweet Dove said softly, a curve to her bow lips. "He looked just like this while watching that woman during the performance at Engles's home. I wonder if he's thinking about me again?"

She met Angelica's gaze and showed her fangs in a satisfied grin.

Part of Angelica wanted to rip Sweet Dove's face off, but there were more important things to do. Angelica ignored the woman and began wrestling with Reyes's hand. If he didn't let go he'd break her bones. She sent some of the power she siphoned to her fingers and gradually built up enough strength to disengage.

Once disconnected she held her hand but kept up the healing flow. This would not be the way to start an encounter with Sweet Dove, to show any kind of weakness.

"He hurt you then? I take that as a good sign."

Angelica didn't rise to the bait; instead she rubbed Reyes's arm, up and down. She kept her head bowed, trying to maintain her slave cover. *Come back to me. You've got to come back.*

He moved slowly forward, however, as if in a trance, but ignored her completely. She stayed with him, though, until they both stood in the center of the space.

The room had a peculiar odor, something she couldn't place at first, except that it smelled very old, almost ancient. The room held a throne-like chair and a barred grate over what was an arched cavern opening the size of an average window. Beyond she could hear water rushing at what must have been a great depth. Yet the resulting fresh air still didn't soften the odor.

She supposed many of the cavern systems around the world would have lots of older parts and even bad smells like this one. But why had this room shut Reyes down so completely?

He turned slowly in Sweet Dove's direction.

Glancing past his shoulder, Angelica saw that a second archway led to another space, also lit by candlelight.

Within were a series of old rusted chains and hooks, like something from an ancient fishing trawler. Below, on a three-foot-high platform, was a wood table stained very dark.

She reached for Reyes's hand once more, because a terrible chill went through her. She almost connected, touching his fingers, but suddenly he levitated toward the doorway and moved swiftly into the room. She hurried to retain the necessary proximity.

He moved to stare down at the table, gripping two of the nearest chains in tight fists. The muscles of his arms flexed and released. His breathing grew rough.

What was he seeing?

Angelica stepped away from him. All she felt from him now, through their shared chains, was a rage that went beyond anything she could possibly comprehend.

She moved off to the side and pressed herself against the wall. She saw him in profile and that his face had broken out in a sweat as he stared at the table.

Then she understood and horror descended on her.

This was where it had all happened, repeatedly, over a century. Maybe this had even been the first room.

She watched Sweet Dove move to join them near the platform, easing off to the opposite side. She moved slowly, slithering like a snake, taking deep breaths, watching Reyes. She didn't fear him, not even a little. But Angelica could tell that Sweet Dove's drive to possess Reyes again, to once more make him her slave, exceeded every other purpose the woman had. She'd lied about a partnership.

"Are you remembering now?" Sweet Dove asked. "Can you feel how I'm peeling away the disguises deep inside your mind, allowing you to recall the times you'd been here before?"

Reyes nodded slowly.

The woman's lips were parted and her nipples peaked within her bra, tight, hard buds. She was getting off on this, on seeing Reyes here, the youth she'd abused, tortured, raped, and on watching him relive his past.

"You used to like the things I did to you."

A grimace swept over his face, but he didn't shift his gaze.

"I know how badly you've wanted to join the Starlin Group, to partake of all the delights of my world. I'm offering you so much, Reyes, and all I need from you is to do this one little thing for me.

"You see, Engles disrupted the performance earlier and I wanted to watch you explode with passion, to really feel your pleasure as you dominated your slave."

She took a few steps closer to the table. "But that moment has passed and maybe it was for the best, because now what I desire tonight will be so much better, for you and for me."

At that, he slowly pivoted in her direction.

Angelica moved at the same time, closer to the table but adjacent to Reyes so that she could see him and watch his expressions. How Reyes responded in this situation had just become a matter of life and death to Angelica. If rage took him over and he attempted to kill Sweet Dove, something he'd fail at because he couldn't prevail over an Ancestral, Angelica knew she'd die. They both would.

She had to do the thinking for both of them right now, since Sweet Dove had taken away Reyes's rational mind by bringing him here. Angelica had the impression that the woman hadn't used this room since Reyes left, which was maybe part of the smell. The scent reminded Angelica of the back rooms of a house that hadn't been cleaned or aired in a long time.

She leaned closer and realized the smell came from the table itself. She wondered if pain and violation developed a redolence over time.

But as she stared at the stained wood she realized what had caused the uneven stain.

Blood.

And lots of it.

She stepped back, horror piercing her once more.

For a time, she couldn't breathe and couldn't think. But she had to pull herself together.

Reyes had worked hard to build a life for himself after his subjugation in this dungeon, honest work with an honest wage on which he'd built his wealth. Only then had he set his sights on Starlin, when he could afford to buy into the expensive lifestyle. And he had only one purpose, to bring this diseased, perverse organization down.

But he could lose it all right now.

"What do you want me to do?" he asked.

"It's simple. I want you on your back, naked, the way you used to be for me. And I want your slave to dominate you, to give the performance I've been denied all these decades since you left. If you do that, I'll make you a board member this very night and in the coming days and weeks, if you once more become the lover I've craved all this time, I'll make you my partner over the entire organization. You'll be wealthy beyond what even you can imagine, and the power, Reyes, trust me, the power is intoxicating."

He shook his head slowly from side to side. "I can never be bound again. Don't you understand that? I can never return to you."

She pouted. "But why, when I brought you to ecstasy

every time we were together? I made sure you knew pleasure. I was a good mistress to you."

Angelica's chain trembled at her throat, vibrating with Reyes's emotion. "While you chained me, cut me, and beat me? While you had others pulling and sucking on me or shoving their dicks into every orifice I possess? You can't imagine why I wouldn't want to return to that?"

"You're kidding yourself, Reyes. Don't you see? You've found your way back to me. This is what you've wanted since you left my home. You need to be here."

Angelica made a quick decision. She joined Reyes and slid her hand up his arm. "I want to do this, master."

He whipped his head in her direction. "What?"

She caressed his muscles, hoping to give an appearance of arousal. She swept a hand the length of the wood. "I want you here, master. I want you laid out. I want to ride you while you're chained. You've already given me so much pleasure and taught me the joys of pain, but now I want more." She shifted her gaze to Sweet Dove. "And I want your mistress to watch, because mostly I want to survive, and what better way than to please the Starlin leadership?"

Sweet Dove narrowed her gaze at Angelica. "You're smarter than I suspected. And I admire anyone who chooses to live."

Reyes stared at Angelica. He didn't fully understand what was going on, which meant his brain wasn't quite functioning yet. But he did know that Angelica's professed desire to do what Sweet Dove wanted made no sense at all. He'd never caused Angelica that kind of pain, so why was she talking like this?

He shifted his gaze back to the table, where he'd been raped times beyond counting, and knew he couldn't go through with Sweet Dove's demands. Here was the one thing he'd promised himself: Never to allow again anyone to chain him down. Ever.

"I won't do it."

Angelica turned toward him and pressed herself up against his body. "Please, master." She sounded desperate, but her telepathic words carried profound resolve. *Reyes, together we can do this. You and I. Forget Sweet Dove right now. Focus on me. Just me. We have to do this.*

He turned and held her gaze and his mind began to clear a little more. *I can't. Try to understand. She took everything from me, here in this room. Everything.*

*I know that. But she's also Scorpion and she just earned a fortune on the death of the Russian slave. We owe it to that woman to keep going. Reyes, you have to do this, but it will be very different because I'll be with you every step of the way. I'll be the one commanding you and riding you. Not her. I'll be making love to you, and that's not the same thing as what happened before.*

Aloud she said, "I want to live, master. Do this for the head of Starlin. Please."

He shook his head. *I can't do this. I won't.*

Angelica kept her head bowed, still playing her role. *Reyes, you must. Don't you see? If you do this one thing you'll be on the Starlin board. You'll finally have access to all the information you've been seeking. The game can be won or lost here.*

His mind finally ordered itself, and he shifted his gaze to the table. But one final element came into view, something he was sure Angelica hadn't considered: Once he was bound in chains, if Sweet Dove decided to kill Angelica or to give her to Engles there'd be nothing he could do to save her.

*Reyes, tell me I'm wrong, but if you refuse isn't it possible, even likely, that Sweet Dove will never make the offer again? Isn't this your only hope, our only hope?*

As if to confirm Angelica's take on the situation, Sweet Dove drew close. "I'll only offer this once, Reyes. Accept the chains here and now or I'll rescind your membership immediately. And you'll be out for good."

# CHAPTER 13

Reyes gripped two dangling rusted iron chains, one in each hand, as he stared down at Sweet Dove's bondage platform. She'd tortured him in exactly this place for an entire century. She'd bound and hurt him at other locations as well, but this had been her favorite.

The platform smelled damn familiar, old blood and sex. His nostrils flared.

Remembered pain flowed through him, and his brain misfired all over again, his rational mind winking in and out.

He struggled to hold it together, something he needed to do if he wanted to keep Angelica out of Sweet Dove's hands.

Sweet Dove had pulled them out of the Starlin masked ball so that he still wore his Roman military costume complete with breastplate. But on Sweet Dove's orders, Angelica had changed into a black dominatrix outfit.

Sweet Dove seemed out of character in a cream silk skirt and sheer, long-sleeved white blouse displaying a gold bra beneath. She looked more like a sexy businesswoman than a vile sadist. But then she'd just revealed the truth to him that she was Scorpion, the owner and founder of the Starlin slaver organization that had abducted Angelica and sold her at auction a little over a week ago.

Slowly he shifted his gaze to Sweet Dove, who stood to the right of the platform staring at him, and smiling from her cruel, curved-bow lips. Such a small mouth for a sadist. Her dark-blue eyes glinted with malevolent hope. Her light-red hair, almost ethereal as it flowed away from her face, gave her a strangely innocent look as did her pale skin.

Sweet Dove wanted him to say yes to her, so that like old times, he'd be chained down and under her control again.

Once he was bound, she would be free to do whatever she wanted. She could hurt him as much as she liked. She could even kill him.

In former times she'd come close again and again during her sessions with him, and he'd begged for death.

But she always brought him back, and at times she even wept at how close she'd come to losing him. He was under no illusions about the woman. Incapable of normal feelings, she'd been a rabid dog upset she might lose a favorite chew toy.

Angelica's voice entered his mind, a sudden quiet

sound that pierced the cacophony. *Reyes, come back to me. I'm here. I'm with you. You're not alone.*

Still holding the chains he pivoted slightly toward her.

Angelica. All too human in his dangerous vampire world and the biggest surprise of his long-lived life.

She stood on the left side of the platform, meeting his gaze and wearing her black leather dominatrix costume, the one Sweet Dove had insisted she wear. She was so beautiful with large warm brown eyes. Her dark hair, pulled back in a Grecian arrangement, heightened her strong cheekbones, giving her a vulnerable appearance. She was Sweet Dove's opposite in every way.

He didn't want her to die, but because Sweet Dove was an Ancestral and powerful beyond words, there was a strong chance neither of them would make it out of this room alive.

Sweet Dove had made it clear that he either let her bind him in chains on this table once more or he'd be kicked out of the Starlin Group for good.

The decision seemed an impossible one to make. If he left right now, he'd forfeit decades of effort spent positioning himself within Starlin, a slaver group that abducted tens of thousands of human females each year. Most of the slaves died within the first two years of captivity, and Starlin made it their extremely profitable business to replace those numbers as needed.

But if he stayed, he risked Angelica's life and most certainly his own freedom, if not his mortality.

He held Angelica's gaze. *I can't keep you safe. If I'm chained down, and she chooses to hurt you, there's nothing I can do.*

*I know, but we have to take the chance. If we do this,*

*you'll be on the Starlin Board and you'll have access to all the information you need to bring down this wretched organization. Please, Reyes. Besides, you heard what she said. If you don't do this, she'll revoke your membership. Then what will we do?*

*You'll go home and be safe. I'll start over.*

Sweet Dove interjected. "Interesting. The two of you are communicating telepathically. That's an exceptional level of power. But what are you saying to each other, I wonder? And why does your slave look you directly in the eye? This one needs a lesson or two in proper submissive behavior."

Reyes heard the threat. *She'll hurt you, Angelica, if you don't respond accordingly right now.*

*I've got this.* Angelica shifted to face the table, then lowered the upper half of her body onto the platform, extending her arms in Sweet Dove's direction. "Forgive me, mistress."

The table was so large that her fingertips just breached the halfway mark, but he feared what Sweet Dove would do next. If she decided to inflict pain, Angelica would get badly hurt.

Reyes started to warn Angelica to move away, that she was in danger. But the next moment Sweet Dove launched and caught her by the wrists.

Angelica started to scream.

Reyes could feel Sweet Dove's preternatural power, the charge that flowed up both Angelica's arms so that she screamed in pain. But he felt immobilized, unable to do anything to help her. If he acted, Sweet Dove would start to suspect his loyalty to the slaver lifestyle. But hearing Angelica in pain was tearing at his heart.

"Don't you love that sound, Reyes? The timbre of your

slave's pain grips me between my legs. I could listen to this for hours." Sweet Dove's lids were low, her lips swollen.

Reyes had to make a decision.

Once more, however, Angelica reached into his mind, surprising him all over again. *We can do this, Reyes.*

He stared at Angelica, at her bowed head, at the strained appearance of her neck as Sweet Dove continued to hurt her. She panted between screams, yet her thoughts were clear, her intentions unwavering.

*Reyes, say yes.* She winced, then screamed again. After a moment she added, *I want to go down this path with you. I have a strong premonition that we must do this thing.*

He couldn't believe it. Despite the pain she endured, she wanted to move forward. He would be bound in chains, Angelica would dominate him and have sex with him, and Sweet Dove would watch.

Sweat beaded on his forehead. Because he and Angelica wore matching blood-chains around their necks, he felt her pain as well as her conviction about the situation. But he hated the thought of his former captor having this much power over him again.

As Sweet Dove continued to pummel her with painful energy, Angelica slowly turned her head to once more meet Reyes's gaze.

He saw her determination, and suddenly his own decision was clear. "So you want to ride me, slave? To treat me as I've treated you? To chain me down on this table?"

"Yes, master." *More than anything, Reyes.* She shook now from the pain Sweet Dove inflicted, and tears rolled down her face.

"Beautiful," Sweet Dove murmured. She turned to meet Reyes's gaze as well. "You've trained this one so well that she begs for it. I can feel her desire for you. She wants this. She's learning to enjoy the pain."

He made his decision for the simple reason that he wanted to do this with Angelica more than anything else in the world. He wanted to be bound by this worthy woman, whose kind generous spirit soared miles above Sweet Dove's low, sadistic heart. He wanted to allow a woman he trusted to have complete power over him.

To Angelica he sent, *I'll do it, but only because it's you.*

Angelica's eyes lit up, and he felt her siphoning his power more than ever. He watched as a surge of power suddenly entered Angelica's arms and met Sweet Dove's preternatural charge until sparks flew above the point at which her hands gripped Angelica's arms.

How was she doing that?

But Sweet Dove laughed. "I believe this means you've brought her into complete submission, Reyes, because these are sparks of love. Only her love and devotion to you could cause this kind of reaction. I'm very impressed."

"Release her, Sweet Dove. Let her chain me down."

As Reyes unbuckled his metal breastplate Sweet Dove turned her attention to him, releasing Angelica at the same time.

Sweet Dove took a couple of steps in Reyes's direction, and with the intention of keeping her focus off Angelica, he slowly removed his short white tunic.

Sweet Dove licked her lips, her gaze strafing his body. "Reyes," she murmured. "You've grown so muscular over the years, and your tattoos excite me."

* * *

As Sweet Dove lusted after her former slave, Angelica rubbed her wrists. She breathed a sigh of relief when the intense pain vanished as quickly as it had come. She drew herself upright and wiped her cheeks, then turned her attention to Reyes as well.

The sudden turn of events, when she and Reyes had discovered that Sweet Dove was the powerful force behind Starlin, that she was the terrible entity known as Scorpion, still had her head reeling. Beyond that, the woman's Ancestral power stunned her.

Angelica's connection to Reyes and her siphoning of his power on an almost constant basis had served to condition her more and more to this hidden vampire world. For that reason she understood the gravity of her situation more clearly than she otherwise would have.

Sweet Dove had weight in this world and terrible power. Reyes would never be able to stand against her unless he, too, embraced his Ancestral abilities. Yet he resisted, fearing that he would become corrupt like Sweet Dove or the woman's equally sadistic right-hand man, Engles.

She forced herself to focus, to think. The masked ball had turned into a minefield that she had to learn to navigate very quickly or she'd die.

Somehow she and Reyes had to find a way to survive the bondage performance, because he'd said it exactly right: Once Sweet Dove had control over them she could do whatever she wanted, and Reyes wouldn't be able to lift a finger to stop her.

Angelica held the flogger in her hand, the one with the strange, snake-head handle. Her tight black leather bustier pushed her breasts into full mounds and cinched in her already small waist. The pants, made up of strips of black leather, were open at the crotch. She hated the way they felt, but they at least had the advantage that she wouldn't be completely naked during the performance.

But she'd never done anything like this before.

Sweet Dove sidled up to Reyes. He was completely naked now, the swirls of the hawk tattoos spread over his back now visible. Sweet Dove traced a finger over his tats.

He looked magnificent as he held his former captor's gaze, his expression hard, commanding, no longer her slave.

The blood-chain at Angelica's neck vibrated heavily with his emotion, a deep hatred that swelled through him. Angelica felt how much he despised the woman's touch.

When Sweet Dove placed her hand on his shoulder, something deep inside Angelica began to writhe, then sharpen with rage. She moved swiftly, faster than a human, another sign she was bonded to Reyes and siphoning his power.

Placing herself between Reyes and Sweet Dove, Angelica laid the flogger against Sweet Dove's throat. "This is my show. I'm the dom here. Got it?"

She held Sweet Dove's gaze and felt the woman's power like a storm against her skin. She continued to draw from Reyes, pulling his power into her and strengthening the muscles of her arms. It would take so little for Sweet Dove to kill her.

Because Sweet Dove didn't attack, Angelica took quick charge of the situation, whirling to face Reyes. "Get on the table, slave, and do it now. You are mine to command."

What possessed her to be so bold? Maybe a strong survival instinct, because if she didn't play this exactly right she would die. And she knew one thing about bullies of every kind: they give way for demonstrations of strength, at least for a time.

*Reyes, I'm yours right now. I'm going to ride you and make you come. Do you want me?*

Reyes held her gaze, his nostrils flaring. The scent of his desire flowed around Angelica as he focused his attention solely on her. He even slid his hand to his arousal and stroked himself. *More than you can imagine.*

But she had a role to play, so she slapped his hand with the flogger. "You're not to touch yourself unless I say so."

He withdrew his fingers, but his cock stiffened even more, and her own desire rose.

"On the table, slave." If she was going to pull this off, she had to be tough. But she still kept herself positioned between Reyes and Sweet Dove.

"Yes, get on the table, Reyes." Sweet Dove spoke over Angelica's shoulder.

When Reyes started to move in response to Sweet Dove, Angelica got within inches of his face and all but shouted, "You are mine to command, not hers! You will obey only me! Do you understand, slave?"

His eyes widened slightly in surprise. To his mind she sent, *Follow my lead. I think I know a way out.*

Aloud Reyes said, "Yes, mistress."

Sweet Dove jerked Angelica's shoulder, pulling her around to face her.

But Angelica lifted her chin and stared straight into her eyes. Instinctively she knew the only way this would work was if she faced up to the devil. "You're not in charge, Sweet Dove. If you refuse to let me do this my way, Reyes and I will leave right now."

"You don't have that kind of say. You're a slave."

"Not wearing this outfit. Right now, I'm a dom and I call the shots."

Again Sweet Dove's power felt like a storm against Angelica's body as she let Angelica feel that she could crush her with a thought. Yet she couldn't back down.

When death didn't follow and Sweet Dove didn't lay a hand on her, Angelica turned toward the table. She threaded the flogger through one of the strips of leather on her thigh and passed by Sweet Dove toward the head of the table.

She reached down, ignoring the sickly odor, and slapped the wood platform, her gaze fixed on Reyes. "I want your head here, slave. Now. I'm going to chain you up and do things to you."

Still in an aroused state, Reyes levitated while stretching out. He positioned himself on the table faceup.

*Do you trust me?*

Reyes closed his eyes. *Implicitly. I couldn't do this otherwise.*

*I know.*

Angelica took one of the shackles. Sweet Dove had infused the metal with a preternatural charge. Only at this moment, feeling the unearthly power of the chains, did Angelica hesitate. Reyes could bust out of a regular iron shackle, but not one charged like this. If her plan to keep standing up to Sweet Dove didn't work, she and Reyes really would be in serious trouble.

But she'd already made her decision. Taking the shackle in hand, she clamped it around Reyes's left wrist. He winced as the preternatural charge took hold. The length of the chain stretched his arm a few inches above the table and at a right angle to his body.

She moved swiftly around the platform and clamped

the other shackle to his right wrist. His eyes were slits, but she could see he watched her. She could also feel his pain and even a low level of fear at being bound again.

More than the discomfort, however, she felt his desire. His cock stood upright, and he tracked her as she crossed to the foot of the platform to shackle each ankle.

But once all four limbs were bound, Reyes arched his back and groaned. He was in pain.

She turned toward him, remembering how badly the charged shackles had hurt her once, the same night as the auction. *Are you okay?*

He held her gaze. *I'm fine. Too many memories.*

*How bad is the pain?*

*Tolerable.*

Sweet Dove intruded once more, approaching the table and stroking Reyes's thigh.

Angelica watched Reyes's eyes widen with horror and panic. She couldn't let this continue, and on instinct she opened herself up to his power, letting it flood her this time. Suddenly, and much to her surprise, Angelica levitated across the table and in a swift motion pushed Sweet Dove away.

Her momentum caught Sweet Dove hard in the chest, and the woman flew backward, hitting the old stone wall, then falling on her ass to the floor. Angelica felt her own hair flying around her face, having come completely undone from the tight Grecian rolls she'd worn for the masked ball.

Her voice resonated with a strange vibration as she shouted at Sweet Dove. "You're not to touch him!"

Sweet Dove levitated to her feet, her eyes blazing with rage. "How dare you, slave! I'll do as I please."

"No, you won't." Angelica had never felt like this in

her life, full of power and a fire of her own. She stared down the monster that had hurt Reyes. "You wanted a sex performance and I'll give you one, but only if you keep your hands off and let me have my way. And I swear that if you come near him again, I'll tear every red hair from your head before I let you touch him, my existence be damned."

Sweet Dove froze, her eyes wide. After several long seconds her shoulders finally relaxed and a lascivious expression overtook her face. "Well, aren't you a surprise? I knew you had potential, that you had the capacity to take a lot of pain, but now I'm seeing something else. You could become like me."

"I don't give a fuck if I could become like the god of the underworld, I just want you to back off and let me do my thing. You told me to dominate this man, and that's what I intend to do." Once more she drew Reyes's power into her and let it flow, so that her hair moved around her shoulders.

Sweet Dove finally lifted both hands in surrender. "Please, do whatever it is you wish to do. I won't attempt to intervene again."

Though she could hardly trust Sweet Dove to keep her word, Angelica nodded once firmly, then turned toward Reyes. Glancing down at his hips, she was astonished to find he was still fully aroused. She met his gaze. *You liked this little standoff?*

*It's you, Angelica. I'm hard for you.*

A shiver of pure desire ran through Angelica. *You're hard for me?*

*Only for you.*

She resisted smiling and instead withdrew the flogger from the strip of leather on her thigh. She slapped it against her hand. *Will this hurt? I mean, how much of this can you take?*

*Bring it. I've had a thousand times worse. Slap me hard for effect. Trust me. I'm a vampire, remember?*

Angelica knew that if she didn't make this good, make it a real show, the bitch wouldn't buy it. *Forgive me,* she sent. She lifted her arm and brought the flogger down hard once on his left pec, then his right.

*Like a butterfly wing,* Reyes responded. *Can't you do any better?*

She met his gaze, wanting to know the truth, but his eyes were at half-mast and his cock twitched. *You're enjoying this.*

*I'm enjoying you.*

Another shiver traveled through her. She couldn't believe her harmless attempt at flirtation all those weeks ago at the Ocean Club had led her here.

She forced herself to forget about Sweet Dove and instead to savor the body she'd come to know so thoroughly over the past week.

For the next several minutes Angelica used the flogger on Reyes, slapping his arms and chest, building a rhythm into the calculated series of strikes. His body reddened, but the whole time Reyes writhed and his arousal stiffened.

She stroked his cock with the flogger and watched the tip weep, then she went to work on his legs.

By the time she reached his feet most of his body had a red hue, but he writhed and was breathing hard, his eyes closed. She had no doubt he was in a profound state of arousal.

She secured the flogger once more between strips of leather, then moved to the side of the platform. She dragged a finger up his body, digging in slightly with her fingernail, and took a long moment to look at him. She slid her palm over the muscular contours of his arms, his pecs, his chest.

She leaned close and kissed him on the lips, then sucked his nipples in turn. Her body was already heated up; still she took her time to explore him with her lips and tongue. She started biting him hard, which caused grunts to leave his throat. She came close many times to drawing blood, but he kept encouraging her to make a show of it.

*Reyes, you're magnificent.*

*And I love what you're doing to me, that you have control of me. I didn't think it could be like this, so erotic. But it's all because of you.*

His words, the beauty of his body, the taste of his skin as she bit him, had built an inferno of desire within her.

*I need you, Reyes.*

*Then take me.*

She climbed up on the platform to straddle him, guiding her wet body over his thick cock. She moaned as she eased down on him, then arched her back and ground her hips. She savored all that he was, the size and feel of him.

*Angelica, my God.*

She opened her eyes and met his gaze.

His lids low, he pushed up with his hips, letting her feel him. *Oh, Reyes, I want more, but you'd better stop.* Aloud she said, "You don't move unless I tell you to move, slave."

"Yes, mistress."

She leaned over him and kissed him on the lips. *Open for me.*

*Yes, mistress.* He sounded teasing.

*Don't do that, not in my head, or you'll have me*

*laughing.* She worked him with her hips, setting a steady rhythm.

Reyes parted his lips and she drove her tongue inside. He groaned.

After a moment she rose up, flexing her hips. Meeting his gaze, she said, "Take over, slave, and make it good. Make me come."

The chains jangled as Reyes started to pump into her, lifting his hips in quick, pleasurable jabs. She cried out, the sensation deep and hitting her just right.

*I'm close.* She trembled.

*Scream if you can. The louder the better.*

*No problem.*

He moved vampire fast, which brought her orgasm flowing in a stream of intense pleasure. She screamed long and loud, as the ecstasy flowed up her well and abdomen, gripping her stomach and tightening her breasts. She rocked her hips against what was still so hard, taking the last of her pleasure.

She leaned over him, breathing hard, her hands on the wood platform.

"You haven't lost your touch, Reyes." Sweet Dove's voice sent a sudden jolt of fear through Angelica. She'd forgotten the woman was even there.

But with his cock buried inside her, Angelica was in a vulnerable place. She started to rise up, to place herself in a more powerful position physically, but Sweet Dove's hand was on her shoulder. The woman let her power flow in a hot, painful arc. Angelica groaned, her body twisting, trying to get away. But Sweet Dove had her pinned in place with just the pressure of her hand.

"Sweet Dove, stop this right now," Reyes shouted. "We've done what you wanted."

"Even though your slave performed adequately, she has misbehaved and needs to be disciplined."

This was just what Reyes had feared, that Sweet Dove would take charge and he'd be unable to protect Angelica. "You've gotten what you wanted. Now release us both."

"Don't be a fool. We're just getting started."

"I'm not your slave anymore." He took his cue from Angelica's earlier attitude toward Sweet Dove and matched the woman's haughtiness with his own. "You owned me for a century, but those days are gone. I like being a slaver. You taught me extremely well."

Tears now flowed down Angelica's cheeks.

Sweet Dove released Angelica's shoulder and transferred the same flow of power to Reyes's chest. He barely held back a serious shout of pain, but the last thing he wanted was for Sweet Dove to gain even a moment of pleasure from hurting him.

*Reyes, fight her. I have a feeling you can break free right now.*

*What do you mean?*

*I don't know. But I sense something within you, something I've never felt before. I think it might be your Ancestral power.*

He felt it as well, that Angelica fed him in ways he didn't understand and made him want to be more than he was.

Ignoring the pulses of pain that radiated through his chest because of Sweet Dove's hold on him, he shifted his gaze to Angelica. His Ancestral power rose in response, calling to him, begging for release.

*Reyes, the sensations have grown stronger. Can you*

*tap into your power? Maybe you can even break free of these bonds.*

*I feel them, I do, but I'm not sure.* Despite his current predicament, Reyes held back. He'd fought becoming like Sweet Dove for so long, always rejecting even the idea of embracing his Ancestral power.

*Reyes, please listen to me. I can tell that Sweet Dove won't let us go. You have to do something. I feel her vile intentions like a fire on my skin.*

He knew Angelica was right, but he had to try a different tack first. Shifting his gaze to Sweet Dove, his body now trembling with pain, he said, "Let us go. You've accomplished what you'd hoped for. You made me in your image. So let me continue on my slaver path, Sweet Dove. You owe me this."

"I owe you?" She trilled her laughter. "I owe you nothing, Reyes. You owe me. You are my slave, now and forever."

Angelica's voice punched through his mind. *Find that power, Reyes. Do it now. She's gearing up.*

Angelica was right. Sweet Dove had never intended to let him go. But how the hell could he break free?

The only way he'd have the smallest chance would be to use his latent Ancestral ability. He knew that a double blood-chain would gain him instant access to his Ancestral power, but there was another way. Before the blood-chains were invented to speed up the process, those with latent Ancestral DNA could connect with the power, usually in times of great stress, and bring the ability to life.

And even Angelica sensed he could do it.

Sweet Dove began slowly increasing her power. His body shook now with pain, but he held back.

Closing his eyes, he grew very still. He dove deep

within himself, focusing on his Ancestral power. He'd never considered the possibility before of having anything to do with this power since so many of the Ancestrals were heavily corrupt, like both Engles and Sweet Dove.

But right now, his life as well as Angelica's depended on him finding the strength to break free of the preternatural chains.

As though coming from far away, he heard Sweet Dove's voice as she issued command after command. "Obey me, Reyes. Submit to me." But he ignored her.

He had to tap into his Ancestral power or he'd die on this table, because the last thing he'd ever do was place himself in Sweet Dove's hands again.

*Reyes, she'll kill you. I can feel it in her. She'll let you die before she releases you from these chains.*

He wanted to reassure Angelica, but he had to stay focused.

He reached his Ancestral power, which resided like a deep water table within his body and his soul combined.

At the same moment Angelica screamed. Sweet Dove must have figured out what he was doing and, in an attempt to distract him, was hurting Angelica again.

He struggled to stay focused. His primary instinct shouted at him to stop Sweet Dove from torturing Angelica. But what could he do if he didn't have added power?

He turned all his attention back to his Ancestral storehouse. He began to sink within it and felt an absolute rush of sensation, like nothing he'd ever known before. He felt strengthened from within and without at the same time.

A second sensation followed, like the tightening of a bond, which he knew would complete his rise to Ancestral status if he allowed it to form. But he didn't want that, at least not now. He didn't trust the Ancestrals he knew and wouldn't allow himself to become one of them.

By pulling back slightly the impulse of the bond melted away, yet he could still draw from his power. When he felt he'd gained enough to break free of the preternaturally charged shackles, he began the long glide back to consciousness.

*Angelica, if you can, reach down and grab hold of me. Can you do that?*

*Too . . . much . . . pain . . .*

She couldn't move. Sweet Dove had her trapped in pain. He knew that sensation. He'd lived with it for a century.

He flooded every muscle in his body with the stream of Ancestral power. He focused on the shackles at his arms and wrists.

As the power coalesced, Reyes opened his eyes and saw that Sweet Dove was distracted by Angelica's pain, that she was feeding off her suffering. Her attention side-tracked, in one burst of energy Reyes broke out of each shackle, rushed toward Angelica, and gathered her up in his arms.

Before Sweet Dove had the time to react, he shifted to altered flight and flew straight up and out of the cavern system.

He wanted to keep going, but he had a powerful instinct about the situation that if he didn't play this moment right, he'd get kicked out of Starlin then and there.

*Angelica, we have to return. I must speak with Sweet Dove. I'm sorry.*

She trembled in his arms. *No, I get it. You have to mend this bridge right now or she'll revoke your membership.*

*Exactly, but I hate taking you back there.*

*Please, don't worry about me. I'm siphoning your power and healing as we speak.*

He circled back quickly to Sweet Dove's torture cave and found her crumpled on the floor, against the cave wall.

As he touched down in front of Sweet Dove, the woman's eyes rolled in her head as she worked to recover.

She looked up at him, squinting. "You broke free."

"I did. You'll never own me again, Sweet Dove. But you've made me what I am today. I'm a slaver now and this slave belongs to me, to use as I see fit. I wouldn't mind becoming your lover, though, if you're open to it."

Sweet Dove sat up and her vision finally came together. "Even after I tried to enslave you, then to kill you?"

"Now that I know I can occasionally tap into my Ancestral power, that you can't hold me, I'm open to a relationship. Your ruthlessness excites me."

She got a look on her face that he'd seen before, a very calculating expression. At one time he would have shuddered, knowing that nothing good could follow. But after having escaped just now, he had no fear that she could ever capture and hold him again, not like before.

"I'll have to think about it, Reyes. I've never thought of you as true lover potential, but it might work."

"We could be excellent partners as well. I have a head for business and already have ideas about ways we could expand the Starlin enterprise."

"You did quite well for yourself after you escaped me, and I'll admit I'm impressed by that. I suppose this means I'll need to adjust my thinking, but you'll have to give me time. I've thought of you as just a slave for so long, it never occurred to me you could become something else in my life."

He used words she could understand. "But I want more, Sweet Dove, so much more. I have ambitions and want to fulfill them."

She gained her feet and stroked his arm. "I guess we're more alike than I ever understood. We'll talk again. Soon. Perhaps when the final event of the festival is over."

He almost pressed her about the one thing she'd promised, a place on the Starlin Board of Governors, but he knew he'd reached his bargaining limit.

"Yes, we'll talk after the masked ball at the Crystal Dome."

She glanced at Angelica. "And maybe by then you won't be so encumbered. It would please me if you would get rid of your slave."

Reyes actually smiled, because he had every intention of faking Angelica's death immediately following the masked ball. "That won't be a problem."

With that he returned to altered flight and shot toward his home in the Como Cavern system.

Once arrived, however, he recalled that Angelica couldn't handle flying that fast. When he touched down in his bedroom, he released her, apologizing. "I forgot. Angelica, I'm so sorry. Are you all right?"

She blinked at him. "I'm not hurting anymore. Once you tore me away from Sweet Dove, the pain stopped."

"No, I mean, don't you have a headache?" Previously when he didn't take altered flight slow enough, Angelica would experience a pounding headache that made her sick for a long time after.

She shook her head, then her eyes went wide. "Oh, because you moved so fast during altered flight." She put a hand to her head. "I'm not. I'm fine. Why?"

"I guess because I tapped into my Ancestral power."

She held both his arms and frowned slightly. "That's right. Does this mean you're an Ancestral now? Although I'm not sensing much of a difference."

He shook his head. "No, I'm not, but I did make use of the power."

Her lips curved slowly. "You broke out of those chains."

He nodded. "I did." He still couldn't believe he'd accomplished the impossible.

"While it was happening I felt so much from you, what you were going through, even while that bitch was hurting me. I could sense you reaching deep, and I knew the moment you connected. Everything began to shift. Most of the pain Sweet Dove was inflicting drifted away. And the way you looked when you were free, like a triumphant warrior."

He turned in a circle. "You have no idea how wonderful this feels. All those years with Sweet Dove I was powerless, but now I feel as though I could do anything."

"You know, there were a couple of times I didn't think we'd make it out alive."

Reyes reached for her, pulling her into his arms. He kissed her deeply. *I'm so grateful to you.*

She drew back, smiling. "We did it, Reyes, and you were damn brilliant going back like that, saying what you did just to keep her hooked."

He searched her face, her brown eyes, how wild her hair looked because of all that she'd done. "And the way you siphoned my power. You even levitated. Did you know that?"

"Oh, that's right, I did. I was just so intent on keeping Sweet Dove away from you." She shuddered.

He held her waist and pulled her close, connecting his hips with hers. "You stunned me, Angelica. She could have decimated you with one carefully aimed thought, but you faced up to her like a warrior."

"I suppose it was foolish, but I'd reached this point where I didn't care if I lived or died. I just knew I couldn't have her anywhere near you, not with you chained down."

His heart swelled as he kissed her again. He'd never been so happy, so full of excitement, in his life. After a moment he drew back, his body on fire once more. "I'm not sure you remember this, but before we went to the masked ball I promised you something, and right now I intend to deliver."

She looked wonderfully confused. "What's that?"

"Maybe I should just show you."

He lifted her in his arms and carried her to the bed. Throwing the comforter back, he settled her near the edge.

"Should I get out of this costume?" Her hand fell to the bustier.

He shook his head. "Not yet, because *we'll* be taking care of you."

She put a hand to her chest, her eyes widening. "What do you mean, 'we'?"

# CHAPTER 14

Desire poured through Angelica, a rush of sensation that brought a warm flush to her cheeks. She remembered now. Reyes had spoken about being able to split into two beings.

Apparently he was going to do that now, but she couldn't imagine what it would be like to have two Reyeses tending to her.

Her breathing grew labored as he stepped away from the bed. She felt his power sing through the blood-chains. As she watched him closely, he became a blur first, then suddenly there were two of him.

The first one moved toward her. "I'm the primary and

I'll do the speaking. My secondary self just engages. So what I want to know first is, what's your pleasure?"

Her lips parted, but her mind got jammed with all the images of the ways she wanted to touch him, or rather them, and to be touched. Finally she just shook her head. "I don't know. Everything."

Reyes smiled, a wonderful smirk that let her know she was in for an extraordinary treat.

More of Reyes, a lot more.

His primary self drew up close and leaned down to her kiss her, his hands fondling the swell of her breasts. After a moment he drew back, moving his hands lower. "You have one of the smallest waists I've ever seen."

"I like your hands around me."

When he rose up unexpectedly, his secondary self, now at the foot of the bed, levitated just enough to catch her at her waist as well, only he dragged her to the end of the bed. He began working the leather pants off her hips.

Angelica knew where this was headed, and desire streamed once more. Reyes leaned close, and while his secondary self continued to work the strange leather pants off her, Reyes kissed the swell of her breasts. He slid one hand beneath the lace, fondling her, then finally freed each nipple from the lace. He settled in to nurse on her, which of course caused flames of pleasure between her legs.

When the secondary Reyes had removed her stilettos and the snug pants, he moved between her legs. She cried out as his mouth settled on her down low and he began to suck.

The pleasure of her nipples and her clitoris being sucked at the same time had her on the brink so fast, she clutched at the sheet beneath her fingers. The sounds of the suckling alone were almost too much.

"Reyes, what are you doing to me?"

He kept tugging on her nipple. *How close are you? Can you come like this?*

*Very close and yes, it would take so little.*

At the exact same moment, both Reyeses sped up their movements, the secondary's tongue flicking her down low so fast that she was coming before she knew what was happening.

She released a series of cries and gasps. Because she'd orgasmed so recently, her flesh was still tender, which made the sensation sharper and even better than before.

She writhed on the bed.

Both Reyeses slowed their movements, but continued to lave her low and kiss and suckle her breasts in turn. After about a minute they settled in as before, and began nursing on her in earnest in both locations.

She whimpered and grabbed at his shoulders with one hand and reached low to caress his head with her other.

*Reyes,* she whispered through his mind.

And again he sped up suckling her nipple fast and at the same time flicking her with his tongue low. Just like that, yet another orgasm sped through her so that she groaned and arched her neck. She couldn't believe this was happening.

This time he eased back from both places, watching her and smiling. "What would you like now?"

She glanced from one to the other. "How are you doing this?"

He shrugged. "I can battle like this as well, but I don't really know the physics. I just can."

"I guess I don't really care. I love having two of you here, tending to me. Come close, one on each side."

He lifted her toward the center of the bed. The secondary Reyes stretched out on her left, the primary on her right.

She kissed each of them in turns, two mouths to savor, two bodies. Using her hands, she once more savored his muscular dips and swells. She took her time, sucking on nipples and pecs, tracing her tongue down abdomens.

Two cocks as well.

She rose up on her knees and took one in each hand, rubbing slowly, thumbing each crown. She watched their shared pleasure as each gaze roved her chest, the swell of her breasts.

She released their cocks and unhooked her bustier, letting her breasts free. Each sat up and took a breast. Two mouths feasted on her, causing her to clench hard between her legs.

She hadn't thought making love with Reyes could get better, yet here she was, ready to lose her mind from so much pleasure.

"Make love to me," she whispered, her voice hoarse.

Each lay back down, and she resumed her place between them. The primary Reyes pulled her toward him, kissing her as he moved his cock between her legs. He angled his hips and found her entrance, pushing inside.

She cried out. He felt so good buried inside her.

The Reyes at her back kissed her neck, her shoulders, and drifted his lips to her buttocks. He nibbled and licked until she was panting.

"Do you want my blood?" she asked.

Both men groaned.

The one now behind her positioned himself at her neck

and bit down with his fangs, then began to suck. In front of her, Reyes held an arm over her chest, keeping her in place. At the same time he slowly rocked his hips into her, driving his cock in and out. He kissed her eyelids, her cheeks, her lips.

She was overcome with sensation, especially when the secondary Reyes moved in closer, nestling his thick cock between the cleft of her bottom. He rubbed himself in quickening thrusts. She reached behind her to caress his shoulder.

*Reyes, this is so wonderful. And I'm close again.*

*So am I. Your blood is like heaven, and feeling your body in so many places at the same time is erotic as hell.*

*Faster.*

Both men moved faster, sucked harder. The primary Reyes thrust his tongue deep into her mouth, the secondary, wedged between her cheeks, used the pressure to work his cock.

Suddenly ecstasy arrived, like a powerful wave crashing down on her. They were three, moving as one, shouting, screaming, crying out. The secondary Reyes moved swiftly behind, his cock tight between her butt cheeks and jerking hard. Primary Reyes curled his hips, pumping between her legs in quick thrusts, shouting as he came. She'd never known such pleasure.

And the sensation kept rolling, so that the bed shook and her heart ached. She loved this so much, being surrounded by two powerful male bodies, both Reyeses. Affection, maybe even love, flowed through her as she reached the pinnacle once more.

Was this love? Did she love the man who drank her blood and plowed into her body in the most wonderful way?

She felt possessed, even enchanted, by the vampire holding her captive in his arms.

Only after a long euphoric minute did the bed begin to settle.

Angelica breathed hard, as did both men.

A soft vibration ran through Reyes, and she watched as the secondary form joined the primary and became one body again. Angelica could barely keep her eyes open as Reyes rolled her onto her back. She felt as though she could float, and her mind was suffused with a delicate euphoria that kept every thought at bay.

She savored the fact that Reyes was still buried deep inside her, that in this moment they were one, they were equals, they were bound.

She wrapped him up in her arms and he kissed her repeatedly. There was an eternal feel to the moment, helping her to believe that no matter what happened in the coming days or weeks, this time with Reyes could never be taken away from her.

*This was wonderful.*

He drew back, still connected low, and thumbed her cheek. "I feel the same way. You've changed everything for me, Angelica, and for that I'll always be grateful."

He made love to her again and again that night. And more than once, she fell into deep conversation with him about his family life and his home in Venezuela where he'd grown up. He shared that when he'd made his fortune and bought the property back, he'd also worked to retrieve all their family possessions, many of which went back several centuries.

His mother's family was Celtic with red hair and blue eyes, though his father had a Spanish heritage, which explained Reyes's coloring: dark hair, light eyes. "My mother had a large collection of small silver boxes, handed down through generations. I was able to get most of them back."

"They have great meaning to you."

"My mother treasured them, so yes, great meaning."

Angelica felt an odd tingling sensation pass through her. "What was her name?"

"Faylen. She had dark auburn hair and was very beautiful."

"I have no doubt." But there it was again, some kind of tingling, but she didn't know what it was, like a memory that just wouldn't surface. He had told her that Faylen had died shortly after Sweet Dove had enslaved Reyes, yet something about that nagged at Angelica. She just didn't know why.

The conversation moved on, and she forgot about the odd sensation. Reyes told her about the rock shelf that overlooked a rich tropical valley below, and she wished she could see his South American home. But she probably wouldn't. She'd be going home soon, right after the last Starlin event at the Crystal Dome.

Over the next couple of weeks and through the continuous stream of Starlin events, she accompanied Reyes to a host of parties. They stayed only long enough to support Reyes's cover as a slaver before leaving.

Reyes would then take her back to his bedroom and, before long, back to his bed.

She was sore in the best way and treasured every joining, though she tried hard not to think about the fact that soon she would be heading home, back to California. Although it was likely Reyes would insist on relocating both her and her mother to a different state. He feared someone from Starlin would happen to see her and the nightmare would start all over again.

How far away that world seemed to her now: her simple accountant's life, her mother's infirm condition, the boredom she'd endured in her day-to-day routine. The thought of returning didn't hold even a spark of interest for her, except to be with her mother. And she really hated the thought that once she left Reyes's world, he might be forced to resume some sort of physical relationship with Sweet Dove in order to gain access to the information he needed to take Starlin down.

She shuddered at the thought.

Each day, usually at mealtime, Reyes would spend an hour or two on the Starlin Web site to familiarize himself with the organization. He'd also exchanged several e-mails with Sweet Dove since he'd broken out of his chains.

Angelica read the e-mails as well, and would have been appalled by the sadistic nature of the content if she hadn't come to understand how vile Sweet Dove really was.

Reyes continued to play Sweet Dove by tempting her with explicit, sexual suggestions, but at the same time dwelling on the importance of an equal partnership with her. Sweet Dove in turn seemed to have gotten over her rage that Reyes had escaped her shackles and would never be returning to her as her slave.

Angelica knew the careful line Reyes walked with Sweet Dove. He had to convince her that acting as a consensual partner could be more fulfilling than the slave-slaver relationship Sweet Dove really wanted. And with each exchange Sweet Dove seemed to be relenting a little more.

It seemed Sweet Dove wanted him even more, now that she couldn't have him.

The day before the masked ball at the Crystal Dome, the finale for the three weeks of Starlin events, Reyes surfaced from studying the organization's Web site. He sat at the table in the sitting room, his laptop open. "I think we need to do something to corroborate my plan to fake your death following the masquerade tomorrow night."

Angelica didn't mind discussing the details, but she had no heart for thinking about how soon she'd be separating from Reyes.

She sat on the nearby couch, sewing a long black cat's tail onto the back of her bustier. The simple costume would serve for the masked ball: bustier and thong, a headband with a pair of cat's ears, a few whiskers glued to her face. But the tail had come loose.

Without looking up at him, she asked, "You mean something beyond telling your fellow sadists that you got overzealous in one of our bondage sessions and I died?"

He drummed his fingers on the table. "I think I have to add something. I mean, part of the way I kept Engles away from you all this time was by making it clear I didn't hurry the torturing of my slaves."

Remembering this part of his charade, she smiled a little. "You mean all those times you boasted about liking to 'season your meat over a long period of time'?"

He shook his head and she could feel his dismay through the shared chains. "I had to say something to explain your lack of bruises and cuts, and for the most part I think it worked."

Angelica tied the final knot, then set the thread and needle aside. She gave a tug on the tail and, satisfied, finally met his gaze. "So what do you have in mind?"

"I think I know a way we can effectively create some realistic bruising without actually hurting you."

Her lips curved. "Is this a new Ancestral power you haven't told me about?"

He returned her smile, and for just a moment she was caught all over again. He was gorgeous when he smiled, and his blue eyes lit up in a way that actually made her heart hurt. For the first time she realized she really didn't want to leave Reyes.

He answered her question. "No, this has nothing to do with any newly acquired abilities from having tapped into my Ancestral power for that very brief moment. Actually this is a trick I once saw Eve do. She has a way of using makeup to create exactly this kind of effect." As the owner of the Ruby Cave and a famous stage personality in the sex-club trade, Eve would know all the tricks.

"Does she actually add bruising for her performances?" From what Reyes had told her, Eve might be into BDSM, but she had strict rules governing her shows.

"No, she doesn't believe in any kind of torture, just dominance. But on Halloween she likes to plant a few zombies in her audience just for fun, and let me tell you those monsters look real."

Angelica smoothed her hand down the soft cat's tail. "And after I'm all dressed up in black-and-blue, you'll show me off at the masked ball."

"I think it would add to my credibility since I intend to fake your death. If it looks like I've lost control with you before, the whole thing will be more plausible when I suddenly announce that I lost it again in one of my bondage sessions and you didn't make it."

Angelica thought for a moment. "You know, I think this is a really good idea. And after the masked ball, we can come straight back here and set the stage in your game room. Maybe you could hang me from the chains or something."

He nodded. "That's an excellent idea. And with the right makeup, trust me, you'd look really dead." He thought for a moment. "Afterward, I could post the pics on the Starlin Web site, maybe blog about it. Yep, this will go a long way to support my claims that I've killed you and dumped you in the ocean."

Angelica barely blinked about the dumping part. Reyes had told her more than once that the middle of the ocean had become the favorite disposal ground for the sadist set.

With the matter settled Reyes opened the laptop once more, but a minute later he gave a shout of triumph. "Listen to this. Sweet Dove has agreed to meet with me in private during the masked ball. She wants to begin discussions about our long-term relationship on both a business and a personal level." He turned to meet her gaze. "Angelica, she's agreed to bring me in as a partner. Do you know what this means?"

She felt his excitement and couldn't help but smile. "You'll have access to all the information you'll need to tear down Starlin."

"That's exactly what it means."

But Angelica felt uneasy. She didn't trust Sweet Dove, and something about the proposed meeting made her skin crawl.

The next night, with a few hours to go before the masked ball, Reyes's housekeeper informed him that Eve had arrived.

Reyes had known Eve a long time, decades in fact. She was one of the key attractions at the Erotic Passage, a vast sex-club network in the Como Cavern system which he had often visited over the years. He counted her as a friend, and she was one of the few people in his world he trusted without question.

With Angelica beside him, he greeted the blond beauty.

She was an Amazonian type and, with stilettos on, was even taller than Reyes. She wore her long blond hair held away from her face with a simple headband. Even without her usually extravagant stage makeup she was a striking beauty, with ice-blue cat eyes, a straight nose, strong cheekbones, and arched brows. She had a direct way of looking at everyone that spoke of her confidence.

She kissed Reyes on each cheek, then turned to offer her hand to Angelica. "I'm Eve. I saw what you did for Reyes at the after-auction party, just after the performance of my acting troupe, when he'd mentally checked out. You did good." She smiled, showing lovely straight teeth. "But you really should bind him to a table, wear a little leather, make use of a flogger." She broke off, glancing from one to the other. "Wait a minute. What's with those smiles?"

Reyes took Angelica's hand and shook his head. "Can't get much past you." Going through the recent experience with Angelica had changed something for him, as though breaking free of the chains had truly ended the decades of slavery for him.

Eve's smile broadened. "So you really did it? I'd love some details."

Reyes wagged his finger. "Not gonna happen. But you were right. It worked for both of us, I think." He looked down at Angelica who smiled up at him, her eyes shining. They'd escaped death together on that table, but it was all the lovemaking afterward, day after day, that had his heart aching right now.

"So where would you like to do this?" Eve glanced around.

Reyes gestured toward the staircase. "How about we take this to my bedroom?"

"Now that's a place I've begged to see all this time. I'm honored."

Reyes had refused a dozen entreaties to share Eve's bed. He valued her friendship too much to cloud it with sex, even though she'd assured him repeatedly that she wasn't a clingy sort and would never have had expectations of him beyond sex.

Had he been tempted? Hell, yes, but right now he was glad he'd stuck to his guns.

He pulled Angelica close to his side, lifting her off her feet, then levitated to the second story, Eve close behind.

Once within he closed the door, and after settling both Eve and Angelica in the sitting room, he swore Eve to secrecy. He then told her about his desire and efforts to destroy the Starlin Group.

Eve listened wide-eyed. "So let me understand. You bought Angelica at auction and now both of you are pretending to support a slave-slaver relationship because you're undercover?"

"Exactly. But this group is heavy into torture, and I need some kind of proof that I've been hurting Angelica or I won't be able to move higher up in the organization." Though the last bit wasn't the entire truth, given that he'd soon be Sweet Dove's partner, he felt it necessary to keep Eve in the dark, especially where Sweet Dove was concerned. The less she knew, the better.

Eve leaned close to Reyes. "I want you to know how much I appreciate that you're going after Starlin. I never said anything all this time about the company you've kept, but now I understand and I'm so proud of what you're doing." She included Angelica as well, grabbing for her hand and giving a squeeze. "For what you're both trying to accomplish."

Reyes nodded. "The moment I escaped my own slavery, I set my mind to it."

Eve nodded several times, but said nothing more. Reyes let the moment breathe as his own dedication to the mission filled his mind all over again. Eve often purchased slaves, but always with the end goal of setting them free. They were like-minded.

Finally he asked, "So you think you can create some realistic bruising?"

Eve rose to her feet and placed her oversized makeup case on the table, then turned to look Angelica over. "This will work best and be more accurate if the bruises are all over the body, which means, my dear, that you'll need to take your clothes off. You can keep your underwear on."

"Whatever it takes." Angelica reached down and slid the long T-shirt she wore over her head, kicked off her shoes, then stripped out of her pants.

A shiver went through Reyes. He'd made love to her a lot over the past two weeks, but the sight of her wearing just her bra and a very sheer black thong worked on him all over again.

Angelica turned toward him, her cheeks flushed. She covered the blood-chain at her neck with her fingers. "What's going on?" But she laughed.

He shook his head back and forth several times. "It's just that . . . what can I say . . . I mean look at you . . ." He waved a hand toward her several times, looking her up and down.

Eve laughed at him and said, "Reyes, maybe you could focus on some paperwork or something."

He cleared his throat, grabbed his laptop, and moved to a nearby club chair. "I'll leave you to it."

Of course he might have had his gaze glued to his laptop screen, but he could still hear the two women.

Eve said, "There's just one thing. To make this as realistic as possible, I should add a preternatural charge to each bruise. It'll cause some mild discomfort, but the charge will invade the skin and deepen the appearance of the wound."

Reyes glanced at Eve and intervened. "No. I don't want anything like that. You're not to hurt Angelica."

But Angelica pivoted slightly in his direction. "Nonsense. We want this to be realistic. I say do it."

Eve smiled. "I like your spirit. How about I try out a preternatural punch, then you can tell me how many of these you think you can take."

"Done."

"Hey," Reyes called out, trying to stop the madness. "Don't I get a say?"

But the women ignored him. Eve placed her fist against Angelica's abdomen and let loose, but Angelica barely flinched.

"Easy-peasy," Angelica said. She touched her abdomen. "That hurt a little, but look at the redness." She glanced at Reyes. "I can take it, really I can. This isn't bad at all. I just wish I'd known about this technique. We could have done this sooner, starting at the after-auction party."

"Fine," Reyes said, though he scowled.

Angelica turned back to Eve. "Try a cut this time."

At that Reyes jumped from his seat, setting his laptop

aside, and drew close to Angelica once more. "I'm drawing the line. No cuts."

Both women stared at him, brows raised.

"I'm serious."

Eve exchanged a glance with Angelica. "We can see that."

"How about just one cut?" Angelica suggested.

Reyes shook his head. "What's with you?"

"It's simple. We've got Scorpion's attention and we should capitalize on that." Even though Sweet Dove was Scorpion, he knew Angelica couldn't mention Sweet Dove's name without arousing Eve's curiosity. And right now Reyes didn't want anyone to know about Sweet Dove. Getting as close as he could to the woman was the key to gaining access to Starlin's internal organization. Once he had that information, he could take Starlin down piece by piece.

But he hated the thought of Angelica being cut in any way.

Reyes turned to Angelica. "Please don't do this. I can't explain it, but I don't want to see you cut. Maybe you can handle it, but I can't. The bruises will be hard enough for me to look at."

Angelica put her hand on his face. "Fine, no cuts, not even fake ones. I wasn't thinking of how this might affect you, only of the end result."

She reached up and kissed him, a gesture that brought his breath up short. He wanted more and again became acutely aware that she wore only a bra and a miniscule thong.

If Eve hadn't been in the room . . .

Angelica smiled. "Go back to your laptop because right now my blood-chain is singing."

He shook his head, turning away from her once more, and headed back to his chair to explore the latest posts on the Starlin Web site.

With each charged punch, Angelica took a deep breath and let the resulting pain flow out of her. Eve would then spread on a layer of makeup in different shades of purple, blue, gray, and even some pink. Some of the splotches were small and others large to indicate she'd been hit by different kinds of objects.

When Eve was satisfied with the look of each bruise she added another preternatural charge, which would act like a tattoo and make the effect semipermanent. A series of showers would fade and then eventually cause the wounds to disappear.

Adding a dusting of light cream powder to Angelica's face and just a hint of blue beneath her eyes gave the impression that Angelica had been brutalized.

When Eve was done Angelica turned toward Reyes. "So how do I look? Damaged enough?"

Reyes, who'd been buried in the laptop and scowling, glanced up. If she'd had any doubt how well Eve had done, Reyes's horrified reaction as he stood up and nearly dropped his laptop spoke of the success of the project.

"Holy shit," he murmured. "Are you all right?"

"Of course I am. Eve didn't really hurt me." Angelica turned toward Eve. "She's just that good."

"I am," Eve said. Having packed up her case, she closed it with a snap. "Sorry, kids, but I have to go. I have a performance in an hour and my own makeup to do." She turned toward Angelica. "You're a damn fine soldier and I'm proud to have known you. I hope you'll stick around, and if you're smart, you'll get Reyes to take on the double-chains. Which reminds me . . ."

Eve pulled out the bottom drawer of the large case, and withdrew a familiar-looking red leather box. Before Eve could tell her what was inside, Angelica's single chain vibrated heavily. "Wait. You've got the double-chains in there, don't you? The ones that would take Reyes to Ancestral in the blink of an eye."

"Yes, I do." Eve extended the case to her.

But before Angelica could lift the lid to see what the chains even looked like, Reyes moved in and grabbed the box.

He barked at Eve. "How the hell did you get these and why would you think I'd want them here even for a second? Or that Angelica would want a permanent relationship with me? And you know how I feel about the Ancestral calling."

Angelica stared up at him. She knew he'd resisted rising to Ancestral status for a long time, but she'd never seen him so worked up.

Eve said, "Not all Ancestrals are bad, and a majority of the traditions are worth reviving. I use some of the ancient Ancestral chants in my shows, you know I do. Our society has just hit a bad stretch, but that will change, especially with men like you taking charge. The Ancestrals at the top of the slaver food chain have brought us all down. They've perverted the use and meaning of their power. And though I appreciate that you've keep me ignorant of much of what's going on within the Starlin slaver organization, and I do know it's for my own protection, I'm convinced you'll need a lot more power to face them. You should at least consider embracing your Ancestral status."

Reyes stared at the box, shaking his head. "Not gonna happen. And I still don't understand how you even got these."

"Rumy sent them over and told me to give them to you the next time I saw you. And no, I don't know how he got them or how he obtained your blood to make them. But you know Rumy. He's so well-connected because of owning the entire Erotic Passage network that I've come to believe he could do anything he set his mind to."

"You should just take them back."

When he shoved them at Eve, however, Angelica took hold of the box, wrested it from Reyes's grip, and pressed it to her chest.

She stepped away from him, lowering her chin. "I don't care what you say, we're keeping these. It doesn't mean we have to use them, but just in case this whole damn thing goes south, I want them close by. Got it?"

Reyes blinked a couple of times, his mouth agape. "I'll ask again, what's gotten into you?"

"I'm not sure I can explain. But when you were bound in those horrible, rusted, smelly chains, I felt your Ancestral power. It was beautiful and I didn't fear you at all. And Eve's right. Your world needs men like you, good men, full of this kind of power and taking charge."

He took on his stubborn look, the one that moved his jaw from side to side as he ground his molars. "Fine, keep them. But it doesn't mean I intend to put them on anytime soon."

"And I would never force you to, but I'm with Eve. I think you should consider rising to Ancestral status. I know you, Reyes. I know your heart, your character, everything you are. To me, you will always be the young man with a dozen stacks of books in his room intent on changing your world. That's the man who should wear the double bonding chains."

Reyes held her gaze for a long moment, and the chain at her neck vibrated with a new emotion, something she had trouble identifying. But it fell somewhere close to Reyes being stunned by what she'd just said. She knew he had trouble believing that anyone could think highly of him. She understood the cause as well, which made her furious with Sweet Dove all over again.

Reyes glanced down at the box she held in her hands and, though he grimaced, muttered, "Fine. I'll think about it." To Eve he added, "Thanks for bringing them by."

Eve kissed Reyes on the cheek. "Hang in there."

Turning to Angelica, she did the same, adding, "Glad you're here taking care of our guy. If you can stomach it, stick around. We can use you right now." With that she stepped away, waved to each of them, then shifted to altered flight.

Angelica watched her disappear through Reyes's desk. She was now so used to seeing people come and go like ghosts that she barely blinked.

For some reason, as she turned back to Reyes, it hit her that after tonight's gala event she and Reyes would start the process of separating. She'd always known this moment would come, but after making love with him as much as she had over the past couple of weeks, she didn't want to leave. In fact it felt as though they were just getting started.

But on so many levels she'd already pushed the bounds of her own safety, and to continue on past the final event would really be tempting fate.

She was going to suggest they get ready for the masked ball when Reyes took the box from her and set it on the table. He then took hold of her hands. "It's really hard for me to see you like this, even if the bruises are mostly fake."

"I know. But Eve did a wonderful job, and it will give credence to the upcoming ruse that we'll be staging."

Reyes stared into her familiar warm brown eyes and for some inexplicable reason his chest grew abnormally tight and his throat hurt. He repressed a heavy sigh as he nodded. "I guess our time together is almost over. It's been wonderful, Angelica, to have you with me, I want you to know that. And I'll take every precaution to keep you and your mother safe, and if we need to I'll help relocate you both to a different part of the country."

"I know you will." Her gaze flitted away from his, then back. "But I'll miss you, more than I can say. I just wish this wasn't such a mess, I'd want to stay otherwise."

"You would?" He couldn't explain exactly how he felt or why he was so surprised. From the first, Angelica had expressed admiration for him, and sharing his bed with her over the past couple of weeks had been one of the finest experiences of his life. He'd come to know every inch of her body, and he loved looking deep into her eyes when he brought her to ecstasy or when his own body shook with passion.

The blood-chains he shared with her might have enhanced the experience, but the bond couldn't manufacture what wasn't there. And right now, as he held her gaze, he wished that he could build a life with her.

But that was impossible. His body and soul were deeply scarred, brutalized by his captivity. He wasn't truly fit to be with a woman. Besides, all his energy for years to come had to be focused on making his world right.

Taking Angelica home would relieve him of the false hope her presence in his life continually pressed on him, and he'd be better able to fulfill his Starlin takedown goals without her.

Putting his relationship with her back into its careful mental compartment, Reyes took a long look at all the bruises, his expression solemn. "These have such a realistic appearance. Are you sure you're okay? You're not hurt?"

"I'm fine. And remember, I'm siphoning your power all the time. I might not heal as fast as you do, but I can feel a low level of healing going on right now."

He touched her shoulder. "I can see that you are, but I wish now I'd never suggested this."

Angelica shook her head. "I completely disagree. This will cement your reputation, especially after all the fuss you made about 'seasoned meat' and 'auctioning me off at my six-month transition.'" She shuddered.

He smiled down at her, then pulled her into his arms. He kissed her, a deep penetrating kiss. He wanted her to feel just how much he appreciated all that she'd done, especially how bravely she'd carried off her role as his slave from the time he'd bought her at auction.

Drawing back slightly, but still holding her close, he said, "You've done so well. I've said this often, but you've amazed me. You've shown such tremendous courage, when you should have fallen apart. And now this, letting yourself essentially take on some tattoos to prove that I'm into the lifestyle."

She flung her arms around his neck and kissed him hard in return. He loved this about Angelica, that she never held back, not in her role as his slave, not in bed, not in her obvious affection for him.

The word *love* rolled around in his head as he held her tightly. He didn't want to let her go, and as the kiss continued he once more let her feel the depth of his admiration for her.

His body heated up, and the cooing sounds she made let him know he could have carried her then and there back to the bed. But he feared he'd forget all about the ball and, because Sweet Dove was expecting him, he had to go.

The final act must be played out.

Drawing back slowly and reluctantly, Reyes pressed his forehead to hers. "I will miss you more than I can say."

"I know. Same here." She released a heavy sigh, then added, "I guess we'd better get ready for the ball."

An hour later he flew Angelica to the Crystal Dome, a place he'd never been before, though it was legendary in Starlin circles. The cavern was magnificent and huge, a giant geode of white crystal, carved and polished for the most part, with a few crystals left upright for unique seating and decor.

The entire ceiling was a smooth dome, lit from behind, an engineering feat all by itself.

He walked her through the archway, then drew her off to the side. She wore a simple cat's costume, adding at the last minute a pair of long black gloves, and he'd opted for a bodyguard look with a snug black T-shirt, leather pants, steel-toed boots, and a simple black mask.

The din from the ball in full swing made conversation impossible except through telepathy.

Angelica squeezed his arm. *This place is amazing and so beautiful. Too bad this group has charge of the room.*

He knew what she meant. They stood just to the side of the opening against the wall. The floor sloped in an easy grade toward a low stage about thirty yards distant where the band stood in disarray, guitars on the floor.

*Is everyone here drunk?* she asked.

*Or high.*

*I would say I'm disgusted, but I need a harsher word. I just don't think there is one. All this beauty wasted on such a useless set of people.*

*Just keep your eyes lowered if you can.*

*Will do.*

Though he was once again attached to Angelica with a leash, he held her arm tightly and kept her close to him. They'd arrived at the Crystal Dome late, hoping to make an entrance, but instead found a drunken orgy in progress and not much dancing.

Half the band was engaged in either fellatio or full-on intercourse.

As though attempting to earn his keep, the drummer sustained a sultry rhythm.

Most of the slaves were naked, bruised, and cut-up.

Screams rang out here and there.

*This is the finale?* Angelica glanced around, but scowled. *If anyone throws up on me, we're outta here.*

*I see Engles. He's waving to us from the left of the stage and he's looking you over. Ah, now he's smiling and nodding. He approves of the bruises.*

*Bastard! And could he have worn a larger codpiece for his Renaissance costume? I believe I now understand the concept of hatred. I detest that man.*

Reyes leaned close. *Just keep the fire from your eyes.* He then kissed her ear, nibbling. *Although that fire is my favorite part of who you are.*

*Reyes.*

Her voice, whispering his name through his mind,

put a fist around his heart that squeezed hard. He would miss that as well, the woman speaking telepathically with him.

*Do we have to go to Engles?* she asked. *Here's a thought. Maybe you should just take me back to bed and keep me there for, oh, I don't know, the next century.*

*Don't tempt me.* And he was tempted, especially since she wore a short black bustier and thong, as well as long black fingerless gloves. Her black cat costume consisted of a pair of ears, a few whiskers glued to her cheeks, and a tail she kept wrapped around her arm the way she'd once wrapped up her auction scarf. He remembered her then, completely nude, her eyes flashing with rage against the audience, and yes, he was tempted.

*Engles will break his arm waving that hard at us.*

Reyes shifted his attention back to Engles. He'd be meeting with Sweet Dove soon. *I think we've been summoned.*

*We'll head in his direction.*

But as they began to move, Angelica squeezed his arm. *Reyes, I'm getting one of those visions again. What did you call them?*

*A revisiting vision. You mean about this place?*

*Nearby, in fact very close.*

Reyes's heart rate started to climb. Every time Angelica had experienced a vision, he'd learned something important.

*Tell me which way to go. Engles will just have to wait.*

*Here to the left.*

Reyes touched the wall, but the smooth crystal was a solid panel all the way across. *I'm not seeing a door anywhere along here.*

*Reyes, my head is practically spinning. Can you shift*

*to altered flight and pass through? What I need to see is on the other side of the wall.*

*I'll take it slow.* Even though Engles would probably come after them, Reyes moved slowly and passed into a series of rooms, a long hallway between. *This looks like an accounting setup. Shit, Angelica, I think this is the Starlin Group's main offices.*

*I think you're right. Do you see the arched doorway at the end? We need to go there. Now.*

Reyes followed Angelica's directions, moving faster now. He felt it as well, a profound sense of urgency.

The archway led to a room with a long conference table and tall padded chairs. A wall of bookshelves opposite and a waterfall at the far left end told Reyes exactly where he was.

*I've seen pictures of this place on the Starlin Web site. This is where the Board of Governors meets.* He remained in altered flight, hovering at the end of the table.

This was the hub of the organization, in the outer offices and here in this conference room.

*Reyes, I can't explain it, but I think we're close to Sweet Dove's office. I have a strong sense of her, that the vision is about her but that we need to be in her space to see it.*

*Just tell me which way to go.*

He felt Angelica grow very still. *Pass through the waterfall.*

Reyes's heart pounded now as he put them both in motion. He approached the water, then passed through the solid rock wall behind it. When he reached the other side he knew he'd arrived at the end point of his mission.

Angelica confirmed his suspicion. *This is Sweet Dove's office. I can feel it with every bone in my body.*

He set them both down on what proved to be an antique Turkish carpet over a gray-and-cream marble floor. His eye was drawn upward first, to a long, dangerous fissure in the carved rock ceiling above. If that kind of breach in the rock had been in any of his properties, he would have brought in an engineer to look it over.

But it wasn't the tall ceiling that held his attention. Suspended from the rock, over the center of the space, was a large metal chandelier, made up of antique swords hanging free in places and welded together in others. A large antique desk with scrolled legs sat to the side, another waterfall adjacent. To the right of the desk was a chaise longue and a pair of black leather chairs.

This was a woman's room.

He could feel that Sweet Dove had been here, even recently.

Angelica trembled in his arms. The vision was coming to her. "Reyes," she said softly. "Why were we able to get into this room? Wouldn't Sweet Dove have set up all kinds of security measures to keep people from flying in here?"

"Yes, I suppose she would." He felt uneasy suddenly.

Angelica's sudden swift intake of breath told him the vision had arrived. As soon as it ended, he'd get her out of the office.

Then his gaze landed on the very thing he'd been after all this time.

In the center of Sweet Dove's desk sat a large laptop. He knew with every fiber of his being that the files in this computer held the information he'd need to destroy Starlin.

# CHAPTER 15

Caught in the vision, Angelica saw Sweet Dove reclining on the chaise longue, fingering the curls at the top of her head. She wore a white linen dress of some kind and was chatting with Engles.

He rocked the tumbler in his hand. "And all this time you were Scorpion. I'm dumbfounded, yet in a way, not surprised. You've always had a clever mind. But why have you told me now?"

"Because I'm drawing Reyes into my net once more, but he won't be satisfied just being my slave. He insists on being my lover, and you were right, his ambitions are even larger than your own. You've done well, Engles, and I want to reward you properly."

"Then make me a partner."

Sweet Dove shook her head. "Not yet, but I may in time. Just keep serving me as you have been. And don't pout. You'll get your reward, the one you've been craving for three weeks now. Reyes has hardly touched her, you know. You would have loved seeing how masterful she was on my table."

"I've enjoyed your retelling of the moment again and again. The images are very real in my mind." Engles sipped his drink. "But how did you restrain yourself with Angelica? A slave, speaking to you in that manner? Addressing you as an equal?"

"I was thinking of you, of course. I wanted to kill her with my bare hands for standing up to me, but she'll suffer infinitely worse in your care. That's how I resisted the impulse to lay waste to her then and there." Her small bow lips curved. "You'll enjoy her immensely, Engles, and she will fight you to the very end, to her rasping, dying breath."

Engles's hand trembled and the ice cubes rattled.

It was hard for Angelica to stay connected to the vision when one of the principal players lusted to torture and kill her and the other clearly wanted her dead. But she stayed put, knowing that she would learn something vital.

Engles's nostrils flared. "So you intend to make him your partner in Starlin, don't you?"

"We'll be partners in everything . . . eventually."

Engles glanced at the desk. "I can't believe you leave your laptop just sitting there."

"No one can get into my office without my allowing it."

"But it contains everything about our organization."

Sweet Dove smiled. "Every particle of space surrounding my office is preternaturally charged. I repeat, no one can get in unless I will it so."

Angelica didn't understand. She knew that Sweet Dove had tremendous Ancestral power, and that if she said the space was secured through her power, then it was.

So how had Reyes managed to invade this room?

Then it all made sense: *the revisiting vision had become the trap.*

At that moment Sweet Dove turned in Angelica's direction, confirming her suspicion. Angelica felt a stream of power aimed toward her, and the next thing she knew she made actual eye contact with Sweet Dove, from the past.

She had to warn Reyes, had to get him out of there. Sweet Dove had used Angelica to lure Reyes to her offices through her revisiting vision power.

At that moment the vision terminated so abruptly that Angelica's neck snapped back. When she returned to herself, she was lying on the floor on top of Reyes. He had a blank look on his face, and she couldn't reach him telepathically.

The trap had been sprung.

She smelled something sickly sweet in the air, the same thing she'd smelled when she'd been abducted outside the Ocean Club.

She only had one trick left. As her consciousness began to fade, she reached inside her left glove, pulled out one of the Ancestral double blood-chains, and shoved it down Reyes's T-shirt.

Hands grabbed her shoulders, pulling her away from him.

She heard Engles's voice from behind her. "You're mine now, sweetheart. Everything is as it should be. And if you're good, you'll know pleasure."

Her vision began to blur, then fade, and suddenly she was falling.

Reyes awoke with a burning sensation at his waist he couldn't pinpoint. His mind felt fuzzy, like it had been messed with, an all-too-familiar sensation from decades ago.

He couldn't even open his eyes.

He forced himself to concentrate, to gain a sense of where he was. He couldn't remember exactly what had happened. One moment he'd had his arm around Angelica, and the next he'd fallen to the carpet in Sweet Dove's office.

So where was Angelica?

Adrenaline spiked and finally he could open his eyes. Sweet Dove's preternatural charge flowed through him once more, keeping him chained to the same platform he'd escaped a couple of weeks ago. The smell of old blood and sex returned to him.

He still wore his clothes, though the strange pain at his waist grew stronger, as though something was burning a hole in his skin.

He rolled his head from side to side, trying to force his mind to clear, especially in the face of the reality that the woman he loathed had captured him again.

He had to escape. He had to find Angelica.

Where was she?

He glanced around the room, but she wasn't there.

He tried to contact her telepathically, but nothing returned.

Then he understood two things: Sweet Dove had removed their single-bonding blood-chains, and she'd given Angelica to Engles.

\* \* \*

Angelica awoke slowly. Her head was killing her, and she felt ready to hurl. She'd felt like this more than once when she'd traveled with altered flight, which meant she'd been moved swiftly from Sweet Dove's office to her present location.

She lay facedown on something relatively soft, but her left arm was bent at an uncomfortable angle.

"Good, you're waking up. Are you done vomiting?"

She knew the voice and rubbed her forehead. "Master Engles?"

"Of course."

He came into view and had a glass in his hand. "Here, drink this. You'll feel better. Much better."

She lifted herself up as the glass appeared beneath her nose.

"Drink up, sweetheart. You'll need this because we're just about to get started."

She sniffed and wrinkled her nose. "What is it?"

"Something that will enhance the experience."

Sudden rage flowed through Angelica. Engles had dogged her heels from the first, always after her, always hurting and killing women. She took a sip, rose up, and spat in his face.

He stood up, his eyelids fluttering.

His hands seemed to float away from his body as he pivoted slowly in her direction.

When he opened his round brown eyes to stare at her, he bore a familiar predatory expression.

He rubbed a hand through his thick wavy hair and smiled. "You ready for a fight?"

Angelica's heart pounded heavily against her rib cage.

The man was a sadistic killer and she was caught in his snare with no way to escape.

She had only one hope. She had to somehow contact Reyes, but she had no idea if he was next door or on another continent. She realized as well that Sweet Dove had removed the single-bonding chains. She was no longer connected to Reyes.

She felt the double-chain at her wrist, hidden inside the long black glove. It seemed to be burning as well, maybe because the chains were separated and were never meant to be. Blood-chains always came with a proximity issue.

Engles reached a trembling hand toward her and one by one plucked the cat whiskers from her face. The removal of each stung a little, the barest hint of things to come if Engles had his way with her. Somehow she had to escape, but how?

Suddenly he picked her up, levitated, then began moving swiftly from room to room. When she reached the chamber with the shallow pool and the platform, she knew exactly where she was. This was the place Reyes had tied her down with scarves, where Scorpion had watched her having sex with Reyes, and later where Reyes had attacked Engles when he'd tried to insinuate himself into their sex performance.

Engles took her to the table.

"I wanted you here." His voice was low and hoarse, full of need.

She had only one whisper of a chance to escape.

When he dumped her onto the table, she whisked the double-chain from her glove, then slipped it over her head.

The sudden power that struck her made her scream in

agony. Engles jumped away from her, his eyes wide with horror.

She put her hand to her throat and once more the preternatural sensation shot through her, burning every part of her body as though tearing her apart and rebuilding her at the same time.

"Where the hell did you get that? Stupid woman! It'll kill you."

"See if I care, you bastard."


Pain suddenly shot through Reyes like nothing he'd ever experienced before, not even at Sweet Dove's hands. He shouted, and the burning sensation at his waist beneath his shirt intensified.

Something was wrong because his captor hadn't even gotten started with her usual means of torture.

The next moment a wave of anguish flowed through him, something outside himself and it had the flavor of Angelica.

*Angelica?* He reached for her through the thick rock walls of the torture room.

*I'm here. I just put on the Ancestral chain. Engles says it will kill me, but I don't care. I'd rather die this way.*

Despite the fact that he was in physical agony, Reyes fell to a place of vampire stillness. Angelica was going to die within the next few minutes. She'd done the worst thing she could have done: she'd donned one of the double-chains apart from him. But where was the companion chain? Then he knew. He was in pain because the second chain resided inside his shirt at his waist, and Angelica had put it there. But how could he reach it shackled as he was?

His own agony formed a wall around him. Sweet

Dove jumped up on the table and shouted at him, but he could barely hear her. She seemed to be asking what was wrong.

"You have to let me go," he shouted.

"Never. And this time you won't be able to get away. You'll die here in this chamber before I ever release you."

So it was all a ruse, her e-mails suggesting a relationship with him.

She left the table and opened the cabinet on the wall to his left. Her tools. She wasn't going to wait. She intended to resume their prior relationship right now.

This couldn't be the end. He had work to do, an organization to bring down, and mostly he had Angelica to save.

Suddenly his mind grew sharp and focused. Only one thought mattered right now: to save Angelica no matter the cost. His own life didn't matter. Only she did, because he loved her.

His thoughts thinned out, his focus turning inward.

He loved her.

He loved Angelica.

Some of the pain lessened at this thought, and his heart grew full. Tears burned his eyes. He'd never believed he could love, not after all he'd been through. But right now, knowing that she'd had the foresight to bring the double-chains along took him the distance.

He loved her.

He saw it all now, how from the beginning she'd given him hope that his life could truly be different. Each step of the way, as she laid her dignity in the dirt and accepted the role of his slave, as she performed sexually in public when it was the last thing she would have ever done, as she stood up to Sweet Dove in order to keep his former captor away from him, all these things had given him hope.

And he loved her with every broken fiber of his being.

But was it too late?

Was there anything he could do?

Sweet Dove had him shackled and held in place with her preternatural power.

The only thing he knew for certain in this completely hopeless situation was that he had to tell Angelica how he felt.

*Angelica?*

*I'm here.* She sounded very faint.

*Are you in pain?* Dumb question.

*Immeasurably.*

Reyes's chest hurt, inside and out. *I can hardly hear you.*

*It won't be long now.*

*Angelica, I was a fool. I love you. I need you to know that.*

*You love me?*

*With all my heart, I just didn't think it was possible for me.*

*I love you, too.* Even within his head, her voice caught.

*You love me?*

*I'm crazy about you, Reyes.*

He didn't understand. *But you never said anything. I felt sure you wanted to go home, to resume your life, to be with your mom.*

*That's partly true, especially about my mom. But the rest was about my fears. Until this moment, I was afraid of staying in your world, but right now all I want is you, at any price. Reyes, I don't know why I thought I could leave you. I know now that I belong here. But Reyes, aren't you able to put on the chain?*

*Sweet Dove has me shackled. I can't reach it.*

*Reyes, please try. You have more power than you know.*

She wouldn't last long now.

He grew very still once more and finally said, *Sweet Dove has intensified the preternatural charge in the shackles, but I'm going to try to access my Ancestral power.*

She didn't answer for a long moment. When she spoke, her telepathic voice was little more than a whisper. *Reyes, I love you. If you can do something, hurry, because Engles just put on the cat's claw.*

As rage poured through Reyes he broke communication with Angelica. He had to do something, had to figure something out right now, or his woman would be hurt by that bastard even while she was dying.

Sweet Dove.

Reyes shifted his attention to her. This nightmare was her doing, always hers. And as an Ancestral she would always have the upper hand.

Even with his arms extended in the rusty chains, he focused on the blood-chain that sat in a heap at his waistband, burning his skin. He took deep breaths and closed his eyes. The last time he'd been on this table, with Angelica on top, dominating him yet loving him at the same time, he'd found his Ancestral power and had accessed it sufficiently to break free.

Tonight there would be no holding back.

With the chain next to his skin he began reaching within himself once more, diving deep, and in a split second found the Ancestral layer that belonged to him as his birthright.

This time he plunged into this power, embracing it all, and for a long moment blacked out.

When he came to, power surged through him as he'd never experienced it before. He called to the chain at his waist and felt it respond. He remained focused on it, and the chain moved faster beneath his shirt. Suddenly, without the use of his hands, the chain flew over his head and settled around his neck.

Ancestral power flashed through him in a heavy wave like nothing he'd known before.

He drew his hands into fists and focused on all four shackles at once.

Sweet Dove shouted, "No!"

With a burst of Ancestral power, he shattered the shackles that had held him prisoner. He broke free of Sweet Dove's preternatural charge. She'd never be able to entrap him again. Nothing could ever hold him again.

He didn't stay, however, to have his reckoning with her. Instead he shifted abruptly to altered flight, focused on Angelica, and flew faster than he ever had in his entire life, following the beacon that she'd become.

He found her in Engles's home, on the platform above the long shallow pool.

The bastard was naked, as was she, her knees split, his body ready to pierce hers, the cat's claw suspended above her left shoulder.

Engles, staring into Angelica's eyes and unaware of Reyes's presence, spoke in a commanding voice. "You'll die right now, Angelica, with my cock buried inside you and blood pouring from your body."

A red film covered Reyes's vision as he flew to grab Engles beneath his arms. He pinned him tight against his chest and with altered flight flew him straight up to the carved rock ceiling of the room, shifted back to levitation at the last moment, and slammed Engles's head into the rock.

He repeated this movement over and over, blood and brains flying everywhere until there was little left and nothing to be healed and restored.

At the same time, security alarms sounded through the space.

Reyes dropped Engles to the pool at the far end, flew back to Angelica, and lifted her up in his arms.

He shifted once more to altered flight and headed to his home. *I'll get a healer. You'll be all right. You have to be.*

She gasped several times, and just as he reached his bedroom, she spoke, *Power is flowing through me now instead of hurting me. The chains just needed to be together. The pain has stopped. I'm okay, truly. I'm fine. Reyes, you have to listen to me. We must get Sweet Dove's laptop. Now.*

Reyes shouldn't have been surprised, but he was. Angelica had almost been raped, tortured, and killed, but the moment she was free of peril, she addressed the critical issue of the mission, just as she always had.

He didn't try to argue. He knew she was right. And because of the deepening Ancestral bond between them he also sensed that she was healing swiftly, just as she said she was.

He changed course.

If he'd doubted that he'd risen to Ancestral status, he

didn't anymore, because the moment he thought about the location of Sweet Dove's office, he knew exactly where it was.

Within seconds he penetrated the preternatural shield around the space and touched down in front of the desk.

But Sweet Dove had guessed his maneuver and held the laptop in her hands. "By the look of all the blood on you and the fact that Angelica lives, Engles wasn't so fortunate."

"He's dead."

"Well, that's too bad, but you and I can still continue."

Reyes stared at her in profound disbelief. He sensed from her what he'd always felt, that somewhere in the early years of her life her psyche had become so corrupt that she truly believed Reyes wanted to be with her, that he wanted to be her slave.

On the other hand, she held the laptop, so some part of her must have known the truth.

Reyes knew that she could destroy the laptop right now, with a single preternatural charge from her hands. If she did, the mission would fail.

He ignored the computer and tried a different tack. "I'm bonded with Angelica now, a double-chain bond. And she's staying with me in our world." He turned toward Angelica and saw the glow in her brown eyes.

Angelica nodded. "I am." She smiled and leaned up and kissed him. Then turning to Sweet Dove, she said, "You can't have Reyes, not ever. He's powerful and you can feel his power, which means you'll never be able to capture him or hold him. You're finished, Sweet Dove."

The woman still ignored Angelica, but as if in a fog, she set the laptop on the desk.

Reyes forced himself to stay focused on Sweet Dove.

He felt something powerful emanating from his former captor, a heavy vibration that he knew well, that became a painful tingling on his skin.

*Hold steady,* he telepathed to Angelica. *Looks like the bitch is going to throw a fit.*

Reyes held Angelica close to his side and created an impenetrable disguise around them both, then levitated away from the desk near the waterfall.

*She can't see us, can she?*

*No, she can't.*

Sweet Dove became a whirlwind and tore around the room with tremendous speed. "Where are you?" she shouted.

She screamed obscenities. Froth poured from her mouth. Her eyes were wild and her hair, freed from the usual clip, flowed in angry waves around her body.

"Reyes!" His name came like a hiss from her lips. Her fangs descended, and she began tearing at her arms with the sharp points, pulling out chunks of flesh in her rage.

Reyes was stunned. She was a monster.

Angelica's voice moved through his mind, offering a sensible suggestion. *While she goes all whirling dervish on us, why don't we grab the laptop?*

*Good idea.*

With great care, he tried to maneuver around Sweet Dove, but when she almost hit them, he shifted to altered flight, left the room, then reentered behind the desk.

Angelica whisked the laptop into her arms. *Reyes, look at the ceiling. The fissure is widening. I think the roof of the cave is about to collapse. I think she's doing this without knowing it.*

Reyes glanced at the long chandelier made of swords. It swayed overhead.

*Let's get out of here.*

Returning to altered flight, he hovered not far from the room, close enough to watch as within seconds the ceiling collapsed, burying Sweet Dove.

He waited, expecting her to rise from the rubble, but she didn't.

*Should we leave? What if she pops up out of there and attacks us?* Angelica sounded worried and he didn't blame her. Sweet Dove had been the author of so much misery, she wouldn't stop now, not if she had the chance to do otherwise.

*I think something might have happened to her. I want to have a look, but I'll keep the disguise tight around us and I won't leave altered flight.*

*Sounds like a plan.*

With great care, he passed through the tumbled rock and found her buried. When the ceiling collapsed, the artful chandelier's couple of dozen blades had cut her up, one of them severing her head from her body.

He couldn't believe it, but his captor was finally dead. Scorpion, the founder of Starlin, the woman known as Sweet Dove, was no more.

The feeling of relief that went through him was so profound that he felt light-headed.

*She's gone.* Angelica's voice gave him substance once more. *She's actually dead.*

*I believed her immortal.*

*She seemed immortal, but there's nothing like a beheading to change a perception.*

Reyes glanced at her and saw the wry curve of her lips. *Thank you.*

*For what?* Angelica's brows rose in surprise.

*For being here, for saying exactly what you just said,*

*for making it real when I'm not sure I would ever have believed it.*

With one arm gripping the laptop and her other slung around his neck, she kissed him. *Take me home, Reyes. Take me out of this nightmare and back to your bedroom, where I belong.*

He wasn't sure she could have spoken sweeter words.

As he launched them away from the cave-in, she said, *I just realized that no one else will ever know that Scorpion is dead. And Engles was her only contact. So not a single member of Starlin will have a clue that we have the laptop and therefore the means to do with this organization anything you want to do. Reyes, you did it! You've achieved what you set out to accomplish. You have everything you need now to take down Starlin. You could even pose as Scorpion while you get everything set up.*

Drawing near his home, he squeezed her waist. *You're right, but you know something, I'm not thinking about that right now.* He touched down in his bedroom near the table and took the laptop from her, setting it aside.

She didn't seem to be aware that she was completely naked, which made him admire her all the more. Engles had almost had her, almost taken her life, but she'd kept her wits and brought them both here to this moment.

No, he wasn't thinking about his mission right now, only about her.

And right now he wanted her in his bed.

Angelica wasn't surprised that Reyes had something specific on his mind, so she said the only thing that made sense. "How about we get you out of your bodyguard clothes, although I must say I like you in a snug T-shirt."

He smiled. She'd never seen such a light in his clear

blue eyes before. He lifted his shirt off, his muscles flexing and making her take deeper breaths. Here was Reyes, the man she'd desired for months. She felt his Ancestral power resonating from him and through the double-chain at her neck.

He reached toward her, tracing her chain with his fingers. "I never would have believed this could happen. But you have to know that I have contacts who can work to remove your chain, if you want. It might take some time, but it can be done." He frowned as he spoke, and she felt his concern for her.

Angelica smiled. "You're what I want, Reyes, with or without the chains. But given the state your world is in and that you'll become a target as soon as you start taking Starlin apart, I think I'd like to keep this on. I'm stunned by the level of power that I feel right now and how much I can siphon from you."

She glanced down at her feet and made a mental decision to levitate. And just like that, she floated.

"Wow." He caught her around the waist but held on loosely so she could continue to experience the new-found ability.

After a moment she slid her arms around his neck, let go of the levitation, and fell against him.

He laughed and swung her in a circle. "You're alive. I thought I'd lost you."

"I know." She held him tightly, even worrying that she was hurting him, a silly thought because he was so physically strong.

He gripped her in return, not setting her on her feet, but just keeping her pressed against him.

Angelica's eyes filled with tears.

"We almost died, both of us, didn't we?"

He nodded, his cheek sliding against her hair, his chest rising and falling. She felt the depth of his emotion, the near loss for each of them and the relief that they'd survived.

"She's dead," Angelica murmured.

"I know. I'm so glad. She won't be able to hurt anyone else ever again or to use her abilities to create another auction, or betting Web site, or method of torture."

Angelica pulled back and her feet finally touched the carpet. She cupped his face with both hands. "We made it."

He nodded. "I have so much I want to say to you that I hardly know where to start, except that I love you. I should have realized it sooner, but I couldn't wrap my head around what was really happening between us. Part of me knew and wanted to believe, the part of me that had known love as a child. Yet I'd gone through so much, I wasn't sure I had the capacity to feel anything ever again."

"I can't imagine what that was like for you. I can only speak for myself." She chuckled softly. "I was kidding myself, Reyes, when I spoke of leaving, of going back to my old life. I think there was a part of me that was uncertain whether I could measure up in your world."

"Well, you certainly proved yourself. What made you take the chains with you, and where the hell did you keep them?"

"In my gloves. That's why I chose this pair that went almost to my elbows. As for the why of it, you were being justifiably stubborn about not making use of them, and for very noble reasons. But remember how Sweet Dove hurt me that first week of my captivity? I felt her power then, and I knew its flavor and its scope. I believed with all my heart that the only way we would survive, if Sweet

Dove chose as she did tonight to act against us, was if we had her level of power.

"And Reyes, my God, your power. It surpasses hers. Did you know that's how it would be?"

He shook his head. "I'm convinced that I kept myself blind to my potential. Of course being her slave all that time and kept in a subservient position helped me feel constantly less than Sweet Dove. But I feared so much that I would become corrupt like her or like Engles. Even now, I know I'll need to be vigilant."

She sensed his fear that being an Ancestral would change him, but she also knew his character and that so long as he lived he'd work hard to stay true to his deepest values, the ones his parents had taught him when he was young. "All I can say is, welcome home, Reyes. That's what I want to say to you. Welcome home."

"That's one of the most wonderful things you could say to me, and that's how I feel. It's taken all this time, from the first day of my captivity until now, to meet you and be with you in order to find my way home. You're my home, Angelica. In fact, that's where I want to go."

"But this is your home."

A slow smile overtook his face. "Venezuela. In the Cordillera system, high in the mountains near the Caribbean coast."

"Oh, you mean your family home. The one you took back when you made your fortune."

He nodded. "How about we get cleaned up, pack some clothes, and head there now?"

"Sounds like a plan."

Angelica soon learned that the double-chain had changed the proximity issue so that while she showered,

Reyes could remain in the sitting room as he continued to explore Sweet Dove's laptop.

By the time she'd emerged wearing jeans and a tank top, her makeup restored and her hair brushed out, she found Reyes at the table, in a robe. He still sat at the table, staring at the laptop, chin in hand.

He glanced up at her, and she put her hand on the double-chain. He seemed to be in a state of shock.

"What is it?"

"It's all here. Every last bit of information I need. It's clear to me that Sweet Dove didn't feel in the least threatened."

"Was it even password protected?"

Reyes shook his head. "She seemed to have a love of numbers, though. The records here are careful to the penny. Her crimes are legion."

She rounded the table and sat on his lap. He surrounded her with his arms. "I like you in jeans."

She kissed him. "I'm all packed. Ready when you are."

He closed the laptop lid and headed for his turn in the shower.

She stared at the laptop for a long time. Part of her was curious, and no doubt in the coming days and weeks she'd become completely familiar with Sweet Dove's organization.

For now, however, the horror could rest. More than anything she needed this time with Reyes, to just be with him.

A half hour later he carried her in one arm, her satchel dangling from his free hand, and flew her at top speed to South America.

*I have no pain.*

*What?* He squeezed her waist.

*There's no more pain when I fly.*

*Nor should there be because of my Ancestral power. But the truth is I didn't even think about it. Although if you'd suffered in any way, the chains would have told me in a split second.*

Within minutes he slowed, flying into the coastal range of Venezuela where the mountains ran along the northernmost section of the country.

He flew her to the highest elevation and passed through a forest, then finally drifted through the hard rock walls of the cavern system.

*My housekeeper has come and gone, so we'll have privacy. But she's left a meal of spicy chicken-filled empanadas and a salad. And beer.*

*And suddenly I'm starved.*

Reyes touched down in the middle of the living room. A thin but very wide waterfall made up the wall opposite, tucked behind a low stone barrier. Soft lights lit the dark rock that sparkled with gold-colored minerals.

Heavy, carved-wood chests and tables sat against the walls but a cream sectional lightened the space. A brightly colored woven rug anchored a solid coffee table. Branches of antique candelabra and ornate silver boxes completed the decor.

Faylen's boxes.

She moved toward one that sat on a dark wood chest. It was one of the larger ones and had intricate carvings on each drawer. "This belonged to your mother, didn't it?" Oddly she could almost feel Faylen's presence in the space, and for a long moment she wished, for Reyes's sake, that his mother was still alive.

With her hand on the box the room began to spin, faster

than ever, a sure sign that a revisiting vision was upon her. Again.

"Reyes." She gestured for him to come to her.

"A vision?"

"Yes, an important one. Please hold me." She just had a feeling.

An image swept through her of a woman with auburn hair sitting on a cot, her legs shackled. The room had a stand with a pitcher of water and a chamber pot in the corner.

Angelica's heart beat hard in her chest. "I think I'm seeing your mother. Tell me what she looked like."

Reyes took a deep breath as he leaned his head close to hers. "Show me. I have a sense that I'll be able to see her because of the Ancestral chains."

Angelica relaxed against him and let her mind flow.

The woman rocked softly on the cot.

"I can see the vision. Oh, God, it is her. That's my mother."

"Reyes, where is this? Do you know where this is?"

"No, that is, it feels familiar. But can you tell me when this took place?" Revisiting visions were always in the past.

Angelica was shocked as she turned in his arms, forcing the vision to disappear. "This vision is of something that occurred just a few minutes ago. Reyes, your mother is still alive."

Reyes felt hot and cold at exactly the same moment. He'd grieved his mother's death for well over a century. Sweet Dove had relayed the progress of her demise step by step, how she'd stopped eating and taking blood and had devolved into blood madness, afterward dying.

Sweet Dove had lied to him.

Maybe it was the blood-chains or his increasing Ancestral power, but he could feel his mother now. He just couldn't believe it was true.

His mother lived.

"Can you sense where she is?" Angelica asked.

He closed his eyes and focused at the same time, letting his Ancestral power surge through him. "She's alone. Dear God, Sweet Dove kept her sequestered all this time."

"Do you think she hurt your mother?"

"Almost two centuries of solitary imprisonment would have been torture enough. But let's go. She wasn't far from Sweet Dove's office."

He held out his arm, and Angelica climbed onto his booted foot. The moment she secured a hold on his neck, he shifted to altered flight and sped through rock and into the air.

A few minutes later he slowed his approach, diving through more rock, centering his path on the image of his mother. Angelica had touched the silver box and the vision had come to her. She had given him so much and now this.

A moment later he passed through the final layer of rock.

When his boots hit the solid rock floor, he stared at the woman in the white, sack-like dress, still sitting on the edge of her cot. She looked as young as he remembered, and her blue eyes were as full of life.

"You found me," she whispered, rising to her feet. "I knew you would. I never gave up hope." She opened her arms, her eyes filling with tears.

He gathered her up, holding her tightly against his

chest, tears coursing down his cheeks. She clung to him and wept. He didn't think he ever wanted to let her go.

At last he murmured, "I bought our home back, the one at Cordillera."

She drew back and planted her hands on his face. "You did?"

He nodded. "As soon as I escaped my captor I began building my fortune. The moment I had enough money to tempt the owner to sell, I bought it back and recovered as many of your things as I could. Remember your silver boxes?"

"Yes. Treasures that belonged to the women of my family for centuries."

"I found most of them."

"Brogan Reyes, my darling son."

More tears followed, until eventually she asked, "But how did you find me? After all this time?"

Reyes finally released her and turned slightly so that Angelica came into his line of sight. "My woman found you. I had just taken her to Cordillera and she touched one of the boxes. She has the revisiting vision gift and saw you here. Right here, not fifteen minutes ago."

His mother left Reyes's side and moved in Angelica's direction. She lifted her hands to Angelica, who in turn took them. "Thank you, my dear."

"Angelica, I'd like you to meet my mother, Faylen Reyes."

Angelica nodded as more tears slipped down her cheeks. "I'm so happy to meet you, Mrs. Reyes."

"Faylen please." Her gaze fell to Angelica's throat. "And you're bonded to Reyes?"

Angelica met Reyes's gaze. "I am."

Reyes felt as though nothing had been so real in his life

as what stood before him: a mother believed dead and now come to life, and a woman to whom he would give himself for the rest of his days.

"Let me take you home, Mother. I'll go very slowly, which means this will take some time."

"I have all the time in the world."

Later that night, with Reyes's mother asleep in a real bed for the first time in almost two centuries, Angelica lay in the arms of the man she loved.

She knew that, in time, she would reunite with her own mother, though she had no idea how she would explain her vampire husband, the constant wearing of the blood-chains, or that over the years her aging would slow to match Reyes's. But those were small issues to be worked out in the larger scheme of things.

She had every confidence that Reyes would take down Starlin, piece by piece, as he'd sworn to do.

For herself Angelica had only one desire, at least for the present, and that was to continue to be a comfort to Reyes.

She felt a profound sense of wonder from Reyes and an ever-flowing wave of emotion that moved back and forth, like the waves at the shore's edge, rising up on the sand, drifting back, a constant push-pull.

She was content, deeply so, and awestruck. She still couldn't believe that she'd been instrumental in metaphorically bringing a woman back from the dead. Reyes had never believed she'd survived the deaths of both her husband and her son. Sweet Dove's recounting had seemed entirely plausible to Reyes.

She stared up at a beautiful piece of red crystal that lay embedded in the slate-colored ceiling, the natural shade of the mountain stone.

She shifted onto her side slightly, turning toward Reyes and drawing close. She was naked, as was Reyes, but he hadn't made love to her yet. Right now she lay next to him, as each settled into the extraordinary moment of coming home.

They'd spent hours in his mother's company, sharing the empanadas with her, talking and talking. Faylen was very thin and ate only a few bites. Her body would take months to fully recover from her captivity.

Reyes wasn't asleep. He lay on his back, also looking up at the ceiling.

She rose up slightly. "You know I've been turning this over in my mind, and what I don't get is why Sweet Dove kept your mother alive."

He shook his head. "I don't really know. Maybe Sweet Dove had planned on using her, or she might have forgotten all about her. You heard what mother said, that a group of caregivers had been in charge of her for decades. She'd only actually seen Sweet Dove three times in all those years."

"You know what? I believe in grace. I believe your mother lived so that your life could be restored in just this way."

He shifted this time, turning to face her. He took her chin in his hand. "You were the first evidence of grace, more than I ever deserved."

Angelica kissed him softly. "I have a feeling that we will have many arguments on the subject of what you deserve before you finally give way to my superior opinion of who you are. Because if a man ever deserved grace, and all good things, it's you."

He searched her eyes and pushed her hair away from her temples. He kissed her forehead and her cheeks.

"I love you, Angelica, more than I'll ever be able to express."

He made love to her after that, moving slowly over her body, holding her gaze while he brought her to ecstasy. The double-chains added a new layer of intensity. She could even feel his pleasure as he released into her, which brought her crying out as once more she reached the pinnacle.

As she fell asleep within the warm comfort of Reyes's embrace, a different kind of vision came to her, something that surprised her beyond words and made her smile. She held a dark-haired baby in her arms, and when he opened his eyes they were as crystal clear as the mountain sky.

She'd been abducted into the vampire world, fallen in love with one of their kind, and would one day give birth to a child who would know only love and security in their care.

In the vision Reyes came to her, moving in close behind and embracing them both. "I don't deserve this bounty," he whispered.

She smiled. Their only real argument, what the man deserved. She turned her head and kissed him. The baby cooed his pleasure. And life was good.